MISS MACKENZIE

Anthony Trollope 1815-1882

Cover Painting:

"A Lady in Black with Pink Roses" by Gunnar Berndtson, 1879.

Cover Design Copyright © 2008 by Vera Nazarian

ISBN-13: 978-1-934648-82-7
ISBN-10: 1-934648-82-5

First Publication (in book form): 1865.

Reprint Trade Paperback Edition

August 2008

A Publication of
Norilana Books
P. O. Box 2188
Winnetka, CA 91396
www.norilana.com

Printed in the United States of America

Miss Mackenzie

Norilana Books

Classics

www.norilana.com

Miss Mackenzie

Anthony Trollope

Contents

Chapter I

The Mackenzie Family

I fear I must trouble my reader with some few details as to the early life of Miss Mackenzie,—details which will be dull in the telling, but which shall be as short as I can make them. Her father, who had in early life come from Scotland to London, had spent all his days in the service of his country. He became a clerk in Somerset House at the age of sixteen, and was a clerk in Somerset House when he died at the age of sixty. Of him no more shall be said than that his wife had died before him, and that he, at dying, left behind him two sons and a daughter.

Thomas Mackenzie, the eldest of those two sons, had engaged himself in commercial pursuits—as his wife was accustomed to say when she spoke of her husband's labours; or went into trade, and kept a shop, as was more generally asserted by those of the Mackenzie circle who were wont to speak their minds freely. The actual and unvarnished truth in the matter shall now be made known. He, with his partner, made and sold oilcloth, and was possessed of premises in the New Road, over which the names of "Rubb and Mackenzie" were posted in large letters. As you, my reader, might enter therein, and purchase a yard and a half of oilcloth, if you were so minded, I think that the free-spoken friends of the family were not far wrong. Mrs. Thomas Mackenzie, however, declared that she was calumniated, and her husband cruelly injured; and she based her assertions on the fact that "Rubb and Mackenzie" had wholesale dealings, and that they sold their article to the trade, who re-sold it. Whether or no she was ill-treated in the matter, I will leave my readers to decide, having told them all that it is necessary for them to know, in order that a judgement may be formed.

Walter Mackenzie, the second son, had been placed in his father's office, and he also had died before the time at which our story is supposed to commence. He had been a poor sickly creature, always ailing, gifted with an affectionate nature, and a great respect for the blood of the Mackenzies, but not gifted with much else that was intrinsically his own. The blood of the Mackenzies was, according to his way of thinking, very pure blood indeed; and he had felt strongly that his brother had disgraced the family by connecting himself with that man Rubb, in the New Road. He had felt this the more strongly, seeing that "Rubb and Mackenzie" had not done great things in their trade. They had kept their joint commercial head above water, but had sometimes barely succeeded in doing that. They had never been bankrupt, and that, perhaps, for some years was all that could be said. If a Mackenzie did go into trade, he should, at any rate, have done better than this. He certainly should have done better than this, seeing that he started in life with a considerable sum of money.

Old Mackenzie,—he who had come from Scotland,—had been the first-cousin of Sir Walter Mackenzie, baronet, of Incharrow, and he had married the sister of Sir John Ball, baronet, of the Cedars, Twickenham. The young Mackenzies, therefore, had reason to be proud of their blood. It is true that Sir John Ball was the first baronet, and that he had simply been a political Lord Mayor in strong political days,—a political Lord Mayor in the leather business; but, then, his business had been undoubtedly wholesale; and a man who gets himself to be made a baronet cleanses himself from the stains of trade, even though he have traded in leather. And then, the present Mackenzie baronet was the ninth of the name; so that on the higher and nobler side of the family, our Mackenzies may be said to have been very strong indeed. This strength the two clerks in Somerset House felt and enjoyed very keenly; and it may therefore be understood that the oilcloth manufactory was much out of favour with them.

When Tom Mackenzie was twenty-five—"Rubb and Mackenzie" as he afterwards became—and Walter, at the age of twenty-one, had been for a year or two placed at a desk in Somerset House, there died one Jonathan Ball, a brother of the baronet Ball, leaving all he had in the world to the two brother Mackenzies. This all was by no means a trifle, for each brother received about twelve thousand pounds when the opposing lawsuits instituted by the Ball family were finished. These opposing lawsuits were carried on with great vigour, but with no success on the Ball side, for three years. By that time, Sir John Ball, of the Cedars, was half ruined, and the Mackenzies got their money. It is needless to say much to the reader of the manner in which Tom Mackenzie found his way into trade— how, in the first place, he endeavoured to resume his Uncle Jonathan's share in the leather business, instigated thereto by a desire to oppose his Uncle John,—Sir John, who was opposing him in the matter of the will,—how he lost money in this attempt, and ultimately embarked, after some other fruitless speculations, the residue of his fortune in partnership with Mr. Rubb. All that happened long ago. He was now a man of nearly fifty, living with his wife and family,—a family of six or seven children,—in a house in Gower Street, and things had not gone with him very well.

Nor is it necessary to say very much of Walter Mackenzie, who had been four years younger than his brother. He had stuck to the office in spite of his wealth; and as he had never married, he had been a rich man. During his father's lifetime, and when he was quite young, he had for a while shone in the world of fashion, having been patronised by the Mackenzie baronet, and by others who thought that a clerk from Somerset House with twelve thousand pounds must be a very estimable fellow. He had not, however, shone in a very brilliant way. He had gone to parties for a year or two, and during those years had essayed the life of a young man about town, frequenting theatres and billiard-rooms, and doing a few things which he should have left undone, and leaving undone a few things which should not have been so left. But, as I have said, he was weak in body as well as weak in mind. Early in life he became an invalid; and though he kept his place in Somerset House till he died, the period of his shining in the fashionable world came to a speedy end.

Now, at length, we will come to Margaret Mackenzie, the sister, our heroine, who was eight years younger than her brother Walter, and twelve years younger than Mr. Rubb's partner. She had been little more than a child when her father died; or I might more correctly say, that though she had then reached an age which makes some girls young women, it had not as yet had that effect upon her. She was then nineteen; but her life in her father's house had been dull and monotonous; she had gone very little into company, and knew very little of the ways of the world. The Mackenzie baronet people had not noticed her. They had failed to make much of Walter with his twelve thousand pounds, and did not trouble themselves with Margaret, who had no fortune of her own. The Ball baronet people were at extreme variance with all her family, and, as a matter of course, she received no countenance from them. In those early days she did not receive much countenance from any one; and perhaps I may say that she had not shown much claim for such countenance as is often given to young ladies by their richer relatives. She was neither beautiful nor clever, nor was she in any special manner made charming by any of those softnesses and graces of youth which to some girls seem to atone for a want of beauty and cleverness. At the age of nineteen, I may almost say that Margaret Mackenzie was ungainly. Her brown hair was rough, and did not form itself into equal lengths. Her cheek-bones were somewhat high, after the manner of the Mackenzies. She was thin and straggling in her figure, with bones larger than they should have been for purposes of youthful grace. There was not wanting a certain brightness to her grey eyes, but it was a brightness as to the use of which she had no early knowledge. At this time her father lived at Camberwell, and I doubt whether the education which Margaret received at Miss Green's establishment for young ladies in that suburb was of a kind to make up by art for that which nature had not given her. This school, too, she left at an early age—at a very early age, as her age went. When she was nearly sixteen, her father, who was then almost an old man, became ill, and the next three years she spent in nursing him. When he died, she was transferred to her younger brother's house,—to a house which he had taken in one of the quiet streets leading down from the Strand to the river, in order that he might be near his office. And here for fifteen years she had lived, eating his bread and nursing him, till he also died, and so she was alone in the world.

During those fifteen years her life had been very weary. A moated grange in the country is bad enough for the life of any Mariana, but a moated grange in town is much worse. Her life in London had been altogether of the moated grange kind, and long before her brother's death it had been very wearisome to her. I will not say that she was always waiting for some one that came not, or that she declared herself to be aweary, or that she wished that she were dead. But the mode of her life was as near that as prose may be near to poetry, or truth to romance. For the coming of one, who, as things fell out in that matter, soon ceased to come at all to her, she had for a while been anxious. There was a young clerk then in Somerset House, one Harry Handcock by name, who had visited her brother in the early days of that long sickness. And Harry Handcock had seen beauty in those grey eyes, and the straggling, uneven locks had by that time settled themselves into some form of tidiness, and the big joints, having been covered, had taken upon themselves softer womanly motions, and the sister's tenderness to the brother had been appreciated. Harry Handcock had spoken a word or two, Margaret being then five-and-twenty, and Harry ten years her senior. Harry had spoken, and Margaret had listened only too willingly. But the sick brother upstairs had become cross and peevish. Such a thing should never take place with his consent, and Harry Handcock had ceased to speak tenderly.

He had ceased to speak tenderly, though he didn't cease to visit the quiet house in Arundel Street. As far as Margaret was concerned he might as well have ceased to come; and in her heart she sang that song of Mariana's, complaining bitterly of her weariness; though the man was seen then in her brother's sickroom regularly once a week. For years this went on. The brother would crawl out to his office in summer, but would never leave his bedroom in the winter months. In those days these things were allowed in public offices; and it was not till very near the end of his life that certain stern official reformers hinted at the necessity of his retiring on a pension. Perhaps it was that hint that killed him. At any rate, he died in harness—if it can in truth be said of him that he ever wore harness. Then, when he was dead, the days were gone in which Margaret Mackenzie cared for Harry Handcock. Harry Handcock was still a bachelor, and when the nature of his late friend's will was ascertained, he said a word or two to show that he thought he was not yet too old for matrimony. But Margaret's weariness could not now be cured in that way. She would have taken him while she had nothing, or would have taken him in those early days had fortune filled her lap with gold. But she had seen Harry Handcock at least weekly for the last ten years, and having seen him without any speech of love, she was not now prepared for the renewal of such speaking.

When Walter Mackenzie died there was a doubt through all the Mackenzie circle as to what was the destiny of his money. It was well known that he had been a prudent man, and that he was possessed of a freehold estate which gave him at least six hundred a year. It was known also that he had money saved beyond this. It was known, too, that Margaret had nothing, or next to nothing, of her own. The old Mackenzie had had no fortune left to him, and had felt it to be a grievance that his sons had not joined their richer lots to his poorer lot. This, of course, had been no fault of Margaret's, but it had made him feel justified in leaving his daughter as a burden upon his younger son. For the last fifteen years she had eaten bread to which she had no positive claim; but if ever woman earned the morsel which she required, Margaret Mackenzie had earned her morsel during her untiring attendance upon her brother. Now she was left to her own resources, and as she went silently about the house during those sad hours which intervened between the death of her brother and his burial, she was altogether in ignorance whether any means of subsistence had been left to her. It was known that Walter Mackenzie had more than once altered his will—that he had, indeed, made many wills—according as he was at such moments on terms of more or less friendship with his brother; but he had never told to any one what was the nature of any bequest that he had made. Thomas Mackenzie had thought of both his brother and sister as poor creatures, and had been thought of by them as being but a poor creature himself. He had become a shopkeeper, so they declared, and it must be admitted that Margaret had shared the feeling which regarded her brother Tom's trade as being disgraceful. They, of Arundel Street, had been idle, reckless, useless beings—so Tom had often declared to his wife—and only by fits and starts had there existed any friendship between him and either of them. But the firm of Rubb and Mackenzie was not growing richer in those days, and both Thomas and his wife had felt themselves forced into a certain amount of conciliatory demeanour by the claims of their seven surviving children. Walter, however, said no word to any one of his money; and when he was followed to his grave by his brother and nephews, and by Harry Handcock, no one knew of what nature would be the provision made for his sister.

"He was a great sufferer," Harry Handcock had said, at the only interview which took place between him and Margaret after the death of her brother and before the reading of the will.

"Yes indeed, poor fellow," said Margaret, sitting in the darkened dining-room, in all the gloom of her new mourning.

"And you yourself, Margaret, have had but a sorry time of it." He still called her Margaret from old acquaintance, and had always done so.

"I have had the blessing of good health," she said, "and have been very thankful. It has been a dull life, though, for the last ten years."

"Women generally lead dull lives, I think." Then he had paused for a while, as though something were on his mind which he wished to consider before he spoke again. Mr. Handcock, at this time, was bald and very stout. He was a strong healthy man, but had about him, to the outward eye, none of the aptitudes of a lover. He was fond of eating and drinking, as no one knew better than Margaret Mackenzie; and had altogether dropped the poetries of life, if at any time any of such poetries had belonged to him. He was, in fact, ten years older than Margaret Mackenzie; but he now looked to be almost twenty years her senior. She was a woman who at thirty-five had more of the graces of womanhood than had belonged to her at twenty. He was a man who at forty-five had lost all that youth does for a man. But still I think that she would have fallen back upon her former love, and found that to be sufficient, had he asked her to do so even now. She would have felt herself bound by her faith to do so, had he said that such was his wish, before the reading of her brother's will. But he did no such thing. "I hope he will have made you comfortable," he said.

"I hope he will have left me above want," Margaret had replied—and that had then been all. She had, perhaps, half-expected something more from him, remembering that the obstacle which had separated them was now removed. But nothing more came, and it would hardly be true to say that she was disappointed. She had no strong desire to marry Harry Handcock whom no one now called Harry any longer; but yet, for the sake of human nature, she bestowed a sigh upon his coldness, when he carried his tenderness no further than a wish that she might be comfortable.

There had of necessity been much of secrecy in the life of Margaret Mackenzie. She had possessed no friend to whom she could express her thoughts and feelings with confidence. I doubt whether any living being knew that there now existed, up in that small back bedroom in Arundel Street, quires of manuscript in which Margaret had written her thoughts and feelings,—hundreds of rhymes which had never met any eye but her own; and outspoken words of love contained in letters which had never been sent, or been intended to be sent, to any destination. Indeed these letters had been commenced with no name, and finished with no signature. It would be hardly true to say that they had been intended for Harry Handcock, even at the warmest period of her love. They had rather been trials of her strength,—proofs of what she might do if fortune should ever be so kind to her as to allow of her loving. No one had ever guessed all this, or had dreamed of accusing Margaret of romance. No one capable of testing her character had known her. In latter days she had now and again dined in Gower Street, but her sister-in-law, Mrs. Tom, had declared her to be a silent, stupid old maid. As a silent, stupid old maid, the Mackenzies of Rubb and Mackenzie were disposed to regard her. But how should they treat this stupid old maid of an aunt, if it should now turn out that all the wealth of the family belonged to her?

When Walter's will was read such was found to be the case. There was no doubt, or room for doubt, in the matter. The will was dated but two months before his death, and left everything to Margaret, expressing a conviction on the part of the testator that it was his duty to do so, because of his sister's unremitting attention to himself. Harry Handcock was requested to act as executor, and was requested also to accept a gold watch and a present of two hundred pounds. Not a word was there in the whole will of his brother's family; and Tom, when he went home with a sad heart, told his wife that all this had come of certain words which she had spoken when last she had visited the sick man. "I knew it would be so," said Tom to his wife. "It can't be helped now, of course. I knew you could not keep your temper quiet, and always told you not to go near him." How the wife answered, the course of our story at the present moment does not require me to tell. That she did answer with sufficient spirit, no one, I should say, need doubt; and it may be surmised that things in Gower Street were not comfortable that evening.

Tom Mackenzie had communicated the contents of the will to his sister, who had declined to be in the room when it was opened. "He has left you everything,—just everything," Tom had said. If Margaret made any word of reply, Tom did not hear it. "There will be over eight hundred a year, and he has left you all the furniture," Tom continued. "He has been very good," said Margaret, hardly knowing how to express herself on such an occasion. "Very good to you," said Tom, with some little sarcasm in his voice. "I mean good to me," said Margaret. Then he told her that Harry Handcock had been named as executor. "There is no more about him in the will, is there?" said Margaret. At the moment, not knowing much about executors, she had fancied that her brother had, in making such appointment, expressed some further wish about Mr. Handcock. Her brother explained to her that the executor was to have two hundred pounds and a gold watch, and then she was satisfied.

"Of course, it's a very sad look-out for us," Tom said; "but I do not on that account blame you."

"If you did you would wrong me," Margaret answered, "for I never once during all the years that we lived together spoke to Walter one word about his money."

"I do not blame you," the brother rejoined; and then no more had been said between them.

He had asked her even before the funeral to go up to Gower Street and stay with them, but she had declined. Mrs. Tom Mackenzie had not asked her. Mrs. Tom Mackenzie had hoped, then—had hoped and had inwardly resolved—that half, at least, of the dying brother's money would have come to her husband; and she had thought that if she once encumbered herself with the old maid, the old maid might remain longer than was desirable. "We should never get rid of her," she had said to her eldest daughter, Mary Jane. "Never, mamma," Mary Jane had replied. The mother and daughter had thought that they would be on the whole safer in not pressing any such invitation. They had not pressed it, and the old maid had remained in Arundel Street.

Before Tom left the house, after the reading of the will, he again invited his sister to his own home. An hour or two had intervened since he had told her of her position in the world, and he was astonished at finding how composed and self-assured she was in the tone and manner of her answer. "No, Tom, I think I had better not," she said. "Sarah will be somewhat disappointed."

"You need not mind that," said Tom.

"I think I had better not. I shall be very glad to see her if she will come to me; and I hope you will come, Tom; but I think I will remain here till I have made up my mind what to do." She remained in Arundel Street for the next three months, and her brother saw her frequently; but Mrs. Tom Mackenzie never went to her, and she never went to Mrs. Tom Mackenzie. "Let it be even so," said Mrs. Tom; "they shall not say that I ran after her and her money. I hate such airs." "So do I, mamma," said Mary

Jane, tossing her head. "I always said that she was a nasty old maid."

On that same day,—the day on which the will was read,—Mr. Handcock had also come to her. "I need not tell you," he had said, as he pressed her hand, "how rejoiced I am— for your sake, Margaret." Then she had returned the pressure, and had thanked him for his friendship. "You know that I have been made executor to the will," he continued. "He did this simply to save you from trouble. I need only promise that I will do anything and everything that you can wish." Then he left her, saying nothing of his suit on that occasion.

Two months after this,—and during those two months he had necessarily seen her frequently,—Mr. Handcock wrote to her from his office in Somerset House, renewing his old proposals of marriage. His letter was short and sensible, pleading his cause as well, perhaps, as any words were capable of pleading it at this time; but it was not successful. As to her money he told her that no doubt he regarded it now as a great addition to their chance of happiness, should they put their lots together; and as to his love for her, he referred her to the days in which he had desired to make her his wife without a shilling of fortune. He had never changed, he said; and if her heart was as constant as his, he would make good now the proposal which she had once been willing to accept. His income was not equal to hers, but it was not inconsiderable, and therefore as regards means they would be very comfortable. Such were his arguments, and Margaret, little as she knew of the world, was able to perceive that he expected that they would succeed with her.

Little, however, as she might know of the world, she was not prepared to sacrifice herself and her new freedom, and her new power and her new wealth, to Mr. Harry Handcock. One word said to her when first she was free and before she was rich, would have carried her. But an argumentative, well-worded letter, written to her two months after the fact of her freedom and the fact of her wealth had sunk into his mind, was powerless on her. She had looked at her glass and had perceived that years had improved her, whereas years had not improved Harry Handcock. She had gone back over her old aspirations, aspirations of which no whisper had ever been uttered, but which had not the less been strong within her, and had told herself that she could not gratify them by a union with Mr. Handcock. She thought, or rather hoped, that society might still open to her its portals,—not simply the society of the Handcocks from Somerset House, but that society of which she had read in novels during the day, and of which she had dreamed at night. Might it not yet be given to her to know clever people, nice people, bright people, people who were not heavy and fat like Mr. Handcock, or sick and wearisome like her poor brother Walter, or vulgar and quarrelsome like her relatives in Gower Street? She reminded herself that she was the niece of one baronet, and the first-cousin once removed of another, that she had eight hundred a year, and liberty to do with it whatsoever she pleased; and she reminded herself, also, that she had higher tastes in the world than Mr. Handcock. Therefore she wrote to him an answer, much longer than his letter, in which she explained to him that the more than ten years' interval which had elapsed since words of love had passed between them had—had—had—changed the nature of her regard. After much hesitation, that was the phrase which she used.

And she was right in her decision. Whether or no she was doomed to be disappointed in her aspirations, or to be partially disappointed and partially gratified, these pages are written to tell. But I think we may conclude that she would hardly have made herself happy by marrying Mr. Handcock while such aspirations were strong upon her. There was nothing on her side in favour of such a marriage but a faint remembrance of auld lang syne.

She remained three months in Arundel Street, and before that period was over she made a proposition to her brother Tom, showing to what extent she was willing to burden herself on behalf of his family. Would he allow her, she asked, to undertake the education and charge of his second daughter, Susanna? She would not offer to adopt her niece, she said, because it was on the cards that she herself might marry; but she would promise to take upon herself the full expense of the girl's education, and all charge of her till such education should be completed. If then any future guardianship on her part should have become incompatible with her own circumstances, she should give Susanna five hundred pounds. There was an air of business about this which quite startled Tom Mackenzie, who, as has before been said, had taught himself in old days to regard his sister as a poor creature. There was specially an air of business about her allusion to her own future state. Tom was not at all surprised that his sister should think of marrying, but he was much surprised that she should dare to declare her thoughts. "Of course she will marry the first fool that asks her," said Mrs. Tom. The father of the large family, however, pronounced the offer to be too good to be refused. "If she does, she will keep her word about the five hundred pounds," he said. Mrs. Tom, though she demurred, of course gave way; and when Margaret Mackenzie left London for Littlebath, where lodgings had been taken for her, she took her niece Susanna with her.

Chapter II

Miss Mackenzie Goes to Littlebath

I fear that Miss Mackenzie, when she betook herself to Littlebath, had before her mind's eye no sufficiently settled plan of life. She wished to live pleasantly, and perhaps fashionably; but she also desired to live respectably, and with a due regard to religion. How she was to set about doing this at Littlebath, I am afraid she did not quite know. She told herself over and over again that wealth entailed duties as well as privileges; but she had no clear idea what were the duties so entailed, or what were the privileges. How could she have obtained any clear idea on the subject in that prison which she had inhabited for so many years by her brother's bedside?

She had indeed been induced to migrate from London to Littlebath by an accident which should not have been allowed to actuate her. She had been ill, and the doctor, with that solicitude which doctors sometimes feel for ladies who are well to do in the world, had recommended change of air. Littlebath, among the Tantivy hills, would be the very place for her. There were waters at Littlebath which she might drink for a month or two with great advantage to her system. It was then the end of July, and everybody that was anybody was going out of town.

Suppose she were to go to Littlebath in August, and stay there for a month, or perhaps two months, as she might feel inclined. The London doctor knew a Littlebath doctor, and would be so happy to give her a letter. Then she spoke to the clergyman of the church she had lately attended in London who also had become more energetic in his assistance since her brother's death than he had been before, and he also could give her a letter to a gentleman of his cloth at Littlebath. She knew very little in private life of the doctor or of the clergyman in London, but not the less, on that account, might their introductions be of service to her in forming a circle of acquaintance at Littlebath. In this way she first came to think of Littlebath, and from this beginning she had gradually reached her decision.

Another little accident, or two other little accidents, had nearly induced her to remain in London—not in Arundel Street, which was to her an odious locality, but in some small genteel house in or about Brompton. She had written to the two baronets to announce to them her brother's death, Tom Mackenzie, the surviving brother, having positively refused to hold any communication with either of them. To both these letters, after some interval, she received courteous replies. Sir Walter Mackenzie was a very old man, over eighty, who now never stirred away from Incharrow, in Ross-shire. Lady Mackenzie was not living. Sir Walter did not write himself, but a letter came from Mrs. Mackenzie, his eldest son's wife, in which she said that she and her husband would be up in London in the course of the next spring, and hoped that they might then have the pleasure of making their cousin's acquaintance. This letter, it was true, did not come till the beginning of August, when the Littlebath plan was nearly formed; and Margaret knew that her cousin, who was in Parliament, had himself been in London almost up to the time at which it was written, so that he might have called had he chosen. But she was prepared to forgive much. There had been cause for offence; and if her great relatives were now prepared to take her by the hand, there could be no reason why she should not consent to be so taken. Sir John Ball, the other baronet, had absolutely come to her, and had seen her. There had been a regular scene of reconciliation, and she had gone down for a day and night to the Cedars. Sir John also was an old man, being over seventy, and Lady Ball was nearly as old. Mr. Ball, the future baronet, had also been there. He was a widower, with a large family and small means. He had been, and of course still was, a barrister; but as a barrister he had never succeeded, and was now waiting sadly till he should inherit the very moderate fortune which would come to him at his father's death. The Balls, indeed, had not done well with their baronetcy, and their cousin found them living with a degree of strictness, as to small expenses, which she herself had never been called upon to exercise. Lady Ball indeed had a carriage—for what would a baronet's wife do without one?—but it did not very often go out. And the Cedars was an old place, with grounds and paddocks appertaining; but the ancient solitary gardener could not make much of the grounds, and the grass of the paddocks was always sold. Margaret, when she was first asked to go to the Cedars, felt that it would be better for her to give up her migration to Littlebath. It would be much, she thought, to have her relations near to her. But she had found Sir John and Lady Ball to be very dull, and her cousin, the father of the large family, had spoken to her about little except money. She was not much in love with the Balls when she returned to London, and the Littlebath plan was allowed to go on.

She made a preliminary journey to that place, and took furnished lodgings in the Paragon. Now it is known to all the world that the Paragon is the nucleus of all that is pleasant and fashionable at Littlebath. It is a long row of houses with two short rows abutting from the ends of the long row, and every house in it looks out upon the Montpelier Gardens. If not built of stone, these houses are built of such stucco that the Margaret Mackenzies of the world do not know the difference. Six steps, which are of undoubted stone, lead up to each door. The areas are grand with high railings. The flagged way before the houses is very broad, and at each corner there is an extensive sweep, so that the carriages of the Paragonites may be made to turn easily. Miss Mackenzie's heart sank a little within her at the sight of all this grandeur, when she was first taken to the Paragon by her new friend the doctor. But she bade her heart be of good courage, and looked at the first floor—divided into dining-room and drawing-room—at the large bedroom upstairs for herself, and two small rooms for her niece and her maid-servant—at the kitchen in which she was to have a partial property, and did not faint at the splendour. And yet how different it was from those dingy rooms in Arundel Street! So different that she could hardly bring herself to think that this bright abode could become her own.

"And what is the price, Mrs. Richards?" Her voice almost did fail her as she asked this question. She was determined to be liberal; but money of her own had hitherto been so scarce with her that she still dreaded the idea of expense.

"The price, mem, is well beknown to all as knows Littlebath. We never alters. Ask Dr Pottinger else."

Miss Mackenzie did not at all wish to ask Dr Pottinger, who was at this moment standing in the front room, while she and her embryo landlady were settling affairs in the back room.

"But what is the price, Mrs. Richards?"

"The price, mem, is two pound ten a week, or nine guineas if taken by the month—to include the kitchen fire."

Margaret breathed again. She had made her little calculations over and over again, and was prepared to bid as high as the sum now named for such a combination of comfort and splendour as Mrs. Richards was able to offer to her. One little question she asked, putting her lips close to Mrs. Richards' ear so that her friend the doctor should not hear her through the doorway, and then jumped back a yard and a half, awe-struck by the energy of her landlady's reply.

"B—— in the Paragon!" Mrs. Richards declared that Miss Mackenzie did not as yet know Littlebath. She bethought herself that she did know Arundel Street, and again thanked Fortune for all the good things that had been given to her.

Miss Mackenzie feared to ask any further questions after this, and took the rooms out of hand by the month.

"And very comfortable you'll find yourself," said Dr Pottinger, as he walked back with his new friend to the inn. He had perhaps been a little disappointed when he saw that Miss Mackenzie showed every sign of good health; but he bore it like a man and a Christian, remembering, no doubt, that let a lady's health be ever so good, she likes to see a doctor sometimes, especially if she be alone in the world. He offered her, therefore, every assistance in his power.

"The assembly rooms were quite close to the Paragon," he said.

"Oh, indeed!" said Miss Mackenzie, not quite knowing the purport of assembly rooms.

"And there are two or three churches within five minutes' walk." Here Miss Mackenzie was more at home, and mentioned the name of the Rev. Mr. Stumfold, for whom she had a letter of introduction, and whose church she would like to attend.

Now Mr. Stumfold was a shining light at Littlebath, the man of men, if he was not something more than mere man, in the eyes of the devout inhabitants of that town. Miss Mackenzie had never heard of Mr. Stumfold till her clergyman in London had mentioned his name, and even now had no idea that he was remarkable for any special views in Church matters. Such special views of her own she had none. But Mr. Stumfold at Littlebath had very special views, and was very specially known for them. His friends said that he was evangelical, and his enemies said that he was Low Church. He himself was wont to laugh at these names—for he was a man who could laugh—and to declare that his only ambition was to fight the devil under

whatever name he might be allowed to carry on that battle. And
he was always fighting the devil by opposing those pursuits
which are the life and mainstay of such places as Littlebath. His
chief enemies were card-playing and dancing as regarded the
weaker sex, and hunting and horse-racing—to which, indeed,
might be added everything under the name of sport—as regarded
the stronger. Sunday comforts were also enemies which he hated
with a vigorous hatred, unless three full services a day, with
sundry intermediate religious readings and exercitations of the
spirit, may be called Sunday comforts. But not on this account
should it be supposed that Mr. Stumfold was a dreary, dark,
sardonic man. Such was by no means the case. He could laugh
loud. He could be very jovial at dinner parties. He could make
his little jokes about little pet wickednesses. A glass of wine, in
season, he never refused. Picnics he allowed, and the flirtation
accompanying them. He himself was driven about behind a pair
of horses, and his daughters were horsewomen. His sons, if the
world spoke truth, were Nimrods; but that was in another
county, away from the Tantivy hills, and Mr. Stumfold knew
nothing of it. In Littlebath Mr. Stumfold reigned over his own
set as a tyrant, but to those who obeyed him he was never
austere in his tyranny.

When Miss Mackenzie mentioned Mr. Stumfold's name
to the doctor, the doctor felt that he had been wrong in his
allusion to the assembly rooms. Mr. Stumfold's people never
went to assembly rooms. He, a doctor of medicine, of course
went among saints and sinners alike, but in such a place as
Littlebath he had found it expedient to have one tone for the
saints and another for the sinners. Now the Paragon was
generally inhabited by sinners, and therefore he had made his
hint about the assembly rooms. He at once pointed out Mr.
Stumfold's church, the spire of which was to be seen as they
walked towards the inn, and said a word in praise of that good
man. Not a syllable would he again have uttered as to the

wickednesses of the place, had not Miss Mackenzie asked some questions as to those assembly rooms.

"How did people get to belong to them? Were they pleasant? What did they do there? Oh—she could put her name down, could she? If it was anything in the way of amusement she would certainly like to put her name down." Dr Pottinger, when on that afternoon he instructed his wife to call on Miss Mackenzie as soon as that young lady should be settled, explained that the stranger was very much in the dark as to the ways and manners of Littlebath.

"What! go to the assembly rooms, and sit under Mr. Stumfold!" said Mrs. Pottinger. "She never can do both, you know."

Miss Mackenzie went back to London, and returned at the end of a week with her niece, her new maid, and her boxes. All the old furniture had been sold, and her personal belongings were very scanty. The time had now come in which personal belongings would accrue to her, but when she reached the Paragon one big trunk and one small trunk contained all that she possessed. The luggage of her niece Susanna was almost as copious as her own. Her maid had been newly hired, and she was almost ashamed of the scantiness of her own possessions in the eyes of her servant.

The way in which Susanna had been given up to her had been oppressive, and at one moment almost distressing. That objection which each lady had to visit the other,—Miss Mackenzie, that is, and Susanna's mamma,—had never been overcome, and neither side had given way. No visit of affection or of friendship had been made. But as it was needful that the transfer of the young lady should be effected with some solemnity, Mrs. Mackenzie had condescended to bring her to her future guardian's lodgings on the day before that fixed for the journey to Littlebath. To so much degradation—for in her eyes it was degradation—Mrs. Mackenzie had consented to subject herself; and Mr. Mackenzie was to come on the following morning, and take his sister and daughter to the train.

The mother, as soon as she found herself seated and almost before she had recovered the breath lost in mounting the lodging-house stairs, began the speech which she had prepared for delivery on the occasion. Miss Mackenzie, who had taken Susanna's hand, remained with it in her own during the greater part of the speech. Before the speech was done the poor girl's hand had been dropped, but in dropping it the aunt was not guilty of any unkindness. "Margaret," said Mrs. Mackenzie, "this is a trial, a very great trial to a mother, and I hope that you feel it as I do."

"Sarah," said Miss Mackenzie, "I will do my duty by your child."

"Well; yes; I hope so. If I thought you would not do your duty by her, no consideration of mere money would induce me to let her go to you. But I do hope, Margaret, you will think of the greatness of the sacrifice we are making. There never was a better child than Susanna."

"I am very glad of that, Sarah."

"Indeed, there never was a better child than any of 'em; I will say that for them before the child herself; and if you do your duty by her, I'm quite sure she'll do hers by you. Tom thinks it best that she should go; and, of course, as all the money which should have gone to him has come to you"—it was here, at this point that Susanna's hand was dropped—"and as you haven't got a chick nor a child, nor yet anybody else of your own, no doubt it is natural that you should wish to have one of them."

"I wish to do a kindness to my brother," said Miss Mackenzie—"and to my niece."

"Yes; of course; I understand. When you would not come up to see us, Margaret, and you all alone, and we with a comfortable home to offer you, of course I knew what your feelings were towards me. I don't want anybody to tell me that! Oh dear, no! 'Tom,' said I when he asked me to go down to

Arundel Street, 'not if I know it.' Those were the very words I uttered: 'Not if I know it, Tom!' And your papa never asked me to go again—did he, Susanna? Nor I couldn't have brought myself to. As you are so frank, Margaret, perhaps candour is the best on both sides. Now I am going to leave my darling child in your hands, and if you have got a mother's heart within your bosom, I hope you will do a mother's duty by her."

More than once during this oration Miss Mackenzie had felt inclined to speak her mind out, and to fight her own battle; but she was repressed by the presence of the girl. What chance could there be of good feeling, of aught of affection between her and her ward, if on such an occasion as this the girl were made the witness of a quarrel between her mother and her aunt? Miss Mackenzie's face had become red, and she had felt herself to be angry; but she bore it all with good courage.

"I will do my best," said she. "Susanna, come here and kiss me. Shall we be great friends?" Susanna went and kissed her; but if the poor girl attempted any answer it was not audible. Then the mother threw herself on the daughter's neck, and the two embraced each other with many tears.

"You'll find all her things very tidy, and plenty of 'em," said Mrs. Mackenzie through her tears. "I'm sure we've worked hard enough at 'em for the last three weeks."

"I've no doubt we shall find it all very nice," said the aunt.

"We wouldn't send her away to disgrace us, were it ever so; though of course in the way of money it would make no difference to you if she had come without a thing to her back. But I've that spirit I couldn't do it, and so I told Tom." After this Mrs. Mackenzie once more embraced her daughter, and then took her departure.

Miss Mackenzie, as soon as her sister-in-law was gone, again took the girl's hand in her own. Poor Susanna was in tears, and indeed there was enough in her circumstances at the present moment to justify her in weeping. She had been given over to her new destiny in no joyous manner.

"Susanna," said Aunt Margaret, with her softest voice, "I'm so glad you have come to me. I will love you very dearly if you will let me."

The girl came and clustered close against her as she sat on the sofa, and so contrived as to creep in under her arm. No one had ever crept in under her arm, or clung close to her before. Such outward signs of affection as that had never been hers, either to give or to receive.

"My darling," she said, "I will love you so dearly."

Susanna said nothing, not knowing what words would be fitting for such an occasion, but on hearing her aunt's assurance of affection, she clung still closer to her, and in this way they became happy before the evening was over.

This adopted niece was no child when she was thus placed under her aunt's charge. She was already fifteen, and though she was young-looking for her age,—having none of that precocious air of womanhood which some girls have assumed by that time,—she was a strong healthy well-grown lass, standing stoutly on her legs, with her head well balanced, with a straight back, and well-formed though not slender waist. She was sharp about the shoulders and elbows, as girls are—or should be—at that age; and her face was not formed into any definite shape of beauty, or its reverse. But her eyes were bright—as were those of all the Mackenzies—and her mouth was not the mouth of a fool. If her cheek-bones were a little high, and the lower part of her face somewhat angular, those peculiarities were probably not distasteful to the eyes of her aunt.

"You're a Mackenzie all over," said the aunt, speaking with some little touch of the northern burr in her voice, though she herself had never known anything of the north.

"That's what mamma's brothers and sisters always tell me. They say I am Scotchy."

Then Miss Mackenzie kissed the girl again. If Susanna had been sent to her because she had in her gait and appearance more of the land of cakes than any of her brothers and sisters, that at any rate should do her no harm in the estimation of her aunt. Thus in this way they became friends.

On the following morning Mr. Mackenzie came and took them down to the train.

"I suppose we shall see you sometimes up in London?" he said, as he stood by the door of the carriage.

"I don't know that there will be much to bring me up," she answered.

"And there won't be much to keep you down in the country," said he. "You don't know anybody at Littlebath, I believe?"

"The truth is, Tom, that I don't know anybody anywhere. I'm likely to know as many people at Littlebath as I should in London. But situated as I am, I must live pretty much to myself wherever I am."

Then the guard came bustling along the platform, the father kissed his daughter for the last time, and kissed his sister also, and our heroine with her young charge had taken her departure, and commenced her career in the world.

For many a mile not a word was spoken between Miss Mackenzie and her niece. The mind of the elder of the two travellers was very full of thought,—of thought and of feeling too, so that she could not bring herself to speak joyously to the young girl. She had her doubts as to the wisdom of what she was doing. Her whole life, hitherto, had been sad, sombre, and, we may almost say, silent. Things had so gone with her that she had had no power of action on her own behalf. Neither with her father, nor with her brother, though both had been invalids, had anything of the management of affairs fallen into her hands. Not even in the hiring or discharging of a cookmaid had she possessed any influence. No power of the purse had been with her—none of that power which belongs legitimately to a wife because a wife is a partner in the business. The two sick men whom she had nursed had liked to retain in their own hands the little privileges which their position had given them. Margaret, therefore, had been a nurse in their houses, and nothing more than a nurse. Had this gone on for another ten years she would have lived down the ambition of any more exciting career, and would have been satisfied, had she then come into the possession of the money which was now hers, to have ended her days nursing herself—or more probably, as she was by nature unselfish, she would have lived down her pride as well as her ambition, and would have gone to the house of her brother and have expended herself in nursing her nephews and nieces. But luckily for her—or unluckily, as it may be—this money had come to her before her time for withering had arrived. In heart, and energy, and desire, there was still much of strength left to her. Indeed it may be said of her, that she had come so late in life to whatever of ripeness was to be vouchsafed to her, that perhaps the period of her thraldom had not terminated itself a day too soon for her advantage. Many of her youthful verses she had destroyed in the packing up of those two modest trunks; but there were effusions of the spirit which had flown into rhyme within the last twelve months, and which she still preserved. Since her brother's death she had confined herself to simple prose, and for this purpose she kept an ample journal. All this is mentioned to show that at the age of thirty-six Margaret Mackenzie was still a young woman.

She had resolved that she would not content herself with a lifeless life, such as those few who knew anything of her evidently expected from her. Harry Handcock had thought to make her his head nurse; and the Tom Mackenzies had also indulged some such idea when they gave her that first invitation to come and live in Gower Street. A word or two had been said at the Cedars which led her to suppose that the baronet's family there would have admitted her, with her eight hundred a year, had she chosen to be so admitted. But she had declared to herself that she would make a struggle to do better with herself and with her money than that. She would go into the world, and see if she could find any of those pleasantnesses of which she had read in books. As for dancing, she was too old, and never yet in her life had she stood up as a worshipper of Terpsichore. Of cards she knew nothing; she had never even seen them used. To the performance of plays she had been once or twice in her early days, and now regarded a theatre not as a sink of wickedness after the manner of the Stumfoldians, but as a place of danger because of difficulty of ingress and egress, because the ways of a theatre were far beyond her ken. The very mode in which it would behove her to dress herself to go out to an ordinary dinner party, was almost unknown to her. And yet, in spite of all this, she was resolved to try.

Would it not have been easier for her—easier and more comfortable—to have abandoned all ideas of the world, and have put herself at once under the tutelage and protection of some clergyman who would have told her how to give away her money, and prepare herself in the right way for a comfortable death-bed? There was much in this view of life to recommend it. It would be very easy, and she had the necessary faith. Such a clergyman, too, would be a comfortable friend, and, if a married man, might be a very dear friend. And there might, probably, be a clergyman's wife, who would go about with her, and assist in that giving away of her money. Would not this be the best life after all? But in order to reconcile herself altogether to such a life as that, it was necessary that she should be convinced that the other life was abominable, wicked, and damnable. She had seen enough of things—had looked far enough into the ways of the world—to perceive this. She knew that she must go about such work with strong convictions, and as yet she could not bring herself to think that "dancing and delights" were damnable. No doubt she would come to have such belief if told so often enough by some persuasive divine; but she was not sure that she wished to believe it.

After doubting much, she had determined to give the world a trial, and, feeling that London was too big for her, had resolved upon Littlebath. But now, having started herself upon her journey, she felt as some mariner might who had put himself out alone to sea in a small boat, with courage enough for the attempt, but without that sort of courage which would make the attempt itself delightful.

And then this girl that was with her! She had told herself that it would not be well to live for herself alone, that it was her duty to share her good things with some one, and therefore she had resolved to share them with her niece. But in this guardianship there was danger, which frightened her as she thought of it.

"Are you tired yet, my dear?" said Miss Mackenzie, as they got to Swindon.

"Oh dear, no; I'm not at all tired."

"There are cakes in there, I see. I wonder whether we should have time to buy one."

After considering the matter for five minutes in doubt, Aunt Margaret did rush out, and did buy the cakes.

Chapter III

Miss Mackenzie's First Acquaintances

In the first fortnight of Miss Mackenzie's sojourn at Littlebath, four persons called upon her; but though this was a success as far as it went, those fourteen days were very dull. During her former short visit to the place she had arranged to send her niece to a day school which had been recommended to her as being very genteel, and conducted under moral and religious auspices of most exalted character. Hither Susanna went every morning after breakfast, and returned home in these summer days at eight o'clock in the evening. On Sundays also, she went to morning church with the other girls; so that Miss Mackenzie was left very much to herself.

Mrs. Pottinger was the first to call, and the doctor's wife contented herself with simple offers of general assistance. She named a baker to Miss Mackenzie, and a dressmaker; and she told her what was the proper price to be paid by the hour for a private brougham or for a public fly. All this was useful, as Miss Mackenzie was in a state of densest ignorance; but it did not seem that much in the way of amusement would come from the acquaintance of Mrs. Pottinger. That lady said nothing about the assembly rooms, nor did she speak of the Stumfoldian manner of life. Her husband had no doubt explained to her that the stranger was not as yet a declared disciple in either school. Miss Mackenzie had wished to ask a question about the assemblies, but had been deterred by fear. Then came Mr. Stumfold in person, and, of course, nothing about the assembly rooms was said by him. He made himself very pleasant, and Miss Mackenzie almost resolved to put herself into his hands. He did not look sour at her, nor did he browbeat her with severe words, nor did he exact from her the performance of any hard duties. He promised to find her a seat in his church, and told her what were the hours of service. He had three "Sabbath services," but he thought that regular attendance twice every Sunday was enough for people in general. He would be delighted to be of use, and Mrs. Stumfold should come and call. Having promised this, he went his way. Then came Mrs. Stumfold, according to promise, bringing with her one Miss Baker, a maiden lady. From Mrs. Stumfold our friend got very little assistance. Mrs. Stumfold was hard, severe, and perhaps a little grand. She let fall a word or two which intimated her conviction that Miss Mackenzie was to become at all points a Stumfoldian, since she had herself invoked the countenance and assistance of the great man on her first arrival; but beyond this, Mrs. Stumfold afforded no comfort. Our friend could not have explained to herself why it was so, but after having encountered Mrs. Stumfold, she was less inclined to become a disciple than she had been when she had seen only the great master himself. It was not only that Mrs. Stumfold, as judged by externals, was felt to be more severe than her husband evangelically, but she was more severe also ecclesiastically. Miss Mackenzie thought that she could probably obey the ecclesiastical man, but that she would certainly rebel against the ecclesiastical woman.

There had been, as I have said, a Miss Baker with the female minister, and Miss Mackenzie had at once perceived that had Miss Baker called alone, the whole thing would have been much more pleasant. Miss Baker had a soft voice, was given to a good deal of gentle talking, was kind in her manner, and prone to quick intimacies with other ladies of her own nature. All this Miss Mackenzie felt rather than saw, and would have been delighted to have had Miss Baker without Mrs. Stumfold. She could, she knew, have found out all about everything in five minutes, had she and Miss Baker been able to sit close together and to let their tongues loose. But Miss Baker, poor soul, was in these days thoroughly subject to the female Stumfold influence, and went about the world of Littlebath in a repressed manner that was truly pitiable to those who had known her before the days of her slavery.

But, as she rose to leave the room at her tyrant's bidding, she spoke a word of comfort. "A friend of mine, Miss Mackenzie, lives next door to you, and she has begged me to say that she will do herself the pleasure of calling on you, if you will allow her."

The poor woman hesitated as she made her little speech, and once cast her eye round in fear upon her companion.

"I'm sure I shall be delighted," said Miss Mackenzie.

"That's Miss Todd, is it?" said Mrs. Stumfold; and it was made manifest by Mrs. Stumfold's voice that Mrs. Stumfold did not think much of Miss Todd.

"Yes; Miss Todd. You see she is so close a neighbour," said Miss Baker, apologetically.

Mrs. Stumfold shook her head, and then went away without further speech.

Miss Mackenzie became at once impatient for Miss Todd's arrival, and was induced to keep an eye restlessly at watch on the two neighbouring doors in the Paragon, in order that she might see Miss Todd at the moment of some entrance or exit. Twice she did see a lady come out from the house next her own on the right, a stout jolly-looking dame, with a red face and a capacious bonnet, who closed the door behind her with a slam, and looked as though she would care little for either male Stumfold or female. Miss Mackenzie, however, made up her mind that this was not Miss Todd. This lady, she thought, was a married lady; on one occasion there had been children with her, and she was, in Miss Mackenzie's judgment, too stout, too decided, and perhaps too loud to be a spinster. A full week passed by before this question was decided by the promised visit,—a week during which the new comer never left her house at any hour at which callers could be expected to call, so anxious was she to become acquainted with her neighbour; and she had almost given the matter up in despair, thinking that Mrs. Stumfold had interfered with her tyranny, when, one day immediately after lunch—in these days Miss Mackenzie always lunched, but seldom dined—when one day immediately after lunch, Miss Todd was announced.

Miss Mackenzie immediately saw that she had been wrong. Miss Todd was the stout, red-faced lady with the children. Two of the children, girls of eleven and thirteen, were with her now. As Miss Todd walked across the room to shake hands with her new acquaintance, Miss Mackenzie at once recognised the manner in which the street door had been slammed, and knew that it was the same firm step which she had heard on the pavement half down the Paragon.

"My friend, Miss Baker, told me you had come to live next door to me," began Miss Todd, "and therefore I told her to tell you that I should come and see you. Single ladies, when they come here, generally like some one to come to them. I'm single myself, and these are my nieces. You've got a niece, I believe, too. When the Popes have nephews, people say all manner of ill-natured things. I hope they ain't so uncivil to us."

Miss Mackenzie smirked and smiled, and assured Miss Todd that she was very glad to see her. The allusion to the Popes she did not understand.

"Miss Baker came with Mrs. Stumfold, didn't she?" continued Miss Todd. "She doesn't go much anywhere now without Mrs. Stumfold, unless when she creeps down to me. She and I are very old friends. Have you known Mr. Stumfold long? Perhaps you have come here to be near him; a great many ladies do."

In answer to this, Miss Mackenzie explained that she was not a follower of Mr. Stumfold in that sense. It was true that she had brought a letter to him, and intended to go to his church. In consequence of that letter, Mrs. Stumfold had been good enough to call upon her.

"Oh yes: she'll come to you quick enough. Did she come with her carriage and horses?"

"I think she was on foot," said Miss Mackenzie.

"Then I should tell her of it. Coming to you, in the best house in the Paragon, on your first arrival, she ought to have come with her carriage and horses."

"Tell her of it!" said Miss Mackenzie.

"A great many ladies would, and would go over to the enemy before the month was over, unless she brought the carriage in the meantime. I don't advise you to do so. You haven't got standing enough in the place yet, and perhaps she could put you down."

"But it makes no difference to me how she comes."

"None in the least, my dear, or to me either. I should be glad to see her even in a wheelbarrow for my part. But you mustn't suppose that she ever comes to me. Lord bless you! no. She found me out to be past all grace ever so many years ago."

"Mrs. Stumfold thinks that Aunt Sally is the old gentleman himself," said the elder of the girls.

"Ha, ha, ha," laughed the aunt. "You see, Miss Mackenzie, we run very much into parties here, as they do in most places of this kind, and if you mean to go thoroughly in with the Stumfold party you must tell me so, candidly, and there won't be any bones broken between us. I shan't like you the less for saying so: only in that case it won't be any use our trying to see much of each other."

Miss Mackenzie was somewhat frightened, and hardly knew what answer to make. She was very anxious to have it understood that she was not, as yet, in bond under Mrs. Stumfold—that it was still a matter of choice to herself whether she would be a saint or a sinner; and she would have been so glad to hint to her neighbour that she would like to try the sinner's line, if it were only for a month or two; only Miss Todd frightened her! And when the girl told her that Miss Todd was regarded, ex parte Stumfold, as being the old gentleman himself, Miss Mackenzie again thought for an instant that there would be safety in giving way to the evangelico-ecclesiastical influence, and that perhaps life might be pleasant enough to her if she could be allowed to go about in couples with that soft Miss Baker.

"As you have been so good as to call," said Miss Mackenzie, "I hope you will allow me to return your visit."

"Oh, dear, yes—shall be quite delighted to see you. You can't hurt me, you know. The question is, whether I shan't ruin you. Not that I and Mr. Stumfold ain't great cronies. He and I meet about on neutral ground, and are the best friends in the world. He knows I'm a lost sheep—a gone 'coon, as the Americans say—so he pokes his fun at me, and we're as jolly as sandboys. But St Stumfolda is made of sterner metal, and will not put up with any such female levity. If she pokes her fun at any sinners, it is at gentlemen sinners; and grim work it must be for them, I should think. Poor Mary Baker! the best creature in the world. I'm afraid she has a bad time of it. But then, you know, perhaps that is the sort of thing you like."

"You see I know so very little of Mrs. Stumfold," said Miss Mackenzie.

"That's a misfortune will soon be cured if you let her have her own way. You ask Mary Baker else. But I don't mean to be saying anything bad behind anybody's back; I don't indeed. I have no doubt these people are very good in their way; only their ways are not my ways; and one doesn't like to be told

so often that one's own way is broad, and that it leads—you
know where. Come, Patty, let us be going. When you've made
up your mind, Miss Mackenzie, just you tell me. If you say,
'Miss Todd, I think you're too wicked for me,' I shall
understand it. I shan't be in the least offended. But if my way
isn't—isn't too broad, you know, I shall be very happy to see
you."

Hereupon Miss Mackenzie plucked up courage and asked
a question.

"Do you ever go to the assembly rooms, Miss Todd?"

Miss Todd almost whistled before she gave her answer.
"Why, Miss Mackenzie, that's where they dance and play cards,
and where the girls flirt and the young men make fools of
themselves. I don't go there very often myself, because I don't
care about flirting, and I'm too old for dancing. As for cards, I
get plenty of them at home. I think I did put down my name and
paid something when I first came here, but that's ever so many
years ago. I don't go to the assembly rooms now."

As soon as Miss Todd was gone, Miss Mackenzie went
to work to reflect seriously upon all she had just heard. Of
course, there could be no longer any question of her going to the
assembly rooms. Even Miss Todd, wicked as she was, did not go
there. But should she, or should she not, return Miss Todd's
visit? If she did she would be thereby committing herself to what
Miss Todd had profanely called the broad way. In such case any
advance in the Stumfold direction would be forbidden to her.
But if she did not call on Miss Todd, then she would have
plainly declared that she intended to be such another disciple as
Miss Baker, and from that decision there would be no recall. On
this subject she must make up her mind, and in doing so she
laboured with all her power. As to any charge of incivility which
might attach to her for not returning the visit of a lady who had
been so civil to her, of that she thought nothing. Miss Todd had
herself declared that she would not be in the least offended. But
she liked this new acquaintance. In owning all the truth about

Miss Mackenzie, I must confess that her mind hankered after the things of this world. She thought that if she could only establish herself as Miss Todd was established, she would care nothing for the Stumfolds, male or female.

But how was she to do this? An establishment in the Stumfold direction might be easier.

In the course of the next week two affairs of moment occurred to Miss Mackenzie. On the Wednesday morning she received from London a letter of business which caused her considerable anxiety, and on the Thursday afternoon a note was brought to her from Mrs. Stumfold,—or rather an envelope containing a card on which was printed an invitation to drink tea with that lady on that day week. This invitation she accepted without much doubt. She would go and see Mrs. Stumfold in her house, and would then be better able to decide whether the mode of life practised by the Stumfold party would be to her taste. So she wrote a reply, and sent it by her maid-servant, greatly doubting whether she was not wrong in writing her answer on common note-paper, and whether she also should not have supplied herself with some form or card for the occasion.

The letter of business was from her brother Tom, and contained an application for the loan of some money,—for the loan, indeed, of a good deal of money. But the loan was to be made not to him but to the firm of Rubb and Mackenzie, and was not to be a simple lending of money on the faith of that firm, for purposes of speculation or ordinary business. It was to be expended in the purchase of the premises in the New Road, and Miss Mackenzie was to have a mortgage on them, and was to receive five per cent for the money which she should advance. The letter was long, and though it was manifest even to Miss Mackenzie that he had written the first page with much hesitation, he had waxed strong as he had gone on, and had really made out a good case. "You are to understand," he said, "that this is, of course, to be done through your own lawyer, who will not allow you to make the loan unless he is satisfied with the security. Our landlords are compelled to sell the premises, and unless we purchase them ourselves, we shall in all probability be turned out, as we have only a year or two more under our present lease. You could purchase the whole thing yourself, but in that case you would not be sure of the same interest for your money." He then went on to say that Samuel Rubb, junior, the son of old Rubb, should run down to Littlebath in the course of next week, in order that the whole thing might be made clear to her. Samuel Rubb was not the partner whose name was included in the designation of the firm, but was a young man,—"a comparatively young man,"—as her brother explained, who had lately been admitted to a share in the business.

This letter put Miss Mackenzie into a twitter. Like all other single ladies, she was very nervous about her money. She was quite alive to the beauty of a high rate of interest, but did not quite understand that high interest and impaired security should go hand in hand together. She wished to oblige her brother, and was aware that she had money as to which her lawyers were looking out for an investment. Even this had made her unhappy, as she was not quite sure whether her lawyers would not spend the money. She knew that lone women were terribly robbed sometimes, and had almost resolved upon insisting that the money should be put into the Three per Cents. But she had gone to work with figures, and having ascertained that by doing so twenty-five pounds a year would be docked off from her computed income, she had given no such order. She now again went to work with her figures, and found that if the loan were accomplished it would add twenty-five pounds a year to her computed income. Mortgages, she knew, were good things, strong and firm, based upon landed security, and very respectable. So she wrote to her lawyers, saying that she would be glad to oblige her brother if there were nothing amiss. Her lawyers wrote back, advising her to refer Mr. Rubb, junior, to them. On the day named in her brother's letter, Mr. Samuel

Rubb, junior, arrived at Littlebath, and called upon Miss
Mackenzie in the Paragon.

Miss Mackenzie had been brought up with contempt and
almost with hatred for the Rubb family. It had, in the first
instance, been the work of old Samuel Rubb to tempt her brother
Tom into trade; and he had tempted Tom into a trade that had
not been fat and prosperous, and therefore pardonable, but into a
trade that had been troublesome and poor. Walter Mackenzie
had always spoken of these Rubbs with thorough disgust, and
had persistently refused to hold any intercourse with them.
When, therefore, Mr. Samuel Rubb was announced, our heroine
was somewhat inclined to seat herself upon a high horse.

Mr. Samuel Rubb, junior, came upstairs, and was by no
means the sort of person in appearance that Miss Mackenzie had
expected to see. In the first place, he was, as well as she could
guess, about forty years of age; whereas she had expected to see
a young man. A man who went about the world especially
designated as junior, ought, she thought, to be very young. And
then Mr. Rubb carried with him an air of dignity, and had about
his external presence a something of authority which made her at
once seat herself a peg lower than she had intended. He was a
good-looking man, nearly six feet high, with great hands and
feet, but with a great forehead also, which atoned for his hands
and feet. He was dressed throughout in black, as tradesmen
always are in these days; but, as Miss Mackenzie said to herself,
there was certainly no knowing that he belonged to the oilcloth
business from the cut of his coat or the set of his trousers. He
began his task with great care, and seemed to have none of the
hesitation which had afflicted her brother in writing his letter.
The investment, he said, would, no doubt, be a good one. Two
thousand four hundred pounds was the sum wanted, and he
understood that she had that amount lying idle. Their lawyer had
already seen her lawyer, and there could be no doubt as to the
soundness of the mortgage. An assurance company with whom
the firm had dealings was quite ready to advance the money on

the proposed security, and at the proposed rate of interest, but in such a matter as that, Rubb and Mackenzie did not wish to deal with an assurance company. They desired that all control over the premises should either be in their own hands, or in the hands of someone connected with them.

By the time that Mr. Samuel Rubb had done, Miss Mackenzie found herself to have dismounted altogether from her horse, and to be pervaded by some slight fear that her lawyers might allow so favourable an opportunity for investing her money to slip through their hands.

Then, on a sudden, Mr. Rubb dropped the subject of the loan, and Miss Mackenzie, as he did so, felt herself to be almost disappointed. And when she found him talking easily to her about matters of external life, although she answered him readily, and talked to him also easily, she entertained some feeling that she ought to be offended. Mr. Rubb, junior, was a tradesman who had come to her on business, and having done his business, why did he not go away? Nevertheless, Miss Mackenzie answered him when he asked questions, and allowed herself to be seduced into a conversation.

"Yes, upon my honour," he said, looking out of the window into the Montpelier Gardens, "a very nice situation indeed. How much better they do these things in such a place as this than we do up in London! What dingy houses we live in, and how bright they make the places here!"

"They are not crowded so much, I suppose," said Miss Mackenzie.

"It isn't only that. The truth is, that in London nobody cares what his house looks like. The whole thing is so ugly that anything not ugly would be out of place. Now, in Paris—you have been in Paris, Miss Mackenzie?"

In answer to this, Miss Mackenzie was compelled to own that she had never been in Paris.

"Ah, you should go to Paris, Miss Mackenzie; you should, indeed. Now, you're a lady that have nothing to prevent your going anywhere. If I were you, I'd go almost everywhere; but above all, I'd go to Paris. There's no place like Paris."

"I suppose not," said Miss Mackenzie.

By this time Mr. Rubb had returned from the window, and had seated himself in the easy chair in the middle of the room. In doing so he thrust out both his legs, folded his hands one over the other, and looked very comfortable.

"Now I'm a slave to business," he said. "That horrid place in the New Road, which we want to buy with your money, has made a prisoner of me for the last twenty years. I went into it as the boy who was to do the copying, when your brother first became a partner. Oh dear, how I did hate it!"

"Did you now?"

"I should rather think I did. I had been brought up at the Merchant Taylors' and they intended to send me to Oxford. That was five years before they began the business in the New Road. Then came the crash which our house had at Manchester; and when we had picked up the pieces, we found that we had to give up university ideas. However, I'll make a business of it before I'm done; you see if I don't, Miss Mackenzie. Your brother has been with us so many years that I have quite a pleasure in talking to you about it."

Miss Mackenzie was not quite sure that she reciprocated the pleasure; for, after all, though he did look so much better than she had expected, he was only Rubb, junior, from Rubb and Mackenzie's; and any permanent acquaintance with Mr. Rubb would not suit the line of life in which she was desirous of moving. But she did not in the least know how to stop him, or how to show him that she had intended to receive him simply as a man of business. And then it was so seldom that anyone came to talk to her, that she was tempted to fall away from her high resolves. "I have not known much of my brother's concerns," she said, attempting to be cautious.

Then he sat for another hour, making himself very agreeable, and at the end of that time she offered him a glass of wine and a biscuit, which he accepted. He was going to remain two or three days in the neighbourhood, he said, and might he call again before he left? Miss Mackenzie told him that he might. How was it possible that she should answer such a question in any other way? Then he got up, and shook hands with her, told her that he was so glad he had come to Littlebath, and was quite cordial and friendly. Miss Mackenzie actually found herself laughing with him as they stood on the floor together, and though she knew that it was improper, she liked it. When he was gone she could not remember what it was that had made her laugh, but she remembered that she had laughed. For a long time past very little laughter had come to her share.

When he was gone she prepared herself to think about him at length. Why had he talked to her in that way? Why was he going to call again? Why was Rubb, junior, from Rubb and Mackenzie's, such a pleasant fellow? After all, he retailed oilcloth at so much a yard; and little as she knew of the world, she knew that she, with ever so much good blood in her veins, and with ever so many hundreds a year of her own, was entitled to look for acquaintances of a higher order than that. She, if she were entitled to make any boast about herself—and she was by no means inclined to such boastings—might at any rate boast that she was a lady. Now, Mr. Rubb was not a gentleman. He was not a gentleman by position. She knew that well enough, and she thought that she had also discovered that he was not quite a gentleman in his manners and mode of speech. Nevertheless she had liked him, and had laughed with him, and the remembrance of this made her sad.

That same evening she wrote a letter to her lawyer, telling him that she was very anxious to oblige her brother, if the security was good. And then she went into the matter at length, repeating much of what Mr. Rubb had said to her, as to the excellence of mortgages in general, and of this mortgage in particular. After that she dressed herself with great care, and went out to tea at Mrs. Stumfold's. This was the first occasion in her life in which she had gone to a party, the invitation to which had come to her on a card, and of course she felt herself to be a little nervous.

Chapter IV

Miss Mackenzie Commences Her Career

Miss Mackenzie had been three weeks at Littlebath when the day arrived on which she was to go to Mrs. Stumfold's party, and up to that time she had not enjoyed much of the society of that very social place. Indeed, in these pages have been described with accuracy all the advancement which she had made in that direction. She had indeed returned Miss Todd's call, but had not found that lady at home. In doing this she had almost felt herself to be guilty of treason against the new allegiance which she seemed to have taken upon herself in accepting Mrs. Stumfold's invitation; and she had done it at last not from any firm resolve of which she might have been proud, but had been driven to it by ennui, and by the easy temptation of Miss Todd's neighbouring door. She had, therefore, slipped out, and finding her wicked friend to be not at home, had hurried back again. She had, however, committed herself to a card, and she knew that Mrs. Stumfold would hear of it through Miss Baker. Miss Baker's visit she had not returned, being in doubt where Miss Baker lived, being terribly in doubt also whether the

Median rules of fashion demanded of her that she should return the call of a lady who had simply come to her with another caller. Her hesitation on this subject had been much, and her vacillations many, but she had thought it safer to abstain. For the last day or two she had been expecting the return of Mr. Rubb, junior—keeping herself a prisoner, I fear, during the best hours of the day, so that she might be there to receive him when he did come; but though she had so acted, she had quite resolved to be very cold with him, and very cautious, and had been desirous of seeing him solely with a view to the mercantile necessities of her position. It behoved her certainly to attend to business when business came in her way, and therefore she would take care to be at home when Mr. Rubb should call.

She had been to church twice a day on each of the Sundays that she had passed in Littlebath, having in this matter strictly obeyed the hints which Mr. Stumfold had given for her guidance. No doubt she had received benefit from the discourses which she had heard from that gentleman each morning; and, let us hope, benefit also from the much longer discourses which she had heard from Mr. Stumfold's curate on each evening. The Rev. Mr. Maguire was very powerful, but he was also very long; and Miss Mackenzie, who was hardly as yet entitled to rank herself among the thoroughly converted, was inclined to think that he was too long. She was, however, patient by nature, and willing to bear much, if only some little might come to her in return. What of social comfort she had expected to obtain from her churchgoings I cannot quite define; but I think that she had unconsciously expected something from them in that direction, and that she had been disappointed.

But now, at nine o'clock on this appointed evening, she was of a certainty and in very truth going into society. The card said half-past eight; but the Sun had not yoked his horses so far away from her Tyre, remote as that Tyre had been, as to have left her in ignorance that half-past eight meant nine. When her watch showed her that half-past eight had really come, she was fidgety, and rang the bell to inquire whether the man might have probably forgotten to send the fly; and yet she had been very careful to tell the man that she did not wish to be at Mrs. Stumfold's before nine.

"He understands, Miss," said the servant; "don't you be afeard; he's a-doing of it every night."

Then she became painfully conscious that even the maidservant knew more of the social ways of the place than did she.

When she reached the top of Mrs. Stumfold's stairs, her heart was in her mouth, for she perceived immediately that she had kept people waiting. After all, she had trusted to false intelligence in that matter of the hour. Half-past eight had meant half-past eight, and she ought to have known that this would be so in a house so upright as that of Mrs. Stumfold. That lady met her at the door, and smiling—blandly, but, perhaps I might be permitted to say, not so blandly as she might have smiled—conducted the stranger to a seat.

"We generally open with a little prayer, and for that purpose our dear friends are kind enough to come to us punctually."

Then Mr. Stumfold got up, and pressed her hand very kindly.

"I'm so sorry," Miss Mackenzie had uttered.

"Not in the least," he replied. "I knew you couldn't know, and therefore we ventured to wait a few minutes. The time hasn't been lost, as Mr. Maguire has treated us to a theological argument of great weight."

Then all the company laughed, and Miss Mackenzie perceived that Mr. Stumfold could joke in his way. She was introduced to Mr. Maguire, who also pressed her hand; and then Miss Baker came and sat by her side. There was, however, at that moment no time for conversation. The prayer was begun immediately, Mr. Stumfold taking this duty himself. Then Mr. Maguire read half a chapter in the Bible, and after that Mr. Stumfold explained it. Two ladies asked Mr. Stumfold questions with great pertinacity, and these questions Mr. Stumfold answered very freely, walking about the room the while, and laughing often as he submitted himself to their interrogations. And Miss Mackenzie was much astonished at the special freedom of his manner,—how he spoke of St Paul as Paul, declaring the saint to have been a good fellow; how he said he liked Luke better than Matthew, and how he named even a holier name than these with infinite ease and an accustomed familiarity which seemed to delight the other ladies; but which at first shocked her in her ignorance.

"But I'm not going to have anything more to say to Peter and Paul at present," he declared at last. "You'd keep me here all night, and the tea will be spoilt."

Then they all laughed again at the absurd idea of this great and good man preferring his food,—his food of this world,—to that other food which it was his special business to dispense. There is nothing which the Stumfoldian ladies of Littlebath liked so much as these little jokes which bordered on the profanity of the outer world, which made them feel themselves to be almost as funny as the sinners, and gave them a slight taste, as it were, of the pleasures of iniquity.

"Wine maketh glad the heart of woman, Mrs. Jones," Mr. Stumfold would say as he filled for the second time the glass of some old lady of his set; and the old lady would chirrup and wink, and feel that things were going almost as jollily with her as they did with that wicked Mrs. Smith, who spent every night of her life playing cards, or as they had done with that horrid Mrs. Brown, of whom such terrible things were occasionally whispered when two or three ladies found themselves sufficiently private to whisper them; that things were going almost as pleasant here in this world, although accompanied by so much safety as to the future in her own case, and so much danger in those other cases! I think it was this aptitude for feminine rakishness which, more than any of his great virtues, more even than his indomitable industry, made Mr. Stumfold the most popular man in Littlebath. A dozen ladies on the present occasion skipped away to the tea-table in the back drawing-room with a delighted alacrity, which was all owing to the unceremonious treatment which St Peter and St Paul had received from their pastor.

Miss Mackenzie had just found time to cast an eye round the room and examine the scene of Mr. Stumfold's pleasantries while Mr. Maguire was reading. She saw that there were only three gentlemen there besides the two clergymen. There was a very old man who sat close wedged in between Mrs. Stumfold and another lady, by whose joint dresses he was almost obliterated. This was Mr. Peters, a retired attorney. He was Mrs. Stumfold's father, and from his coffers had come the superfluities of comfort which Miss Mackenzie saw around her. Rumour, even among the saintly people of Littlebath, said that Mr. Peters had been a sharp practitioner in his early days;—that he had been successful in his labours was admitted by all.

"No doubt he has repented," Miss Baker said one day to Miss Todd.

"And if he has not, he has forgotten all about it, which generally means the same thing," Miss Todd had answered.

Mr. Peters was now very old, and I am disposed to think he had forgotten all about it.

The other two gentlemen were both young, and they stood very high in the graces of all the company there assembled. They were high in the graces of Mr. Stumfold, but higher still in the graces of Mrs. Stumfold, and were almost worshipped by one or two other ladies whose powers of external adoration were not diminished by the possession of husbands. They were, both of them, young men who had settled themselves for a time at Littlebath that they might be near Mr. Stumfold, and had sufficient of worldly wealth to enable them to pass their time in semi-clerical pursuits.

Mr. Frigidy, the elder, intended at some time to go into the Church, but had not as yet made sufficient progress in his studies to justify him in hoping that he could pass a bishop's examination. His friends told him of Islington and St Bees, of Durham, Birkenhead, and other places where the thing could be done for him; but he hesitated, fearing whether he might be able to pass even the initiatory gates of Islington. He was a good young man, at peace with all the world—except Mr. Startup. With Mr. Startup the veracious chronicler does not dare to assert that Mr. Frigidy was at peace. Now Mr. Startup was the other young man whom Miss Mackenzie saw in that room.

Mr. Startup was also a very good young man, but he was of a fiery calibre, whereas Frigidy was naturally mild. Startup was already an open-air preacher, whereas Frigidy lacked nerve to speak a word above his breath. Startup was not a clergyman because certain scruples impeded and prevented him, while in the bosom of Frigidy there existed no desire so strong as that of having the word reverend attached to his name. Startup, though he was younger than Frigidy, could talk to seven ladies at once with ease, but Frigidy could not talk to one without much assistance from that lady herself. The consequence of this was that Mr. Frigidy could not bring himself to love Mr. Startup,— could not enable himself to justify a veracious chronicler in saying that he was at peace with all the world, Startup included.

The ladies were too many for Miss Mackenzie to notice them specially as she sat listening to Mr. Maguire's impressive voice. Mr. Maguire she did notice, and found him to be the possessor of a good figure, of a fine head of jet black hair, of a perfect set of white teeth, of whiskers which were also black and very fine, but streaked here and there with a grey hair,—and of the most terrible squint in his right eye which ever disfigured a face that in all other respects was fitted for an Apollo. So egregious was the squint that Miss Mackenzie could not keep herself from regarding it, even while Mr. Stumfold was expounding. Had she looked Mr. Maguire full in the face at the beginning, I do not think it would so much have mattered to her; but she had seen first the back of his head, and then his profile, and had unfortunately formed a strong opinion as to his almost perfect beauty. When, therefore, the defective eye was disclosed to her, her feelings were moved in a more than ordinary manner. How was it that a man graced with such a head, with such a mouth and chin and forehead, nay, with such a left eye, could be cursed with such a right eye! She was still thinking of this when the frisky movement into the tea-room took place around her.

When at this moment Mr. Stumfold offered her his arm to conduct her through the folding doors, this condescension on his part almost confounded her. The other ladies knew that he always did so to a newcomer, and therefore thought less of it. No other gentleman took any other lady, but she was led up to a special seat,—a seat of honour as it were, at the left hand side of a huge silver kettle. Immediately before the kettle sat Mrs. Stumfold. Immediately before another kettle, at another table, sat Miss Peters, a sister of Mrs. Stumfold's. The back drawing-room in which they were congregated was larger than the other, and opened behind into a pretty garden. Mr. Stumfold's lines in falling thus among the Peters, had fallen to him in pleasant places. On the other side of Miss Mackenzie sat Miss Baker, and on the other side of Mrs. Stumfold stood Mr. Startup, talking aloud and administering the full tea-cups with a conscious grace. Mr. Stumfold and Mr. Frigidy were at the other table, and Mr. Maguire was occupied in passing promiscuously from one to the other. Miss Mackenzie wished with all her heart that he would seat himself somewhere with his face turned away from her, for she found it impossible to avert her eyes from his eye. But he was always there, before her sight, and she began to feel that he was an evil spirit,—her evil spirit, and that he would be too many for her.

Before anybody else was allowed to begin, Mrs. Stumfold rose from her chair with a large and completely filled bowl of tea, with a plate also laden with buttered toast, and with her own hands and on her own legs carried these delicacies round to her papa. On such an occasion as this no servant, no friend, no Mr. Startup, was allowed to interfere with her filial piety.

"She does it always," said an admiring lady in an audible whisper from the other side of Miss Baker. "She does it always."

The admiring lady was the wife of a retired coachbuilder, who was painfully anxious to make her way into good evangelical society at Littlebath.

"Perhaps you will put in the sugar for yourself," said Mrs. Stumfold to Miss Mackenzie as soon as she returned. On this occasion Miss Mackenzie received her cup the first after the father of the house, but the words spoken to her were stern to the ear.

"Perhaps you will put in the sugar yourself. It lightens the labour."

Miss Mackenzie expressed her willingness to do so and regretted that Mrs. Stumfold should have to work so hard. Could she be of assistance?

"I'm quite used to it, thank you," said Mrs. Stumfold.

The words were not uncivil, but the tone was dreadfully severe, and Miss Mackenzie felt painfully sure that her hostess was already aware of the card that had been left at Miss Todd's door.

Mr. Startup was now actively at work.

"Lady Griggs's and Miss Fleebody's—I know. A great deal of sugar for her ladyship, and Miss Fleebody eats muffin. Mrs. Blow always takes pound-cake, and I'll see that there's one near her. Mortimer,"—Mortimer was the footman,—"is getting more bread and butter. Maguire, you have two dishes of sweet biscuits over there; give us one here. Never mind me, Mrs. Stumfold; I'll have my innings presently."

All this Mr. Frigidy heard with envious ears as he sat with his own tea-cup before him at the other table. He would have given the world to have been walking about the room like Startup, making himself useful and conspicuous; but he couldn't do it—he knew that he couldn't do it. Later in the evening, when he had been sitting by Miss Trotter for two hours—and he had very often sat by Miss Trotter before—he ventured upon a remark.

"Don't you think that Mr. Startup makes himself a little forward?"

"Oh dear yes, very," said Miss Trotter. "I believe he's an excellent young man, but I always did think him forward, now you mention it. And sometimes I've wondered how dear Mrs. Stumfold could like so much of it. But do you know, Mr. Frigidy, I am not quite sure that somebody else does like it. You know who I mean."

Miss Trotter said much more than this, and Mr. Frigidy was comforted, and believed that he had been talking.

When Mrs. Stumfold commenced her conversation with Mr. Startup, Miss Baker addressed herself to Miss Mackenzie; but there was at first something of stiffness in her manner,—as became a lady whose call had not been returned.

"I hope you like Littlebath," said Miss Baker.

Miss Mackenzie, who began to be conscious that she had done wrong, hesitated as she replied that she liked it pretty well.

"I think you'll find it pleasant," said Miss Baker; and then there was a pause. There could not be two women more fitted for friendship than were these, and it was much to be hoped, for the sake of our poor, solitary heroine especially, that this outside crust of manner might be broken up and dispersed.

"I dare say I shall find it pleasant, after a time," said Miss Mackenzie. Then they applied themselves each to her own bread and butter.

"You have not seen Miss Todd, I suppose, since I saw you?" Miss Baker asked this question when she perceived that Mrs. Stumfold was deep in some secret conference with Mr. Startup. It must, however, be told to Miss Baker's credit, that she had persistently maintained her friendship with Miss Todd, in spite of all the Stumfoldian influences. Miss Mackenzie, at the moment less brave, looked round aghast, but seeing that her hostess was in deep conference with her prime minister, she took heart of grace. "I called, and I did not see her."

"She promised me she would call," said Miss Baker.

"And I returned her visit, but she wasn't at home," said Miss Mackenzie.

"Indeed," said Miss Baker; and then there was silence between them again.

But, after a pause, Miss Mackenzie again took heart of grace. I do not think that there was, of nature, much of the coward about her. Indeed, the very fact that she was there alone at Littlebath, fighting her own battle with the world, instead of having allowed herself to be swallowed up by the Harry Handcocks, and Tom Mackenzies, proved her to be anything but a coward. "Perhaps, Miss Baker, I ought to have returned your visit," said she.

"That was just as you like," said Miss Baker with her sweetest smile.

"Of course, I should have liked it, as I thought it so good of you to come. But as you came with Mrs. Stumfold, I was not quite sure whether it might be intended; and then I didn't know,—did not exactly know,—where you lived."

After this the two ladies got on very comfortably, so long as they were left sitting side by side. Miss Baker imparted to Miss Mackenzie her full address, and Miss Mackenzie, with that brightness in her eyes which they always assumed when she was eager, begged her new friend to come to her again.

"Indeed, I will," said Miss Baker. After that they were parted by a general return to the front room.

And now Miss Mackenzie found herself seated next to Mr. Maguire. She had been carried away in the crowd to a further corner, in which there were two chairs, and before she had been able to consider the merits or demerits of the position, Mr. Maguire was seated close beside her. He was seated close beside her in such a way as to make the two specially separated from all the world beyond, for in front of them stood a wall of crinoline,—a wall of crinoline divided between four or five owners, among whom was shared the eloquence of Mr. Startup, who was carrying on an evangelical flirtation with the whole of them in a manner that was greatly pleasing to them, and enthusiastically delightful to him. Miss Mackenzie, when she found herself thus entrapped, looked into Mr. Maguire's eye with dismay. Had that look been sure to bring down upon her the hatred of that reverend gentleman, she could not have helped it. The eye fascinated her, as much as it frightened her. But Mr. Maguire was used to have his eye inspected, and did not hate her. He fixed it apparently on the corners of the wall, but in truth upon her, and then he began:

"I am so glad that you have come among us, Miss Mackenzie."

"I'm sure that I'm very much obliged."

"Well; you ought to be. You must not be surprised at my saying so, though it sounds uncivil. You ought to feel obliged, and the obligation should be mutual. I am not sure, that when all things are considered, you could find yourself in any better place in England, than in the drawing-room of my friend Stumfold; and, if you will allow me to say so, my friend Stumfold could hardly use his drawing-room better, than by entertaining you."

"Mr. Stumfold is very good, and so is she."

"Mr. Stumfold is very good; and as for Mrs. Stumfold, I look upon her as a very wonderful woman,—quite a wonderful woman. For grasp of intellect, for depth of thought, for tenderness of sentiment—perhaps you mightn't have expected that, but there it is—for tenderness of sentiment, for strength of faith, for purity of life, for genial hospitality, and all the domestic duties, Mrs. Stumfold has no equal in Littlebath, and perhaps few superiors elsewhere."

Here Mr. Maguire paused, and Miss Mackenzie, finding herself obliged to speak, said that she did not at all doubt it.

"You need not doubt it, Miss Mackenzie. She is all that, I tell you; and more, too. Her manners may seem a little harsh to you at first. I know it is so sometimes with ladies before they know her well; but it is only skin-deep, Miss Mackenzie,—only skin-deep. She is so much in earnest about her work, that she cannot bring herself to be light and playful as he is. Now, he is as full of play as a young lamb."

"He seems to be very pleasant."

"And he is always just the same. There are people, you know, who say that religion is austere and melancholy. They never could say that if they knew my friend Stumfold. His life is devoted to his clerical duties. I know no man who works harder in the vineyard than Stumfold. But he always works with a smile on his face. And why not, Miss Mackenzie? when you think of it, why not?"

"I dare say it's best not to be unhappy," said Miss Mackenzie. She did not speak till she perceived that he had paused for her answer.

"Of course we know that this world can make no one happy. What are we that we should dare to be happy here?"

Again he paused, but Miss Mackenzie feeling that she had been ill-treated and trapped into a difficulty at her last reply, resolutely remained silent.

"I defy any man or woman to be happy here," said Mr. Maguire, looking at her with one eye and at the corner of the wall with the other in a manner that was very terrible to her. "But we may be cheerful,—we may go about our work singing psalms of praise instead of songs of sorrow. Don't you agree with me, Miss Mackenzie, that psalms of praise are better than songs of sorrow?"

"I don't sing at all, myself," said Miss Mackenzie.

"You sing in your heart, my friend; I am sure you sing in your heart. Don't you sing in your heart?" Here again he paused.

"Well; perhaps in my heart, yes."

"I know you do, loud psalms of praise upon a ten-stringed lute. But Stumfold is always singing aloud, and his lute has twenty strings." Here the voice of the twenty-stringed singer was heard across the large room asking the company a riddle.

"Why was Peter in prison like a little boy with his shoes off?"

"That's so like him," said Mr. Maguire.

All the ladies in the room were in a fever of expectation, and Mr. Stumfold asked the riddle again.

"He won't tell them till we meet again; but there isn't one here who won't study the life of St Peter during the next week. And what they'll learn in that way they'll never forget."

"But why was he like a little boy with his shoes off?" asked Miss Mackenzie.

"Ah! that's Stumfold's riddle. You must ask Mr. Stumfold, and he won't tell you till next week. But some of the ladies will be sure to find it out before then. Have you come to settle yourself altogether at Littlebath, Miss Mackenzie?"

This question he asked very abruptly, but he had a way of looking at her when he asked a question, which made it impossible for her to avoid an answer.

"I suppose I shall stay here for some considerable time."

"Do, do," said he with energy. "Do; come and live among us, and be one of us; come and partake with us at the feast which we are making ready; come and eat of our crusts, and dip with us in the same dish; come and be of our flock, and go with us into the pleasant pastures, among the lanes and green hedges which appertain to the farm of the Lord. Come and walk with us through the Sabbath cornfields, and pluck the ears when you are a-hungered, disregarding the broad phylacteries. Come and sing with us songs of a joyful heart, and let us be glad together. What better can you do, Miss Mackenzie? I don't believe there is a more healthy place in the world than Littlebath, and, considering that the place is fashionable, things are really very reasonable."

He was rapid in his utterance, and so full of energy, that Miss Mackenzie did not quite follow him in his quick transitions. She hardly understood whether he was advising her to take up an abode in a terrestrial Eden or a celestial Paradise; but she presumed that he meant to be civil, so she thanked him and said she thought she would. It was a thousand pities that he should squint so frightfully, as in all other respects he was a good-looking man. Just at this moment there seemed to be a sudden breaking up of the party.

"We are all going away," said Mr. Maguire. "We always do when Mrs. Stumfold gets up from her seat. She does it when she sees that her father is nodding his head. You must let me out, because I've got to say a prayer. By-the-bye, you'll allow me to walk home with you, I hope. I shall be so happy to be useful."

Miss Mackenzie told him that the fly was coming for her, and then he scrambled away into the middle of the room.

"We always walk home from these parties," said Miss Baker, who had, however, on this occasion, consented to be taken away by Miss Mackenzie in the fly. "It makes it come so much cheaper, you know."

"Of course it does; and it's quite as nice if everybody does it. But you don't walk going there?"

"Not generally," said Miss Baker; "but there are some of them who do that. Miss Trotter always walks both ways, if it's ever so wet." Then there were a few words said about Miss Trotter which were not altogether good-natured.

Miss Mackenzie, as soon as she was at home, got down her Bible and puzzled herself for an hour over that riddle of Mr. Stumfold's; but with all her trouble she could not find why St Peter in prison was like a little boy with his shoes off.

Chapter V

Showing How Mr. Rubb, Junior, Progressed at Littlebath

A full week had passed by after Mrs. Stumfold's tea-party before Mr. Rubb called again at the Paragon; and in the meantime Miss Mackenzie had been informed by her lawyer that there did not appear to be any objection to the mortgage, if she liked the investment for her money.

"You couldn't do better with your money,—you couldn't indeed," said Mr. Rubb, when Miss Mackenzie, meaning to be cautious, started the conversation at once upon matters of business.

Mr. Rubb had not been in any great hurry to repeat his call, and Miss Mackenzie had resolved that if he did come again she would treat him simply as a member of the firm with whom she had to transact certain monetary arrangements. Beyond that she would not go; and as she so resolved, she repented herself of the sherry and biscuit.

The people whom she had met at Mr. Stumfold's had been all ladies and gentlemen; she, at least, had supposed them to be so, not having as yet received any special information respecting the wife of the retired coachbuilder. Mr. Rubb was not a gentleman; and though she was by no means inclined to give herself airs,—though, as she assured herself, she believed Mr. Rubb to be quite as good as herself,—yet there was, and must always be, a difference among people. She had no inclination to be proud; but if Providence had been pleased to place her in one position, it did not behove her to degrade herself by assuming a position that was lower. Therefore, on this account, and by no means moved by any personal contempt towards Mr. Rubb, or the Rubbs of the world in general, she was resolved that she would not ask him to take any more sherry and biscuits.

Poor Miss Mackenzie! I fear that they who read this chronicle of her life will already have allowed themselves to think worse of her than she deserved. Many of them, I know, will think far worse of her than they should think. Of what faults, even if we analyse her faults, has she been guilty? Where she has been weak, who among us is not, in that, weak also? Of what vanity has she been guilty with which the least vain among us might not justly tax himself? Having been left alone in the world, she has looked to make friends for herself; and in seeking for new friends she has wished to find the best that might come in her way.

Mr. Rubb was very good-looking; Mr. Maguire was afflicted by a terrible squint. Mr. Rubb's mode of speaking was pleasant to her; whereas she was by no means sure that she liked Mr. Maguire's speech. But Mr. Maguire was by profession a gentleman. As the discreet young man, who is desirous of rising in the world, will eschew skittles, and in preference go out to tea at his aunt's house—much more delectable as skittles are to his own heart—so did Miss Mackenzie resolve that it would become her to select Messrs Stumfold and Maguire as her male friends, and to treat Mr. Rubb simply as a man of business. She was denying herself skittles and beer, and putting up with tea and an old aunt, because she preferred the proprieties of life to its pleasures. Is it right that she should be blamed for such self-denial? But now the skittles and beer had come after her, as those delights will sometimes pursue the prudent youth who would fain avoid them. Mr. Rubb was there, in her drawing-room, looking extremely well, shaking hands with her very comfortably, and soon abandoning his conversation on that matter of business to which she had determined to confine herself. She was angry with him, thinking him to be very free and easy; but, nevertheless, she could not keep herself from talking to him.

"You can't do better than five per cent," he had said to her, "not with first-class security, such as this is."

All that had been well enough. Five per cent and first-class security were, she knew, matters of business; and though Mr. Rubb had winked his eye at her as he spoke of them, leaning forward in his chair and looking at her not at all as a man of business, but quite in a friendly way, yet she had felt that she was so far safe. She nodded her head also, merely intending him to understand thereby that she herself understood something about business. But when he suddenly changed the subject, and asked her how she liked Mr. Stumfold's set, she drew herself up suddenly and placed herself at once upon her guard.

"I have heard a great deal about Mr. Stumfold," continued Mr. Rubb, not appearing to observe the lady's altered manner, "not only here and where I have been for the last few days, but up in London also. He is quite a public character, you know."

"Clergymen in towns, who have large congregations, always must so be, I suppose."

"Well, yes; more or less. But Mr. Stumfold is decidedly more, and not less. People say he is going in for a bishopric."

"I had not heard it," said Miss Mackenzie, who did not quite understand what was meant by going in for a bishopric.

"Oh, yes, and a very likely man he would have been a year or two ago. But they say the prime minister has changed his tap lately."

"Changed his tap!" said Miss Mackenzie.

"He used to draw his bishops very bitter, but now he draws them mild and creamy. I dare say Stumfold did his best, but he didn't quite get his hay in while the sun shone."

"He seems to me to be very comfortable where he is," said Miss Mackenzie.

"I dare say. It must be rather a bore for him having to live in the house with old Peters. How Peters scraped his money together, nobody ever knew yet; and you are aware, Miss Mackenzie, that old as he is, he keeps it all in his own hands. That house, and everything that is in it, belongs to him; you know that, I dare say."

Miss Mackenzie, who could not keep herself from being a little interested in these matters, said that she had not known it.

"Oh dear, yes! and the carriage too. I've no doubt Stumfold will be all right when the old fellow dies. Such men as Stumfold don't often make mistakes about their money. But as long as old Peters lasts I shouldn't think it can be quite serene. They say that she is always cutting up rough with the old man."

"She seemed to me to behave very well to him," said Miss Mackenzie, remembering the carriage of the tea-cup.

"I dare say it is so before company, and of course that's all right; it's much better that the dirty linen should be washed in private. Stumfold is a clever man, there's no doubt about that. If you've been much to his house, you've probably met his curate, Mr. Maguire."

"I've only been there once, but I did meet Mr. Maguire."

"A man that squints fearfully. They say he's looking out for a wife too, only she must not have a father living, as Mrs. Stumfold has. It's astonishing how these parsons pick up all the good things that are going in the way of money." Miss Mackenzie, as she heard this, could not but remember that she might be regarded as a good thing going in the way of money, and became painfully aware that her face betrayed her consciousness.

"You'll have to keep a sharp look out," continued Mr. Rubb, giving her a kind caution, as though he were an old familiar friend.

"I don't think there's any fear of that kind," said Miss Mackenzie, blushing.

"I don't know about fear, but I should say that there is great probability; of course I am only joking about Mr. Maguire. Like the rest of them, of course, he wishes to feather his own nest; and why shouldn't he? But you may be sure of this, Miss Mackenzie, a lady with your fortune, and, if I may be allowed to say so, with your personal attractions, will not want for admirers."

Miss Mackenzie was very strongly of opinion that Mr. Rubb might not be allowed to say so. She thought that he was behaving with an unwarrantable degree of freedom in saying anything of the kind; but she did not know how to tell him either by words or looks that such was the case. And, perhaps, though the impertinence was almost unendurable, the idea conveyed was not altogether so grievous; it had certainly never hitherto occurred to her that she might become a second Mrs. Stumfold; but, after all, why not? What she wanted was simply this, that something of interest should be added to her life. Why should not she also work in the vineyard, in the open quasiclerical vineyard of the Lord's people, and also in the private vineyard of some one of the people's pastors? Mr. Rubb was very impertinent, but it might, perhaps, be worth her while to think of what he said. As regarded Mr. Maguire, the gentleman whose name had been specially mentioned, it was quite true that he did squint awfully.

"Mr. Rubb," said she, "if you please, I'd rather not talk about such things as that."

"Nevertheless, what I say is true, Miss Mackenzie; I hope you don't take it amiss that I venture to feel an interest about you."

"Oh! no," said she; "not that I suppose you do feel any special interest about me."

"But indeed I do, and isn't it natural? If you will remember that your only brother is the oldest friend that I have in the world, how can it be otherwise? Of course he is much older than me, and very much older than you, Miss Mackenzie."

"Just twelve years," said she, very stiffly.

"I thought it had been more, but in that case you and I are nearly of an age. As that is so, how can I fail to feel an interest about you? I have neither mother, nor sister, nor wife of my own; a sister, indeed, I have, but she's married at Singapore, and I have not seen her for seventeen years."

"Indeed."

"No, not for seventeen years; and the heart does crave for some female friend, Miss Mackenzie."

"You ought to get a wife, Mr. Rubb."

"That's what your brother always says. 'Samuel,' he said to me just before I left town, 'you're settled with us now; your father has as good as given up to you his share of the business, and you ought to get married.' Now, Miss Mackenzie, I wouldn't take that sort of thing from any man but your brother; it's very odd that you should say exactly the same thing too."

"I hope I have not offended you."

"Offended me! no, indeed, I'm not such a fool as that. I'd sooner know that you took an interest in me than any woman living. I would, indeed. I dare say you don't think much of it, but when I remember that the names of Rubb and Mackenzie have been joined together for more than twenty years, it seems natural to me that you and I should be friends."

Miss Mackenzie, in the few moments which were allowed to her for reflection before she was obliged to answer, again admitted to herself that he spoke the truth. If there was any fault in the matter the fault was with her brother Tom, who had joined the name of Mackenzie with the name of Rubb in the first instance. Where was this young man to look for a female friend if not to his partner's family, seeing that he had neither wife nor mother of his own, nor indeed a sister, except one out at Singapore, who was hardly available for any of the purposes of family affection? And yet it was hard upon her. It was through no negligence on her part that poor Mr. Rubb was so ill provided. "Perhaps it might have been so if I had continued to live in London," said Miss Mackenzie; "but as I live at Littlebath—" Then she paused, not knowing how to finish her sentence.

"What difference does that make? The distance is nothing if you come to think of it. Your hall door is just two hours and a quarter from our place of business in the New Road; and it's one pound five and nine if you go by first-class and cabs, or sixteen and ten if you put up with second-class and omnibuses. There's no other way of counting. Miles mean nothing now-a-days."

"They don't mean much, certainly."

"They mean nothing. Why, Miss Mackenzie, I should think it no trouble at all to run down and consult you about anything that occurred, about any matter of business that weighed at all heavily, if nothing prevented me except distance. Thirty shillings more than does it all, with a return ticket, including a bit of lunch at the station."

"Oh! and as for that—"

"I know what you mean, Miss Mackenzie, and I shall never forget how kind you were to offer me refreshment when I was here before."

"But, Mr. Rubb, I hope you won't think of doing such a thing. What good could I do you? I know nothing about business; and really, to tell the truth, I should be most unwilling to interfere—that is, you know, to say anything about anything of the kind."

"I only meant to point out that the distance is nothing. And as to what you were advising me about getting married—"

"I didn't mean to advise you, Mr. Rubb!"

"I thought you said so."

"But, of course, I did not intend to discuss such a matter seriously."

"It's a most serious subject to me, Miss Mackenzie."

"No doubt; but it's one I can't know anything about. Men in business generally do find, I think, that they get on better when they are married."

"Yes, they do."

"That's all I meant to say, Mr. Rubb."

After this he sat silent for a few minutes, and I am inclined to think that he was weighing in his mind the expediency of asking her to become Mrs. Rubb, on the spur of the moment. But if so, his mind finally gave judgment against the attempt, and in giving such judgment his mind was right. He would certainly have so startled her by the precipitancy of such a proposition, as to have greatly endangered the probability of any further intimacy with her. As it was, he changed the conversation, and began to ask questions as to the welfare of his partner's daughter. At this period of the day Susanna was at school, and he was informed that she would not be home till the evening. Then he plucked up courage and begged to be allowed to come again,—just to look in at eight o'clock, so that he might see Susanna. He could not go back to London comfortably, unless he could give some tidings of Susanna to the family in Gower Street. What was she to do? Of course she was obliged to ask him to drink tea with them. "That would be so pleasant," he said; and Miss Mackenzie owned to herself that the gratification expressed in his face as he spoke was very becoming.

When Susanna came home she did not seem to know much of Mr. Rubb, junior, or to care much about him. Old Mr. Rubb lived, she knew, near the place of business in the New Road, and sometimes he came to Gower Street, but nobody liked him. She didn't remember that she had ever seen Mr. Rubb, junior, at her mother's house but once, when he came to dinner. When she was told that Mr. Rubb was very anxious to see her, she chucked up her head and said that the man was a goose.

He came, and in a very few minutes he had talked over Susanna. He brought her a little present,—a work-box,—which he had bought for her at Littlebath; and though the work-box itself did not altogether avail, it paved the way for civil words, which were more efficacious. On this occasion he talked more to his partner's daughter than to his partner's sister, and promised to tell her mamma how well she was looking, and that the air of Littlebath had brought roses to her cheeks.

"I think it is a healthy place," said Miss Mackenzie.

"I'm quite sure it is," said Mr. Rubb. "And you like Mrs. Crammer's school, Susanna?"

She would have preferred to have been called Miss Mackenzie, but was not disposed to quarrel with him on the point.

"Yes, I like it very well," she said. "The other girls are very nice; and if one must go to school, I suppose it's as good as any other school."

"Susanna thinks that going to school at all is rather a nuisance," said Miss Mackenzie.

"You'd think so too, aunt, if you had to practise every day for an hour in the same room with four other pianos. It's my belief that I shall hate the sound of a piano the longest day that I shall live."

"I suppose it's the same with all young ladies," said Mr. Rubb.

"It's the same with them all at Mrs. Crammer's. There isn't one there that does not hate it."

"But you wouldn't like not to be able to play," said her aunt.

"Mamma doesn't play, and you don't play; and I don't see what's the use of it. It won't make anybody like music to hear four pianos all going at the same time, and all of them out of tune."

"You must not tell them in Gower Street, Mr. Rubb, that Susanna talks like that," said Miss Mackenzie.

"Yes, you may, Mr. Rubb. But you must tell them at the same time that I am quite happy, and that Aunt Margaret is the dearest woman in the world."

"I'll be sure to tell them that," said Mr. Rubb. Then he went away, pressing Miss Mackenzie's hand warmly as he took his leave; and as soon as he was gone, his character was of course discussed.

"He's quite a different man, aunt, from what I thought; and he's not at all like old Mr. Rubb. Old Mr. Rubb, when he comes to drink tea in Gower Street, puts his handkerchief over his knees to catch the crumbs."

"There's no great harm in that, Susanna."

"I don't suppose there's any harm in it. It's not wicked. It's not wicked to eat gravy with your knife."

"And does old Mr. Rubb do that?"

"Always. We used to laugh at him, because he is so clever at it. He never spills any; and his knife seems to be quite as good as a spoon. But this Mr. Rubb doesn't do things of that sort."

"He's younger, my dear."

"But being younger doesn't make people more ladylike of itself."

"I did not know that Mr. Rubb was exactly ladylike."

"That's taking me up unfairly; isn't it, aunt? You know what I meant; and only fancy that the man should go out and buy me a work-box. That's more than old Mr. Rubb ever did for any of us, since the first day he knew us. And, then, didn't you think that young Mr. Rubb is a handsome man, aunt?"

"He's all very well, my dear."

"Oh; I think he is downright handsome; I do, indeed. Miss Dumpus,—that's Mrs. Crammer's sister,—told us the other day, that I was wrong to talk about a man being handsome; but that must be nonsense, aunt?"

"I don't see that at all, my dear. If she told you so, you ought to believe that it is not nonsense."

"Come, aunt; you don't mean to tell me that you would believe all that Miss Dumpus says. Miss Dumpus says that girls should never laugh above their breath when they are more than fourteen years old. How can you make a change in your laughing just when you come to be fourteen? And why shouldn't you say a man's handsome, if he is handsome?"

"You'd better go to bed, Susanna."

"That won't make Mr. Rubb ugly. I wish you had asked him to come and dine here on Sunday, so that we might have seen whether he eats his gravy with his knife. I looked very hard to see whether he'd catch his crumbs in his handkerchief."

Then Susanna went to her bed, and Miss Mackenzie was left alone to think over the perfections and imperfections of Mr. Samuel Rubb, junior.

From that time up to Christmas she saw no more of Mr. Rubb; but she heard from him twice. His letters, however, had reference solely to business, and were not of a nature to produce either anger or admiration. She had also heard more than once from her lawyer; and a question had arisen as to which she was called upon to trust to her own judgment for a decision. Messrs Rubb and Mackenzie had wanted the money at once, whereas the papers for the mortgage were not ready. Would Miss Mackenzie allow Messrs Rubb and Mackenzie to have the money under these circumstances? To this inquiry from her lawyer she made a rejoinder asking for advice. Her lawyer told her that he could not recommend her, in the ordinary way of business, to make any advance of money without positive security; but, as this was a matter between friends and near relatives, she might perhaps be willing to do it; and he added that, as far as his own opinion went, he did not think that there would be any great risk. But then it all depended on this:—did she want to oblige her friends and near relatives? In answer to this question she told herself that she certainly did wish to do so; and she declared,—also to herself,—that she was willing to advance the money to her brother, even though there might be some risk. The upshot of all this was that Messrs Rubb and Mackenzie got the money some time in October, but that the mortgage was not completed when Christmas came. It was on this matter that Mr. Rubb, junior, had written to Miss Mackenzie, and his letter had been of a nature to give her a feeling of perfect security in the transaction. With her brother she had had no further correspondence; but this did not surprise her, as her brother was a man much less facile in his modes of expression than his younger partner.

As the autumn had progressed at Littlebath, she had become more and more intimate with Miss Baker, till she had almost taught herself to regard that lady as a dear friend. She had fallen into the habit of going to Mrs. Stumfold's tea-parties every fortnight, and was now regarded as a regular Stumfoldian by all those who interested themselves in such matters. She had begun a system of district visiting and Bible reading with Miss Baker, which had at first been very agreeable to her. But Mrs. Stumfold had on one occasion called upon her and taken her to task,—as Miss Mackenzie had thought, rather abruptly,—with reference to some lack of energy or indiscreet omission of which she had been judged to be guilty by that highly-gifted lady. Against this Miss Mackenzie had rebelled mildly, and since that things had not gone quite so pleasantly with her. She had still been honoured with Mrs. Stumfold's card of invitation, and had still gone to the tea-parties on Miss Baker's strenuously-urged advice; but Mrs. Stumfold had frowned, and Miss Mackenzie had felt the frown; Mrs. Stumfold had frowned, and the retired coachbuilder's wife had at once snubbed the culprit, and Mr. Maguire had openly expressed himself to be uneasy.

"Dearest Miss Mackenzie," he had said, with charitable zeal, "if there has been anything wrong, just beg her pardon, and you will find that everything has been forgotten at once; a more forgiving woman than Mrs. Stumfold never lived."

"But suppose I have done nothing to be forgiven," urged Miss Mackenzie.

Mr. Maguire looked at her, and shook his head, the exact meaning of the look she could not understand, as the peculiarity of his eyes created confusion; but when he repeated twice to her the same words, "The heart of man is exceeding treacherous," she understood that he meant to condemn her.

"So it is, Mr. Maguire, but that is no reason why Mrs. Stumfold should scold me."

Then he got up and left her, and did not speak to her again that evening, but he called on her the next day, and was very affectionate in his manner. In Mr. Stumfold's mode of treating her she had found no difference.

With Miss Todd, whom she met constantly in the street, and who always nodded to her very kindly, she had had one very remarkable interview.

"I think we had better give it up, my dear," Miss Todd had said to her. This had been in Miss Baker's drawing-room.

"Give what up?" Miss Mackenzie had asked.

"Any idea of our knowing each other. I'm sure it never can come to anything, though for my part I should have been so glad. You see you can't serve God and Mammon, and it is settled beyond all doubt that I'm Mammon. Isn't it, Mary?"

Miss Baker, to whom this appeal was made, answered it only by a sigh.

"You see," continued Miss Todd, "that Miss Baker is allowed to know me, though I am Mammon, for the sake of auld lang syne. There have been so many things between us that it wouldn't do for us to drop each other. We have had the same lovers; and you know, Mary, that you've been very near coming over to Mammon yourself. There's a sort of understanding that Miss Baker is not to be required to cut me. But they would not allow that sort of liberty to a new comer; they wouldn't, indeed."

"I don't know that anybody would be likely to interfere with me," said Miss Mackenzie.

"Yes, they would, my dear. You didn't quite know yourself which way it was to be when you first came here, and if it had been my way, I should have been most happy to have made myself civil. You have chosen now, and I don't doubt but what you have chosen right. I always tell Mary Baker that it does very well for her, and I dare say it will do very well for you too. There's a great deal in it, and only that some of them do tell such lies I think I should have tried it myself. But, my dear Miss Mackenzie, you can't do both."

After this Miss Mackenzie used to nod to Miss Todd in the street, but beyond that there was no friendly intercourse between those ladies.

At the beginning of December there came an invitation to Miss Mackenzie to spend the Christmas holidays away from Littlebath, and as she accepted this invitation, and as we must follow her to the house of her friends, we will postpone further mention of the matter till the next chapter.

Chapter VI

Miss Mackenzie Goes to the Cedars

About the middle of December Mrs. Mackenzie, of Gower Street, received a letter from her sister-in-law at Littlebath, in which it was proposed that Susanna should pass the Christmas holidays with her father and mother. "I myself," said the letter, "am going for three weeks to the Cedars. Lady Ball has written to me, and as she seems to wish it, I shall go. It is always well, I think, to drop family dissensions." The letter said a great deal more, for Margaret Mackenzie, not having much business on hand, was fond of writing long letters; but the upshot of it was, that she would leave Susanna in Gower Street, on her way to the Cedars, and call for her on her return home.

"What on earth is she going there for?" said Mrs. Tom Mackenzie.

"Because they have asked her," replied the husband.

"Of course they have asked her; but that's no reason she should go. The Balls have behaved very badly to us, and I should think much better of her if she stayed away."

To this Mr. Mackenzie made no answer, but simply remarked that he would be rejoiced in having Susanna at home on Christmas Day.

"That's all very well, my dear," said Mrs. Tom, "and of course so shall I. But as she has taken the charge of the child I don't think she ought to drop her down and pick her up just whenever she pleases. Suppose she was to take it into her head to stop at the Cedars altogether, what are we to do then?—just have the girl returned upon our hands, with all her ideas of life confused and deranged. I hate such ways."

"She has promised to provide for Susanna, whenever she may not continue to give her a home."

"What would such a promise be worth if John Ball got hold of her money? That's what they're after, as sure as my name is Martha; and what she's after too, very likely. She was there once before she went to Littlebath at all. They want to get their uncle's money back, and she wants to be a baronet's wife."

The same view of the matter was perhaps taken by Mr. Rubb, junior, when he was told that Miss Mackenzie was to pass through London on her way to the Cedars, though he did not express his fears openly, as Mrs. Mackenzie had done.

"Why don't you ask your sister to stay in Gower Street?" he said to his partner.

"She wouldn't come."

"You might at any rate ask her."

"What good would it do?"

"Well; I don't know that it would do any good; but it wouldn't do any harm. Of course it's natural that she should wish to have friends about her; and it will only be natural too that she should marry some one."

"She may marry whom she pleases for me."

"She will marry whom she pleases; but I suppose you don't want to see her money go to the Balls."

"I shouldn't care a straw where her money went," said Thomas Mackenzie, "if I could only know that this sum which we have had from her was properly arranged. To tell you the truth, Rubb, I'm ashamed to look my sister in the face."

"That's nonsense. Her money is as right as the bank; and if in such matters as that brothers and sisters can't take liberties with each other, who the deuce can?"

"In matters of money nobody should ever take a liberty with anybody," said Mr. Mackenzie.

He knew, however, that a great liberty had been taken with his sister's money, and that his firm had no longer the power of providing her with the security which had been promised to her.

Mr. Mackenzie would take no steps, at his partner's instance, towards arresting his sister in London; but Mr. Rubb was more successful with Mrs. Mackenzie, with whom, during the last month or two, he had contrived to establish a greater intimacy than had ever previously existed between the two families. He had been of late a good deal in Gower Street, and Mrs. Mackenzie had found him to be a much pleasanter and better educated man than she had expected. Such was the language in which she expressed her praise of him, though I am disposed to doubt whether she herself was at all qualified to judge of the education of any man. He had now talked over the affairs of Margaret Mackenzie with her sister-in-law, and the result of that talking was that Mrs. Mackenzie wrote a letter to Littlebath, pressing Miss Mackenzie to stay a few days in Gower Street, on her way through London. She did this as well as she knew how to do it; but still there was that in the letter which plainly told an apt reader that there was no reality in the professions of affection made in it. Miss Mackenzie became well aware of the fact as she read her sister's words. Available hypocrisy is a quality very difficult of attainment and of all hypocrisies, epistolary hypocrisy is perhaps the most difficult. A man or woman must have studied the matter very thoroughly, or be possessed of great natural advantages in that direction, who can so fill a letter with false expressions of affection, as to make any reader believe them to be true. Mrs. Mackenzie was possessed of no such skill.

"Believe her to be my affectionate sister-in-law! I won't believe her to be anything of the kind," Margaret so spoke of the writer to herself, when she had finished the letter; but, nevertheless, she answered it with kind language, saying that she could not stay in town as she passed through to the Cedars, but that she would pass one night in Gower Street when she called to pick up Susanna on her return home.

It is hard to say what pleasure she promised herself in going to the Cedars, or why she accepted that invitation. She had, in truth, liked neither the people nor the house, and had felt herself to be uncomfortable while she was there. I think she felt it to be a duty to force herself to go out among people who, though they were personally disagreeable to her, might be socially advantageous. If Sir John Ball had not been a baronet, the call to the Cedars would not have been so imperative on her. And yet she was not a tufthunter, nor a toady. She was doing what we all do,—endeavouring to choose her friends from the best of those who made overtures to her of friendship. If other things be equal, it is probable that a baronet will be more of a gentleman and a pleasanter fellow than a manufacturer of oilcloth. Who is there that doesn't feel that? It is true that she had tried the baronet, and had not found him very pleasant, but that might probably have been her own fault. She had been shy and stiff, and perhaps ill-mannered, or had at least accused herself of these faults; and therefore she resolved to go again.

She called with Susanna as she passed through London, and just saw her sister-in-law.

"I wish you could have stayed," said Mrs. Mackenzie.

"I will for one night, as I return, on the 10th of January," said Miss Mackenzie.

Mrs. Mackenzie could not understand what Mr. Rubb had meant by saying that that old maid was soft and pleasant, nor could she understand Susanna's love for her aunt. "I suppose men will put up with anything for the sake of money," she said to herself; "and as for children, the truth is, they'll love anybody who indulges them."

"Aunt is so kind," Susanna said. "She's always kind. If you wake her up in the middle of the night, she's kind in a moment. And if there's anything good to eat, it will make her eyes quite shine if she sees that anybody else likes it. I have known her sit for half an hour ever so uncomfortable, because she would not disturb the cat."

"Then she must be a fool, my dear," said Mrs. Mackenzie.

"She isn't a fool, mamma; I'm quite sure of that," said Susanna.

Miss Mackenzie went on to the Cedars, and her mind almost misgave her in going there, as she was driven up through the dull brick lodges, which looked as though no paint had touched them for the last thirty years, up to the front door of the dull brick house, which bore almost as dreary a look of neglect as the lodges. It was a large brick house of three stories, with the door in the middle, and three windows on each side of the door, and a railed area with a kitchen below the ground. Such houses were built very commonly in the neighbourhood of London some hundred and fifty years ago, and they may still be pleasant enough to the eye if there be ivy over them, and if they be clean with new paint, and spruce with the outer care of gardeners and the inner care of housemaids; but old houses are often like old ladies, who require more care in their dressing than they who are younger. Very little care was given to the Cedars, and the place therefore always looked ill-dressed. On the right hand as you entered was the dining-room, and the three windows to the left were all devoted to the hall. Behind the dining-room was Sir John's study, as he called it, and behind or beyond the hall was the drawing-room, from which four windows looked out into the garden. This might have been a pretty room had any care been taken to make anything pretty at the Cedars. But the furniture was old, and the sofas were hard, and the tables were rickety, and the curtains which had once been red had become brown with the sun. The dinginess of the house had not struck Miss Mackenzie so forcibly when she first visited it, as it did now. Then she had come almost direct from Arundel Street, and the house in Arundel Street had itself been very dingy. Mrs. Stumfold's drawing-rooms were not dingy, nor were her own rooms in the Paragon. Her eye had become accustomed to better things, and she now saw at once how old were the curtains, and how lamentably the papers wanted to be renewed on the walls. She had, however, been drawn from the neighbouring station to the house in the private carriage belonging to the establishment, and if there was any sense of justice in her, it must be presumed that she balanced the good things with the bad.

But her mind misgave her, not because the house was outwardly dreary, but in fear of the inward dreariness of the people—or in fear rather of their dreariness and pride combined. Old Lady Ball, though naturally ill-natured, was not ill-mannered, nor did she give herself any special airs; but she knew that she was a baronet's wife, that she kept her carriage, and that it was an obligation upon her to make up for the poverty of her house by some little haughtiness of demeanour. There are women, high in rank, but poor in pocket, so gifted with the peculiar grace of aristocracy, that they show by every word spoken, by every turn of the head, by every step taken, that they are among the high ones of the earth, and that money has nothing to do with it. Old Lady Ball was not so gifted, nor had she just claim to such gifts. But some idea on the subject pervaded her mind, and she made efforts to be aristocratic in her poverty. Sir John was a discontented, cross old man, who had succeeded greatly in early life, having been for nearly twenty years in Parliament, but had fallen into adversity in his older days. The loss of that very money of which his niece, Miss Mackenzie was possessed, was, in truth, the one great misfortune which he deplored; but that misfortune had had ramifications and extensions with which the reader need not trouble himself; but which, altogether, connected as they were with certain liberal aspirations which he had entertained in early life, and certain political struggles made during his parliamentary career, induced him to regard himself as a sort of Prometheus. He had done much for the world, and the world in return had made him a baronet without any money! He was a very tall, thin, gray-haired, old man, stooping much, and worn with age, but still endowed with some strength of will, and great capability of making himself unpleasant. His son was a bald-headed, stout man, somewhat past forty, who was by no means without cleverness, having done great things as a young man at Oxford; but in life he had failed. He was a director of certain companies in London, at which he used to attend, receiving his guinea for doing so, and he had some small capital,—some remnant of his father's trade wealth, which he nursed with extreme care, buying shares here and there and changing his money about as his keen outlook into City affairs directed him. I do not suppose that he had much talent for the business, or he would have grown rich; but a certain careful zeal carried him on without direct loss, and gave him perhaps five per cent for his capital, whereas he would have received no more than four and a half had he left it alone and taken his dividends without troubling himself. As the difference did not certainly amount to a hundred a-year, it can hardly be said that he made good use of his time. His zeal deserved a better success. He was always thinking of his money, excusing himself to himself and to others by the fact of his nine children. For myself I think that his children were no justification to him; as they would have been held to be none, had he murdered and robbed his neighbours for their sake.

There had been a crowd of girls in the house when Miss Mackenzie had paid her former visit to the Cedars,—so many that she had carried away no remembrance of them as individuals. But at that time the eldest son, a youth now just of age, was not at home. This hope of the Balls, who was endeavouring to do at Oxford as his father had done, was now with his family, and came forward to meet his cousin as the old carriage was driven up to the door. Old Sir John stood within, in the hall, mindful of the window air, and Lady Ball, a little mindful of her dignity, remained at the drawing-room door. Even though Miss Mackenzie had eight hundred a-year, and was nearly related to the Incharrow family, a further advance than the drawing-room door would be inexpedient; for the lady, with all her virtues, was still sister to the man who dealt in retail oilcloth in the New Road!

Miss Mackenzie thought nothing of this, but was well contented to be received by her hostess in the drawing-room.

"It's a dull house to come to, my dear," said Lady Ball; "but blood is thicker than water, they say, and we thought that perhaps you might like to be with your cousins at Christmas."

"I shall like it very much," said Miss Mackenzie.

"I suppose you must find it rather sad, living alone at Littlebath, away from all your people?"

"I have my niece with me, you know."

"A niece, have you? That's one of the girls from Gower Street, I suppose? It's very kind of you, and I dare say, very proper."

"But Littlebath is a very gay place, I thought," said John Ball, the third and youngest of the name. "We always hear of it at Oxford as being the most stunning place for parties anywhere near."

"I suppose you play cards every night of your life," said the baronet.

"No; I don't play cards," said Miss Mackenzie. "Many ladies do, but I'm not in that set."

"What set are you in?" said Sir John.

"I don't think I am in any set. I know Mr. Stumfold, the clergyman there, and I go to his house sometimes."

"Oh, ah; I see," said Sir John. "I beg your pardon for mentioning cards. I shouldn't have done it, if I had known that you were one of Mr. Stumfold's people."

"I am not one of Mr. Stumfold's people especially," she said, and then she went upstairs.

The other John Ball came back from London just in time for dinner—the middle one of the three, whom we will call Mr. Ball. He greeted his cousin very kindly, and then said a word or two to his mother about shares. She answered him, assuming a look of interest in his tidings.

"I don't understand it; upon my word, I don't," said he. "Some of them will burn their fingers before they've done. I don't dare do it; I know that."

In the evening, when John Ball,—or Jack, as he was called in the family,—had left the drawing-room, and the old man was alone with his son, they discussed the position of Margaret Mackenzie.

"You'll find she has taken up with the religious people there," said the father.

"It's just what she would do," said the son.

"They're the greatest thieves going. When once they have got their eyes upon money, they never take them off again."

"She's not been there long enough yet to give any one a hold upon her."

"I don't know that, John; but, if you'll take my advice, you'll find out the truth at once. She has no children, and if you've made up your mind about it, you'll do no good by delay."

"She's a very nice woman, in her way."

"Yes, she's nice enough. She's not a beauty; eh, John? and she won't set the Thames on fire."

"I don't wish her to do so; but I think she'd look after the girls, and do her duty."

"I dare say; unless she has taken to run after prayer-meetings every hour of her life."

"They don't often do that after they're married, sir."

"Well; I know nothing against her. I never thought much of her brothers, and I never cared to know them. One's dead now, and as for the other, I don't suppose he need trouble you much. If you've made up your mind about it, I think you might as well ask her at once." From all which it may be seen that Miss Mackenzie had been invited to the Cedars with a direct object on the part of Mr. Ball.

But though the old gentleman thus strongly advised instant action, nothing was done during Christmas week, nor had any hint been given up to the end of the year. John Ball, however, had not altogether lost his time, and had played the part of middle-aged lover better than might have been expected from one the whole tenor of whose life was so thoroughly unromantic. He did manage to make himself pleasant to Miss Mackenzie, and so far ingratiated himself with her that he won much of her confidence in regard to money matters.

"But that's a very large sum of money?" he said to her one day as they were sitting together in his father's study. He was alluding to the amount which she had lent to Messrs Rubb and Mackenzie, and had become aware of the fact that as yet Miss Mackenzie held no security for the loan. "Two thousand five hundred pounds is a very large sum of money."

"But I'm to get five per cent, John." They were first cousins, but it was not without some ceremonial difficulty that they had arrived at each other's Christian names.

"My dear Margaret, their word for five per cent is no security. Five per cent is nothing magnificent. A lady situated as you are should never part with her money without security—never: but if she does, she should have more than five per cent."

"You'll find it's all right, I don't doubt," said Miss Mackenzie, who, however, was beginning to have little inward tremblings of her own.

"I hope so; but I must say, I think Mr. Slow has been much to blame. I do, indeed." Mr. Slow was the attorney who had for years acted for Walter Mackenzie and his father, and was now acting for Miss Mackenzie. "Will you allow me to go to him and see about it?"

"It has not been his fault. He wrote and asked me whether I would let them have it, before the papers were ready, and I said I would."

"But may I ask about it?"

Miss Mackenzie paused before she answered:

"I think you had better not, John. Remember that Tom is my own brother, and I should not like to seem to doubt him. Indeed, I do not doubt him in the least—nor yet Mr. Rubb."

"I can assure you that it is a very bad way of doing business," said the anxious lover.

By degrees she began to like her cousin John Ball. I do not at all wish the reader to suppose that she had fallen in love with that bald-headed, middle-aged gentleman, or that she even thought of him in the light of a possible husband; but she found herself to be comfortable in his company, and was able to make a friend of him. It is true that he talked to her more of money than anything else; but then it was her money of which he talked, and he did it with an interest that could not but flatter her. He was solicitous about her welfare, gave her bits of advice, did one or two commissions for her in town, called her Margaret, and was kind and cousinly. The Cedars, she thought, was altogether more pleasant than she had found the place before. Then she told herself that on the occasion of her former visit she had not been there long enough to learn to like the place or the people. Now she knew them, and though she still dreaded her uncle and his cross sayings, and though that driving out with her aunt in the old carriage was tedious, she would have been glad to prolong her stay there, had she not bound herself to take Susanna back to school at Littlebath on a certain day. When that day came near— and it did come very near before Mr. Ball spoke out—they pressed her to prolong her stay. This was done by both Lady Ball and by her son.

"You might as well remain with us another fortnight," said Lady Ball during one of these drives. It was the last drive which Miss Mackenzie had through Twickenham lanes during that visit to the Cedars.

"I can't do it, aunt, because of Susanna."

"I don't see that at all. You're not to make yourself a slave to Susanna."

"But I'm to make myself a mother to her as well as I can."

"I must say you have been rather hasty, my dear. Suppose you were to change your mode of life, what would you do?"

Then Miss Mackenzie, blushing slightly in the obscure corner of the carriage as she spoke, explained to Lady Ball that clause in her agreement with her brother respecting the five hundred pounds.

"Oh, indeed," said Lady Ball.

The information thus given had been manifestly distasteful, and the conversation was for a while interrupted; but Lady Ball returned to her request before they were again at home.

"I really do think you might stop, Margaret. Now that we have all got to know each other, it will be a great pity that it all should be broken up."

"But I hope it won't be broken up, aunt."

"You know what I mean, my dear. When people live so far off they can't see each other constantly; and now you are here, I think you might stay a little longer. I know there is not much attraction—"

"Oh, aunt, don't say that! I like being here very much."

"Then, why can't you stay? Write and tell Mrs. Tom that she must keep Susanna at home for another week or so. It can't matter."

To this Miss Mackenzie made no immediate answer.

"It is not only for myself I speak, but John likes having you here with his girls; and Jack is so fond of you; and John himself is quite different while you are here. Do stay!"

Saying which Lady Ball put out her hand caressingly on Miss Mackenzie's arm.

"I'm afraid I mustn't," said Miss Mackenzie, very slowly. "Much as I should like it, I'm afraid I mustn't do it. I've pledged myself to go back with Susanna, and I like to be as good as my word."

Lady Ball drew herself up.

"I never went so much out of my way to ask any one to stay in my house before," she said.

"Dear aunt! don't be angry with me."

"Oh no! I'm not angry. Here we are. Will you get out first?"

Whereupon Lady Ball descended from the carriage, and walked into the house with a good deal of dignity.

"What a wicked old woman she was!" virtuous readers will say; "what a wicked old woman to endeavour to catch that poor old maid's fortune for her son!"

But I deny that she was in any degree a wicked old woman on that score. Why should not the two cousins marry, and do very well together with their joint means? Lady Ball intended to make a baronet's wife of her. If much was to be taken, was not much also to be given?

"You are going to stay, are you not?" Jack said to her that evening, as he wished her good-night. She was very fond of Jack, who was a nice-looking, smooth-faced young fellow, idolised by his sisters over whom he tyrannised, and bullied by his grandfather, before whom he quaked.

"I'm afraid not, Jack; but you shall come and see me at Littlebath, if you will."

"I should like it, of all things; but I do wish you'd stay: the house is so much nicer when you are in it!"

But of course she could not stay at the request of the young lad, when she had refused the request of the lad's grandmother.

After this she had one day to remain at the Cedars. It was a Thursday, and on the Friday she was to go to her brother's house on her way to Littlebath. On the Thursday morning Mr. Ball waylaid her on the staircase, as she came down to breakfast, and took her with him into the drawing-room. There he made his request, standing with her in the middle of the room.

"Margaret," he said, "must you go away and leave us?"

"I'm afraid I must, John," she said.

"I wish we could make you think better of it."

"Of course I should like to stay, but—"

"Yes, there's always a but. I should have thought that, of all people in the world, you were the one most able to do just what you please with your time."

"We have all got duties to do, John."

"Of course we have; but why shouldn't it be your duty to make your relations happy? If you could only know how much I like your being here?"

Had it not been that she did not dare to do that for the son which she had refused to the mother, I think that she would have given way. As it was, she did not know how to yield, after having persevered so long.

"You are all so kind," she said, giving him her hand, "that it goes to my heart to refuse you; but I'm afraid I can't. I do not wish to give my brother's wife cause to complain of me."

"Then," said Mr. Ball, speaking very slowly, "I must ask this favour of you, that you will let me see you alone for half an hour after dinner this evening."

"Certainly," said Miss Mackenzie.

"Thank you, Margaret. After tea I will go into the study, and perhaps you will follow me."

Chapter VII

Miss Mackenzie Leaves the Cedars

There was something so serious in her cousin's request to her, and so much of gravity in his mode of making it, that Miss Mackenzie could not but think of it throughout the day. On what subject did he wish to speak to her in so solemn and special a manner? An idea of the possibility of an offer no doubt crossed her mind and fluttered her, but it did not do more than this; it did not remain fixed with her, or induce her to resolve what answer she would give if such offer were made. She was afraid to allow herself to think that such a thing could happen, and put the matter away from her,—uneasily, indeed, but still with so much resolution as to leave her with a conviction that she need not give any consideration to such an hypothesis.

And she was not at a loss to suggest to herself another subject. Her cousin had learned something about her money which he felt himself bound to tell her, but which he would not have told her now had she consented to remain at the Cedars. There was something wrong about the loan. This made her seriously unhappy, for she dreaded the necessity of discussing her brother's conduct with her cousin.

During the whole of the day Lady Ball was very courteous, but rather distant. Lady Ball had said to herself that Margaret would have stayed had she been in a disposition favourable to John Ball's hopes. If she should decline the alliance with which the Balls proposed to honour her, then Lady Ball was prepared to be very cool. There would be an ingratitude in such a proceeding after the open-armed affection which had been shown to her which Lady Ball could not readily bring herself to forgive. Sir John, once or twice during the day, took up his little sarcasms against her supposed religious tendencies at Littlebath.

"You'll be glad to get back to Mr. Stumfold," he said.

"I shall be glad to see him, of course," she answered, "as he is a friend."

"Mr. Stumfold has a great many lady friends at Littlebath," he continued.

"Yes, a great many," said Miss Mackenzie, understanding well that she was being bullied.

"What a pity that there can be only one Mrs. Stumfold," snarled the baronet; "it's often a wonder to me how women can be so foolish."

"And it's often a wonder to me," said Miss Mackenzie, "how gentlemen can be so ill-natured."

She had plucked up her spirits of late, and had resented Sir John's ill-humour.

At the usual hour Mr. Ball came home to dinner, and Miss Mackenzie, as soon as she saw him, again became fluttered. She perceived that he was not at his ease, and that made her worse. When he spoke to the girls he seemed hardly to mind what he was saying, and he greeted his mother without any whispered tidings as to the share-market of the day.

Margaret asked herself if it could be possible that anything was very wrong about her own money. If the worst came to the worst she could but have lost that two thousand five hundred pounds and she would be able to live well enough without it. If her brother had asked her for it, she would have given it to him. She would teach herself to regard it as a gift, and then the subject would not make her unhappy.

They all came down to dinner, and they all went in to tea, and the tea-things were taken away, and then John Ball arose. During tea-time neither he nor Miss Mackenzie had spoken a word, and when she got up to follow him, there was a solemnity about the matter which ought to have been ludicrous to any of those remaining, who might chance to know what was about to happen. It must be supposed that Lady Ball at any rate did know, and when she saw her middle-aged niece walk slowly out of the room after her middle-aged son, in order that a love proposal might be made from one to the other with advantage, she must, I should think, have perceived the comic nature of the arrangement. She went on, however, very gravely with her knitting, and did not even make an attempt to catch her husband's eye.

"Margaret," said John Ball, as soon as he had shut the study door; "but, perhaps, you had better sit down."

Then she sat down, and he came and seated himself opposite to her; opposite her, but not so close as to give him any of the advantages of a lover.

"Margaret, I don't know whether you have guessed the subject on which I wish to speak to you; but I wish you had."

"Is it about the money?" she asked.

"The money! What money? The money you have lent to your brother? Oh, no."

Then, at that moment, Margaret did, I think, guess.

"It's not at all about the money," he said, and then he sighed.

He had at one time thought of asking his mother to make the proposition for him, and now he wished that he had done so.

"No, Margaret, it's something else that I want to say. I believe you know my condition in life pretty accurately."

"In what way, John?"

"I am a poor man; considering my large family, a very poor man. I have between eight and nine hundred a year, and when my father and mother are both gone I shall have nearly as much more; but I have nine children, and as I must keep up something of a position, I have a hard time of it sometimes, I can tell you."

Here he paused, as though he expected her to say something; but she had nothing to say and he went on.

"Jack is at Oxford, as you know, and I wish to give him any chance that a good education may afford. It did not do much for me, but he may be more lucky. When my father is dead, I think I shall sell this place; but I have not quite made up my mind about that;—it must depend on circumstances. As for the girls, you see that I do what I can to educate them."

"They seem to me to be brought up very nicely; nothing could be better."

"They are good girls, very good girls, and so is Jack a very good fellow."

"I love Jack dearly," said Miss Mackenzie, who had already come to a half-formed resolution that Jack Ball should be heir to half her fortune, her niece Susanna being heiress to the other half.

"Do you? I'm so glad of that." And there was actually a tear in the father's eye.

"And so I do the girls," said Margaret. "It's something so nice to feel that one has people really belonging to one that one may love. I hope they'll know Susanna some day, for she's a very nice girl,—a very dear girl."

"I hope they will," said Mr. Ball; but there was not much enthusiasm in the expression of this hope.

Then he got up from his chair, and took a turn across the room. "The truth is, Margaret, that there's no use in my beating about the bush. I shan't say what I've got to say a bit the better for delaying it. I want you to be my wife, and to be mother to those children. I like you better than any woman I've seen since

I lost Rachel, but I shouldn't dare to make you such an offer if you had not money of your own. I could not marry unless my wife had money, and I would not marry any woman unless I felt I could love her—not if she had ever so much. There! now you know it all. I suppose I have not said it as I ought to do, but if you're the woman I take you for that won't make much difference."

For my part I think that he said what he had to say very well. I do not know that he could have done it much better. I do not know that any other form of words would have been more persuasive to the woman he was addressing. Had he said much of his love, or nothing of his poverty; or had he omitted altogether any mention of her wealth, her heart would have gone against him at once. As it was he had produced in her mind such a state of doubt, that she was unable to answer him on the moment.

"I know," he went on to say, "that I haven't much to offer you." He had now seated himself again, and as he spoke he looked upon the ground.

"It isn't that, John," she answered; "you have much more to give than I have a right to expect."

"No," he said. "What I offer you is a life of endless trouble and care. I know all about it myself. It's all very well to talk of a competence and a big house, and if you were to take me, perhaps we might keep the old place on and furnish it again, and my mother thinks a great deal about the title. For my part I think it's only a nuisance when a man has not got a fortune with it, and I don't suppose it will be any pleasure to you to be called Lady Ball. You'd have a life of fret and worry, and would not have half so much money to spend as you have now. I know all that, and have thought a deal about it before I could bring myself to speak to you. But, Margaret, you would have duties which would, I think, in themselves, have a pleasure for you. You would know what to do with your life, and would be of inestimable value to many people who would love you dearly.

As for me, I never saw any other woman whom I could bring myself to offer as a mother to my children." All this he said looking down at the floor, in a low, dull, droning voice, as though every sentence spoken were to have been the last. Then he paused, looked into her face for a moment, and after that, allowed his eyes again to fall on the ground.

Margaret was, of course, aware that she must make him some answer, and she was by no means prepared to give him one that would be favourable. Indeed, she thought she knew that she could not marry him, because she felt that she did not love him with affection of the sort which would be due to a husband. She told herself that she must refuse his offer. But yet she wanted time, and above all things, she wished to find words which would not be painful to him. His dull droning voice, and the honest recital of his troubles, and of her troubles if she were to share his lot, had touched her more nearly than any vows of love would have done. When he told her of the heavy duties which might fall to her lot as his wife, he almost made her think that it might be well for her to marry him, even though she did not love him. "I hardly know how to answer you, you have taken me so much by surprise," she said.

"You need not give me an answer at once," he replied; "you can think of it." As she did not immediately say anything, he presumed that she assented to this proposition. "You won't wonder now," he said, "that I wished you to stay here, or that my mother wished it."

"Does Lady Ball know?" she asked.

"Yes, my mother does know."

"What am I to say to her?"

"Shall I tell you, Margaret, what to say? Put your arms round her neck, and tell her that you will be her daughter."

"No, John; I cannot do that; and perhaps I ought to say now that I don't think it will ever be possible. It has all so surprised me, that I haven't known how to speak; and I am afraid

I shall be letting you go from me with a false idea. Perhaps I ought to say at once that it cannot be."

"No, Margaret, no. It is much better that you should think of it. No harm can come of that."

"There will be harm if you are disappointed."

"I certainly shall be disappointed if you decide against me; but not more violently so, if you do it next week than if you do it now. But I do hope that you will not decide against me."

"And what am I to do?"

"You can write to me from Littlebath."

"And how soon must I write?"

"As soon as you can make up your mind. But, Margaret, do not decide against me too quickly. I do not know that I shall do myself any good by promising you that I will love you tenderly." So saying he put out his hand, and she took it; and they stood there looking into each other's eyes, as young lovers might have done,—as his son might have looked into those of her daughter, had she been married young and had children of her own. In the teeth of all those tedious money dealings in the City there was some spice of romance left within his bosom yet!

But how was she to get herself out of the room? It would not do for such a Juliet to stay all the night looking into the eyes of her ancient Romeo. And how was she to behave herself to Lady Ball, when she should again find herself in the drawing-room, conscious as she was that Lady Ball knew all about it? And how was she to conduct herself before all those young people whom she had left there? And her proposed father-in-law, whom she feared so much, and in truth disliked so greatly— would he know all about it, and thrust his ill-natured jokes at her? Her lover should have opened the door for her to pass through; but instead of doing so, as soon as she had withdrawn her hand from his, he placed himself on the rug, and leaned back in silence against the chimney-piece.

"I suppose it wouldn't do," she said, "for me to go off to bed without seeing them."

"I think you had better see my mother," he replied, "else you will feel awkward in the morning."

Then she opened the door for herself, and with frightened feet crept back to the drawing-room. She could hardly bring herself to open the second door; but when she had done so, her heart was greatly released, as, looking in, she saw that her aunt was the only person there.

"Well, Margaret," said the old lady, walking up to her; "well?"

"Dear aunt, I don't know what I am to say to you. I don't know what you want."

"I want you to tell me you have consented to become John's wife."

"But I have not consented. Think how sudden it has been, aunt!"

"Yes, yes; I can understand that. You could not tell him at once that you would take him; but you won't mind telling me."

"I would have told him so in an instant, if I had made up my mind. Do you think I would wish to keep him in suspense on such a matter? If I could have felt that I could love him as his wife, I would have told him so instantly,—instantly."

"And why not love him as his wife—why not?" Lady Ball, as she asked the question, was almost imperious in her eagerness.

"Why not, aunt? It is not easy to answer such a question as that. A woman, I suppose, can't say why she doesn't love a man, nor yet why she does. You see, it's so sudden. I hadn't thought of him in that way."

"You've known him now for nearly a year, and you've been in the house with him for the last three weeks. If you haven't seen that he has been attached to you, you are the only person in the house that has been so blind."

"I haven't seen it at all, aunt."

"Perhaps you are afraid of the responsibility," said Lady Ball.

"I should fear it certainly; but that alone would not deter me. I would endeavour to do my best."

"And you don't like living in the same house with me and Sir John."

"Indeed, yes; you are always good to me; and as to my uncle, I know he does not mean to be unkind. I should not fear that."

"The truth is, I suppose, Margaret, that you do not like to part with your money."

"That's unjust, aunt. I don't think I care more for my money than another woman."

"Then what is it? He can give you a position in the world higher than any you could have had a hope to possess. As Lady Ball you will be equal in all respects to your own far-away cousin, Lady Mackenzie."

"That has nothing to do with it, aunt."

"Then what is it?" asked Lady Ball again. "I suppose you have no absolute objection to be a baronet's wife."

"Suppose, aunt, that I do not love him?"

"Pshaw!" said the old woman.

"But it isn't pshaw," said Miss Mackenzie. "No woman ought to marry a man unless she feels that she loves him."

"Pshaw!" said Lady Ball again.

They had both been standing; and as everybody else was gone Miss Mackenzie had determined that she would go off to bed without settling herself in the room. So she prepared herself for her departure.

"I'll say good-night now, aunt. I have still some of my packing to do, and I must be up early."

"Don't be in a hurry, Margaret. I want to speak to you before you leave us, and I shall have no other opportunity. Sit down, won't you?"

Then Miss Mackenzie seated herself, most unwillingly.

"I don't know that there is anyone nearer to you than I am, my dear; at any rate, no woman; and therefore I can say more than any other person. When you talk of not loving John, does that mean—does it mean that you are engaged to anyone else?"

"No, it does not."

"And it does not mean that there is anyone else whom you are thinking of marrying?"

"I am not thinking of marrying anyone."

"Or that you love any other man?"

"You are cross-questioning me, aunt, more than is fair."

"Then there is some one?"

"No, there is nobody. What I say about John I don't say through any feeling for anybody else."

"Then, my dear, I think that a little talk between you and me may make this matter all right. I'm sure you don't doubt John when he says that he loves you very dearly. As for your loving him, of course that would come. It is not as if you two were two young people, and that you wanted to be billing and cooing. Of course you ought to be fond of each other, and like each other's company; and I have no doubt that you will. You and I would, of course, be thrown very much together, and I'm sure I'm very fond of you. Indeed, Margaret, I have endeavoured to show that I am."

"You've been very kind, aunt."

"Therefore as to your loving him, I really don't think there need be any doubt about that. Then, my dear, as to the other part of the arrangement,—the money and all that. If you were to have any children, your own fortune would be settled on them; at least, that could be arranged, if you required it; though, as your fortune all came from the Balls, and is the very money with which the title was intended to be maintained, you probably would not be very exacting about that. Stop a moment, my dear, and let me finish before you speak. I want you particularly to think of what I say, and to remember that all your money did come from the Balls. It has been very hard upon John,—you must feel that. Look at him with his heavy family, and how he works for them!"

"But my uncle Jonathan died and left his money to my brothers before John was married. It is twenty-five years ago."

"Well I remember it, my dear! John was just engaged to Rachel, and the marriage was put off because of the great cruelty of Jonathan's will. Of course I am not blaming you."

"I was only ten years old, and uncle Jonathan did not leave me a penny. My money came to me from my brother; and, as far as I can understand, it is nearly double as much as he got from Sir John's brother."

"That may be; but John would have doubled it quite as readily as Walter Mackenzie. What I mean to say is this, that as you have the money which in the course of nature would have come to John, and which would have been his now if a great injustice had not been done—"

"It was done by a Ball, and not by a Mackenzie."

"That does not alter the case in the least. Your feelings should be just the same in spite of that. Of course the money is yours and you can do what you like with it. You can give it to young Mr. Samuel Rubb, if you please." Stupid old woman! "But I think you must feel that you should repair the injury which was done, as it is in your power to do so. A fine position is offered you. When poor Sir John goes, you will become Lady Ball, and be the mistress of this house, and have your own carriage." Terribly stupid old woman! "And you would have friends and relatives always round you, instead of being all alone at such a place as Littlebath, which must, I should say, be very sad. Of course there would be duties to perform to the dear children; but I don't think so ill of you, Margaret, as to suppose for an instant that you would shrink from that. Stop one moment, my dear, and I shall have done. I think I have said all now; but I can well understand that when John spoke to you, you could not immediately give him a favourable answer. It was much better to leave it till to-morrow. But you can't have any objection to speaking out to me, and I really think you might make me happy by saying that it shall be as I wish."

It is astonishing the harm that an old woman may do when she goes well to work, and when she believes she can prevail by means of her own peculiar eloquence. Lady Ball had so trusted to her own prestige, to her own ladyship, to her own carriage and horses, and to the rest of it, and had also so misjudged Margaret's ordinary mild manner, that she had thought to force her niece into an immediate acquiescence by her mere words. The result, however, was exactly the contrary to this. Had Miss Mackenzie been left to herself after the interview with Mr. Ball: had she gone upstairs to sleep upon his proposal, without any disturbance to those visions of sacrificial duty which his plain statement had produced: had she been allowed to leave the house and think over it all without any other argument to her than those which he had used, I think that she would have accepted him. But now she was up in arms against the whole thing. Her mind, clear as it was, was hardly lucid enough to allow of her separating the mother and son at this moment. She was claimed as a wife into the family because they thought that they had a right to her fortune; and the temptations offered, by which they hoped to draw her into her duty, were a beggarly title and an old coach! No! The visions of sacrificial duty were all dispelled. There was doubt before, but now there was no doubt.

"I think I will go to bed, aunt," she said very calmly, "and I will write to John from Littlebath."

"And cannot you put me out of my suspense?"

"If you wish it, yes. I know that I must refuse him. I wish that I had told him so at once, as then there would have been an end of it."

"You don't mean that you have made up your mind?"

"Yes, aunt, I do. I should be wrong to marry a man that I do not love; and as for the money, aunt, I must say that I think you are mistaken."

"How mistaken?"

"You think that I am called upon to put right some wrong that you think was done you by Sir John's brother. I don't think that I am under any such obligation. Uncle Jonathan left his money to his sister's children instead of to his brother's children. If his money had come to John, you would not have admitted that we had any claim, because we were nephews and nieces."

"The whole thing would have been different."

"Well, aunt, I am very tired, and if you'll let me, I'll go to bed."

"Oh, certainly."

Then, with anything but warm affection, the aunt and niece parted, and Miss Mackenzie went to her bed with a firm resolution that she would not become Lady Ball.

It had been arranged for some time back that Mr. Ball was to accompany his cousin up to London by the train; and though under the present circumstances that arrangement was not without a certain amount of inconvenience, there was no excuse at hand for changing it. Not a word was said at breakfast as to the scenes of last night. Indeed, no word could very well have been said, as all the family was present, including Jack and the girls. Lady Ball was very quiet, and very dignified; but Miss Mackenzie perceived that she was always called "Margaret," and not "my dear," as had been her aunt's custom. Very little was said by any one, and not a great deal was eaten.

"Well; when are we to see you back again?" said Sir John, as Margaret arose from her chair on being told that the carriage was there.

"Perhaps you and my aunt will come down some day and see me at Littlebath?" said Miss Mackenzie.

"No; I don't think that's very likely," said Sir John.

Then she kissed all the children, till she came to Jack.

"I am going to kiss you, too," she said to him.

"No objection in life," said Jack. "I sha'n't complain about that."

"You'll come and see me at Littlebath?" said she.

"That I will if you'll ask me."

Then she put her face to her aunt, and Lady Ball permitted her cheek to be touched. Lady Ball was still not without hope, but she thought that the surest way was to assume a high dignity of demeanour, and to exhibit a certain amount of displeasure. She still believed that Margaret might be frightened into the match. It was but a mile and a half to the station, and for that distance Mr. Ball and Margaret sat together in the carriage. He said nothing to her as to his proposal till the station was in view, and then only a word.

"Think well of it, Margaret, if you can."

"I fear I cannot think well of it," she answered. But she spoke so low, that I doubt whether he completely heard her words. The train up to London was nearly full, and there he had no opportunity of speaking to her. But he desired no such opportunity. He had said all that he had to say, and was almost well pleased to know that a final answer was to be given to him, not personally, but by letter. His mother had spoken to him that morning, and had made him understand that she was not well pleased with Margaret; but she had said nothing to quench her son's hopes.

"Of course she will accept you," Lady Ball had said, "but women like her never like to do anything without making a fuss about it."

"To me, yesterday, I thought she behaved admirably," said her son.

At the station at London he put her into the cab that was to take her to Gower Street, and as he shook hands with her through the window, he once more said the same words:

"Think well of it, Margaret, if you can."

Chapter VIII

Mrs. Tom Mackenzie's Dinner Party

Mrs. Tom was ever so gracious on the arrival of her sister-in-law, but even in her graciousness there was something which seemed to Margaret to tell of her dislike. Near relatives, when they are on good terms with each other, are not gracious. Now, Mrs. Tom, though she was ever so gracious, was by no means cordial. Susanna, however, was delighted to see her aunt, and Margaret, when she felt the girl's arms round her neck, declared to herself that that should suffice for her,—that should be her love, and it should be enough. If indeed, in after years, she could make Jack love her too, that would be better still. Then her mind went to work upon a little marriage scheme that would in due time make a baronet's wife of Susanna. It would not suit her to become Lady Ball, but it might suit Susanna.

"We are going to have a little dinner party to-day," said Mrs. Tom.

"A dinner party!" said Margaret. "I didn't look for that, Sarah."

"Perhaps I ought not to call it a party, for there are only one or two coming. There's Dr Slumpy and his wife; I don't know whether you ever met Dr Slumpy. He has attended us for ever so long; and there is Miss Colza, a great friend of mine. Mademoiselle Colza I ought to call her, because her father was a Portuguese. Only as she never saw him, we call her Miss. And there's Mr. Rubb,—Samuel Rubb, junior. I think you met him at Littlebath."

"Yes; I know Mr. Rubb."

"That's all; and I might as well say how it will be now. Mr. Rubb will take you down to dinner. Tom will take Mrs. Slumpy, and the doctor will take me. Young Tom,"—Young Tom was her son, who was now beginning his career at Rubb and Mackenzie's,—"Young Tom will take Miss Colza, and Mary Jane and Susanna will come down by themselves. We might have managed twelve, and Tom did think of asking Mr. Handcock and one of the other clerks, but he did not know whether you would have liked it."

"I should not have minded it. That is, I should have been very glad to meet Mr. Handcock, but I don't care about it."

"That's just what we thought, and therefore we did not ask him. You'll remember, won't you, that Mr. Rubb takes you down?" After that Miss Mackenzie took her nieces to the Zoological Gardens, leaving Mary Jane at home to assist her mother in the cares for the coming festival, and thus the day wore itself away till it was time for them to prepare themselves for the party.

Miss Colza was the first to come. She was a young lady somewhat older than Miss Mackenzie; but the circumstances of her life had induced her to retain many of the propensities of her girlhood. She was as young looking as curls and pink bows could make her, and was by no means a useless guest at a small dinner party, as she could chatter like a magpie. Her claims to be called "Mademoiselle" were not very strong, as she had lived in Finsbury Square all her life. Her father was connected in trade with the Rubb and Mackenzie firm, and dealt, I think, in oil. She was introduced with great ceremony, and having heard that Miss Mackenzie lived at Littlebath, went off at score about the pleasures of that delicious place.

"I do so hate London, Miss Mackenzie."

"I lived here all my life, and I can't say I liked it."

"It is such a crowd, isn't it? and yet so dull. Give me Brighton! We were down for a week in November, and it was nice."

"I never saw Brighton."

"Oh, do go to Brighton. Everybody goes there now; you really do see the world at Brighton. Now, in London one sees nothing."

Then came in Mr. Rubb, and Miss Colza at once turned her attention to him. But Mr. Rubb shook Miss Colza off almost unceremoniously, and seated himself by Miss Mackenzie. Immediately afterwards arrived the doctor and his wife. The doctor was a very silent man, and as Tom Mackenzie himself was not given to much talking, it was well that Miss Colza should be there. Mrs. Slumpy could take her share in conversation with an effort, when duly assisted; but she could not lead the van, and required more sprightly aid than her host was qualified to give her. Then there was a whisper between Tom and Mrs. Tom and the bell was rung, and the dinner was ordered. Seven had been the time named, and a quarter past seven saw the guests assembled in the drawing-room. A very dignified person in white cotton gloves had announced the names, and the same dignified person had taken the order for dinner. The dignified person had then retreated downstairs slowly, and what was taking place for the next half-hour poor Mrs. Mackenzie, in the agony of her mind, could not surmise. She longed to go and see, but did not dare. Even for Dr Slumpy, or even for his wife, had they been alone with her she would not have cared much. Miss Colza she could have treated with perfect indifference—could even have taken her down into the kitchen

with her. Rubb, her own junior partner, was nothing, and Miss
Mackenzie was simply her sister-in-law. But together they made
a party. Moreover she had on her best and stiffest silk gown, and
so armed she could not have been effective in the kitchen. And
so came a silence for some minutes, in spite of the efforts of
Miss Colza. At last the hostess plucked up her courage to make a
little effort.

"Tom," she said, "I really think you had better ring
again."

"It will be all right, soon," said Tom, considering that
upon the whole it would be better not to disturb the gentleman
downstairs just yet.

"Upon my word, I never felt it so cold in my life as I did
to-day," he said, turning on Dr Slumpy for the third time with
that remark.

"Very cold," said Dr Slumpy, pulling out his watch and
looking at it.

"I really think you'd better ring the bell," said Mrs. Tom.

Tom, however, did not stir, and after another period of
five minutes dinner was announced. It may be as well, perhaps,
to explain, that the soup had been on the table for the last quarter
of an hour or more, but that after placing the tureen on the table,
the dignified gentleman downstairs had come to words with the
cook, and had refused to go on further with the business of the
night until that ill-used woman acceded to certain terms of his
own in reference to the manner in which the foods should be
served. He had seen the world, and had lofty ideas, and had been
taught to be a tyrant by the weakness of those among whom his
life had been spent. The cook had alleged that the dinner, as
regarded the eating of it, would certainly be spoilt. As to that, he
had expressed a mighty indifference. If he was to have any hand
in them, things were to be done according to certain rules,
which, as he said, prevailed in the world of fashion. The cook,
who had a temper and who regarded her mistress, stood out long
and boldly, but when the housemaid, who was to assist Mr.

Grandairs upstairs, absolutely deserted her, and sitting down
began to cry, saying: "Sairey, why don't you do as he tells you?
What signifies its being greasy if it hain't never to go hup?" then
Sarah's courage gave way, and Mr. Grandairs, with all the
conqueror in his bosom, announced that dinner was served.

It was a great relief. Even Miss Colza's tongue had been
silent, and Mr. Rubb had found himself unable to carry on any
further small talk with Miss Mackenzie. The minds of men and
women become so tuned to certain positions, that they go astray
and won't act when those positions are confused. Almost every
man can talk for fifteen minutes, standing in a drawing-room,
before dinner; but where is the man who can do it for an hour? It
is not his appetite that impedes him, for he could well have
borne to dine at eight instead of seven; nor is it that matter lacks
him, for at other times his eloquence does not cease to flow so
soon. But at that special point of the day he is supposed to talk
for fifteen minutes, and if any prolonged call is then made upon
him, his talking apparatus falls out of order and will not work.
You can sit still on a Sunday morning, in the cold, on a very
narrow bench, with no comfort appertaining, and listen for half
an hour to a rapid outflow of words, which, for any purpose of
instruction or edification, are absolutely useless to you. The
reading to you of the *"Quæ genus,"* or *"As in præsenti,"* could
not be more uninteresting. Try to undergo the same thing in your
own house on a Wednesday afternoon, and see where you will
be. To those ladies and gentlemen who had been assembled in
Mrs. Mackenzie's drawing-room this prolonged waiting had
been as though the length of the sermon had been doubled, or as
if it had fallen on them at some unexpected and unauthorised
time.

But now they descended, each gentleman taking his
allotted lady, and Colza's voice was again heard. At the bottom
of the stairs, just behind the dining-room door, stood the tyrant,
looking very great, repressing with his left hand the housemaid
who was behind him. She having observed Sarah at the top of

the kitchen stairs telegraphing for assistance, had endeavoured to make her way to her friend while Tom Mackenzie and Mrs. Slumpy were still upon the stairs; but the tyrant, though he had seen the cook's distress, had refused and sternly kept the girl a prisoner behind him. Ruat dinner, fiat genteel deportment.

The order of the construction of the dinner was no doubt à la Russe; and why should it not have been so, as Tom Mackenzie either had or was supposed to have as much as eight hundred a year? But I think it must be confessed that the architecture was in some degree composite. It was à la Russe, because in the centre there was a green arrangement of little boughs with artificial flowers fixed on them, and because there were figs and raisins, and little dishes with dabs of preserve on them, all around the green arrangement; but the soups and fish were on the table, as was also the wine, though it was understood that no one was to be allowed to help himself or his neighbour to the contents of the bottle. When Dr Slumpy once made an attempt at the sherry, Grandairs was down upon him instantly, although laden at the time with both potatoes and sea-kale; after that he went round and frowned at Dr Slumpy, and Dr Slumpy understood the frown.

That the soup should be cold, everybody no doubt expected. It was clear soup, made chiefly of Marsala, and purchased from the pastry cook's in Store Street. Grandairs, no doubt, knew all about it, as he was connected with the same establishment. The fish—Mrs. Mackenzie had feared greatly about her fish, having necessarily trusted its fate solely to her own cook—was very ragged in its appearance, and could not be very warm; the melted butter too was thick and clotted, and was brought round with the other condiments too late to be of much service; but still the fish was eatable, and Mrs. Mackenzie's heart, which had sunk very low as the unconsumed soup was carried away, rose again in her bosom. Poor woman! she had done her best, and it was hard that she should suffer. One little effort she made at the moment to induce Elizabeth to carry round the sauce, but Grandairs had at once crushed it; he had rushed at the girl and taken the butter-boat from her hand. Mrs. Mackenzie had seen it all; but what could she do, poor soul?

The thing was badly managed in every way. The whole hope of conversation round the table depended on Miss Colza, and she was deeply offended by having been torn away from Mr. Rubb. How could she talk seated between the two Tom Mackenzies? From Dr Slumpy Mrs. Mackenzie could not get a word. Indeed, with so great a weight on her mind, how could she be expected to make any great effort in that direction? But Mr. Mackenzie might have done something, and she resolved that she would tell him so before he slept that night. She had slaved all day in order that he might appear respectable before his own relatives, at the bottom of his own table—and now he would do nothing! "I believe he is thinking of his own dinner!" she said to herself. If her accusation was just his thoughts must have been very sad.

In a quiet way Mr. Rubb did talk to his neighbour. Upstairs he had spoken a word or two about Littlebath, saying how glad he was that he had been there. He should always remember Littlebath as one of the pleasantest places he had ever seen. He wished that he lived at Littlebath; but then what was the good of his wishing anything, knowing as he did that he was bound for life to Rubb and Mackenzie's counting house!

"And you will earn your livelihood there," Miss Mackenzie had replied.

"Yes; and something more than that I hope. I don't mind telling you,—a friend like you,—that I will either spoil a horn or make a spoon. I won't go on in the old groove, which hardly gives any of us salt to our porridge. If I understand anything of English commerce, I think I can see my way to better things than that." Then the period of painful waiting had commenced, and he was unable to say anything more.

That had been upstairs. Now below, amidst all the troubles of Mrs. Mackenzie and the tyranny of Grandairs, he began again:

"Do you like London dinner parties?"

"I never was at one before."

"Never at one before! I thought you had lived in London all your life."

"So I have; but we never used to dine out. My brother was an invalid."

"And do they do the thing well at Littlebath?"

"I never dined out there. You think it very odd, I dare say, but I never was at a dinner party in my life—not before this."

"Don't the Balls see much company?"

"No, very little; none of that kind."

"Dear me. It comes so often to us here that we get tired of it. I do, at least. I'm not always up to this kind of thing. Champagne—if you please. Miss Mackenzie, you will take some champagne?"

Now had come the crisis of the evening, the moment that was all important, and Grandairs was making his round in all the pride of his vocation. But Mrs. Mackenzie was by no means so proud at the present conjuncture of affairs. There was but one bottle of champagne. "So little wine is drank now, that, what is the good of getting more? Of course the children won't have it." So she had spoken to her husband. And who shall blame her or say where economy ends, or where meanness begins? She had wanted no champagne herself, but had wished to treat her friends well. She had seized a moment after Grandairs had come, and Mrs. Slumpy was not yet there, to give instructions to the great functionary.

"Don't mind me with the champagne, nor yet Mr. Tom, nor the young ladies."

Thus she had reduced the number to six, and had calculated that the bottle would certainly be good for that number, with probably a second glass for the doctor and Mr. Rubb. But Grandairs had not condescended to be put out of his way by such orders as these. The bottle had first come to Miss Colza, and then Tom's glass had been filled, and Susanna's—through no fault of theirs, innocent bairns, "but on purpose!" as Mrs. Mackenzie afterwards declared to her husband when speaking of the man's iniquity. And I think it had been done on purpose. The same thing occurred with Mary Jane—till Mrs. Mackenzie, looking on, could have cried. The girl's glass was filled full, and she did give a little shriek at last. But what availed shrieking? When the bottle came round behind Mrs. Mackenzie back to Dr Slumpy, it was dry, and the wicked wretch held the useless nozzle triumphantly over the doctor's glass.

"Give me some sherry, then," said the doctor.

The little dishes which had been brought round after the fish, three in number,—and they in the proper order of things should have been spoken of before the champagne,—had been in their way successful. They had been so fabricated, that all they who attempted to eat of their contents became at once aware that they had got hold of something very nasty, something that could hardly have been intended by Christian cooks as food for men; but, nevertheless, there had been something of glory attending them. Little dishes require no concomitant vegetables, and therefore there had been no scrambling. Grandairs brought one round after the other with much majesty, while Elizabeth stood behind looking on in wonder. After the second little dish Grandairs changed the plates, so that it was possible to partake of two, a feat which was performed by Tom Mackenzie the younger. At this period Mrs. Mackenzie, striving hard for equanimity, attempted a word or two with the doctor. But immediately upon that came the affair of the champagne, and she was crushed, never to rise again.

Mr. Rubb at this time had settled down into so pleasant a little series of whispers with his neighbour, that Miss Colza resolved once more to exert herself, not with the praiseworthy desire of assisting her friend Mrs. Mackenzie, but with malice prepense in reference to Miss Mackenzie.

Miss Mackenzie seemed to be having "a good time" with her neighbour Samuel Rubb, junior, and Miss Colza, who was a woman of courage, could not see that and not make an effort. It cannot be told here what passages there had been between Mr. Rubb and Miss Colza. That there had absolutely been passages I beg the reader to understand. "Mr. Rubb," she said, stretching across the table, "do you remember when, in this very room, we met Mr. and Mrs. Talbot Green?"

"Oh yes, very well," said Mr. Rubb, and then turning to Miss Mackenzie, he went on with his little whispers.

"Mr. Rubb," continued Miss Colza, "does anybody put you in mind of Mrs. Talbot Green?"

"Nobody in particular. She was a thin, tall, plain woman, with red hair, wasn't she? Who ought she to put me in mind of?"

"Oh dear! how can you forget so? That wasn't her looks at all. We all agreed that she was quite interesting-looking. Her hair was just fair, and that was all. But I shan't say anything more about it."

"But who do you say is like her?"

"Miss Colza means Aunt Margaret," said Mary Jane.

"Of course I do," said Miss Colza. "But Mrs. Talbot Green was not at all the person that Mr. Rubb has described; we all thought her very nice-looking. Mr. Rubb, do you remember how you would go on talking to her, till Mr. Talbot Green did not like it at all?"

"No, I don't."

"Oh, but you did; and you always do."

Then Miss Colza ceased, having finished that effort. But she made others from time to time as long as they remained in the dining-room, and by no means gave up the battle. There are women who can fight such battles when they have not an inch of ground on which to stand.

After the little dishes there came, of course, a saddle of mutton, and, equally of course, a pair of boiled fowls. There was also a tongue; but the à la Russe construction of the dinner was maintained by keeping the tongue on the sideboard, while the mutton and chickens were put down to be carved in the ordinary way. The ladies all partook of the chickens, and the gentlemen all of the mutton. The arrangement was very tedious, as Dr Slumpy was not as clever with the wings of the fowls as he perhaps would have been had he not been defrauded in the matter of the champagne; and then every separate plate was carried away to the sideboard with reference to the tongue. Currant jelly had been duly provided, and, if Elizabeth had been allowed to dispense it, might have been useful. But Grandairs was too much for the jelly, as he had been for the fish-sauce, and Dr Slumpy in vain looked up, and sighed, and waited. A man in such a condition measures the amount of cold which his meat may possibly endure against the future coming of the potatoes, till he falls utterly to the ground between two stools. So was it now with Dr Slumpy. He gave one last sigh as he saw the gravy congeal upon his plate, but, nevertheless, he had finished the unpalatable food before Grandairs had arrived to his assistance.

Why tell of the ruin of the maccaroni, of the fine-coloured pyramids of shaking sweet things which nobody would eat, and by the non-consumption of which nothing was gained, as they all went back to the pastrycook's,—or of the ice-puddings flavoured with onions? It was all misery, wretchedness, and degradation. Grandairs was king, and Mrs. Mackenzie was the lowest of his slaves. And why? Why had she done this thing? Why had she, who, to give her her due, generally held her own in her own house pretty firmly,—why had she lowered her neck and made a wretched thing of herself? She knew that it would be so when she first suggested to herself the attempt. She did it for fashion's sake, you will say. But there was no one there who did not as accurately know as she did herself, how absolutely beyond fashion's way lay her way. She was making no fight to enter some special portal of the world, as a lady may do who takes a house suddenly in Mayfair, having come from God knows where. Her place in the world was fixed, and she made no contest as to the fixing. She hoped for no great change in the direction of society. Why on earth did she perplex her mind and bruise her spirit, by giving a dinner à la anything? Why did she not have the roast mutton alone, so that all her guests might have eaten and have been merry?

She could not have answered this question herself, and I doubt whether I can do so for her. But this I feel, that unless the question can get itself answered, ordinary Englishmen must cease to go and eat dinners at each other's houses. The ordinary Englishman, of whom we are now speaking, has eight hundred a year; he lives in London; and he has a wife and three or four children. Had he not better give it up and go back to his little bit of fish and his leg of mutton? Let him do that boldly, and he will find that we, his friends, will come to him fast enough; yes, and will make a gala day of it. By Heavens, we have no gala time of it when we go to dine with Mrs. Mackenzie à la Russe! Lady Mackenzie, whose husband has ever so many thousands a year, no doubt does it very well. Money, which cannot do everything,—which, if well weighed, cannot in its excess perhaps do much,—can do some things. It will buy diamonds and give grand banquets. But paste diamonds, and banquets which are only would-be grand, are among the poorest imitations to which the world has descended.

"So you really go to Littlebath to-morrow," Mr. Rubb said to Miss Mackenzie, when they were again together in the drawing-room.

"Yes, to-morrow morning. Susanna must be at school the next day."

"Happy Susanna! I wish I were going to school at Littlebath. Then I shan't see you again before you go."

"No; I suppose not."

"I am so sorry, because I particularly wished to speak to you,—most particularly. I suppose I could not see you in the morning? But, no; it would not do. I could not get you alone without making such a fuss of the thing."

"Couldn't you say it now?" asked Miss Mackenzie.

"I will, if you'll let me; only I suppose it isn't quite the thing to talk about business at an evening party; and your sister-in-law, if she knew it, would never forgive me."

"Then she shan't know it, Mr. Rubb."

"Since you are so good, I think I will make bold. Carpe diem, as we used to say at school, which means that one day is as good as another, and, if so why not any time in the day? Look here, Miss Mackenzie—about that money, you know."

And Mr. Rubb got nearer to her on the sofa as he whispered the word money into her ear. It immediately struck her that her own brother Tom had said not a word to her about the money, although they had been together for the best part of an hour before they had gone up to dress.

"I suppose Mr. Slow will settle all that," said Miss Mackenzie.

"Of course;—that is to say, he has nothing further to settle just as yet. He has our bond for the money, and you may be sure it's all right. The property is purchased, and is ours,—our own at this moment, thanks to you. But landed property is so hard to convey. Perhaps you don't understand much about that! and I'm sure I don't. The fact is, the title deeds at present are in other hands, a mere matter of form; and I want you to understand that the mortgage is not completed for that reason."

"I suppose it will be done soon?"

"It may, or it may not; but that won't affect your interest, you know."

"I was thinking of the security."

"Well, the security is not as perfect as it should be. I tell you that honestly; and if we were dealing with strangers we should expect to be called on to refund. And we should refund

instantly, but at a great sacrifice, a ruinous sacrifice. Now, I want
you to put so much trust in us,—in me, if I may be allowed to
ask you to do so,—as to believe that your money is substantially
safe. I cannot explain it all now; but the benefit which you have
done us is immense."

"I suppose it will all come right, Mr. Rubb."

"It will all come right, Miss Mackenzie."

Then there was extracted from her something which he
was able to take as a promise that she would not stir in the
matter for a while, but would take her interest without asking for
any security as to her principal.

The conversation was interrupted by Miss Colza, who
came and stood opposite to them.

"Well, I'm sure," she said; "you two are very
confidential."

"And why shouldn't we be confidential, Miss Colza?"
asked Mr. Rubb.

"Oh, dear! no reason in life, if you both like it."

Miss Mackenzie was not sure that she did like it. But
again she was not sure that she did not, when Mr. Rubb pressed
her hand at parting, and told her that her great kindness had been
of the most material service to the firm. "He felt it," he said, "if
nobody else did." That also might be a sacrificial duty and
therefore gratifying.

The next morning she and Susanna left Gower Street at
eight, spent an interesting period of nearly an hour at the railway
station, and reached Littlebath in safety at one.

Chapter IX

Miss Mackenzie's Philosophy

Miss Mackenzie remained quiet in her room for two days after her return before she went out to see anybody. These last Christmas weeks had certainly been the most eventful period of her life, and there was very much of which it was necessary that she should think. She had, she thought, made up her mind to refuse her cousin's offer; but the deed was not yet done. She had to think of the mode in which she must do it; and she could not but remember, also, that she might still change her mind in that matter if she pleased. The anger produced in her by Lady Ball's claim, as it were, to her fortune, had almost evaporated; but the memory of her cousin's story of his troubles was still fresh. "I have a hard time of it sometimes, I can tell you." Those words and others of the same kind were the arguments which had moved her, and made her try to think that she could love him. Then she remembered his bald head and the weary, careworn look about his eyes, and his little intermittent talk, addressed chiefly to his mother, about the money-market,—little speeches made as he would sit with the newspaper in his hand:

"The Confederate loan isn't so bad, after all. I wish I'd taken a few."

"You know you'd never have slept if you had," Lady
Ball would answer.

All this Miss Mackenzie now turned in her mind, and
asked herself whether she could be happy in hearing such
speeches for the remainder of her life.

"It is not as if you two were young people, and wanted to
be billing and cooing," Lady Ball had said to her the same
evening.

Miss Mackenzie, as she thought of this, was not so sure
that Lady Ball was right. Why should she not want billing and
cooing as well as another? It was natural that a woman should
want some of it in her life, and she had had none of it yet. She
had had a lover, certainly, but there had been no billing and
cooing with him. Nothing of that kind had been possible in her
brother Walter's house.

And then the question naturally arose to her whether her
aunt had treated her justly in bracketing her with John Ball in
that matter of age. John Ball was ten years her senior; and ten
years, she knew, was a very proper difference between a man
and his wife. She was by no means inclined to plead, even to
herself, that she was too young to marry her cousin; there was
nothing in their ages to interfere, if the match was in other
respects suitable. But still, was not he old for his age, and was
not she young for hers? And if she should ultimately resolve to
devote herself and what she had left of youth to his children and
his welfare, should not the sacrifice be recognised? Had Lady
Ball done well to speak of her as she certainly might well speak
of him? Was she beyond all aptitude for billing and cooing, if
billing and cooing might chance to come in her way?

Thinking of this during the long afternoon, when
Susanna was at school, she got up and looked at herself in the
mirror. She moved up her hair from off her ears, knowing where
she would find a few that were grey, and shaking her head, as
though owning to herself that she was old; but as her fingers ran
almost involuntarily across her locks, her touch told her that they

were soft and silken; and she looked into her own eyes, and saw that they were bright; and her hand touched the outline of her cheek, and she knew that something of the fresh bloom of youth was still there; and her lips parted, and there were her white teeth; and there came a smile and a dimple, and a slight purpose of laughter in her eye, and then a tear. She pulled her scarf tighter across her bosom, feeling her own form, and then she leaned forward and kissed herself in the glass.

He was very careworn, soiled as it were with the world, tired out with the dusty, weary life's walk which he had been compelled to take. Of romance in him there was nothing left, while in her the aptitude for romance had only just been born. It was not only that his head was bald, but that his eye was dull, and his step slow. The juices of life had been pressed out of him; his thoughts were all of his cares, and never of his hopes. It would be very sad to be the wife of such a man; it would be very sad, if there were no compensation; but might not the sacrificial duties give her that atonement which she would require? She would fain do something with her life and her money,—some good, some great good to some other person. If that good to another person and billing and cooing might go together, it would be very pleasant. But she knew there was danger in such an idea. The billing and cooing might lead altogether to evil. But there could be no doubt that she would do good service if she married her cousin; her money would go to good purposes, and her care to those children would be invaluable. They were her cousins, and would it not be sweet to make of herself a sacrifice?

And then—Reader! remember that she was no saint, and that hitherto very little opportunity had been given to her of learning to discriminate true metal from dross. Then—she thought of Mr. Samuel Rubb, junior. Mr. Samuel Rubb, junior, was a handsome man, about her own age; and she felt almost sure that Mr. Samuel Rubb, junior, admired her. He was not worn out with life; he was not broken with care; he would look forward into the world, and hope for things to come. One thing she knew to be true—he was not a gentleman. But then, why should she care for that? The being a gentleman was not everything. As for herself, might there not be strong reason to doubt whether those who were best qualified to judge would call her a lady? Her surviving brother kept an oilcloth shop, and the brother with whom she had always lived had been so retired from the world that neither he nor she knew anything of its ways. If love could be gained, and anything of romance; if some active living mode of life could thereby be opened to her, would it not be well for her to give up that idea of being a lady? Hitherto her rank had simply enabled her to become a Stumfoldian; and then she remembered that Mr. Maguire's squint was very terrible! How she should live, what she should do with herself, were matters to her of painful thought; but she looked in the glass again, and resolved that she would decline the honour of becoming Mrs. Ball.

On the following morning she wrote her letter, and it was written thus:

7 Paragon, Littlebath, January, 186—.

MY DEAR JOHN,

I have been thinking a great deal about what you said to me, and I have made up my mind that I ought not to become your wife. I know that the honour you have proposed to me is very great, and that I may seem to be ungrateful in declining it; but I cannot bring myself to feel that sort of love for you which a wife should have for her husband. I hope this will not make you displeased with me. It ought not to do so, as my feelings towards you and to your children are most affectionate.

I know my aunt will be angry with me. Pray tell her from me, with my best love, that I have thought very much of all she said to me, and that I feel sure that I am doing right. It is not that I should be afraid of the duties which would fall upon me as your wife; but that the woman who undertakes those duties should feel for you a wife's love. I think it is best to speak openly, and I hope that you will not be offended.

Give my best love to my uncle and aunt, and to the
girls, and to Jack, who will, I hope, keep his promise of
coming and seeing me.

Your very affectionate cousin,

MARGARET MACKENZIE.

"There," said John Ball to his mother, when he had read the
letter, "I knew it would be so; and she is right. Why should she
give up her money and her comfort and her ease, to look after
my children?"

Lady Ball took the letter and read it, and pronounced it to
be all nonsense.

"It may be all nonsense," said her son; "but such as it is,
it is her answer."

"I suppose you'll have to go down to Littlebath after
her," said Lady Ball.

"I certainly shall not do that. It would do no good; and
I'm not going to persecute her."

"Persecute her! What nonsense you men do talk! As if
any woman in her condition could be persecuted by being asked
to become a baronet's wife. I suppose I must go down."

"I beg that you will not, mother."

"She is just one of those women who are sure to stand
off, not knowing their own minds. The best creature in the
world, and really very clever, but weak in that respect! She has
not had lovers when she was young, and she thinks that a man
should come dallying about her as though she were eighteen. It
only wants a little perseverance, John, and if you'll take my
advice, you'll go down to Littlebath after her."

But John, in this matter, would not follow his mother's
advice, and declared that he would take no further steps. "He
was inclined," he said, "to think that Margaret was right. Why
should any woman burden herself with nine children?"

Then Lady Ball said a great deal more about the Ball
money, giving it as her decided opinion that Margaret owed

herself and her money to the Balls. As she could not induce her son to do anything, she wrote a rejoinder to her niece.

"My dearest Margaret," she said, "Your letter has made both me and John very unhappy. He has set his heart upon making you his wife, and I don't think will ever hold up his head again if you will not consent. I write now instead of John, because he is so much oppressed. I wish you had remained here, because then we could have talked it over quietly. Would it not be better for you to be here than living alone at Littlebath? for I cannot call that little girl who is at school anything of a companion. Could you not leave her as a boarder, and come to us for a month? You would not be forced to pledge yourself to anything further; but we could talk it over."

It need hardly be said that Miss Mackenzie, as she read this, declared to herself that she had no desire to talk over her own position with Lady Ball any further.

"John is afraid," the letter went on to say, "that he offended you by the manner of his proposition; and that he said too much about the children, and not enough about his own affection. Of course he loves you dearly. If you knew him as I do, which of course you can't as yet, though I hope you will, you would be aware that no consideration, either of money or about the children, would induce him to propose to any woman unless he loved her. You may take my word for that."

There was a great deal more in the letter of the same kind, in which Lady Ball pressed her own peculiar arguments; but I need hardly say that they did not prevail with Miss Mackenzie. If the son could not induce his cousin to marry him, the mother certainly never would do so. It did not take her long to answer her aunt's letter. She said that she must, with many thanks, decline for the present to return to the Cedars, as the charge which she had taken of her niece made her presence at Littlebath necessary. As to the answer which she had given to John, she was afraid she could only say that it must stand. She had felt a little angry with Lady Ball; and though she tried not to show this in the tone of her letter, she did show it.

"If I were you I would never see her or speak to her again," said Lady Ball to her son.

"Very likely I never shall," he replied.

"Has your love-making with that old maid gone wrong, John?" the father asked.

But John Ball was used to his father's ill nature, and never answered it.

Nothing special to our story occurred at Littlebath during the next two or three months, except that Miss Mackenzie became more and more intimate with Miss Baker, and more and more anxious to form an acquaintance with Miss Todd. With all the Stumfoldians she was on terms of mitigated friendship, and always went to Mrs. Stumfold's fortnightly tea-drinkings. But with no lady there,—always excepting Miss Baker,—did she find that she grew into familiarity. With Mrs. Stumfold no one was familiar. She was afflicted by the weight of her own position, as we suppose the Queen to be, when we say that her Majesty's altitude is too high to admit of friendships. Mrs. Stumfold never condescended—except to the bishop's wife who, in return, had snubbed Mrs. Stumfold. But living, as she did, in an atmosphere of flattery and toadying, it was wonderful how well she preserved her equanimity, and how she would talk and perhaps think of herself, as a poor, erring human being. When, however, she insisted much upon this fact of her humanity, the coachmaker's wife would shake her head, and at last stamp her foot in anger, swearing that though everybody was of course dust, and grass, and worms; and though, of course, Mrs. Stumfold must, by nature, be included in that everybody; yet dust, and grass, and worms nowhere exhibited themselves with so few of the stains of humanity on them as they did within the bosom of Mrs. Stumfold. So that, though the absolute fact of Mrs. Stumfold being dust, and grass, and worms, could not, in regard to the consistency of things, be denied, yet in her dustiness, grassiness, and worminess she was so little dusty, grassy, and wormy, that it was hardly fair, even in herself, to mention the fact at all.

"I know the deceit of my own heart," Mrs. Stumfold would say.

"Of course you do, Mrs. Stumfold," the coachmaker's wife replied. "It is dreadful deceitful, no doubt. Where's the heart that ain't? But there's a difference in hearts. Your deceit isn't hard like most of 'em. You know it, Mrs. Stumfold, and wrestle with it, and get your foot on the neck of it, so that, as one may say, it's always being killed and got the better of."

During these months Miss Mackenzie learned to value at a very low rate the rank of the Stumfoldian circle into which she had been admitted. She argued the matter with herself, saying that the coachbuilder's wife and others were not ladies. In a general way she was, no doubt, bound to assume them to be ladies; but she taught herself to think that such ladyhood was not of itself worth a great deal. It would not be worth the while of any woman to abstain from having some Mr. Rubb or the like, and from being the lawful mother of children in the Rubb and Mackenzie line of life, for the sake of such exceptional rank as was to be maintained by associating with the Stumfoldians. And, as she became used to the things and persons around her, she indulged herself in a considerable amount of social philosophy, turning over ideas in her mind for which they, who saw merely the lines of her outer life, would hardly have given her credit. After all, what was the good of being a lady? Or was there any good in it at all? Could there possibly be any good in making a struggle to be a lady? Was it not rather one of those things which are settled for one externally, as are the colour of one's hair and the size of one's bones, and which should be taken or left alone, as Providence may have directed? "One cannot add a cubit to one's height, nor yet make oneself a lady;" that was the nature of Miss Mackenzie's argument with herself.

And, indeed, she carried the argument further than that. It was well to be a lady. She recognised perfectly the delicacy and worth of the article. Miss Baker was a lady; as to that there was no doubt. But, then, might it not also be very well not to be a lady; and might not the advantages of the one position be compensated with equal advantages in the other? It is a grand thing to be a queen; but a queen has no friends. It is fine to be a princess; but a princess has a very limited choice of husbands. There was something about Miss Baker that was very nice; but even Miss Baker was very melancholy, and Miss Mackenzie could see that that melancholy had come from wasted niceness. Had she not been so much the lady, she might have been more the woman. And there could be no disgrace in not being a lady, if such ladyhood depended on external circumstances arranged for one by Providence. No one blames one's washerwoman for not being a lady. No one wishes one's housekeeper to be a lady; and people are dismayed, rather than pleased, when they find that their tailors' wives want to be ladies. What does a woman get by being a lady? If fortune have made her so, fortune has done much for her. But the good things come as the natural concomitants of her fortunate position. It is not because she is a lady that she is liked by her peers and peeresses. But those choice gifts which have made her a lady have made her also to be liked. It comes from the outside, and for it no struggle can usefully be made. Such was the result of Miss Mackenzie's philosophy.

One may see that all these self-inquiries tended Rubb-wards. I do not mean that they were made with any direct intention on her part to reconcile herself to a marriage with Mr. Samuel Rubb, or that she even thought of such an event as probable. He had said nothing to her to justify such thought, and as yet she knew but very little of him. But they all went to reconcile her to that sphere of life which her brother Tom had chosen, and which her brother Walter had despised. They taught her to believe that a firm footing below was better than what might, after a life's struggle, be found to be but a false footing above. And they were brightened undoubtedly by an idea that some marriage in which she could love and be loved was possible to her below, though it would hardly be possible to her above.

Her only disputant on the subject was Miss Baker, and she startled that lady much by the things which she said. Now, with Miss Baker, not to be a lady was to be nothing. It was her weakness, and I may also say her strength. Her ladyhood was of that nature that it took no soil from outer contact. It depended, even within her own bosom, on her own conduct solely, and in no degree on the conduct of those among whom she might chance to find herself. She thought it well to pass her evenings with Mr. Stumfold's people, and he at any rate had the manners of a gentleman. So thinking, she felt in no wise disgraced because the coachbuilder's wife was a vulgar, illiterate woman. But there were things, not bad in themselves, which she herself would never have done, because she was a lady. She would have broken her heart rather than marry a man who was not a gentleman. It was not unlady-like to eat cold mutton, and she ate it. But she would have shuddered had she been called on to eat any mutton with a steel fork. She had little generous ways with her, because they were the ways of ladies, and she paid for them from off her own back and out of her own dish. She would not go out to tea in a street cab, because she was a lady and alone; but she had no objection to walk, with her servant with her if it was dark. No wonder that such a woman was dismayed by the philosophy of Miss Mackenzie.

And yet they had been brought together by much that was alike in their dispositions. Miss Mackenzie had now been more than six months an inhabitant of Littlebath, and six months at such places is enough for close intimacies. They were both quiet, conscientious, kindly women, each not without some ambition of activity, but each a little astray as to the way in which that activity should be shown. They were both alone in the world, and Miss Baker during the last year or two had become painfully so from the fact of her estrangement from her old friend Miss Todd. They both wished to be religious, having strong faith in the need of the comfort of religion; but neither of them were quite satisfied with the Stumfoldian creed. They had both, from conscience, eschewed the vanities of the world; but with neither was her conscience quite satisfied that such eschewal was necessary, and each regretted to be losing pleasures which might after all be innocent.

"If I'm to go to the bad place," Miss Todd had said to Miss Baker, "because I like to do something that won't hurt my old eyes of an evening, I don't see the justice of it. As for calling it gambling, it's a falsehood, and your Mr. Stumfold knows that as well as I do. I haven't won or lost ten pounds in ten years, and I've no more idea of making money by cards than I have by sweeping the chimney. Tell me why are cards wicked? Drinking, and stealing, and lying, and backbiting, and naughty love-making,—but especially backbiting—backbiting—backbiting,—those are the things that the Bible says are wicked. I shall go on playing cards, my dear, till Mr. Stumfold can send me chapter and verse forbidding it."

Then Miss Baker, who was no doubt weak, had been unable to answer her, and had herself hankered after the flesh-pots of Egypt and the delights of the unregenerated.

All these things Miss Baker and Miss Mackenzie discussed, and Miss Baker learned to love her younger friend in spite of her heterodox philosophy. Miss Mackenzie was going to give a tea-party,—nothing as yet having been quite settled, as there were difficulties in the way; but she propounded to Miss Baker the possibility of asking Miss Todd and some few of the less conspicuous Toddites. She had her ambition, and she wished to see whether even she might not do something to lessen the gulf which separated those who loved the pleasures of the world in Littlebath from the bosom of Mr. Stumfold.

"You don't know what you are going to do," Miss Baker said.

"I'm not going to do any harm."

"That's more than you can say, my dear." Miss Baker had learnt from Miss Todd to call her friends "my dear."

"You are always so afraid of everything," said Miss Mackenzie.

"Of course I am;—one has to be afraid. A single lady can't go about and do just as she likes, as a man can do, or a married woman."

"I don't know about a man; but I think a single woman ought to be able to do more what she likes than a married woman. Suppose Mrs. Stumfold found that I had got old Lady Ruff to meet her, what could she do to me?"

Old Lady Ruff was supposed to be the wickedest old card-player in all Littlebath, and there were strange stories afloat of the things she had done. There were Stumfoldians who declared that she had been seen through the blinds teaching her own maid piquet on a Sunday afternoon; but any horror will get itself believed nowadays. How could they have known that it was not beggar-my-neighbour? But piquet was named because it is supposed in the Stumfoldian world to be the wickedest of all games.

"I don't suppose she'd do much," said Miss Baker; "no doubt she would be very much offended."

"Why shouldn't I try to convert Lady Ruff?"

"She's over eighty, my dear."

"But I suppose she's not past all hope. The older one is the more one ought to try. But, of course, I'm only joking about her. Would Miss Todd come if you were to ask her?"

"Perhaps she would, but I don't think she'd be comfortable; or if she were, she'd make the others uncomfortable. She always does exactly what she pleases."

"That's just why I think I should like her. I wish I dared to do what I pleased! We all of us are such cowards. Only that I don't dare, I'd go off to Australia and marry a sheep farmer."

"You would not like him when you'd got him;—you'd find him very rough."

"I shouldn't mind a bit about his being rough. I'd marry a shoe-black to-morrow if I thought I could make him happy, and he could make me happy."

"But it wouldn't make you happy."

"Ah! that's just what we don't know. I shan't marry a shoe-black, because I don't dare. So you think I'd better not ask Miss Todd. Perhaps she wouldn't get on well with Mr. Maguire."

"I had them both together once, my dear, and she made herself quite unbearable. You've no idea what kind of things she can say."

"I should have thought Mr. Maguire would have given her as good as she brought," said Miss Mackenzie.

"So he did; and then Miss Todd got up and left him, saying out loud, before all the company, that it was not fair for him to come and preach sermons in such a place as that. I don't think they have ever met since."

All this made Miss Mackenzie very thoughtful. She had thrown herself into the society of the saints, and now there seemed to be no escape for her; she could not be wicked even if she wished it. Having got into her convent, and, as it were, taken the vows of her order, she could not escape from it.

"That Mr. Rubb that I told you of is coming down here," she said, still speaking to Miss Baker of her party.

"Oh, dear! will he be here when you have your friends here?"

"That's what I intended; but I don't think I shall ask anybody at all. It is so stupid always seeing the same people."

"Mr. Rubb is—is—is—?"

"Yes; Mr. Rubb is a partner in my brother's house, and sells oilcloth, and things of that sort, and is not by any means aristocratic. I know what you mean."

"Don't be angry with me, my dear."

"Angry! I am not a bit angry. Why should I be angry? A man who keeps a shop is not, I suppose, a gentleman. But then, you know, I don't care about gentlemen,—about any gentleman, or any gentlemen."

Miss Baker sighed, and then the conversation dropped. She had always cared about gentlemen,—and once in her life, or perhaps twice, had cared about a gentleman.

Yes; Mr. Rubb was coming down again. He had written to say that it was necessary that he should again see Miss Mackenzie about the money. The next morning after the conversation which has just been recorded, Miss Mackenzie got another letter about the same money, of which it will be necessary to say more in the next chapter.

Chapter X

Plenary Absolutions

The letter which Miss Mackenzie received was from old Mr. Slow, her lawyer; and it was a very unpleasant letter. It was so unpleasant that it made her ears tingle when she read it and remembered that the person to whom special allusion was made was one whom she had taught herself to regard as her friend. Mr. Slow's letter was as follows:

7 Little St Dunstan Court, April, 186—.

DEAR MADAM,

I think it proper to write to you specially, about the loan made by you to Messrs Rubb and Mackenzie, as the sum lent is serious, and as there has been conduct on the part of some one which I regard as dishonest. I find that what we have done in the matter has been regulated rather by the fact that you and Mr. Mackenzie are brother and sister, than by the ordinary course of such business; and I perceive that we had special warrant given to us for this by you in your letter of the 23rd November last; but, nevertheless, it is my duty to explain to you that Messrs Rubb and Mackenzie, or,—as I believe to be the case, Mr. Samuel Rubb, junior, of that firm,—have not dealt with you fairly. The money was borrowed for the purpose of buying certain premises, and, I believe, was laid out in that way.

But it was borrowed on the special understanding that you, as the lender, were to have the title-deeds of that property, and the first mortgage upon them. It was alleged, when the purchase was being made, that the money was wanted before the mortgage could be effected, and you desired us to advance it. This we did, aware of the close family connection between yourself and one of the firm. Of course, on your instruction, we should have done this had there been no such relationship, but in that case we should have made further inquiry, and, probably, have ventured to advise you. But though the money was so advanced without the completion of the mortgage, it was advanced on the distinct understanding that the security proffered in the first instance was to be forthcoming without delay. We now learn that the property is mortgaged to other parties to its full value, and that no security for your money is to be had.

I have seen both Mr. Mackenzie and Mr. Rubb, junior. As regards your brother, I believe him to have been innocent of any intention of the deceit, for deceit there certainly has been. Indeed, he does not deny it. He offers to give you any security on the business, such as the stock-in-trade or the like, which I may advise you to take. But such would in truth be of no avail to you as security. He, your brother, seemed to be much distressed by what has been done, and I was grieved on his behalf. Mr. Rubb,—the younger Mr. Rubb,—expressed himself in a very different way. He at first declined to discuss the matter with me; and when I told him that if that was his way I would certainly expose him, he altered his tone a little, expressing regret that there should be delay as to the security, and wishing me to understand that you were yourself aware of all the facts.

There can be no doubt that deceit has been used towards you in getting your money, and that Mr. Rubb has laid himself open to proceedings which, if taken against him, would be absolutely ruinous to him. But I fear they would be also ruinous to your brother. It is my painful duty to tell you that your money so advanced is on a most precarious footing. The firm, in addition to their present liabilities, are not worth half the money; or, I fear I may say, any part of it. I presume there is a working profit, as two families live upon the business. Whether, if you were to come upon them as a creditor, you could get your money out of their assets, I cannot say; but you, perhaps, will not feel yourself disposed to resort to such a measure. I have considered it my duty to tell you all the facts, and though your distinct authority to us to advance the money absolves us from responsibility, I must regret that we did not make further inquiries before we allowed so large a sum of money to pass out of our hands.

I am, dear Madam,

Your faithful servant,

JONATHAN SLOW.

Mr. Rubb's promised visit was to take place in eight or ten days from the date on which this letter was received. Miss Mackenzie's ears, as I have said, tingled as she read it. In the first place, it gave her a terrible picture of the precarious state of her brother's business. What would he do,—he with his wife, and all his children, if things were in such a state as Mr. Slow described them? And yet a month or two ago he was giving champagne and iced puddings for dinner! And then what words that discreet old gentleman, Mr. Slow, had spoken about Mr. Rubb, and what things he had hinted over and above what he had spoken! Was it not manifest that he conceived Mr. Rubb to have been guilty of direct fraud?

Miss Mackenzie at once made up her mind that her money was gone! But, in truth, this did not much annoy her. She had declared to herself once before that if anything was wrong about the money she would regard it as a present made to her brother; and when so thinking of it, she had, undoubtedly, felt that it was, not improbably, lost to her. It was something over a hundred a year to be deducted from her computed income, but she would still be able to live at the Paragon quite as well as she had intended, and be able also to educate Susanna. Indeed, she could do this easily and still save money, and, therefore, as regarded the probable loss, why need she be unhappy?

Before the morning was over she had succeeded in white-washing Mr. Rubb in her own mind. It is, I think, certainly the fact that women are less pervious to ideas of honesty than men are. They are less shocked by dishonesty when they find it, and are less clear in their intellect as to that which constitutes honesty. Where is the woman who thinks it wrong to smuggle? What lady's conscience ever pricked her in that she omitted the armorial bearings on her silver forks from her tax papers? What wife ever ceased to respect her husband because he dealt dishonestly in business? Whereas, let him not go to church, let him drink too much wine, let him go astray in his conversation, and her wrath arises against these faults. But this lack of feminine accuracy in the matter of honesty tends rather to charity in their judgment of others, than to deeds of fraud on the part of women themselves.

Miss Mackenzie, who desired nothing that was not her own, who scrupulously kept her own hands from all picking and stealing, gave herself no peace, after reading the lawyer's letter, till she was able to tell herself that Mr. Rubb was to be forgiven for what he had done. After all, he had, no doubt, intended that she should have the promised security. And had not he himself come to her in London and told her the whole truth,—or, if not the whole truth, as much of it as was reasonable to expect that he should be able to tell her at an evening party after dinner? Of course Mr. Slow was hard upon him. Lawyers always were hard. If she chose to give Messrs Rubb and Mackenzie two thousand five hundred pounds out of her pocket, what was that to him? So she went on, till at last she was angry with Mr. Slow for the language he had used.

It was, however, before all things necessary that she should put Mr. Slow right as to the facts of the case. She had, no doubt, condoned whatever Mr. Rubb had done. Mr. Rubb undoubtedly had her sanction for keeping her money without security. Therefore, by return of post, she wrote the following short letter, which rather astonished Mr. Slow when he received it—

Littlebath, April, 186—.

DEAR SIR,

I am much obliged by your letter about the money; but the truth is that I have known for some time that there was to be no mortgage. When I was in town I saw Mr. Rubb at my brother's house, and it was understood between us then that the matter was to remain as it is. My brother and his partner are very welcome to the money.

Believe me to be,

Yours sincerely,

MARGARET MACKENZIE.

The letter was a false letter; but I suppose Miss Mackenzie did not know that she was writing falsely. The letter was certainly false, because when she spoke of the understanding "between us," having just mentioned her brother and Mr. Rubb, she intended the lawyer to believe that the understanding was between them three; whereas, not a word had been said about the money in her brother's hearing, nor was he aware that his partner had spoken of the money.

Mr. Slow was surprised and annoyed. As regarded his comfort as a lawyer, his client's letter was of course satisfactory. It absolved him not only from all absolute responsibility, but also from the feeling which no doubt had existed within his own breast, that he had in some sort neglected the lady's interest. But, nevertheless, he was annoyed. He did not believe the statement that Rubb and Mackenzie had had permission to hold the money without mortgage, and thought that neither of the partners had themselves so conceived when he had seen them. They had, however, been too many for him—and too many also for the poor female who had allowed herself to be duped out of her money. Such were Mr. Slow's feelings on the matter, and then he dismissed the subject from his mind.

The next day, about noon, Miss Mackenzie was startled almost out of her propriety by the sudden announcement at the drawing-room door of Mr. Rubb. Before she could bethink herself how she would behave herself, or whether it would become her to say anything of Mr. Slow's letter to her, he was in the room.

"Miss Mackenzie," he said, hurriedly—and yet he had paused for a moment in his hurry till the servant had shut the door—"may I shake hands with you?"

There could, Miss Mackenzie thought, be no objection to so ordinary a ceremony; and, therefore, she said, "Certainly," and gave him her hand.

"Then I am myself again," said Mr. Rubb; and having so said, he sat down.

Miss Mackenzie hoped that there was nothing the matter with him, and then she also sat down at a considerable distance.

"There is nothing the matter with me," said he, "as you are still so kind to me. But tell me, have you not received a letter from your lawyer?"

"Yes, I have."

"And he has done all in his power to blacken me? I know it. Tell me, Miss Mackenzie, has he not blackened me? Has he not laid things to my charge of which I am incapable? Has he not accused me of getting money from you under false pretences,—than do which, I'd sooner have seen my own brains blown out? I would, indeed."

"He has written to me about the money, Mr. Rubb."

"Yes; he came to me, and behaved shamefully to me; and he saw your brother, too, and has been making all manner of ignominious inquiries. Those lawyers can never understand that there can be anything of friendly feeling about money. They can't put friendly feelings into their unconscionable bills. I believe the world would go on better if there was no such thing as an attorney in it. I wonder who invented them, and why?"

Miss Mackenzie could give him no information on this point, and therefore he went on:

"But you must tell me what he has said, and what it is he wants us to do. For your sake, if you ask us, Miss Mackenzie, we'll do anything. We'll sell the coats off our backs, if you wish it. You shall never lose one shilling by Rubb and Mackenzie as long as I have anything to do with the firm. But I'm sure you will excuse me if I say that we can do nothing at the bidding of that old cormorant."

"I don't know that there's anything to be done, Mr. Rubb."

"Is not there? Well, it's very generous in you to say so; and you always are generous. I've always told your brother, since I had the honour of knowing you, that he had a sister to be proud of. And, Miss Mackenzie, I'll say more than that; I've flattered myself that I've had a friend to be proud of. But now I must tell you why I've come down to-day; you know I was to have been here next week. Well, when Mr. Slow came to me and I found what was up, I said to myself at once that it was right you should know exactly—exactly—how the matter stands. I was going to explain it next week, but I wouldn't leave you in suspense when I knew that that lawyer was going to trouble you."

"It hasn't troubled me, Mr. Rubb."

"Hasn't it though, really? That's so good of you again! Now the truth is—but it's pretty nearly just what I told you that day after dinner, when you agreed, you know, to what we had done."

Here he paused, as though expecting an answer.

"Yes, I did agree."

"Just at present, while certain other parties have a right to hold the title-deeds, and I can't quite say how long that may be, we cannot execute a mortgage in your favour. The title-deeds represent the property. Perhaps you don't know that."

"Oh yes, I know as much as that."

"Well then, as we haven't the title-deeds, we can't execute the mortgage. Perhaps you'll say you ought to have the title-deeds."

"No, Mr. Rubb, I don't want to say anything of the kind. If my money can be of any assistance to my brother—to my brother and you—you are welcome to the use of it, without any mortgage. I will show you a copy of the letter I sent to Mr. Slow."

"Thanks; a thousand thanks! and may I see the letter which Mr. Slow wrote?"

"No, I think not. I don't know whether it would be right to show it to you."

"I shouldn't think of doing anything about it; that is, resenting it, you know. Only then we should all be on the square together."

"I think I'd better not. Mr. Slow, when he wrote it, probably did not mean that I should show it to you."

"You're right; you're always right. But you'll let me see your answer."

Then Miss Mackenzie went to her desk, and brought him a copy of the note she had written to the lawyer. He read it very carefully, twice over; and then she could see, when he refolded the paper, that his eyes were glittering with satisfaction.

"Miss Mackenzie, Miss Mackenzie," he said, "I think that you are an angel!"

And he did think so. In so much at that moment he was at any rate sincere. She saw that he was pleased, and she was pleased herself.

"There need be no further trouble about it," she said; and as she spoke she rose from her seat.

And he rose, too, and came close to her. He came close to her, hesitated for a moment, and then, putting one hand behind her waist, though barely touching her, he took her hand with his other hand. She thought that he was going to kiss her lips, and for a moment or two he thought so too; but either his courage failed him or else his discretion prevailed. Whether it was the one or the other, must depend on the way in which she would have taken it. As it was, he merely raised her hand and kissed that. When she could look into his face his eyes were full of tears.

"The truth is," said he, "that you have saved us from ruin;—that's the real truth. Damn all lying!"

She started at the oath, but in an instant she had forgiven him that too. There was a sound of reality about it, which reconciled her to the indignity; though, had she been true to her faith as a Stumfoldian, she ought at least to have fainted at the sound.

"I hardly know what I am saying, Miss Mackenzie, and I beg your pardon; but the fact is you could sell us up if you pleased. I didn't mean it when I first got your brother to agree as to asking you for the loan; I didn't indeed; but things were going wrong with us, and just at that moment they went more wrong than ever; and then came the temptation, and we were able to make everything right by giving up the title-deeds of the premises. That's how it was, and it was I that did it. It wasn't your brother; and though you may forgive me, he won't."

This was all true, but how far the truth should be taken towards palliating the deed done, I must leave the reader to decide; and the reader will doubtless perceive that the truth did not appear until Mr. Rubb had ascertained that its appearance would not injure him. I think, however, that it came from his heart, and that it should count for something in his favour. The tear which he rubbed from his eye with his hand counted very much in his favour with Miss Mackenzie; she had not only forgiven him now, but she almost loved him for having given her something to forgive. With many women I doubt whether there be any more effectual way of touching their hearts than ill-using them and then confessing it. If you wish to get the sweetest fragrance from the herb at your feet, tread on it and bruise it.

She had forgiven him, and taken him absolutely into favour, and he had kissed her hand, having all but embraced her as he did so; but on the present occasion he did not get beyond that. He lacked the audacity to proceed at once from the acknowledgment of his fault to a declaration of his love; but I hardly think that he would have injured himself had he done so.

He should have struck while the iron was hot, and it was heated now nearly to melting; but he was abashed by his own position, and having something real in his heart, having some remnant of generous feeling left about him, he could not make such progress as he might have done had he been cool enough to calculate all his advantages.

"Don't let it trouble you any more," Miss Mackenzie said, when he had dropped her hand.

"But it does trouble me, and it will trouble me."

"No," she said, with energy, "it shall not; let there be an end of it. I will write to Tom, and tell him that he is welcome to the money. Isn't he my brother? You are both welcome to it. If it has been of service to you, I am very happy that it should be so. And now, Mr. Rubb, if you please, we won't have another word about it."

"What am I to say?"

"Not another word."

It seemed as though he couldn't speak another word, for he went to the window and stood there silently, looking into the street. As he did so, there came another visitor to Miss Mackenzie, whose ringing at the doorbell had not been noticed by them, and Miss Baker was announced while Mr. Rubb was still getting the better of his feelings. Of course he turned round when he heard the lady's name, and of course he was introduced by his hostess. Miss Mackenzie was obliged to make some apology for the gentleman's presence.

"Mr. Rubb was expected next week, but business brought him down to-day unexpectedly."

"Quite unexpectedly," said Mr. Rubb, making a violent endeavour to recover his equanimity.

Miss Baker looked at Mr. Rubb, and disliked him at once. It should be remembered that she was twenty years older than Miss Mackenzie, and that she regarded the stranger, therefore, with a saner and more philosophical judgment than her friend could use,—with a judgment on which the outward comeliness of the man had no undue influence; and it should be remembered also that Miss Baker, from early age, and by all the association of her youth, had been taught to know a gentleman when she saw him. Miss Mackenzie, who was by nature the cleverer woman of the two, watched her friend's face, and saw by a glance that she did not like Mr. Rubb, and then, within her own bosom, she called her friend an old maid.

"We're having uncommonly fine weather for the time of year," said Mr. Rubb.

"Very fine weather," said Miss Baker. "I've called, my dear, to know whether you'll go in with me next door and drink tea this evening?"

"What, with Miss Todd?" asked Miss Mackenzie, who was surprised at the invitation.

"Yes, with Miss Todd. It is not one of her regular nights, you know, and her set won't be there. She has some old friends with her,—a Mr. Wilkinson, a clergyman, and his wife. It seems that her old enemy and your devoted slave, Mr. Maguire, knows Mr. Wilkinson, and he's going to be there."

"Mr. Maguire is no slave of mine, Miss Baker."

"I thought he was; at any rate his presence will be a guarantee that Miss Todd will be on her best behaviour, and that you needn't be afraid."

"I'm not afraid of anything of that sort."

"But will you go?"

"Oh, yes, if you are going."

"That's right; and I'll call for you as I pass by. I must see her now, and tell her. Good-morning, Sir;" whereupon Miss Baker bowed very stiffly to Mr. Rubb.

"Good-morning, Ma'am," said Mr. Rubb, bowing very stiffly to Miss Baker.

When the lady was gone, Mr. Rubb sat himself again down on the sofa, and there he remained for the next half-hour. He talked about the business of the firm, saying how it would now certainly be improved; and he talked about Tom

Mackenzie's family, saying what a grand thing it was for Susanna to be thus taken in hand by her aunt; and he asked a question or two about Miss Baker, and then a question or two about Mr. Maguire, during which questions he learned that Mr. Maguire was not as yet a married man; and from Mr. Maguire he got on to the Stumfolds, and learned somewhat of the rites and ceremonies of the Stumfoldian faith. In this way he prolonged his visit till Miss Mackenzie began to feel that he ought to take his leave.

Miss Baker had gone at once to Miss Todd, and had told that lady that Miss Mackenzie would join her tea-party. She had also told how Mr. Rubb, of the firm of Rubb and Mackenzie, was at this moment in Miss Mackenzie's drawing-room.

"I'll ask him to come, too," said Miss Todd. Then Miss Baker had hesitated, and had looked grave.

"What's the matter?" said Miss Todd.

"I'm not quite sure you'll like him," said Miss Baker.

"Probably not," said Miss Todd; "I don't like half the people I meet, but that's no reason I shouldn't ask him."

"But he is—that is, he is not exactly—"

"What is he, and what is he not, exactly?" asked Miss Todd.

"Why, he is a tradesman, you know," said Miss Baker.

"There's no harm that I know of in that," said Miss Todd. "My uncle that left me my money was a tradesman."

"No," said Miss Baker, energetically; "he was a merchant in Liverpool."

"You'll find it very hard to define the difference, my dear," said Miss Todd. "At any rate I'll ask the man to come;— that is, if it won't offend you."

"It won't in the least offend me," said Miss Baker.

So a note was at once written and sent in to Miss Mackenzie, in which she was asked to bring Mr. Rubb with her on that evening. When the note reached Miss Mackenzie, Mr. Rubb was still with her.

Of course she communicated to him the invitation. She wished that it had not been sent; she wished that he would not accept it,—though on that head she had no doubt; but she had not sufficient presence of mind to keep the matter to herself and say nothing about it. Of course he was only too glad to drink tea with Miss Todd. Miss Mackenzie attempted some slight manoeuvre to induce Mr. Rubb to go direct to Miss Todd's house; but he was not such an ass as that; he knew his advantage, and kept it, insisting on his privilege of coming there, to Miss Mackenzie's room, and escorting her. He would have to escort Miss Baker also; and things, as he thought, were looking well with him. At last he rose to go, but he made good use of the privilege of parting. He held Miss Mackenzie's hand, and pressed it.

"You mustn't be angry," he said, "if I tell you that you are the best friend I have in the world."

"You have better friends than me," she said, "and older friends."

"Yes; older friends; but none,—not one, who has done for me so much as you have; and certainly none for whom I have so great a regard. May God bless you, Miss Mackenzie!"

"May God bless you, too, Mr. Rubb!"

What else could she say? When his civility took so decorous a shape, she could not bear to be less civil than he had been, or less decorous. And yet it seemed to her that in bidding God bless him with that warm pressure of the hand, she had allowed to escape from her an appearance of affection which she had not intended to exhibit.

"Thank you; thank you," said he; and then at last he went.

She seated herself slowly in her own chair near the window,—the chair in which she was accustomed to sit for many solitary hours, and asked herself what it all meant. Was she allowing herself to fall in love with Mr. Rubb, and if so, was it well that it should be so? This would be bringing to the sternest proof of reality her philosophical theory on social life. It was all very well for her to hold a bold opinion in discussions with Miss Baker as to a "man being a man for a' that," even though he might not be a gentleman; but was she prepared to go the length of preferring such a man to all the world? Was she ready to go down among the Rubbs, for now and ever, and give up the society of such women as Miss Baker? She knew that it was necessary that she should come to some resolve on the matter, as Mr. Rubb's purpose was becoming too clear to her. When an unmarried gentleman of forty tells an unmarried lady of thirty-six that she is the dearest friend he has in the world, he must surely intend that they shall, neither of them, remain unmarried any longer. Then she thought also of her cousin, John Ball; and some vague shadow of thought passed across her mind also in respect of the Rev. Mr. Maguire.

Chapter XI

Miss Todd Entertains Some Friends at Tea

I believe that a desire to get married is the natural state of a woman at the age of—say from twenty-five to thirty-five, and I think also that it is good for the world in general that it should be so. I am now speaking, not of the female population at large, but of women whose position in the world does not subject them to the necessity of earning their bread by the labour of their hands. There is, I know, a feeling abroad among women that this desire is one of which it is expedient that they should become ashamed; that it will be well for them to alter their natures in this respect, and learn to take delight in the single state. Many of the most worthy women of the day are now teaching this doctrine, and are intent on showing by precept and practice that an unmarried woman may have as sure a hold on the world, and a position within it as ascertained, as may an unmarried man. But I confess to an opinion that human nature will be found to be too strong for them. Their school of philosophy may be graced by a few zealous students,—by students who will be subject to the personal influence of their great masters,—but it will not be successful in the outer world. The truth in the matter is too clear. A woman's life is not perfect or whole till she has added herself to a husband.

Nor is a man's life perfect or whole till he has added to himself a wife; but the deficiency with the man, though perhaps more injurious to him than its counterpart is to the woman, does not, to the outer eye, so manifestly unfit him for his business in the world. Nor does the deficiency make itself known to him so early in life, and therefore it occasions less of regret,—less of regret, though probably more of misery. It is infinitely for his advantage that he should be tempted to take to himself a wife; and, therefore, for his sake if not for her own, the philosophic preacher of single blessedness should break up her class-rooms, and bid her pupils go and do as their mothers did before them.

They may as well give up their ineffectual efforts, and know that nature is too strong for them. The desire is there; and any desire which has to be repressed with an effort, will not have itself repressed unless it be in itself wrong. But this desire, though by no means wrong, is generally accompanied by something of a feeling of shame. It is not often acknowledged by the woman to herself, and very rarely acknowledged in simple plainness to another. Miss Mackenzie could not by any means bring herself to own it, and yet it was there strong within her bosom. A man situated in outer matters as she was situated, possessed of good means, hampered by no outer demands, would have declared to himself clearly that it would be well for him to marry. But he would probably be content to wait a while and would, unless in love, feel the delay to be a luxury. But Miss Mackenzie could not confess as much, even to herself,—could not let herself know that she thought as much; but yet she desired to be married, and dreaded delay. She desired to be married, although she was troubled by some half-formed idea that it would be wicked. Who was she, that she should be allowed to be in love? Was she not an old maid by prescription, and, as it were, by the force of ordained circumstances? Had it not been made very clear to her when she was young that she had no right to fall in love, even with Harry Handcock? And although in certain moments of ecstasy, as when she kissed herself in the glass, she almost taught herself to think that feminine charms and feminine privileges had not been all denied to her, such was not her permanent opinion of herself. She despised herself. Why, she knew not; and probably did not know that she did so. But, in truth, she despised herself, thinking herself to be too mean for a man's love.

She had been asked to marry him by her cousin Mr. Ball, and she had almost yielded. But had she married him it would not have been because she thought herself good enough to be loved by him, but because she held herself to be so insignificant that she had no right to ask for love. She would have taken him because she could have been of use, and because she would have felt that she had no right to demand any other purpose in the world. She would have done this, had she not been deterred by the rude offer of other advantages which had with so much ill judgment been made to her by her aunt.

Now, here was a lover who was not old and careworn, who was personally agreeable to her, with whom something of the customary romance of the world might be possible. Should she take him? She knew well that there were drawbacks. Her perceptions had not missed to notice the man's imperfections, his vulgarities, his false promises, his little pushing ways. But why was she to expect him to be perfect, seeing, as she so plainly did, her own imperfections? As for her money, of course he wanted her money. So had Mr. Ball wanted her money. What man on earth could have wished to marry her unless she had had money? It was thus that she thought of herself. And he had robbed her! But that she had forgiven; and, having forgiven it, was too generous to count it for anything. But, nevertheless, she was ambitious. Might there not be a better, even than Mr. Rubb?

Mr. Maguire squinted horribly; so horribly that the form and face of the man hardly left any memory of themselves except the memory of the squint. His dark hair, his one perfect eye, his good figure, his expressive mouth, were all lost in that dreadful perversion of vision. It was a misfortune so great as to justify him in demanding that he should be judged by different laws than those which are used as to the conduct of the world at large. In getting a wife he might surely use his tongue with more freedom than another man, seeing that his eye was so much against him. If he were somewhat romantic in his talk, or even more than romantic, who could find fault with him? And if he used his clerical vocation to cover the terrors of that distorted pupil, can any woman say that he should be therefore condemned? Miss Mackenzie could not forget his eye, but she thought that she had almost brought herself to forgive it. And, moreover, he was a gentleman, not only by Act of Parliament, but in outward manners. Were she to become Mrs. Maguire, Miss Baker would certainly come to her house, and it might be given to her to rival Mrs. Stumfold—in running which race she would be weighted by no Mr. Peters.

It is true that Mr. Maguire had never asked her to marry him, but she believed that he would ask her if she gave him any encouragement. Now it was to come to pass, by a wonderful arrangement of circumstances, that she was to meet these two gentlemen together. It might well be, that on this very occasion, she must choose whether it should be either or neither.

Mr. Rubb came, and she looked anxiously at his dress. He had on bright yellow kid gloves, primrose he would have called them, but, if there be such things as yellow gloves, they were yellow; and she wished that she had the courage to ask him to take them off. This was beyond her, and there he sat, with his gloves almost as conspicuous as Mr. Maguire's eye. Should she, however, ever become Mrs. Rubb, she would not find the gloves to be there permanently; whereas the eye would remain. But then the gloves were the fault of the one man, whereas the eye was simply the misfortune of the other. And Mr. Rubb's hair was very full of perfumed grease, and sat on each side of his head in a conscious arrangement of waviness that was detestable. As she looked at Mr. Rubb in all the brightness of his evening costume, she began to think that she had better not. At last Miss Baker came, and they started off together. Miss Mackenzie saw that Miss Baker eyed the man, and she blushed. When they got down upon the doorstep, Samuel Rubb, junior, absolutely offered an arm simultaneously to each lady! At that moment Miss Mackenzie hated him in spite of her special theory.

"Thank you," said Miss Baker, declining the arm; "it is only a step."

Miss Mackenzie declined it also.

"Oh, of course," said Mr. Rubb. "If it's only next door it does not signify."

Miss Todd welcomed them cordially, gloves and all. "My dear," she said to Miss Baker, "I haven't seen you for twenty years. Miss Mackenzie, this is very kind of you. I hope we sha'n't do you any harm, as we are not going to be wicked to-night."

Miss Mackenzie did not dare to say that she would have preferred to be wicked, but that is what she would have said if she had dared.

"Mr. Rubb, I'm very happy to see you," continued Miss Todd, accepting her guest's hand, glove and all. "I hope they haven't made you believe that you are going to have any dancing, for, if so, they have hoaxed you shamefully." Then she introduced them to Mr. and Mrs. Wilkinson.

Mr. Wilkinson was a plain-looking clergyman, with a very pretty wife. "Adela," Miss Todd said to Mrs. Wilkinson, "you used to dance, but that's all done with now, I suppose."

"I never danced much," said the clergyman's wife, "but have certainly given it up now, partly because I have no one to dance with."

"Here's Mr. Rubb quite ready. He'll dance with you, I'll be bound, if that's all."

Mr. Rubb became very red, and Miss Mackenzie, when she next took courage to look at him, saw that the gloves had disappeared.

There came also a Mr. and Mrs. Fuzzybell, and immediately afterwards Mr. Maguire, whereupon Miss Todd declared her party to be complete.

"Mrs. Fuzzybell, my dear, no cards!" said Miss Todd, quite out loud, with a tragic-comic expression in her face that was irresistible. "Mr. Fuzzybell, no cards!" Mrs. Fuzzybell said that she was delighted to hear it. Mr. Fuzzybell said that it did not signify. Miss Baker stole a glance at Mr. Maguire, and shook in her shoes. Mr. Maguire tried to look as though he had not heard it.

"Do you play cards much here?" asked Mr. Rubb.

"A great deal too much, Sir," said Miss Todd, shaking her head.

"Have you many Dissenters in your parish, Mr. Wilkinson?" asked Mr. Maguire.

"A good many," said Mr. Wilkinson.

"But no Papists?" suggested Mr. Maguire.

"No, we have no Roman Catholics."

"That is such a blessing!" said Mr. Maguire, turning his eyes up to Heaven in a very frightful manner. But he had succeeded for the present in putting down Miss Todd and her cards.

They were now summoned round the tea-table,—a genuine tea-table at which it was expected that they should eat and drink. Miss Mackenzie was seated next to Mr. Maguire on one side of the table, while Mr. Rubb sat on the other between Miss Todd and Miss Baker. While they were yet taking their seats, and before the operations of the banquet had commenced, Susanna entered the room. She also had been specially invited, but she had not returned from school in time to accompany her aunt. The young lady had to walk round the room to shake hands with everybody, and when she came to Mr. Rubb, was received with much affectionate urgency. He turned round in his chair and was loud in his praises. "Miss Mackenzie," said he, speaking across the table, "I shall have to report in Gower Street that Miss Susanna has become quite the lady." From that moment Mr. Rubb had an enemy close to the object of his affections, who was always fighting a battle against him.

Susanna had hardly gained her seat, before Mr. Maguire seized an opportunity which he saw might soon be gone, and sprang to his legs. "Miss Todd," said he, "may I be permitted to ask a blessing?"

"Oh, certainly," said Miss Todd; "but I thought one only did that at dinner."

Mr. Maguire, however, was not the man to sit down without improving the occasion.

"And why not for tea also?" said he. "Are they not gifts alike?"

"Very much alike," said Miss Todd, "and so is a cake at a pastry-cook's. But we don't say grace over our buns."

"We do, in silence," said Mr. Maguire, still standing; "and therefore we ought to have it out loud here."

"I don't see the argument; but you're very welcome."

"Thank you," said Mr. Maguire; and then he said his grace. He said it with much poetic emphasis, and Miss Mackenzie, who liked any little additional excitement, thought that Miss Todd had been wrong.

"You've a deal of society here, no doubt," said Mr. Rubb to Miss Baker, while Miss Todd was dispensing her tea.

"I suppose it's much the same as other places," said Miss Baker. "Those who know many people can go out constantly if they like it."

"And it's so easy to get to know people," said Mr. Rubb. "That's what makes me like these sort of places so much. There's no stiffness and formality, and all that kind of thing. Now in London, you don't know your next neighbour, though you and he have lived there for ten years."

"Nor here either, unless chance brings you together."

"Ah; but there is none of that horrid decorum here," said Mr. Rubb. "There's nothing I hate like decorum. It prevents people knowing each other, and being jolly and happy together. Now, the French know more about society than any people, and I'm told they have none of it."

"I'm sure I can't say," said Miss Baker.

"It's given up to them that they've got rid of it altogether," said Mr. Rubb.

"Who have got rid of what?" asked Miss Todd, who saw that her friend was rather dismayed by the tenor of Mr. Rubb's conversation.

"The French have got rid of decorum," said Mr. Rubb.

"Altogether, I believe," said Miss Todd.

"Of course they have. It's given up to them that they have. They're the people that know how to live!"

"You'd better go and live among them, if that's your way of thinking," said Miss Todd.

"I would at once, only for the business," said Mr. Rubb. "If there's anything I hate, it's decorum. How pleasant it was for me to be asked in to take tea here in this social way!"

"But I hope decorum would not have forbidden that," said Miss Todd.

"I rather think it would though, in London."

"Where you're known, you mean?" asked Miss Todd.

"I don't know that that makes any difference; but people don't do that sort of thing. Do they, Miss Mackenzie? You've lived in London most of your life, and you ought to know."

Miss Mackenzie did not answer the appeal that was made to her. She was watching Mr. Rubb narrowly, and knew that he was making a fool of himself. She could perceive also that Miss Todd would not spare him. She could forgive Mr. Rubb for being a fool. She could forgive him for not knowing the meaning of words, for being vulgar and assuming; but she could hardly bring herself to forgive him in that he did so as her friend, and as the guest whom she had brought thither. She did not declare to herself that she would have nothing more to do with him, because he was an ass; but she almost did come to this conclusion, lest he should make her appear to be an ass also.

"What is the gentleman's name?" asked Mr. Maguire, who, under the protection of the urn, was able to whisper into Miss Mackenzie's ear.

"Rubb," said she.

"Oh, Rubb; and he comes from London?"

"He is my brother's partner in business," said Miss Mackenzie.

"Oh, indeed. A very worthy man, no doubt. Is he staying with—with you, Miss Mackenzie?"

Then Miss Mackenzie had to explain that Mr. Rubb was not staying with her,—that he had come down about business, and that he was staying at some inn.

"An excellent man of business; I'm sure," said Mr. Maguire. "By-the-bye, Miss Mackenzie, if it be not improper to ask, have you any share in the business?"

Miss Mackenzie explained that she had no share in the business; and then blundered on, saying how Mr. Rubb had come down to Littlebath about money transactions between her and her brother.

"Oh, indeed," said Mr. Maguire; and before he had done, he knew very well that Mr. Rubb had borrowed money of Miss Mackenzie.

"Now, Mrs. Fuzzybell, what are we to do?" said Miss Todd, as soon as the tea-things were gone.

"We shall do very well," said Mrs. Fuzzybell; "we'll have a little conversation."

"If we could all banish decorum, like Mr. Rubb, and amuse ourselves, wouldn't it be nice? I quite agree with you, Mr. Rubb; decorum is a great bore; it prevents our playing cards to-night."

"As for cards, I never play cards myself," said Mr. Rubb.

"Then, when I throw decorum overboard, it sha'n't be in company with you, Mr. Rubb."

"We were always taught to think that cards were objectionable."

"You were told they were the devil's books, I suppose," said Miss Todd.

"Mother always objected to have them in the house," said Mr. Rubb.

"Your mother was quite right," said Mr. Maguire; "and I hope that you will never forget or neglect your parent's precepts. I'm not meaning to judge you, Miss Todd—"

"But that's just what you are meaning to do, Mr. Maguire."

"Not at all; very far from it. We've all got our wickednesses and imperfections."

"No, no, not you, Mr. Maguire. Mrs. Fuzzybell, you don't think that Mr. Maguire has any wickednesses and imperfections?"

"I'm sure I don't know," said Mrs. Fuzzybell, tossing her head.

"Miss Todd," said Mr. Maguire, "when I look into my own heart, I see well how black it is. It is full of iniquity; it is a grievous sore that is ever running, and will not be purified."

"Gracious me, how unpleasant!" said Miss Todd.

"I trust that there is no one here who has not a sense of her own wickedness."

"Or of his," said Miss Todd.

"Or of his," and Mr. Maguire looked very hard at Mr. Fuzzybell. Mr. Fuzzybell was a quiet, tame old gentleman, who followed his wife's heels about wherever she went; but even he, when attacked in this way, became very fierce, and looked back at Mr. Maguire quite as severely as Mr. Maguire looked at him.

"Or of his," continued Mr. Maguire; "and therefore far be it from me to think hardly of the amusements of other people. But when this gentleman tells me that his excellent parent warned him against the fascination of cards, I cannot but ask him to remember those precepts to his dying bed."

"I won't say what I may do later in life," said Mr. Rubb.

"When he becomes like you and me, Mrs. Fuzzybell," said Miss Todd.

"When one does get older," said Mr. Rubb.

"And has succeeded in throwing off all decorum," said Miss Todd.

"How can you say such things?" asked Miss Baker, who was shocked by the tenor of the conversation.

"It isn't I, my dear; it's Mr. Rubb and Mr. Maguire, between them. One says he has thrown off all decorum and the other declares himself to be a mass of iniquity. What are two poor old ladies like you and I to do in such company?"

Miss Mackenzie, when she heard Mr. Maguire declare himself to be a running sore, was even more angry with him than with Mr. Rubb. He, at any rate, should have known better. After all, was not Mr. Ball better than either of them, though his head was bald and his face worn with that solemn, sad look of care which always pervaded him?

In the course of the evening she found herself seated apart from the general company, with Mr. Maguire beside her. The eye that did not squint was towards her, and he made an effort to be agreeable to her that was not altogether ineffectual.

"Does not society sometimes make you very sad?" he said.

Society had made her sad to-night, and she answered him in the affirmative.

"It seems that people are so little desirous to make other people happy," she replied.

"It was just that idea that was passing through my own mind. Men and women are anxious to give you the best they have, but it is in order that you may admire their wealth or their taste; and they strive to be witty, amusing, and sarcastic! but that, again, is for the éclat they are to gain. How few really struggle to make those around them comfortable!"

"It comes, I suppose, from people having such different tastes," said Miss Mackenzie, who, on looking round the room, thought that the people assembled there were peculiarly ill-assorted.

"As for happiness," continued Mr. Maguire, "that is not to be looked for from society. They who expect their social hours to be happy hours will be grievously disappointed."

"Are you not happy at Mrs. Stumfold's?"

"At Mrs. Stumfold's? Yes;—sometimes, that is; but even there I always seem to want something. Miss Mackenzie, has it never occurred to you that the one thing necessary in this life, the one thing—beyond a hope for the next, you know, the one thing is—ah, Miss Mackenzie, what is it?"

"Perhaps you mean a competence," said Miss Mackenzie.

"I mean some one to love," said Mr. Maguire.

As he spoke he looked with all the poetic vigour of his better eye full into Miss Mackenzie's face, and Miss Mackenzie, who then could see nothing of the other eye, felt the effect of the glance somewhat as he intended that she should feel it. When a lady who is thinking about getting married is asked by a gentleman who is frequently in her thoughts whether she does not want some one to love, it is natural that she should presume that he means to be particular; and it is natural also that she should be in some sort gratified by that particularity. Miss Mackenzie was, I think, gratified, but she did not express any such feeling.

"Is not that your idea also?" said he,—"some one to love; is not that the great desideratum here below!" And the tone in which he repeated the last words was by no means ineffective.

"I hope everybody has that," said she.

"I fear not; not anyone to love with a perfect love. Who does Miss Todd love?"

"Miss Baker."

"Does she? And yet they live apart, and rarely see each other. They think differently on all subjects. That is not the love of which I am speaking. And you, Miss Mackenzie, are you sure that you love anyone with that perfect all-trusting, love?"

"I love my niece Susanna best," said she.

"Your niece, Susanna! She is a sweet child, a sweet girl; she has everything to make those love her who know her; but—"

"You don't think anything amiss of Susanna, Mr. Maguire?"

"Nothing, nothing; Heaven forbid, dear child! And I think so highly of you for your generosity in adopting her."

"I could not do less than take one of them, Mr. Maguire."

"But I meant a different kind of love from that. Do you feel that your regard for your niece is sufficient to fill your heart?"

"It makes me very comfortable."

"Does it? Ah! me; I wish I could make myself comfortable."

"I should have thought, seeing you so much in Mrs. Stumfold's house—"

"I have the greatest veneration for that woman, Miss Mackenzie! I have sometimes thought that of all the human beings I have ever met, she is the most perfect; she is human, and therefore a sinner, but her sins never meet my eyes."

Miss Mackenzie, who did not herself regard Mrs. Stumfold as being so much better than her neighbours, could not receive this with much rapture.

"But," continued Mr. Maguire, "she is as cold—as cold—as cold as ice."

As the lady in question was another man's wife, this did not seem to Miss Mackenzie to be of much consequence to Mr. Maguire, but she allowed him to go on.

"Stumfold I don't think minds it; he is of that joyous disposition that all things work to good for him. Even when she's most obdurate in her sternness to him—"

"Law! Mr. Maguire, I did not think she was ever stern to him."

"But she is, very hard. Even then I don't think he minds it much. But, Miss Mackenzie, that kind of companion would not do for me at all. I think a woman should be soft and soothing, like a dove."

She did not stop to think whether doves are soothing, but she felt that the language was pretty.

Just at this moment she was summoned by Miss Baker, and looking up she perceived that Mr. and Mrs. Fuzzybell were already leaving the room.

"I don't know why you need disturb Miss Mackenzie," said Miss Todd, "she has only got to go next door, and she seems very happy just now."

"I would sooner go with Miss Baker," said Miss Mackenzie.

"Mr. Maguire would see you home," suggested Miss Todd.

But Miss Mackenzie of course went with Miss Baker, and Mr. Rubb accompanied them.

"Good-night, Mr. Rubb," said Miss Todd; "and don't make very bad reports of us in London."

"Oh! no; indeed I won't."

"For though we do play cards, we still stick to decorum, as you must have observed to-night."

At Miss Mackenzie's door there was an almost overpowering amount of affectionate farewells. Mr. Maguire was there as well as Mr. Rubb, and both gentlemen warmly pressed the hand of the lady they were leaving. Mr. Rubb was not quite satisfied with his evening's work, because he had not been able to get near to Miss Mackenzie; but, nevertheless, he was greatly gratified by the general manner in which he had been received, and was much pleased with Littlebath and its inhabitants. Mr. Maguire, as he walked home by himself, assured himself that he might as well now put the question; he had been thinking about it for the last two months, and had made up his mind that matrimony would be good for him.

Miss Mackenzie, as she went to bed, told herself that she might have a husband if she pleased; but then, which should it be? Mr. Rubb's manners were very much against him; but of Mr. Maguire's eye she had caught a gleam as he turned from her on the doorsteps, which made her think of that alliance with dismay.

Chapter XII

Mrs. Stumfold Interferes

On the morning following Miss Todd's tea-party, Mr. Rubb called on Miss Mackenzie and bade her adieu. He was, he said, going up to London at once, having received a letter which made his presence there imperative. Miss Mackenzie could, of course, do no more than simply say good-bye to him. But when she had said so he did not even then go at once. He was standing with his hat in hand, and had bade her farewell; but still he did not go. He had something to say, and she stood there trembling, half fearing what the nature of that something might be.

"I hope I may see you again before long," he said at last.

"I hope you may," she replied.

"Of course I shall. After all that's come and gone, I shall think nothing of running down, if it were only to make a morning call."

"Pray don't do that, Mr. Rubb."

"I shall, as a matter of course. But in spite of that, Miss Mackenzie, I can't go away without saying another word about the money. I can't indeed."

"There needn't be any more about that, Mr. Rubb."

"But there must be, Miss Mackenzie; there must, indeed; at least, so much as this. I know I've done wrong about that money."

"Don't talk about it. If I choose to lend it to my brother and you without security, there's nothing very uncommon in that."

"No; there ain't; at least perhaps there ain't. Though as far as I can see, brothers and sisters out in the world are mostly as hard to each other where money is concerned as other people. But the thing is, you didn't mean to lend it without security."

"I'm quite contented as it is."

"And I did wrong about it all through; I feel it so that I can't tell you. I do, indeed. But I'll never rest till that money is paid back again. I never will."

Then, having said that, he went away. When early on the preceding evening he had put on bright yellow gloves, making himself smart before the eyes of the lady of his love, it must be presumed that he did so with some hope of success. In that hope he was altogether betrayed. When he came and confessed his fraud about the money, it must be supposed that in doing so he felt that he was lowering himself in the estimation of her whom he desired to win for his wife. But, had he only known it, he thereby took the most efficacious step towards winning her esteem. The gloves had been nearly fatal to him; but those words,—"I feel it so that I can't tell you," redeemed the evil that the gloves had done. He went away, however, saying nothing more then, and failing to strike while the iron was hot.

Some six weeks after this Mrs. Stumfold called on Miss Mackenzie, making a most important visit. But it should be first explained, before the nature of that visit is described, that Miss Mackenzie had twice been to Mrs. Stumfold's house since the evening of Miss Todd's party, drinking tea there on both occasions, and had twice met Mr. Maguire. On the former occasion they two had had some conversation, but it had been of no great moment. He had spoken nothing then of the pleasures of love, nor had he made any allusion to the dove-like softness of women. On the second meeting he had seemed to keep aloof from her altogether, and she had begun to tell herself that that dream was over, and to scold herself for having dreamed at all— when he came close up behind and whispered a word in her ear.

"You know," he said, "how much I would wish to be with you, but I can't now."

She had been startled, and had turned round, and had found herself close to his dreadful eye. She had never been so close to it before, and it frightened her. Then again he came to her just before she left, and spoke to her in the same mysterious way:

"I will see you in a day or two," he said, "but never mind now;" and then he walked away. She had not spoken a word to him, nor did she speak a word to him that evening.

Miss Mackenzie had never before seen Mrs. Stumfold since her first visit of ceremony, except in that lady's drawing-room, and was surprised when she heard the name announced. It was an understood thing that Mrs. Stumfold did not call on the Stumfoldians unless she had some great and special reason for doing so,—unless some erring sister required admonishing, or the course of events in the life of some Stumfoldian might demand special advice. I do not know that any edict of this kind had actually been pronounced, but Miss Mackenzie, though she had not yet been twelve months in Littlebath, knew that this arrangement was generally understood to exist. It was plain to be seen by the lady's face, as she entered the room, that some special cause had brought her now. It wore none of those pretty smiles with which morning callers greet their friends before they begin their first gentle attempts at miscellaneous conversation. It was true that she gave her hand to Miss Mackenzie, but she did even this with austerity; and when she seated herself,—not on the sofa as she was invited to do, but on one of the square, hard, straight-backed chairs,—Miss Mackenzie knew well that pleasantness was not to be the order of the morning.

"My dear Miss Mackenzie," said Mrs. Stumfold, "I hope you will pardon me if I express much tender solicitude for your welfare."

Miss Mackenzie was so astonished at this mode of address, and at the tone in which it was uttered, that she made no reply to it. The words themselves had in them an intention of kindness, but the voice and look of the lady were, if kind, at any rate not tender.

"You came among us," continued Mrs. Stumfold, "and became one of us, and we have been glad to welcome you."

"I'm sure I've been much obliged."

"We are always glad to welcome those who come among us in a proper spirit. Society with me, Miss Mackenzie, is never looked upon as an end in itself. It is only a means to an end. No woman regards society more favourably than I do. I think it offers to us one of the most efficacious means of spreading true gospel teaching. With these views I have always thought it right to open my house in a spirit, as I hope, of humble hospitality;— and Mr. Stumfold is of the same opinion. Holding these views, we have been delighted to see you among us, and, as I have said already, to welcome you as one of us."

There was something in this so awful that Miss Mackenzie hardly knew how to speak, or let it pass without speaking. Having a spirit of her own she did not like being told that she had been, as it were, sat upon and judged, and then admitted into Mrs. Stumfold's society as a child may be admitted into a school after an examination. And yet on the spur of the moment she could not think what words might be appropriate for her answer. She sat silent, therefore, and Mrs. Stumfold again went on.

"I trust that you will acknowledge that we have shown our good will towards you, our desire to cultivate a Christian friendship with you, and that you will therefore excuse me if I ask you a question which might otherwise have the appearance of interference. Miss Mackenzie, is there anything between you and my husband's curate, Mr. Maguire?"

Miss Mackenzie's face became suddenly as red as fire, but for a moment or two she made no answer. I do not know whether I may as yet have succeeded in making the reader understand the strength as well as the weakness of my heroine's character; but Mrs. Stumfold had certainly not succeeded in perceiving it. She was accustomed, probably, to weak, obedient women,—to women who had taught themselves to believe that submission to Stumfoldian authority was a sign of advanced Christianity; and in the mild-looking, quiet-mannered lady who had lately come among them, she certainly did not expect to encounter a rebel. But on such matters as that to which the female hierarch of Littlebath was now alluding, Miss Mackenzie was not by nature adapted to be submissive.

"Is there anything between you and Mr. Maguire?" said Mrs. Stumfold again. "I particularly wish to have a plain answer to that question."

Miss Mackenzie, as I have said, became very red in the face. When it was repeated, she found herself obliged to speak. "Mrs. Stumfold, I do not know that you have any right to ask me such a question as that."

"No right! No right to ask a lady who sits under Mr. Stumfold whether or not she is engaged to Mr. Stumfold's own curate! Think again of what you are saying, Miss Mackenzie!" And there was in Mrs. Stumfold's voice as she spoke an expression of offended majesty, and in her countenance a look of awful authority, sufficient no doubt to bring most Stumfoldian ladies to their bearings.

"You said nothing about being engaged to him."

"Oh, Miss Mackenzie!"

"You said nothing about being engaged to him, but if you had I should have made the same answer. You asked me if there was anything between me and him; and I think it was a very offensive question."

"Offensive! I am afraid, Miss Mackenzie, you have not your spirit subject to a proper control. I have come here in all kindness to warn you against danger, and you tell me that I am offensive! What am I to think of you?"

"You have no right to connect my name with any gentleman's. You can't have any right merely because I go to Mr. Stumfold's church. It's quite preposterous. If I went to Mr. Paul's church"—Mr. Paul was a very High Church young clergyman who had wished to have candles in his church, and of whom it was asserted that he did keep a pair of candles on an inverted box in a closet inside his bedroom—"if I went to Mr. Paul's church, might his wife, if he had one, come and ask me all manner of questions like that?"

Now Mr. Paul's name stank in the nostrils of Mrs. Stumfold. He was to her the thing accursed. Had Miss Mackenzie quoted the Pope, or Cardinal Wiseman or even Dr Newman, it would not have been so bad. Mrs. Stumfold had once met Mr. Paul, and called him to his face the most abject of all the slaves of the scarlet woman. To this courtesy Mr. Paul, being a good-humoured and somewhat sportive young man, had replied that she was another. Mrs. Stumfold had interpreted the gentleman's meaning wrongly, and had ever since gnashed with her teeth and fired great guns with her eyes whenever Mr. Paul was named within her hearing. "Ribald ruffian," she had once said of him; "but that he thinks his priestly rags protect him, he would not have dared to insult me." It was said that she had complained to Stumfold; but Mr. Stumfold's sacerdotal clothing, whether ragged or whole, prevented him also from interfering, and nothing further of a personal nature had occurred between the opponents.

But Miss Mackenzie, who certainly was a Stumfoldian by her own choice, should not have used the name. She probably did not know the whole truth as to that passage of arms between Mr. Paul and Mrs. Stumfold, but she did know that no name in

Littlebath was so odious to the lady as that of the rival
clergyman.

"Very well, Miss Mackenzie," said she, speaking loudly
in her wrath; "then let me tell you that you will come by your
ruin,—yes, by your ruin. You poor unfortunate woman, you are
unfit to guide your own steps, and will not take counsel from
those who are able to put you in the right way!"

"How shall I be ruined?" said Miss Mackenzie, jumping
up from her seat.

"How? Yes. Now you want to know. After having
insulted me in return for my kindness in coming to you, you ask
me questions. If I tell you how, no doubt you will insult me
again."

"I haven't insulted you, Mrs. Stumfold. And if you don't
like to tell me, you needn't. I'm sure I did not want you to come
to me and talk in this way."

"Want me! Who ever does want to be reproved for their
own folly? I suppose what you want is to go on and marry that
man, who may have two or three other wives for what you
know, and put yourself and your money into the hands of a
person whom you never saw in your life above a few months
ago, and of whose former life you literally know nothing. Tell
the truth, Miss Mackenzie, isn't that what you desire to do?"

"I find him acting as Mr. Stumfold's curate."

"Yes; and when I come to warn you, you insult me. He is
Mr. Stumfold's curate, and in many respects he is well fitted for
his office."

"But has he two or three wives already, Mrs. Stumfold?"

"I never said that he had."

"I thought you hinted it."

"I never hinted it, Miss Mackenzie. If you would only be
a little more careful in the things which you allow yourself to
say, it would be better for yourself; and better for me too, while I
am with you."

"I declare you said something about two or three wives; and if there is anything of that kind true of a gentleman and a clergyman, I don't think he ought to be allowed to go about as a single gentleman. I mean as a curate. Mr. Maguire is nothing to me,—nothing whatever; and I don't see why I should have been mixed up with him; but if there is anything of that sort—"

"But there isn't."

"Then, Mrs. Stumfold, I don't think you ought to have mentioned two or three wives. I don't, indeed. It is such a horrid idea,—quite horrid! And I suppose, after all, the poor man has not got one?"

"If you had allowed me, I should have told you all, Miss Mackenzie. Mr. Maguire is not married, and never has been married, as far as I know."

"Then I do think what you said of him was very cruel."

"I said nothing; as you would have known, only you are so hot. Miss Mackenzie, you quite astonish me; you do, indeed. I had expected to find you temperate and calm; instead of that, you are so impetuous, that you will not listen to a word. When it first came to my ears that there might be something between you and Mr. Maguire—"

"I will not be told about something. What does something mean, Mrs. Stumfold?"

"When I was told of this," continued Mrs. Stumfold, determined that she would not be stopped any longer by Miss Mackenzie's energy; "when I was told of this, and, indeed, I may say saw it—"

"You never saw anything, Mrs. Stumfold."

"I immediately perceived that it was my duty to come to you; to come to you and tell you that another lady has a prior claim upon Mr. Maguire's hand and heart."

"Oh, indeed."

"Another young lady,"—with an emphasis on the word young,—"whom he first met at my house, who was introduced to him by me,—a young lady not above thirty years of age, and quite suitable in every way to be Mr. Maguire's wife. She may not have quite so much money as you; but she has a fair provision, and money is not everything; a lady in every way suitable—"

"But is this suitable young lady, who is only thirty years of age, engaged to him?"

"I presume, Miss Mackenzie, that in speaking to you, I am speaking to a lady who would not wish to interfere with another lady who has been before her. I do hope that you cannot be indifferent to the ordinary feelings of a female Christian on that subject. What would you think if you were interfered with, though, perhaps, as you had not your fortune in early life, you may never have known what that was."

This was too much even for Miss Mackenzie.

"Mrs. Stumfold," she said, again rising from her seat, "I won't talk about this any more with you. Mr. Maguire is nothing to me; and, as far as I can see, if he was, that would be nothing to you."

"But it would,—a great deal."

"No, it wouldn't. You may say what you like to him, though, for the matter of that, I think it a very indelicate thing for a lady to go about raising such questions at all. But perhaps you have known him a long time, and I have nothing to do with what you and he choose to talk about. If he is behaving bad to any friend of yours, go and tell him so. As for me, I won't hear anything more about it."

As Miss Mackenzie continued to stand, Mrs. Stumfold was forced to stand also, and soon afterwards found herself compelled to go away. She had, indeed, said all that she had come to say, and though she would willingly have repeated it again had Miss Mackenzie been submissive, she did not find herself encouraged to do so by the rebellious nature of the lady she was visiting.

"I have meant well, Miss Mackenzie," she said as she took her leave, "and I hope that I shall see you just the same as ever on my Thursdays."

To this Miss Mackenzie made answer only by a curtsey, and then Mrs. Stumfold went her way.

Miss Mackenzie, as soon as she was left to herself, began to cry. If Mrs. Stumfold could have seen her, how it would have soothed and rejoiced that lady's ruffled spirit! Miss Mackenzie would sooner have died than have wept in Mrs. Stumfold's presence, but no sooner was the front door closed than she began. To have been attacked at all in that way would have been too much for her, but to have been called old and unsuitable— for that was, in truth, the case; to hear herself accused of being courted solely for her money, and that when in truth she had not been courted at all; to have been informed that a lover for her must have been impossible in those days when she had no money! was not all this enough to make her cry? And then, was it the truth that Mr. Maguire ought to marry some one else? If so, she was the last woman in Littlebath to interfere between him and that other one. But how was she to know that this was not some villainy on the part of Mrs. Stumfold? She felt sure, after what she had now seen and heard, that nothing in that way would be too bad for Mrs. Stumfold to say or do. She never would go to Mrs. Stumfold's house again; that was a matter of course; but what should she do about Mr. Maguire? Mr. Maguire might never speak to her in the way of affection,—probably never would do so; that she could bear; but how was she to bear the fact that every Stumfoldian in Littlebath would know all about it? On one thing she finally resolved, that if ever Mr. Maguire spoke to her on the subject, she would tell him everything that had occurred. After that she cried herself to sleep.

On that afternoon she felt herself to be very desolate and much in want of a friend. When Susanna came back from school in the evening she was almost more desolate than before. She could say nothing of her troubles to one so young, nor yet could she shake off the thought of them. She had been bold enough while Mrs. Stumfold had been with her, but now that she was alone, or almost worse than alone, having Susanna with her,—now that the reaction had come, she began to tell herself that a continuation of this solitary life would be impossible to her. How was she to live if she was to be trampled upon in this way? Was it not almost necessary that she should leave Littlebath? And yet if she were to leave Littlebath, whither should she go, and how should she muster courage to begin everything over again? If only it had been given her to have one friend,—one female friend to whom she could have told everything! She thought of Miss Baker, but Miss Baker was a staunch Stumfoldian; and what did she know of Miss Baker that gave her any right to trouble Miss Baker on such a subject? She would almost rather have gone to Miss Todd, if she had dared.

She laid awake crying half the night. Nothing of the kind had ever occurred to her before. No one had ever accused her of any impropriety; no one had ever thrown it in her teeth that she was longing after fruit that ought to be forbidden to her. In her former obscurity and dependence she had been safe. Now that she had begun to look about her and hope for joy in the world, she had fallen into this terrible misfortune! Would it not have been better for her to have married her cousin John Ball, and thus have had a clear course of duty marked out for her? Would it not have been better for her even to have married Harry Handcock than to have come to this misery? What good would her money do her, if the world was to treat her in this way?

And then, was it true? Was it the fact that Mr. Maguire was ill-treating some other woman in order that he might get her money? In all her misery she remembered that Mrs. Stumfold would not commit herself to any such direct assertion, and she remembered also that Mrs. Stumfold had especially insisted on her own part of the grievance,—on the fact that the suitable young lady had been met by Mr. Maguire in her drawing-room.

As to Mr. Maguire himself, she could reconcile herself to the loss of him. Indeed she had never yet reconciled herself to the idea of taking him. But she could not endure to think that Mrs. Stumfold's interference should prevail, or, worse still, that other people should have supposed it to prevail.

The next day was Thursday,—one of Mrs. Stumfold's Thursdays,—and in the course of the morning Miss Baker came to her, supposing that, as a matter of course, she would go to the meeting.

"Not to-night, Miss Baker," said she.

"Not going! and why not?"

"I'd rather not go out to-night."

"Dear me, how odd. I thought you always went to Mrs. Stumfold's. There's nothing wrong, I hope?"

Then Miss Mackenzie could not restrain herself, and told Miss Baker everything. And she told her story, not with whines and lamentations, as she had thought of it herself while lying awake during the past night, but with spirited indignation. "What right had she to come to me and accuse me?"

"I suppose she meant it for the best," said Miss Baker.

"No, Miss Baker, she meant it for the worst. I am sorry to speak so of your friend, but I must speak as I find her. She intended to insult me. Why did she tell me of my age and my money? Have I made myself out to be young? or misbehaved myself with the means which Providence has given me? And as to the gentleman, have I ever conducted myself so as to merit reproach? I don't know that I was ever ten minutes in his company that you were not there also."

"It was the last accusation I should have brought against you," whimpered Miss Baker.

"Then why has she treated me in this way? What right have I given her to be my advisor, because I go to her husband's church? Mr. Maguire is my friend, and it might have come to that, that he should be my husband. Is there any sin in that, that I should be rebuked?"

"It was for the other lady's sake, perhaps."

"Then let her go to the other lady, or to him. She has forgotten herself in coming to me, and she shall know that I think so."

Miss Baker, when she left the Paragon, felt for Miss Mackenzie more of respect and more of esteem also than she had ever felt before. But Miss Mackenzie, when she was left alone, went upstairs, threw herself on her bed, and was again dissolved in tears.

Chapter XIII

Mr. Maguire's Courtship

After the scene between Miss Mackenzie and Miss Baker more than a week passed by before Miss Mackenzie saw any of her Littlebath friends; or, as she called them with much sadness when speaking of them to herself, her Littlebath acquaintances. Friends, or friend, she had none. It was a slow, heavy week with her, and it is hardly too much to say that every hour in it was spent in thinking of the attack which Mrs. Stumfold had made upon her. When the first Sunday came, she went to church, and saw there Miss Baker, and Mrs. Stumfold, and Mr. Stumfold and Mr. Maguire. She saw, indeed, many Stumfoldians, but it seemed that their eyes looked at her harshly, and she was quite sure that the coachmaker's wife treated her with marked incivility as they left the porch together. Miss Baker had frequently waited for her on Sunday mornings, and walked the length of two streets with her; but she encountered no Miss Baker near the church gate on this morning, and she was sure that Mrs. Stumfold had prevailed against her. If it was to be thus with her, had she not better leave Littlebath as soon as possible? In the same solitude she lived the whole of the next week; with the same feelings did she go to church on the next

Sunday; and then again was she maltreated by the upturned nose and half-averted eyes of the coachmaker's wife.

Life such as this would be impossible to her. Let any of my readers think of it, and then tell themselves whether it could be possible. Mariana's solitude in the moated grange was as nothing to hers. In granges, and such like rural retreats, people expect solitude; but Miss Mackenzie had gone to Littlebath to find companionship. Had she been utterly disappointed, and found none, that would have been bad; but she had found it and then lost it. Mariana, in her desolateness, was still waiting for the coming of some one; and so was Miss Mackenzie waiting, though she hardly knew for whom. For me, if I am to live in a moated grange, let it be in the country. Moated granges in the midst of populous towns are very terrible.

But on the Monday morning,—the morning of the second Monday after the Stumfoldian attach,—Mr. Maguire came, and Mariana's weariness was, for the time, at an end. Susanna had hardly gone, and the breakfast things were still on the table, when the maid brought her up word that Mr. Maguire was below, and would see her if she would allow him to come up. She had heard no ring at the bell, and having settled herself with a novel in the arm-chair, had almost ceased for the moment to think of Mr. Maguire or of Mrs. Stumfold. There was something so sudden in the request now made to her, that it took away her breath.

"Mr. Maguire, Miss, the clergyman from Mr. Stumfold's church," said the girl again.

It was necessary that she should give an answer, though she was ever so breathless.

"Ask Mr. Maguire to walk up," she said; and then she began to bethink herself how she would behave to him.

He was there, however, before her thoughts were of much service to her, and she began by apologising for the breakfast things.

"It is I that ought to beg your pardon for coming so early," said he; "but my time at present is so occupied that I hardly know how to find half an hour for myself; and I thought you would excuse me."

"Oh, certainly," said she; and then sitting down she waited for him to begin.

It would have been clear to any observer, had there been one present, that Mr. Maguire had practised his lesson. He could not rid himself of those unmistakable signs of preparation which every speaker shows when he has been guilty of them. But this probably did not matter with Miss Mackenzie, who was too intent on the part she herself had to play to notice his imperfections.

"I saw that you observed, Miss Mackenzie," he said, "that I kept aloof from you on the two last evenings on which I met you at Mrs. Stumfold's."

"That's a long time ago, Mr. Maguire," she answered. "It's nearly a month since I went to Mrs. Stumfold's house."

"I know that you were not there on the last Thursday. I noticed it. I could not fail to notice it. Thinking so much of you as I do, of course I did notice it. Might I ask you why you did not go?"

"I'd rather not say anything about it," she replied, after a pause.

"Then there has been some reason? Dear Miss Mackenzie, I can assure you I do not ask you without a cause."

"If you please, I will not speak upon that subject. I had much rather not, indeed, Mr. Maguire."

"And shall I not have the pleasure of seeing you there on next Thursday?"

"Certainly not."

"Then you have quarrelled with her, Miss Mackenzie?"

He said nothing now of the perfections of that excellent woman, of whom not long since he had spoken in terms almost too strong for any simple human virtues.

"I'd rather not speak of it. It can't do any good. I don't know why you should ask me whether I intend to go there any more, but as you have, I have answered you."

Then Mr. Maguire got up from his chair, and walked about the room, and Miss Mackenzie, watching him closely, could see that he was much moved. But, nevertheless, I think he had made up his mind to walk about the room beforehand. After a while he paused, and, still standing, spoke to her again across the table.

"May I ask you this question? Has Mrs. Stumfold said anything to you about me?"

"I'd rather not talk about Mrs. Stumfold."

"But, surely, I may ask that. I don't think you are the woman to allow anything said behind a person's back to be received to his detriment."

"Whatever one does hear about people one always hears behind their backs."

"Then she has told you something, and you have believed it?"

She felt herself to be so driven by him that she did not know how to protect herself. It seemed to her that these clerical people of Littlebath had very little regard for the feelings of others in their modes of following their own pursuits.

"She has told you something of me, and you have believed her?" repeated Mr. Maguire. "Have I not a right to ask you what she has said?"

"You have no right to ask me anything."

"Have I not, Miss Mackenzie? Surely that is hard. Is it not hard that I should be stabbed in the dark, and have no means of redressing myself? I did not expect such an answer from you;—indeed I did not."

"And is not it hard that I should be troubled in this way? You talk of stabbing. Who has stabbed you? Is it not your own particular friend, whom you described to me as the best person in all the world? If you and she fall out why should I be brought into it? Once for all, Mr. Maguire, I won't be brought into it."

Now he sat down and again paused before he went on with his talk.

"Miss Mackenzie," he said, when he did speak. "I had not intended to be so abrupt as I fear you will think me in that which I am about to say; but I believe you will like plain measures best."

"Certainly I shall, Mr. Maguire."

"They are the best, always. If, then, I am plain with you, will you be plain with me also? I think you must guess what it is I have to say to you."

"I hate guessing anything, Mr. Maguire."

"Very well; then I will be plain. We have now known each other for nearly a year, Miss Mackenzie."

"A year, is it? No, not a year. This is the beginning of June, and I did not come here till the end of last August. It's about nine months, Mr. Maguire."

"Very well; nine months. Nine months may be as nothing in an acquaintance, or it may lead to the closest friendship."

"I don't know that we have met so very often. You have the parish to attend to, Mr. Maguire."

"Of course I have—or rather I had, for I have left Mr. Stumfold."

"Left Mr. Stumfold! Why, I heard you preach yesterday."

"I did preach yesterday, and shall till he has got another assistant. But he and I are parted as regards all friendly connection."

"But isn't that a pity?"

"Miss Mackenzie, I don't mind telling you that I have found it impossible to put up with the impertinence of that woman"—and now, as he spoke, there came a distorted fire out of his imperfect eye—"impossible! If you knew what I have gone through in attempting it! But that's over. I have the greatest respect for him in the world; a very thorough esteem. He is a hard-working man, and though I do not always approve the style of his wit,—of which, by-the-bye, he thinks too much himself,—still I acknowledge him to be a good spiritual pastor. But he has been unfortunate in his marriage. No doubt he has got money, but money is not everything."

"Indeed, it is not, Mr. Maguire."

"How he can live in the same house with that Mr. Peters, I can never understand. The quarrels between him and his daughter are so incessant that poor Mr. Stumfold is unable to conceal them from the public."

"But you have spoken so highly of her."

"I have endeavoured, Miss Mackenzie—I have endeavoured to think well of her. I have striven to believe that it was all gold that I saw. But let that pass. I was forced to tell you that I am going to leave Mr. Stumfold's church, or I should not now have spoken about her or him. And now comes the question, Miss Mackenzie."

"What is the question, Mr. Maguire?"

"Miss Mackenzie—Margaret, will you share your lot with mine? It is true that you have money. It is true that I have none,—not even a curacy now. But I don't think that any such consideration as that would weigh with you for a moment, if you can find it in your heart to love me."

Miss Mackenzie sat thinking for some minutes before she gave her answer—or striving to think; but she was so completely under the terrible fire of his eye, that any thought was very difficult.

"I am not quite sure about that," she said after a while. "I think, Mr. Maguire, that there should be a little money on both sides. You would hardly wish to live altogether on your wife's fortune."

"I have my profession," he replied, quickly.

"Yes, certainly; and a noble profession it is,—the most noble," said she.

"Yes, indeed; the most noble."

"But somehow—"

"You mean the clergymen are not paid as they should be. No, they are not, Miss Mackenzie. And is it not a shame for a Christian country like this that it should be so? But still, as a profession, it has its value. Look at Mrs. Stumfold; where would she be if she were not a clergyman's wife? The position has its value. A clergyman's wife is received everywhere, you know."

"A man before he talks of marriage ought to have something of his own, Mr. Maguire, besides—"

"Besides what?"

"Well, I'll tell you. As you have done me this honour, I think that I am now bound to tell you what Mrs. Stumfold said to me. She had no right to connect my name with yours or with that of any other gentleman, and my quarrel with her is about that. As to what she said about you, that is your affair and not mine."

Then she told him the whole of that conversation which was given in the last chapter, not indeed repeating the hint about the three or four wives, but recapitulating as clearly as she could all that had been said about the suitable young lady.

"I knew it," said he; "I knew it. I knew it as well as though I had heard it. Now what am I to think of that woman, Miss Mackenzie?"

"Of which woman?"

"Of Mrs. Stumfold, of course. It's all jealousy: every bit of it jealousy."

"Jealousy! Do you mean that she—that she—"

"Not jealousy of that kind, Miss Mackenzie. Oh dear, no. She's as pure as the undriven snow, I should say, as far as that goes. But she can't bear to think that I should rise in the world."

"I thought she wanted to marry you to a suitable lady, and young, with a fair provision."

"Pshaw! The lady has about seventy pounds a-year! But that would signify nothing if I loved her, Miss Mackenzie."

"There has been something, then?"

"Yes; there has been something. That is, nothing of my doing,—nothing on earth. Miss Mackenzie, I am as innocent as the babe unborn."

As he said this she could not help looking into the horrors of his eyes, and thinking that innocent was not the word for him.

"I'm as innocent as the babe unborn. Why should I be expected to marry a lady merely because Mrs. Stumfold tells me that there she is? And it's my belief that old Peters has got their money somewhere, and won't give it up, and that that's the reason of it."

"But did you ever say you would marry her?"

"What! Miss Floss, never! I'll tell you the whole story, Miss Mackenzie; and if you want to ask any one else, you can ask Mrs. Perch." Mrs. Perch was the coachbuilder's wife. "You've seen Miss Floss at Mrs. Stumfold's, and must know yourself whether I ever noticed her any more than to be decently civil."

"Is she the lady that's so thin and tall?"

"Yes."

"With the red hair?"

"Well, it's sandy, certainly. I shouldn't call it just red myself."

"Some people like red hair, you know," said Miss Mackenzie, thinking of the suitable lady. Miss Mackenzie was willing at that moment to forfeit all her fortune if Miss Floss was not older than she was! "And that is Miss Floss, is it?"

"Yes, and I don't blame Mrs. Stumfold for wishing to get a husband for her friend, but it is hard upon me."

"Really, Mr. Maguire, I think that perhaps you couldn't do better."

"Better than what?"

"Better than take Miss Floss. As you say, some people like red hair. And she is very suitable, certainly. And, Mr.

Maguire, I really shouldn't like to interfere;—I shouldn't indeed."

"Miss Mackenzie, you're joking, I know."

"Not in the least, Mr. Maguire. You see there has been something about it."

"There has been nothing."

"There's never smoke without fire; and I don't think a lady like Mrs. Stumfold would come here and tell me all that she did, if it hadn't gone some way. And you owned just now that you admired her."

"I never owned anything of the kind. I don't admire her a bit. Admire her! Oh, Miss Mackenzie, what do you think of me?"

Miss Mackenzie said that she really didn't know what to think.

Then, having as he thought altogether disposed of Miss Floss, he began again to press his suit. And she was weak; for though she gave him no positive encouragement, neither did she give him any positive denial. Her mind was by no means made up, and she did not know whether she wished to take him or to leave him. Now that the thing had come so near, what guarantee had she that he would be good to her if she gave him everything that she possessed? As to her cousin John Ball, she would have had many guarantees. Of him she could say that she knew what sort of a man he was; but what did she know of Mr. Maguire? At that moment, as he sat there pleading his own cause with all the eloquence at his command, she remembered that she did not even know his Christian name. He had always in her presence been called Mr. Maguire. How could she say that she loved a man whose very name she had not as yet heard?

But still, if she left all her chances to run from her, what other fate would she have but that of being friendless all her life? Of course she must risk much if she was ever minded to change her mode of life. She had said something to him as to the expediency of there being money on both sides, but as she said it she knew that she would willingly have given up her money could she only have been sure of her man. Was not her income enough for both? What she wanted was companionship, and love if it might be possible; but if not love, then friendship. This, had she known where she could purchase it with certainty, she would willingly have purchased with all her wealth.

"If I have surprised you, will you say that you will take time to think of it?" pleaded Mr. Maguire.

Miss Mackenzie, speaking in the lowest possible voice, said that she would take time to think of it.

When a lady says that she will take time to think of such a proposition, the gentleman is generally justified in supposing that he has carried his cause. When a lady rejects a suitor, she should reject him peremptorily. Anything short of such peremptory reaction is taken for acquiescence. Mr. Maguire consequently was elated, called her Margaret, and swore that he loved her as he had never loved woman yet.

"And when may I come again?" he asked.

Miss Mackenzie begged that she might be allowed a fortnight to think of it.

"Certainly," said the happy man.

"And you must not be surprised," said Miss Mackenzie, "if I make some inquiry about Miss Floss."

"Any inquiry you please," said Mr. Maguire. "It is all in that woman's brain; it is indeed. Miss Floss, perhaps, has thought of it; but I can't help that, can I? I can't help what has been said to her. But if you mean anything as to a promise from me, Margaret, on my word as a Christian minister of the Gospel, there has been nothing of the kind."

She did not much mind his calling her Margaret; it was in itself such a trifle; but when he made a fuss about kissing her hand it annoyed her.

"Only your hand," he said, beseeching the privilege.

"Pshaw," she said, "what's the good?"

She had sense enough to feel that with such lovemaking as that between her and her lover there should be no kissing till after marriage; or at any rate, no kissing of hands, as is done between handsome young men of twenty-three and beautiful young ladies of eighteen, when they sit in balconies on moonlight nights. A good honest kiss, mouth to mouth, might not be amiss when matters were altogether settled; but when she thought of this, she thought also of his eye and shuddered. His eye was not his fault, and a man should not be left all his days without a wife because he squints; but still, was it possible? could she bring herself to endure it?

He did kiss her hand, however, and then went. As he stood at the door he looked back fondly and exclaimed—

"On Monday fortnight, Margaret; on Monday fortnight."

"Goodness gracious, Mr. Maguire," she answered, "do shut the door;" and then he vanished.

As soon as he was gone she remembered that his name was Jeremiah. She did not know how she had learned it, but she knew that such was the fact. If it did come to pass how was she to call him? She tried the entire word Jeremiah, but it did not seem to answer. She tried Jerry also, but that was worse. Jerry might have been very well had they come together fifteen years earlier in life, but she did not think that she could call him Jerry now. She supposed it must be Mr. Maguire; but if so, half the romance of the thing would be gone at once!

She felt herself to be very much at sea, and almost wished that she might be like Mariana again, waiting and aweary, so grievous was the necessity of having to make up her mind on such a subject. To whom should she go for advice? She had told him that she would make further inquiries about Miss Floss, but of whom was she to make them? The only person to whom she could apply was Miss Baker, and she was almost sure that Miss Baker would despise her for thinking of marrying Mr. Maguire.

But after a day or two she did tell Miss Baker, and she saw at once that Miss Baker did despise her. But Miss Baker, though she manifestly did despise her, promised her some little aid. Miss Todd knew everything and everybody. Might Miss Baker tell Miss Todd? If there was anything wrong, Miss Todd would ferret it out to a certainty. Miss Mackenzie, hanging down her head, said that Miss Baker might tell Miss Todd. Miss Baker, when she left Miss Mackenzie, turned at once into Miss Todd's house, and found her friend at home.

"It surprises me that any woman should be so foolish," said Miss Baker.

"Come, come, my dear, don't you be hard upon her. We have all been foolish in our days. Do you remember, when Sir Lionel used to be here, how foolish you and I were?"

"It's not the same thing at all," said Miss Baker. "Did you ever see a man with such an eye as he has got?"

"I shouldn't mind his eye, my dear; only I'm afraid he's got no money."

Miss Todd, however, promised to make inquiries, and declared her intention of communicating what intelligence she might obtain direct to Miss Mackenzie. Miss Baker resisted this for a little while, but ultimately submitted, as she was wont to do, to the stronger character of her friend.

Miss Mackenzie had declared that she must have a fortnight to think about it, and Miss Todd therefore knew that she had nearly a fortnight for her inquiries. The reader may be sure that she did not allow the grass to grow under her feet. With Miss Mackenzie the time passed slowly enough, for she could only sit on her sofa and doubt, resolving first one way and then another; but Miss Todd went about Littlebath, here and there, among friends and enemies, filling up all her time; and before the end of the fortnight she certainly knew more about Mr. Maguire than did anybody else in Littlebath.

She did not see Miss Mackenzie till the Saturday, the last Saturday before the all-important Monday; but on that day she went to her.

"I suppose you know what I'm come about, my dear," she said.

Miss Mackenzie blushed, and muttered something about Miss Baker.

"Yes, my dear; Miss Baker was speaking to me about Mr. Maguire. You needn't mind speaking out to me, Miss Mackenzie. I can understand all about it; and if I can be of any assistance, I shall be very happy. No doubt you feel a little shy, but you needn't mind with me."

"I'm sure you're very good."

"I don't know about that, but I hope I'm not very bad. The long and the short of it is, I suppose, that you think you might as well—might as well take Mr. Maguire."

Miss Mackenzie felt thoroughly ashamed of herself. She could not explain to Miss Todd all her best motives; and then, those motives which were not the best were made to seem so very weak and mean by the way in which Miss Todd approached them. When she thought of the matter alone, it seemed to her that she was perfectly reasonable in wishing to be married, in order that she might escape the monotony of a lonely life; and she thought that if she could talk to Miss Todd about the subject gently, for a quarter of an hour at a time every day for two or three months, it was possible that she might explain her views with credit to herself; but how could she do this to anyone so very abruptly? She could only confess that she did want to marry the man, as the child confesses her longing for a tart.

"I have thought about it, certainly," she said.

"Quite right," said Miss Todd; "quite right if you like him. Now for me, I'm so fond of my own money and my own independence, that I've never had a fancy that way,—not since I was a girl."

"But you're so different, Miss Todd; you've got such a position of your own."

And Miss Mackenzie, who was at present desirous of marrying a very strict evangelical clergyman, thought with envy of the social advantages and pleasant iniquities of her wicked neighbour.

"Oh, I don't know. I've a few friends, but that comes of being here so long. And then, you see, I ain't particular as you are. I always see that when a lady goes in to be evangelical, she soon finds a husband to take care of her; that is, if she has got any money. It all goes on very well, and I've no doubt they're right. There's my friend Mary Baker, she's single still; but then she began very late in life. Now about Mr. Maguire."

"Well, Miss Todd."

"In the first place, I really don't think he has got much that he can call his own."

"He hasn't got anything, Miss Todd; he told me so himself."

"Did he, indeed?" said Miss Todd; "then let me tell you he is a deal honester than they are in general."

"Oh, he told me that. I know he's got no income in the world besides his curacy, and that he has thrown up."

"And therefore you are going to give him yours."

"I don't know about that, Miss Todd; but it wasn't about money that I was doubting. What I've got is enough for both of us, if his wants are not greater than mine. What is the use of money if people cannot be happy together with it? I don't care a bit for money, Miss Todd; that is, not for itself. I shouldn't like to be dependent on a stranger; I don't know that I would like to be dependent again even on a brother; but I should take no shame to be dependent on a husband if he was good to me."

"That's just it; isn't it?"

"There's quite enough for him and me."

"I must say you look at the matter in the most disinterested way. I couldn't bring myself to take it up like that."

"You haven't lived the life that I have, Miss Todd, and I don't suppose you ever feel solitary as I do."

"Well, I don't know. We single women have to be solitary sometimes—and sometimes sad."

"But you're never sad, Miss Todd."

"Have you never heard there are some animals, that, when they're sick, crawl into holes, and don't ever show themselves among the other animals? Though it is only the animals that do it, there's a pride in that which I like. What's the good of complaining if one's down in the mouth? When one gets old and heavy and stupid, one can't go about as one did when one was young; and other people won't care to come to you as they did then."

"But I had none of that when I was young, Miss Todd."

"Hadn't you? Then I won't say but what you may be right to try and begin now. But, law! what am I talking of? I am old enough to be your mother."

"I think it so kind of you to talk to me at all."

"Well, now about Mr. Maguire. I don't think he's possessed of much of the fat of the land; but that you say you know already?"

"Oh yes, I know all that."

"And it seems he has lost his curacy?"

"He threw that up himself."

"I shouldn't be surprised—but mind I don't say this for certain—but I shouldn't be surprised if he owed a little money."

Miss Mackenzie's face became rather long.

"What do you call a little, Miss Todd?"

"Two or three hundred pounds. I don't call that a great deal."

"Oh dear, no!" and Miss Mackenzie's face again became cheerful. "That could be settled without any trouble."

"Upon my word you are the most generous woman I ever saw."

"No, I'm not that."

"Or else you must be very much in love?"

"I don't think I am that either, Miss Todd; only I don't care much about money if other things are suitable. What I chiefly wanted to know was—"

"About that Miss Floss?"

"Yes, Miss Todd."

"My belief is there never was a greater calumny, or what I should call a stronger attempt at a do. Mind I don't think much of your St Stumfolda, and never did. I believe the poor man has never said a word to the woman. Mrs. Stumfold has put it into her head that she could have Mr. Maguire if she chose to set her cap at him, and, I dare say, Miss Floss has been dutiful to her saint. But, Miss Mackenzie, if nothing else hinders you, don't let that hinder you." Then Miss Todd, having done her business and made her report, took her leave.

This was on Saturday. The next day would be Sunday, and then on the following morning she must make her answer. All that she had heard about Mr. Maguire was, to her thinking, in his favour. As to his poverty, that he had declared himself, and that she did not mind. As to a few hundred pounds of debt, how was a poor man to have helped such a misfortune? In that matter of Miss Floss he had been basely maligned,—so much maligned, that Miss Mackenzie owed him all her sympathy. What excuse could she now have for refusing him?

When she went to bed on the Sunday night such were her thoughts and her feelings.

Chapter XIV

Tom Mackenzie's Bed-Side

There was a Stumfoldian edict, ultra-Median-and-Persian in its strictness, ordaining that no Stumfoldian in Littlebath should be allowed to receive a letter on Sundays. And there also existed a coordinate rule on the part of the Postmaster-General,—or, rather, a privilege granted by that functionary,—in accordance with which Stumfoldians, and other such sects of Sabbatarians, were empowered to prohibit the letter-carriers from contaminating their special knockers on Sunday mornings. Miss Mackenzie had given way to this easily, seeing nothing amiss in the edict, and not caring much for her Sunday letters. In consequence, she received on the Monday mornings those letters which were due to her on Sundays, and on this special Monday morning she received a letter, as to which the delay was of much consequence. It was to tell her that her brother Tom was dying, and to pray that she would be up in London as early on the Monday as was practicable. Mr. Samuel Rubb, junior, who had written the letter in Gower Street, had known nothing of the Sabbatical edicts of the Stumfoldians.

"It is an inward tumour," said Mr. Rubb, "and has troubled him long, though he has said nothing about it. It is now breaking, and the doctor says he can't live. He begs that you will come to him, as he has very much to say to you. Mrs. Tom would have written, but she is so much taken up, and is so much beside herself, that she begs me to say that she is not able; but I hope it won't be less welcome coming from me. The second pair back will be ready for you, just as if it were your own. I would be waiting at the station on Monday, if I knew what train you would come by."

This she received while at breakfast on the Monday morning, having sat down a little earlier than usual, in order that the tea-things might be taken away so as to make room for Mr. Maguire.

Of course she must go up to town instantly, by the first practicable train. She perceived at once that she would have to send a message by telegraph, as they would have expected to hear from her that morning. She got the railway guide, and saw that the early express train had already gone. There was, however, a mid-day train which would reach Paddington in the afternoon. She immediately got her bonnet and went off to the telegraph office, leaving word with the servant, that if any one called "he" was to be told that she had received sudden tidings which took her up to London. On her return she found that "he" had not been there yet, and now she could only hope that he would not come till after she had started. It would, of course, be impossible, at such a moment as this, to make any answer to such a proposition as Mr. Maguire's.

He came, and when the servant gave him the message at the door, he sent up craving permission to see her but for a moment. She could not refuse him, and went down to him in the drawing-room, with her shawl and bonnet.

"Dearest Margaret," said he, "what is this?" and he took both her hands.

"I have received word that my brother, in London, is very ill,—that he is dying, and I must go to him."

He still held her hands, standing close to her, as though he had some special right to comfort her.

"Cannot I go with you?" he said. "Let me; do let me."

"Oh, no, Mr. Maguire; it is impossible. What could you do? I am going to my brother's house."

"But have I not a right to be of help to you at such a time?" he asked.

"No, Mr. Maguire; no right; certainly none as yet."

"Oh! Margaret."

"I'm sure you will see that I cannot talk of anything of that sort now."

"But you will not be back for ever so long."

"I cannot tell."

"Oh! Margaret; you will not leave me in suspense? After bidding me wait a fortnight, you will not go away without telling me that you will be mine when you come back? One word will do it."

"Mr. Maguire, you really must excuse me now."

"One word, Margaret; only one word," and he still held her.

"Mr. Maguire," she said, tearing her hand from him, "I am astonished at you. I tell you that my brother is dying and you hold me here, and expect me to give you an answer about nonsense. I thought you were more manly."

He saw that there was a flash in her eye as he stepped back; so he begged her pardon, and muttering something about hoping to hear from her soon, took his leave. Poor man! I do not see why she should not have accepted him, as she had made up her mind to do so. And to him, with his creditors, and in his present position, any certainty in this matter would have made so much difference!

At the Paddington station Miss Mackenzie was met by her other lover, Mr. Rubb. Mr. Rubb, however, had never yet declared himself as holding this position, and did not do so on the present occasion. Their conversation in the cab was wholly

concerning her brother's state, or nearly so. It seemed that there
was no hope. Mr. Rubb said that very clearly. As to time the
doctor would say nothing certain; but he had declared that it
might occur any day. The patient could never leave his bed
again; but as his constitution was strong, he might remain in his
present condition some weeks. He did not suffer much pain, or,
at any rate, did not complain of much; but was very sad. Then
Mr. Rubb said one other word.

"I am afraid he is thinking of his wife and children."

"Would there be nothing for them out of the business?"
asked Miss Mackenzie.

The junior partner at first shook his head, saying nothing.
After a few minutes he did speak in a low voice. "If there be
anything, it will be very little,—very little."

Miss Mackenzie was rejoiced that she had given no
definite promise to Mr. Maguire. There seemed to be now a job
for her to do in the world which would render it quite
unnecessary that she should look about for a husband. If her
brother's widow were left penniless, with seven children, there
would be no longer much question as to what she would do with
her money. Perhaps the only person in the world that she
cordially disliked was her sister-in-law. She certainly knew no
other woman whose society would be so unpalatable to her. But
if things were so as Mr. Rubb now described them, there could
be no doubt about her duty. It was very well indeed that her
answer to Mr. Maguire had been postponed to that Monday.

She found her sister-in-law in the dining-room, and Mrs.
Mackenzie, of course, received her with a shower of tears. "I did
think you would have come, Margaret, by the first train."

Then Margaret was forced to explain all about the letter
and the Sunday arrangements at Littlebath; and Mrs. Tom was
stupid and wouldn't understand, but persisted in her grievance,
declaring that Tom was killing himself with disappointment.

"And there's Dr Slumpy just this moment gone without a
word to comfort one,—not even to say about when it will be. I

suppose you'll want your dinner before you go up to see him. As for us we've had no dinners, or anything regular; but, of course, you must be waited on." Miss Mackenzie simply took off her bonnet and shawl, and declared herself ready to go upstairs as soon as her brother would be ready to see her.

"It's fret about money has done it all, Margaret," said the wife. "Since the day that Walter's shocking will was read, he's never been himself for an hour. Of course he wouldn't show it to you; but he never has."

Margaret turned short round upon her sister-in-law on the stairs.

"Sarah," said she, and then she stopped herself. "Never mind; it is natural, no doubt, you should feel it; but there are times and places when one's feelings should be kept under control."

"That's mighty fine," said Mrs. Mackenzie; "but, however, if you'll wait here, I'll go up to him."

In a few minutes more Miss Mackenzie was standing by her brother's bedside, holding his hand in hers.

"I knew you would come, Margaret," he said.

"Of course I should come; who doubted it? But never mind that, for here I am."

"I only told her that we expected her by the earlier train," said Mrs. Tom.

"Never mind the train as long as she's here," said Tom. "You've heard how it is with me, Margaret?"

Then Margaret buried her face in the bed-clothes and wept, and Mrs. Tom, weeping also, hid herself behind the curtains.

There was nothing said then about money or the troubles of the business, and after a while the two women went down to tea. In the dining-room they found Mr. Rubb, who seemed to be quite at home in the house. Cold meat was brought up for Margaret's dinner, and they all sat down to one of those sad sick-house meals which he or she who has not known must have

been lucky indeed. To Margaret it was nothing new. All the life
that she remembered, except the last year, had been spent in
nursing her other brother; and now to be employed about the
bed-side of a sufferer was as natural to her as the air she
breathed.

"I will sit with him to-night, Sarah, if you will let me,"
she said; and Sarah assented.

It was still daylight when she found herself at her post.
Mrs. Mackenzie had just left the room to go down among the
children, saying that she would return again before she left him
for the night. To this the invalid remonstrated, begging his wife
to go to bed.

"She has not had her clothes off for the last week," said
the husband.

"It don't matter about my clothes," said Mrs. Tom, still
weeping. She was always crying when in the sick room, and
always scolding when out of it; thus complying with the two
different requisitions of her nature. The matter, however, was
settled by an assurance on her part that she would go to bed, so
that she might be stirring early.

There are women who seem to have an absolute pleasure
in fixing themselves for business by the bedside of a sick man.
They generally commence their operations by laying aside all
fictitious feminine charms, and by arraying themselves with a
rigid, unconventional, unenticing propriety. Though they are still
gentle,—perhaps more gentle than ever in their movements,—
there is a decision in all they do very unlike their usual mode of
action. The sick man, who is not so sick but what he can ponder
on the matter, feels himself to be like a baby, whom he has seen
the nurse to take from its cradle, pat on the back, feed, and then
return to its little couch, all without undue violence or tyranny,
but still with a certain consciousness of omnipotence as far as
that child was concerned. The vitality of the man is gone from
him, and he, in his prostrate condition, debarred by all the
features of his condition from spontaneous exertion, feels

himself to be more a woman than the woman herself. She, if she be such a one as our Miss Mackenzie, arranges her bottles with precision; knows exactly how to place her chair, her lamp, and her teapot; settles her cap usefully on her head, and prepares for the night's work certainly with satisfaction. And such are the best women of the world,—among which number I think that Miss Mackenzie has a right to be counted.

A few words of affection were spoken between the brother and sister, for at such moments brotherly affection returns, and the estrangements of life are all forgotten in the old memories. He seemed comforted to feel her hand upon the bed, and was glad to pronounce her name, and spoke to her as though she had been the favourite of the family for years, instead of the one member of it who had been snubbed and disregarded. Poor man, who shall say that there was anything hypocritical or false in this? And yet, undoubtedly, it was the fact that Margaret was now the only wealthy one among them, which had made him send to her, and think of her, as he lay there in his sickness.

When these words of love had been spoken, he turned himself on his pillow, and lay silent for a long while,—for hours, till the morning sun had risen, and the daylight was again seen through the window curtain. It was not much after midsummer, and the daylight came to them early. From time to time she had looked at him, and each hour in the night she had crept round to him, and given him that which he needed. She did it all with a certain system, noiselessly, but with an absolute assurance on her own part that she carried with her an authority sufficient to ensure obedience. On that ground, in that place, I think that even Miss Todd would have succumbed to her.

But when the morning sun had driven the appearance of night from the room, making the paraphernalia of sickness more ghastly than they had been under the light of the lamp, the brother turned himself back again, and began to talk of those things which were weighing on his mind.

"Margaret," he said, "it's very good of you to come, but as to myself, no one's coming can be of any use to me."

"It is all in the hands of God, Tom."

"No doubt, no doubt," said he, sadly, not daring to argue such a point with her, and yet feeling but little consolation from her assurance. "So is the bullock in God's hands when the butcher is going to knock him on the head, but yet we know that the beast will die. Men live and die from natural causes, and not by God's interposition."

"But there is hope; that is what I mean. If God pleases—"

"Ah, well. But, Margaret, I fear that he will not please; and what am I to do about Sarah and the children?"

This was a question that could be answered by no general platitude,—by no weak words of hopeless consolation. Coming from him to her, it demanded either a very substantial answer, or else no answer at all. What was he to do about Sarah and the children? Perhaps there came a thought across her mind that Sarah and the children had done very little for her,—had considered her very little, in those old, weary days, in Arundel Street. And those days were not, as yet, so very old. It was now not much more than twelve months since she had sat by the deathbed of her other brother,—since she had expressed to herself, and to Harry Handcock, a humble wish that she might find herself to be above absolute want.

"I do not think you need fret about that, Tom," she said, after turning these things over in her mind for a minute or two.

"How, not fret about them? But I suppose you know nothing of the state of the business. Has Rubb spoken to you?"

"He did say some word as we came along in the cab."

"What did he say?"

"He said—"

"Well, tell me what he said. He said, that if I died—what then? You must not be afraid of speaking of it openly. Why,

Margaret, they have all told me that it must be in a month or two. What did Rubb say?"

"He said that there would be very little coming out of the business—that is, for Sarah and the children—if anything were to happen to you."

"I don't suppose they'd get anything. How it has been managed I don't know. I have worked like a galley slave at it, but I haven't kept the books, and I don't know how things have gone so badly. They have gone badly,—very badly."

"Has it been Mr. Rubb's fault?"

"I won't say that; and, indeed, if it has been any man's fault it has been the old man's. I don't want to say a word against the one that you know. Oh, Margaret!"

"Don't fret yourself now, Tom."

"If you had seven children, would not you fret yourself? And I hardly know how to speak to you about it. I know that we have already had ever so much of your money, over two thousand pounds; and I fear you will never see it again."

"Never mind, Tom; it is yours, with all my heart. Only, Tom, as it is so badly wanted, I would rather it was yours than Mr. Rubb's. Could I not do something that would make that share of the building yours?"

He shifted himself uneasily in his bed, and made her understand that she had distressed him.

"But perhaps it will be better to say nothing more about that," said she.

"It will be better that you should understand it all. The property belongs nominally to us, but it is mortgaged to the full of its value. Rubb can explain it all, if he will. Your money went to buy it, but other creditors would not be satisfied without security. Ah, dear! it is so dreadful to have to speak of all this in this way."

"Then don't speak of it, Tom."

"But what am I to do?"

"Are there no proceeds from the business?"

"Yes, for those who work in it; and I think there will be something coming out of it for Sarah,—something, but it will be very small. And if so, she must depend for it solely on Mr. Rubb."

"On the young one?"

"Yes; on the one that you know."

There was a great deal more said, and of course everyone will know how such a conversation was ended, and will understand with what ample assurance as to her own intentions Margaret promised that the seven children should not want. As she did so, she made certain rapid calculations in her head. She must give up Mr. Maguire. There was no doubt about that. She must give up all idea of marrying any one, and, as she thought of this, she told herself that she was perhaps well rid of a trouble. She had already given away to the firm of Rubb and Mackenzie above a hundred a-year out of her income. If she divided the remainder with Mrs. Tom, keeping about three hundred and fifty pounds a-year for herself and Susanna, she would, she thought, keep her promise well, and yet retain enough for her own comfort and Susanna's education. It would be bad for the prospects of young John Ball, the third of the name, whom she had taught herself to regard as her heir; but young John Ball would know nothing of the good things he had lost. As to living with her sister-in-law Sarah, and sharing her house and income with the whole family, that she declared to herself nothing should induce her to do. She would give up half of all that she had, and that half would be quite enough to save her brother's children from want. In making the promise to her brother she said nothing about proportions, and nothing as to her own future life. "What I have," she said, "I will share with them and you may rest assured that they shall not want." Of course he thanked her as dying men do thank those who take upon themselves such charges; but she perceived as he did so, or thought that she perceived, that he still had something more upon his mind.

Mrs. Tom came and relieved her in the morning, and Miss Mackenzie was obliged to put off for a time that panoply of sick-room armour which made her so indomitable in her brother's bedroom. Downstairs she met Mr. Rubb, who talked to her much about her brother's affairs, and much about the oilcloth business, speaking as though he were desirous that the most absolute confidence should exist between him and her. But she said no word of her promise to her brother, except that she declared that the money lent was now to be regarded as a present made by her to him personally.

"I am afraid that that will avail nothing," said Mr. Rubb, junior, "for the amount now stands as a debt due by the firm to you, and the firm, which would pay you the money if it could, cannot pay it to your brother's estate any more than it can to yours."

"But the interest," said Miss Mackenzie.

"Oh, yes! the interest can be paid," said Mr. Rubb, junior, but the tone of his voice did not give much promise that this interest would be forthcoming with punctuality.

She watched again that night; and on the next day, in the afternoon, she was told that a gentleman wished to see her in the drawing-room. Her thoughts at once pointed to Mr. Maguire, and she went downstairs prepared to be very angry with that gentleman. But on entering the room she found her cousin, John Ball. She was, in truth, glad to see him; for, after all, she thought that she liked him the best of all the men or women that she knew. He was always in trouble, but then she fancied that with him she at any rate knew the worst. There was nothing concealed with him,—nothing to be afraid of. She hoped that they might continue to know each other intimately as cousins. Under existing circumstances they could not, of course, be anything more to each other than that.

"This is very kind of you, John," she said, taking his hand. "How did you know I was here?"

"Mr. Slow told me. I was with Mr. Slow about business of yours. I'm afraid from what I hear that you find your brother very ill."

"Very ill, indeed, John,—ill to death."

She then asked after her uncle and aunt, and the children, at the Cedars.

They were much as usual, he said; and he added that his mother would be very glad to see her at the Cedars; only he supposed there was no hope of that.

"Not just at present, John. You see I am wholly occupied here."

"And will he really die, do you think?"

"The doctors say so."

"And his wife and children—will they be provided for?"

Margaret simply shook her head, and John Ball, as he watched her, felt assured that his uncle Jonathan's money would never come in his way, or in the way of his children. But he was a man used to disappointment, and he bore this with mild sufferance.

Then he explained to her the business about which he had specially come to her. She had entrusted him with certain arrangements as to a portion of her property, and he came to tell her that a certain railway company wanted some houses which belonged to her, and that by Act of Parliament she was obliged to sell them.

"But the Act of Parliament will make the railway company pay for them, won't it, John?"

Then he went on to explain to her that she was in luck's way, "as usual," said the poor fellow, thinking of his own misfortunes, and that she would greatly increase her income by the sale. Indeed, it seemed to her that she would regain pretty nearly all she had lost by the loan to Rubb and Mackenzie. "How very singular," thought she to herself. Under these circumstances, it might, after all, be possible that she should marry Mr. Maguire, if she wished it.

When Mr. Ball had told his business he did not stay much longer. He said no word of his own hopes, if hopes they could be called any longer. As he left her, he just referred to what had passed between them. "This is no time, Margaret," said he, "to ask you whether you have changed your mind?"

"No, John; there are other things to think of now; are there not? And, besides, they will want here all that I can do for them."

She spoke to him with an express conviction that what was wanted of her by him, as well as by others, was her money, and it did not occur to him to contradict her.

"He might have asked to see me, I do think," said Mrs. Tom, when John Ball was gone. "But there always was an upsetting pride about those people at the Cedars which I never could endure. And they are as poor as church mice. When poverty and pride go together I do detest them. I suppose he came to find out all about us, but I hope you told him nothing."

To all this Miss Mackenzie made no answer at all.

Chapter XV

The Tearing of the Verses

Things went on in Gower Street for three or four weeks in the same way, and then Susanna was fetched home from Littlebath. Miss Mackenzie would have gone down herself but that she was averse to see Mr. Maguire. She therefore kept on her Littlebath lodgings, though Mrs. Tom said much to her of the wasteful extravagance in doing so. It was at last settled that Mr. Rubb should go down to Littlebath and bring Susanna back with him; and this he did, not at all to that young lady's satisfaction. It was understood that Susanna did not leave the school, at which she had lately been received as a boarder; but the holidays had come, and it was thought well that she should see her father. During this time Miss Mackenzie received two letters from Mr. Maguire. In the first he pleaded hard for an answer to his offer. He had, he said, now relinquished his curacy, having found the interference of that terrible woman to be unendurable. He had left his curacy, and was at present without employment. Under such circumstances, "his Margaret" would understand how imperative it was that he should receive an answer. A curacy, or, rather, a small incumbency, had offered itself among the mines in Cornwall; but he could not think of accepting this till he should know what "his Margaret" might say to it.

To this Margaret answered most demurely, and perhaps a little slily. She said that her brother's health and affairs were at present in such a condition as to allow her to think of nothing else; that she completely understood Mr. Maguire's position, and that it was essential that he should not be kept in suspense. Under these combined circumstances she had no alternative but to release him from the offer he had made. This she did with the less unwillingness as it was probable that her pecuniary position would be considerably altered by the change in her brother's family which they were now expecting almost daily. Then she bade him farewell, with many expressions of her esteem, and said that she hoped he might be happy among the mines in Cornwall.

Such was her letter; but it did not satisfy Mr. Maguire, and he wrote a second letter. He had declined, he said, the incumbency among the mines, having heard of something which he thought would suit him better in Manchester. As to that, there was no immediate hurry, and he proposed remaining at Littlebath for the next two months, having been asked to undertake temporary duty in a neighbouring church for that time. By the end of the two months he hoped that "his Margaret" would be able to give him an answer in a different tone. As to her pecuniary position, he would leave that, he said, "all to herself."

To this second letter Miss Mackenzie did not find it necessary to send any reply. The domestics in the Mackenzie family were not at this time numerous, and the poor mother had enough to do with her family downstairs. No nurse had been hired for the sick man, for nurses cannot be hired without money, and money with the Tom Mackenzies was scarce. Our Miss Mackenzie would have hired a nurse, but she thought it better to take the work entirely into her own hands. She did so, and I think we may say that her brother did not suffer by it. As she sat by his bedside, night after night, she seemed to feel that she had fallen again into her proper place, and she looked back upon the year she had spent at Littlebath almost with dismay. Since her brother's death, three men had offered to marry her, and there was a fourth from whom she had expected such an offer. She looked upon all this with dismay, and told herself that she was not fit to sail, under her own guidance, out in the broad sea, amidst such rocks as those. Was not some humbly feminine employment, such as that in which she was now engaged, better for her in all ways? Sad as was the present occasion, did she not feel a satisfaction in what she was doing, and an assurance that she was fit for her position? Had she not always been ill at ease, and out of her element, while striving at Littlebath to live the life of a lady of fortune? She told herself that it was so, and that it would be better for her to be a hard-working, dependent woman, doing some tedious duty day by day, than to live a life of ease which prompted her to longings for things unfitted to her.

She had brought a little writing-desk with her that she had carried from Arundel Street to Littlebath, and this she had with her in the sick man's bedroom. Sitting there through the long hours of night, she would open this and read over and over again those remnants of the rhymes written in her early days which she had kept when she made her great bonfire. There had been quires of such verses, but she had destroyed all but a few leaves before she started for Littlebath. What were left, and were now read, were very sweet to her, and yet she knew that they were wrong and meaningless. What business had such a one as she to talk of the sphere's tune and the silvery moon, of bright stars shining and hearts repining? She would not for worlds have allowed any one to know what a fool she had been—either Mrs. Tom, or John Ball, or Mr. Maguire, or Miss Todd. She would have been covered with confusion if her rhymes had fallen into the hands of any one of them.

And yet she loved them well, as a mother loves her only idiot child. They were her expressions of the romance and poetry that had been in her; and though the expressions doubtless were poor, the romance and poetry of her heart had been high and noble. How wrong the world is in connecting so closely as it does the capacity for feeling and the capacity for expression,—in thinking that capacity for the one implies capacity for the other, or incapacity for the one incapacity also for the other; in confusing the technical art of the man who sings with the unselfish tenderness of the man who feels! But the world does so connect them; and, consequently, those who express themselves badly are ashamed of their feelings.

She read her poor lines again and again, throwing herself back into the days and thoughts of former periods, and telling herself that it was all over. She had thought of encouraging love, and love had come to her in the shape of Mr. Maguire, a very strict evangelical clergyman, without a cure or an income, somewhat in debt, and with, oh! such an eye! She tore the papers, very gently, into the smallest fragments. She tore them again and again, swearing to herself as she did so that there should be an end of all that; and, as there was no fire at hand, she replaced the pieces in her desk. During this ceremony of the tearing she devoted herself to the duties of a single life, to the drudgeries of ordinary utility, to such works as those she was now doing. As to any society, wicked or religious,—wicked after the manner of Miss Todd, or religious after the manner of St Stumfolda,—it should come or not, as circumstances might direct. She would go no more in search of it. Such were the resolves of a certain night, during which the ceremony of the tearing took place.

It came to pass at this time that Mr. Rubb, junior, visited his dying partner almost daily, and was always left alone with him for some time. When these visits were made Miss Mackenzie would descend to the room in which her sister-in-law was sitting, and there would be some conversation between them about Mr. Rubb and his affairs. Much as these two women disliked each other, there had necessarily arisen between them a certain amount of confidence. Two persons who are much thrown together, to the exclusion of other society, will tell each other their thoughts, even though there be no love between them.

"What is he saying to him all these times when he is with him?" said Mrs. Tom one morning, when Miss Mackenzie had come down on the appearance of Mr. Rubb in the sick room.

"He is talking about the business, I suppose."

"What good can that do? Tom can't say anything about that, as to how it should be done. He thinks a great deal about Sam Rubb; but it's more than I do."

"They must necessarily be in each other's confidence, I should say."

"He's not in my confidence. My belief is he's been a deal too clever for Tom; and that he'll turn out to be too clever—for me, and—my poor orphans." Upon which Mrs. Tom put her handkerchief up to her eyes. "There; he's coming down," continued the wife. "Do you go up now, and make Tom tell you what it is that Sam Rubb has been saying to him."

Margaret Mackenzie did go up as she heard Mr. Rubb close the front door; but she had no such purpose as that with which her sister-in-law had striven to inspire her. She had no wish to make the sick man tell her anything that he did not wish to tell. In considering the matter within her own breast, she owned to herself that she did not expect much from the Rubbs in aid of the wants of her nephews and nieces; but what would be the use of troubling a dying man about that? She had agreed with herself to believe that the oilcloth business was a bad affair, and that it would be well to hope for nothing from it. That her brother to the last should harass himself about the business was only natural; but there could be no reason why she should harass him on the same subject. She had recognised the fact that his widow and children must be supported by her; and had she now been told that the oilcloth factory had been absolutely abandoned as being worth nothing, it would not have caused her much disappointment. She thought a great deal more of the railway company that was going to buy her property under such favourable circumstances.

She was, therefore, much surprised when her brother began about the business as soon as she had seated herself. I do not know that the reader need be delayed with any of the details that he gave her, or with the contents of the papers which he showed her. She, however, found herself compelled to go into the matter, and compelled also to make an endeavour to understand it. It seemed that everything hung upon Samuel Rubb, junior, except the fact that Samuel Rubb's father, who now never went near the place, got more than half the net profits; and the further fact, that the whole thing would come to an end if this payment to old Rubb were stopped.

"Tom," said she, in the middle of it all, when her head was aching with figures, "if it will comfort you, and enable you to put all these things away, you may know that I will divide everything I have with Sarah."

He assured her that her kindness did comfort him; but he hoped better than that; he still thought that something better might be arranged if she would only go on with her task. So she went on painfully toiling through figures.

"Sam drew them up on purpose for you, yesterday afternoon," said he.

"Who did it?" she asked.

"Samuel Rubb."

He then went on to declare that she might accept all Samuel Rubb's figures as correct.

She was quite willing to accept them, and she strove hard to understand them. It certainly did seem to her that when her money was borrowed somebody must have known that the promised security would not be forthcoming; but perhaps that somebody was old Rubb, whom, as she did not know him, she was quite ready to regard as the villain in the play that was being acted. Her own money, too, was a thing of the past. That fault, if fault there had been, was condoned; and she was angry with herself in that she now thought of it again.

"And now," said her brother, as soon as she had put the papers back, and declared that she understood them. "Now I have something to say to you which I hope you will hear without being angry." He raised himself on his bed as he said this, doing so with difficulty and pain, and turning his face upon her so that he could look into her eyes. "If I didn't know that I was dying I don't think that I could say it to you."

"Say what, Tom?"

She thought of what most terrible thing it might be possible that he should have to communicate. Could it be that he had got hold, or that Rubb and Mackenzie had got hold, of all her fortune, and turned it into unprofitable oilcloth? Could they in any way have made her responsible for their engagements? She wished to trust them; she tried to avoid suspicion; but she feared that things were amiss.

"Samuel Rubb and I have been talking of it, and he thinks it had better come from me," said her brother.

"What had better come?" she asked.

"It is his proposition, Margaret." Then she knew all about it, and felt great relief. Then she knew all about it, and let him go on till he had spoken his speech.

"God knows how far he may be indulging a false hope, or deceiving himself altogether; but he thinks it possible that you might—might become fond of him. There, Margaret, that's the long and the short of it. And when I told him that he had better say that himself, he declared that you would not bring yourself to listen to him while I am lying here dying."

"Of course I would not."

"But, look here, Margaret; I know you would do much to comfort me in my last moments."

"Indeed, I would, Tom."

"I wouldn't ask you to marry a man you didn't like,—not even if it were to do the children a service; but if that can be got

over, the other feeling should not restrain you when it would be
the greatest possible comfort to me."

"But how could it serve you, Tom?"

"If that could be arranged, Rubb would give up to Sarah
during his father's life all the proceeds of the business, after
paying the old man. And when he dies, and he is very old now,
the five hundred a-year would be continued to her. Think what
that would be, Margaret."

"But, Tom, she shall have what will make her
comfortable without waiting for any old man's death. It shall be
quite half of my income. If that is not enough it shall be more.
Will not that do for her?"

Then her brother strove to explain as best he could that
the mere money was not all he wanted. If his sister did not like
this man, if she had no wish to become a married woman, of
course, he said, the plan must fall to the ground. But if there was
anything in Mr. Rubb's belief that she was not altogether
indifferent to him, if such an arrangement could be made
palatable to her, then he would be able to think that he, by the
work of his life, had left something behind him to his wife and
family.

"And Sarah would be more comfortable," he pleaded.
"Of course, she is grateful to you, as I am, and as we all are. But
given bread is bitter bread, and if she could think it came to her,
of her own right—"

He said ever so much more, but that ever so much more
was quite unnecessary. His sister understood the whole matter. It
was desirable that she, by her fortune, should enable the widow
and orphans of her brother to live in comfort; but it was not
desirable that this dependence on her should be plainly
recognised. She did not, however, feel herself to be angry or
hurt. It would, no doubt, be better for the family that they should
draw their income in an apparently independent way from their
late father's business than that they should owe their support to
the charity of an aunt. But then, how about herself? A month or

two ago, before the Maguire feature in her career had displayed itself so strongly, an overture from Mr. Rubb might probably not have been received with disfavour. But now, while she was as it were half engaged to another man, she could not entertain such a proposition. Her womanly feeling revolted from it. No doubt she intended to refuse Mr. Maguire. No doubt she had made up her mind to that absolutely, during the ceremony of tearing up her verses. And she had never had much love for Mr. Maguire, and had felt some—almost some, for Mr. Rubb. In either case she was sure that, had she married the man,—the one man or the other,—she would instantly have become devoted to him. And I, who chronicle her deeds and endeavour to chronicle her thoughts, feel equally sure that it would have been so. There was something harsh in it, that Mr. Maguire's offer to her should, though never accepted, debar her from the possibility of marrying Mr. Rubb, and thus settling all the affairs of her family in a way that would have been satisfactory to them and not altogether unsatisfactory to her; but she was aware that it did so. She felt that it was so, and then threw herself back for consolation upon the security which would still be hers, and the want of security which must attach itself to a marriage with Mr. Rubb. He might make ducks, and drakes, and oilcloth of it all; and then there would be nothing left for her, for her sister-in-law, or for the children.

"May I tell him to speak to yourself?" her brother asked, while she was thinking of all this.

"No, Tom; it would do no good."

"You do not fancy him, then."

"I do not know about fancying; but I think it will be better for me to remain as I am. I would do anything for you and Sarah, almost anything; but I cannot do that."

"Then I will say nothing further."

"Don't ask me to do that."

And he did not ask her again, but turned his face from her and thought of the bitterness of his death-bed.

That evening, when she went down to tea, she met Samuel Rubb standing at the drawing-room door.

"There is no one here," he said; "will you mind coming in? Has your brother spoken to you?"

She had followed him into the room, and he had closed the door as he asked the question.

"Yes, he has spoken to me."

She could see that the man was trembling with anxiety and eagerness, and she almost loved him that he was anxious and eager. Mr. Maguire, when he had come a wooing, had not done it badly altogether, but there had not been so much reality as there was about Sam Rubb while he stood there shaking, and fearing, and hoping.

"Well," said he, "may I hope—may I think it will be so? may I ask you to be mine?"

He was handsome in her eyes, though perhaps, delicate reader, he would not have been handsome in yours. She knew that he was not a gentleman; but what did that matter? Neither was her sister-in-law Sarah a lady. There was not much in that house in Gower Street that was after the manner of gentlemen and ladies. She was ready to throw all that to the dogs, and would have done so but for Mr. Maguire. She felt that she would like to have allowed herself to love him in spite of the tearing of the verses. She felt this, and was very angry with Mr. Maguire. But the facts were stern, and there was no hope for her.

"Mr. Rubb," she said, "there can be nothing of that kind."

"Can't there really, now?" said he.

She assured him in her strongest language, that there could be nothing of that kind, and then went down to the dining-room.

He did not venture to follow her, but made his way out of the house without seeing anyone else.

Another fortnight went by, and then, towards the close of September, came the end of all things in this world for poor Tom

Mackenzie. He died in the middle of the night in his wife's arms, while his sister stood by holding both their hands. Since the day on which he had endeavoured to arrange a match between his partner and his sister he had spoken no word of business, at any rate to the latter, and things now stood on that footing which she had then attempted to give them. We all know how silent on such matters are the voices of all in the bereft household, from the hour of death till that other hour in which the body is consigned to its kindred dust. Women make mourning, and men creep about listlessly, but during those few sad days there may be no talk about money. So it was in Gower Street. The widow, no doubt, thought much of her bitter state of dependence, thought something, perhaps, of the chance there might be that her husband's sister would be less good than her word, now that he was gone—meditated with what amount of submission she must accept the generosity of the woman she had always hated; but she was still mistress of that house till the undertakers had done their work; and till that work had been done, she said little of her future plans.

"I'd earn my bread, if I knew how," she began, putting her handkerchief up to her eyes, on the afternoon of the very day on which he was buried.

"There will be no occasion for that, Sarah," said Miss Mackenzie, "there will be enough for us all."

"But I would if I knew how. I wouldn't mind what I did; I'd scour floors rather than be dependent, I've that spirit in me; and I've worked, and moiled, and toiled with those children; so I have."

Miss Mackenzie then told her that she had solemnly promised her brother to divide her income with his widow, and informed her that she intended to see Mr. Slow, the lawyer, on the following day, with reference to the doing of this.

"If there is anything from the factory, that can be divided too," said Miss Mackenzie.

"But there won't. The Rubbs will take all that; of course they will. And Tom put into it near upon ten thousand pounds!"

Then she began to cry again, but soon interrupted her tears to ask what was to become of Susanna. Susanna, who was by, looked anxiously up into her aunt's eyes.

"Susanna and I," said the aunt, "have thrown in our lot together, and we mean to remain so; don't we, dear?"

"If mamma will let me."

"I'm sure it's very good of you to take one off my hands," said the mother, "for even one will be felt."

Then came a note to Miss Mackenzie from Lady Ball, asking her to spend a few days at the Cedars before she returned to Littlebath,—that is, if she did return,—and she consented to do this. While she was there Mr. Slow could prepare the necessary arrangements for the division of the property, and she could then make up her mind as to the manner and whereabouts of her future life. She was all at sea again, and knew not how to choose. If she were a Romanist, she would go into a convent; but Protestant convents she thought were bad, and peculiarly unfitted for the followers of Mr. Stumfold. She had nothing to bind her to any spot, and something to drive her from every spot of which she knew anything.

Before she went to the Cedars Mr. Rubb came to Gower Street and bade her farewell.

"I had allowed myself to hope, Miss Mackenzie," said he, "I had, indeed; I suppose I was very foolish."

"I don't know as to being foolish, Mr. Rubb, unless it was in caring about such a person as me."

"I do care for you, very much; but I suppose I was wrong to think you would put up with such as I am. Only I did think that perhaps, seeing that we had been partners with your brother so long—All the same, I know that the Mackenzies are different from the Rubbs."

"That has nothing to do with it; nothing in the least."

"Hasn't it now? Then, perhaps, Miss Mackenzie, at some future time—"

Miss Mackenzie was obliged to tell him that there could not possibly be any other answer given to him at any future time than that which she gave him now. He suggested that perhaps he might be allowed to try again when the first month or two of her grief for her brother should be over; but she assured him that it would be useless. At the moment of her conference with him, she did this with all her energy; and then, as soon as she was alone, she asked herself why she had been so energetical. After all, marriage was an excellent state in which to live. The romance was doubtless foolish and wrong, and the tearing of the papers had been discreet, yet there could be no good reason why she should turn her back upon sober wedlock. Nevertheless, in all her speech to Mr. Rubb she did do so. There was something in her position as connected with Mr. Maguire which made her feel that it would be indelicate to entertain another suitor before that gentleman had received a final answer.

As she went away from Gower Street to the Cedars she thought of this very sadly, and told herself that she had been like the ass who starved between two bundles of hay, or as the boy who had fallen between two stools.

Chapter XVI

Lady Ball's Grievance

Miss Mackenzie, before she left Gower Street, was forced to make some arrangements as to her affairs at Littlebath, and these were ultimately settled in a manner that was not altogether palatable to her. Mr. Rubb was again sent down, having Susanna in his charge, and he was empowered to settle with Miss Mackenzie's landlady and give up the lodgings. There was much that was disagreeable in this. Miss Mackenzie having just rejected Mr. Rubb's suit, did not feel quite comfortable in giving him a commission to see all her stockings and petticoats packed up and brought away from the lodgings. Indeed, she could give him no commission of the kind, but intimated her intention of writing to the lodging-house keeper. He, however, was profuse in his assurances that nothing should be left behind, and if Miss Mackenzie would tell him anything of the way in which the things ought to be packed, he would be so happy to attend to her! To him Miss Mackenzie would give no such instructions, but, doubtless, she gave many to Susanna.

As to Susanna, it was settled that she should remain as a boarder at the Littlebath school, at any rate for the next half-year. After that there might be great doubt whether her aunt could bear the expense of maintaining her in such a position.

Miss Mackenzie had reconciled herself to going to the Cedars because she would thus have an opportunity of seeing her lawyer and arranging about her property, whereas had she been down at Littlebath there would have been a difficulty. And she wanted some one whom she could trust to act for her, some one besides the lawyer, and she thought that she could trust her cousin, John Ball. As to getting away from all her suitors that was impossible. Had she gone to Littlebath there was one there; had she remained with her sister-in-law, she would have been always near another; and, on going to the Cedars, she would meet the third. But she could not on that account absolutely isolate herself from everybody that she knew in the world. And, perhaps, she was getting somewhat used to her suitors, and less liable than she had been to any fear that they could force her into action against her own consent. So she went to the Cedars, and, on arriving there, received from her uncle and aunt but a moderate amount of condolence as to the death of her brother.

Her first and second days in her aunt's house were very quiet. Nothing was said of John's former desires, and nothing about her own money or her brother's family. On the morning of the third day she told her cousin that she would, on the next morning, accompany him to town if he would allow her. "I am going to Mr. Slow's," said she, "and perhaps you could go with me." To this he assented willingly, and then, after a pause, surmised that her visit must probably have reference to the sale of her houses to the railway company. "Partly to that," she said, "but it chiefly concerns arrangements for my brother's family."

To this John Ball said nothing, nor did Lady Ball, who was present, then speak. But Miss Mackenzie could see that her aunt looked at her cousin, opening her eyes, and expressing concern. John Ball himself allowed no change to come upon his face, but went on deliberately with his bread and butter. "I shall be very happy to go with you," he said, "and will either come and call for you when you have done, or stay with you while you are there, just as you like."

"I particularly want you to stay with me," said she, "and as we go up to town I will tell you all about it."

She observed that before her cousin left the house on that day, his mother got hold of him and was alone with him for nearly half an hour. After that, Lady Ball was alone with Sir John, in his own room, for another half hour. The old baronet had become older, of course, and much weaker, since his niece had last been at the Cedars, and was now seldom seen about the house till the afternoon.

Of all the institutions at the Cedars that of the carriage was the most important. Miss Mackenzie found that the carriage arrangement had been fixed upon a new and more settled basis since her last visit. Then it used to go out perhaps as often as three times a week. But there did not appear to be any fixed rule. Like other carriages, it did, to a certain degree, come when it was wanted. But now there was, as I have said, a settled basis. The carriage came to the door on Tuesdays, Thursdays, and Saturdays, exactly at two o'clock, and Sir John with Lady Ball were driven about till four.

On the first Tuesday of her visit Miss Mackenzie had gone with her uncle and aunt, and even she had found the pace to be very slow, and the whole affair to be very dull. Her uncle had once enlivened the thing by asking her whether she had found any lovers since she went to Littlebath, and this question had perplexed her very much. She could not say that she had found none, and as she was not prepared to acknowledge that she had found any, she could only sit still and blush.

"Women have plenty of lovers when they have plenty of money," said the baronet.

"I don't believe that Margaret thinks of anything of the kind," said Lady Ball.

After that Margaret determined to have as little to do with the carriage as possible, and on that evening she learned from her cousin that the horses had been sold to the man who farmed the land, and were hired every other day for two hours' work.

It was on the Thursday morning that Miss Mackenzie had spoken of going into town on the morrow, and on that day when her aunt asked her about the driving, she declined.

"I hope that nothing your uncle said on Tuesday annoyed you?"

"Oh dear, no; but if you don't mind it, I'd rather stay at home."

"Of course you shall if you like it," said her aunt; "and by-the-by, as I want to speak to you, and as we might not find time after coming home, if you don't mind it I'll do it now."

Of course Margaret said that she did not mind it, though in truth she did mind it, and was afraid of her aunt.

"Well then, Margaret, look here. I want to know something about your brother's affairs. From what I have heard, I fear they were not very good."

"They were very bad, aunt,—very bad indeed."

"Dear, dear; you don't say so. Sir John always feared that it would be so when Thomas Mackenzie mixed himself up with those Rubbs. And there has gone half of Jonathan Ball's money,—money which Sir John made! Well, well!"

Miss Mackenzie had nothing to say to this; and as she had nothing to say to it she sat silent, making no attempt at any words.

"It does seem hard; don't it, my dear?"

"It wouldn't make any difference to anybody now—to my uncle, I mean, or to John, if the money was not gone."

"That's quite true; quite true; only it does seem to be a pity. However, that half of Jonathan's money which you have got, is not lost, and there's some comfort in that."

Miss Mackenzie was not called upon to make any answer to this; for although she had lost a large sum of money by lending it to her brother, nevertheless she was still possessed of a larger sum of money than that which her brother Walter had received from Jonathan Ball.

"And what are they going to do, my dear—the children, I mean, and the widow? I suppose there'll be something for them out of the business?"

"I don't think there'll be anything, aunt. As far as I can understand there will be nothing certain. They may probably get a hundred and twenty-five pounds a-year." This she named, as being the interest of the money she had lent—or given.

"A hundred and twenty-five pounds a-year. That isn't much, but it will keep them from absolute want."

"Would it, aunt?"

"Oh, yes; at least, I suppose so. I hope she's a good manager. She ought to be, for she's a very disagreeable woman. You told me that yourself, you know."

Then Miss Mackenzie, having considered for one moment, resolved to make a clean breast of it all, and this she did with the fewest possible words.

"I'm going to divide what I've got with them, and I hope it will make them comfortable."

"What!" exclaimed her aunt.

"I'm going to give Sarah half what I've got, for her and her children. I shall have enough to live on left."

"Margaret, you don't mean it?"

"Not mean it? why not, aunt? You would not have me let them starve. Besides, I promised my brother when he was dying."

"Then I must say he was very wrong, very wicked, I may say, to exact any such promise from you; and no such promise is binding. If you ask Sir John, or your lawyer, they will tell you so. What! exact a promise from you to the amount of half your income. It was very wrong."

"But, aunt, I should do the same if I had made no promise."

"No, you wouldn't, my dear. Your friends wouldn't let you. And indeed your friends must prevent it now. They will not hear of such a sacrifice being made."

"But, aunt—"

"Well, my dear."

"It's my own, you know." And Margaret, as she said this, plucked up her courage, and looked her aunt full in the face.

"Yes, it is your own, by law; but I don't suppose, my dear, that you are of that disposition or that character that you'd wish to set all the world at defiance, and make everybody belonging to you feel that you had disgraced yourself."

"Disgraced myself by relieving my brother's family!"

"Disgraced yourself by giving to that woman money that has come to you as your fortune has come. Think of it, where it came from!"

"It came to me from my brother Walter."

"And where did he get it? And who made it? And don't you know that your brother Tom had his share of it, and wasted it all? Did it not all come from the Balls? And yet you think so little of that, that you are going to let that woman rob you of it— rob you and my grandchildren; for that, I tell you, is the way in which the world will look at it. Perhaps you don't know it, but all that property was as good as given to John at one time. Who was it first took you by the hand when you were left all alone in Arundel Street? Oh, Margaret, don't go and be such an ungrateful, foolish creature!"

Margaret waited for a moment, and then she answered—

"There's nobody so near to me as my own brother's children."

"As to that, Margaret, there isn't much difference in nearness between your uncle and your nephews and nieces. But there's a right and a wrong in these things, and when money is concerned, people are not justified in indulging their fancies. Everything here has been told to you. You know how John is situated with his children. And after what there has been between you and him, and after what there still might be if you would have it so, I own that I am astonished—fairly astonished. Indeed, my dear, I can only look on it as simple weakness on your part. It was but the other day that you told me you had done all that you thought necessary by your brother in taking Susanna."

"But that was when he was alive, and I thought he was doing well."

"The fact is, you have been there and they've talked you over. It can't be that you love children that you never saw till the other day; and as for the woman, you always hated her."

"Whether I love her or hate her has nothing to do with it."

"Margaret, will you promise me this, that you will see Mr. Slow and talk to him about it before you do anything?"

"I must see Mr. Slow before I can do anything; but whatever he says, I shall do it all the same."

"Will you speak to your uncle?"

"I had rather not."

"You are afraid to tell him of this; but of course he must be told. Will you speak to John?"

"Certainly; I meant to do so going to town to-morrow."

"And if he tells you you are wrong—"

"Aunt, I know I am not wrong. It is nonsense to say that I am wrong in—"

"That's disrespectful, Margaret!"

"I don't want to be disrespectful, aunt; but in such a case as this I know that I have a right to do what I like with my own money. If I was going to give it away to any other friend, if I was going to marry, or anything like that,"—she blushed at the remembrance of the iniquities she had half intended as she said this—"then there might be some reason for you to scold me; but with a brother and a brother's family it can't be wrong. If you had a brother, and had been with him when he was dying, and he had left his wife and children looking to you, you would have done the same."

Upon this Lady Ball got up from her chair and walked to the door. Margaret had been more impetuous and had answered her with much more confidence than she had expected. She was determined now to say one more word, but so to say it that it should not be answered—to strike one more blow, but so to strike it that it should not be returned.

"Margaret," she said, as she stood with the door open in her hands, "if you will reflect where the money came from, your conscience will tell you without much difficulty where it should go to. And when you think of your brother's children, whom this time last year you had hardly seen, think also of John Ball's children, who have welcomed you into this house as their dearest relative. In one sense, certainly, the money is yours, Margaret; but in another sense, and that the highest sense, it is not yours to do what you please with it."

Then Lady Ball shut the door rather loudly, and sailed away along the hall. When the passages were clear, Miss Mackenzie made her way up into her own room, and saw none of the family till she came down just before dinner.

She sat for a long time in the chair by her bed-side thinking of her position. Was it true after all that she was bound by a sense of justice to give any of her money to the Balls? It was true that in one sense it had been taken from them, but she had had nothing to do with the taking. If her brother Walter had married and had children, then the Balls would have not expected the money back again. It was ever so many years,—five-and-twenty years, and more since the legacy had been made by Jonathan Ball to her brother, and it seemed to her that her aunt had no common sense on her side in the argument. Was it possible that she should allow her own nephews and nieces to starve while she was rich? She had, moreover, made a promise,—a promise to one who was now dead, and there was a solemnity in that which carried everything else before it. Even though the thing might be unjust, still she must do it.

But she was to give only half her fortune to her brother's family; there would still be the half left for herself, for herself or for these Balls if they wanted it so sorely. She was beginning to hate her money. It had brought to her nothing but tribulation and disappointment. Had Walter left her a hundred a year, she would, not having then dreamed of higher things, have been amply content. Would it not be better that she should take for herself some modest competence, something on which she might live without trouble to her relatives, without trouble to her friends she had first said,—but as she did so she told herself with scorn that friends she had none,—and then let the Balls have what was left her after she had kept her promise to her brother? Anything would be better than such persecution as that to which her aunt had subjected her.

At last she made up her mind to speak of it all openly to her cousin. She had an idea that in such matters men were more trustworthy than women, and perhaps less greedy. Her cousin would, she thought, be more just to her than her aunt had been. That her aunt had been very unjust,—cruel and unjust,—she felt assured.

She came down to dinner, and she could see by the manner of them all that the matter had been discussed since John Ball's return from London. Jack, the eldest son, was not at home, and the three girls who came next to Jack dined with their father and grandfather. To them Margaret endeavoured to talk easily, but she failed. They had never been favourites with her as Jack was, and, on this occasion, she could get very little from them that was satisfactory to her. John Ball was courteous to her, but he was very silent throughout the whole evening. Her aunt showed her displeasure by not speaking to her, or speaking barely with a word. Her uncle, of whose voice she was always in fear, seemed to be more cross, and when he did speak, more sarcastic than ever. He asked her whether she intended to go back to Littlebath.

"I think not," said she.

"Then that has been a failure, I suppose," said the old man.

"Everything is a failure, I think," said she, with tears in her eyes.

This was in the drawing-room, and immediately her cousin John came and sat by her. He came and sat there, as though he had intended to speak to her; but he went away again in a minute or two without having uttered a word. Things went on in the same way till they moved off to bed, and then the formal adieus for the night were made with a coldness that amounted, on the part of Lady Ball, almost to inhospitality.

"Good-night, Margaret," she said, as she just put out the tip of her finger.

"Good-night, my dear," said Sir John. "I don't know what's the matter with you, but you look as though you'd been doing something that you were ashamed of."

Lady Ball was altogether injudicious in her treatment of her niece. As to Sir John, it made probably very little difference. Miss Mackenzie had perceived, when she first came to the Cedars, that he was a cross old man, and that he had to be endured as such by any one who chose to go into that house. But she had depended on Lady Ball for kindness of manner, and had been tempted to repeat her visits to the house because her aunt had, after her fashion, been gracious to her. But now there was rising in her breast a feeling that she had better leave the Cedars as soon as she could shake the dust off her feet, and see nothing more of the Balls. Even the Rubb connection seemed to her to be better than the Ball connection, and less exaggerated in its greediness. Were it not for her cousin John, she would have resolved to go on the morrow. She would have faced the indignation of her aunt, and the cutting taunts of her uncle, and have taken herself off at once to some lodging in London. But

John Ball had meant to be kind to her when he came and sat close to her on the sofa, and her soft heart relented towards him.

Lady Ball had in truth mistaken her niece's character. She had found her to be unobtrusive, gentle, and unselfish; and had conceived that she must therefore be weak and compliant. As to many things she was compliant, and as to some things she was weak; but there was in her composition a power of resistance and self-sustenance on which Lady Ball had not counted. When conscious of absolute ill-usage, she could fight well, and would not bow her neck to any Mrs. Stumfold or to any Lady Ball.

Chapter XVII

Mr. Slow's Chambers

She came down late to breakfast on the following morning, not being present at prayers, and when she came down she wore a bonnet.

"I got myself ready, John, for fear I should keep you waiting."

Her aunt spoke to her somewhat more graciously than on the preceding evening, and accepted her apology for being late.

Just as she was about to start Lady Ball took her apart and spoke one word to her.

"No one can tell you better what you ought to do than your cousin John; but pray remember that he is far too generous to say a word for himself."

Margaret made no answer, and then she and her cousin started on foot across the grounds to the station. The distance was nearly a mile, and during the walk no word was said between them about the money. They got into the train that was to take them up to London, and sat opposite to each other. It happened that there was no passenger in either of the seats next to him or her, so that there was ample opportunity for them to hold a private conversation; but Mr. Ball said nothing to her, and she, not knowing how to begin, said nothing to him. In this way they reached the London station at Waterloo Bridge, and then he asked her what she proposed to do next.

"Shall we go to Mr. Slow's at once?" she asked.

To this he assented, and at her proposition they agreed to walk to the lawyer's chambers. These were on the north side of Lincoln's Inn Fields, near the Turnstile, and Mr. Ball remarked that the distance was again not much above a mile. So they crossed the Strand together, and made their way by narrow streets into Drury Lane, and then under a certain archway into Lincoln's Inn Fields. To Miss Mackenzie, who felt that something ought to be said, the distance and time occupied seemed to be very short.

"Why, this is Lincoln's Inn Fields!" she exclaimed, as she came out upon the west side.

"Yes; this is Lincoln's Inn Fields, and Mr. Slow's chambers are over there."

She knew very well where Mr. Slow's chambers were situated, but she paused on the pavement, not wishing to go thither quite at once.

"John," she said, "I thought that perhaps we might have talked over all this before we saw Mr. Slow."

"Talked over all what?"

"About the money that I want to give to my brother's family. Did not my aunt tell you of it?"

"Yes; she told me that you and she had differed."

"And she told you what about?"

"Yes," said he, slowly; "she told me what about."

"And what ought I to do, John?"

As she asked the question she caught hold of the lappet of his coat, and looked up into his face as though supplicating him to give her the advantage of all his discretion and all his honesty.

They were still standing on the pavement, where the street comes out from under the archway. She was gazing into his face, and he was looking away from her, over towards the inner railings of the square, with heavy brow and dull eye and motionless face. She was very eager, and he seemed to be simply patient, but nevertheless he was working hard with his thoughts, striving to determine how best he might answer her. His mother had told him that he might model this woman to his will, and had repeated to him that story which he had heard so often of the wrong that had been done to him by his uncle Jonathan. It may be said that there was no need for such repetition, as John Ball had himself always thought quite enough of that injury. He had thought of it for the last twenty years, almost hourly, till it was graven upon his very soul. He had been a ruined, wretched, moody man, because of his uncle Jonathan's will. There was no need, one would have said, to have stirred him on that subject. But his mother, on this morning, in the ten minutes before prayer-time, had told him of it all again, and had told him also that the last vestige of his uncle's money would now disappear from him unless he interfered to save it.

"On this very day it must be saved; and she will do anything you tell her," said his mother. "She regards you more than anyone else. If you were to ask her again now, I believe she would accept you this very day. At any rate, do not let those people have the money."

And yet he had not spoken to Margaret on the subject during the journey, and would now have taken her to the lawyer's chambers without a word, had she not interrupted him and stopped him.

Nevertheless he had been thinking of his uncle, and his uncle's will, and his uncle's money, throughout the morning. He was thinking of it at that moment when she stopped him— thinking how hard it all was, how cruel that those people in the New Road should have had and spent half his uncle's fortune, and that now the remainder, which at one time had seemed to be near the reach of his own children, should also go to atone for the negligence and fraud of those wretched Rubbs.

We all know with how strong a bias we regard our own side of any question, and he regarded his side in this question with a very strong bias. Nevertheless he had refrained from a word, and would have refrained, had she not stopped him.

When she took hold of him by the coat, he looked for a moment into her face, and thought that in its trouble it was very sweet. She leaned somewhat against him as she spoke, and he wished that she would lean against him altogether. There was about her a quiet power of endurance, and at the same time a comeliness and a womanly softness which seemed to fit her altogether for his wants and wishes. As he looked with his dull face across into the square, no physiognomist would have declared of him that at that moment he was suffering from love, or thinking of a woman that was dear to him. But it was so with him, and the physiognomist, had one been there, would have been wrong. She had now asked him a question, which he was bound to answer in some way:—"What ought I to do, John?"

He turned slowly round and walked with her, away from their destination, round by the south side of the square, and then up along the blank wall on the east side, nearly to the passage into Holborn, and back again all round the enclosed space. She, while she was speaking to him and listening to him, hardly remembered where she was or whither she was going.

"I thought," said he, in answer to her question, "that you intended to ask Mr. Slow's advice?"

"I didn't mean to do more than tell him what should be done. He is not a friend, you know, John."

"It's customary to ask lawyers their advice on such subjects."

"I'd rather have yours, John. But, in truth, what I want you to say is, that I am right in doing this,—right in keeping my promise to my brother, and providing for his children."

"Like most people, Margaret, you want to be advised to follow your own counsel."

"God knows that I want to do right, John. I want to do nothing else, John, but what's right. As to this money, I care but little for it for myself."

"It is your own, and you have a right to enjoy it."

"I don't know much about enjoyment. As to enjoyment, it seems to me to be pretty much the same whether a person is rich or poor. I always used to hear that money brought care, and I'm sure I've found it so since I had any."

"You've got no children, Margaret."

"No; but there are all those orphans. Am I not bound to look upon them as mine, now that he has gone? If they don't depend on me, whom are they to depend on?"

"If your mind is made up, Margaret, I have nothing to say against it. You know what my wishes are. They are just the same now as when you were last with us. It isn't only for the money I say this, though, of course, that must go a long way with a man circumstanced as I am; but, Margaret, I love you dearly, and if you can make up your mind to be my wife, I would do my best to make you happy."

"I hadn't meant you to talk in that way, John," said Margaret.

But she was not much flurried. She was now so used to these overtures that they did not come to her as much out of the common way. And she gave herself none of that personal credit which women are apt to take to themselves when they find they are often sought in marriage. She looked upon her lovers as so many men to whom her income would be convenient, and felt herself to be almost under an obligation to them for their willingness to put up with the incumbrance which was attached to it.

"But it's the only way I can talk when you ask me about this," said he. Then he paused for a moment before he added, "How much is it you wish to give to your brother's widow?"

"Half what I've got left."

"Got left! You haven't lost any of your money have you, Margaret?"

Then she explained to him the facts as to the loan, and took care to explain to him also, very fully, the compensatory fact of the purchase by the railway company. "And my promise to him was made after I had lent it, you know," she urged.

"I do think it ought to be deducted; I do indeed," he said. "I am not speaking on my own behalf now, as for the sake of my children, but simply as a man of business. As for myself, though I do think I have been hardly used in the matter of my uncle's money, I'll try to forget it. I'll try at any rate to do without it. When I first knew you, and found—found that I liked you so much, I own that I did have hopes. But if it must be, there shall be an end of that. The children don't starve, I suppose."

"Oh, John!"

"As for me, I won't hanker after your money. But, for your own sake, Margaret—"

"There will be more than enough for me, you know; and, John—"

She was going to make him some promise; to tell him something of her intention towards his son, and to make some tender of assistance to himself; being now in that mind to live on the smallest possible pittance, of which I have before spoken, when he ceased speaking or listening, and hurried her on to the attorney's chambers.

"Do what you like with it. It is your own," said he. "And we shall do no good by talking about it any longer out here."

So at last they made their way up to Mr. Slow's rooms, on the first floor in the old house in Lincoln's Inn Fields, and were informed that that gentleman was at home. Would they be pleased to sit down in the waiting-room?

There is, I think, no sadder place in the world than the waiting-room attached to an attorney's chambers in London. In this instance it was a three-cornered room, which had got itself wedged in between the house which fronted to Lincoln's Inn

ANTHONY TROLLOPE

Fields, and some buildings in a narrow lane that ran at the back of the row. There was no carpet in it, and hardly any need of one, as the greater part of the floor was strewed with bundles of dusty papers. There was a window in it, which looked out from the point of the further angle against the wall of the opposite building. The dreariness of this aspect had been thought to be too much for the minds of those who waited, and therefore the bottom panes had been clouded, so that there was in fact no power of looking out at all. Over the fireplace there was a table of descents and relationship, showing how heirship went; and the table was very complicated, describing not only the heirship of ordinary real and personal property, but also explaining the wonderful difficulties of gavelkind, and other mysteriously traditional laws. But the table was as dirty as it was complicated, and the ordinary waiting reader could make nothing of it. There was a small table in the room, near the window, which was always covered with loose papers; but these loose papers were on this occasion again covered with sheets of parchment, and a pale-faced man, of about thirty, whose beard had never yet attained power to do more than sprout, was sitting at the table, and poring over the parchments. Round the room, on shelves, there was a variety of iron boxes, on which were written the names of Mr. Slow's clients,—of those clients whose property justified them in having special boxes of their own. But these boxes were there, it must be supposed, for temporary purposes,—purposes which might be described as almost permanently temporary,—for those boxes which were allowed to exist in absolute permanence of retirement, were kept in an iron room downstairs, the trap-door into which had yawned upon Miss Mackenzie as she was shown into the waiting-room. There was, however, one such box open, on the middle of the floor, and sundry of the parchments which had been taken from it were lying around it.

There were but two chairs in the room besides the one occupied by the man at the table, and these were taken by John

Ball and his cousin. She sat herself down, armed with patience, indifferent to the delay and indifferent to the dusty ugliness of everything around her, as women are on such occasions. He, thinking much of his time, and somewhat annoyed at being called upon to wait, sat with his chin resting on his umbrella between his legs, and as he did so he allowed his eyes to roam around among the names upon the boxes. There was nothing on any one of those up on the shelves that attracted him. There was the Marquis of B——, and Sir C. D——, and the Dowager Countess of E——. Seeing this, he speculated mildly whether Mr. Slow put forward the boxes of his aristocratic customers to show how well he was doing in the world. But presently his eye fell from the shelf and settled upon the box on the floor. There, on that box, he saw the name of Walter Mackenzie.

This did not astonish him, as he immediately said to himself that these papers were being searched with reference to the business on which his cousin was there that day; bur suddenly it occurred to him that Margaret had given him to understand that Mr. Slow did not expect her. He stepped over to her, therefore, one step over the papers, and asked her the question, whispering it into her ear.

"No," said she, "I had no appointment. I don't think he expects me."

He returned to his seat, and again sitting down with his chin on the top of his umbrella, surveyed the parchments that lay upon the ground. Upon one of them, that was not far from his feet, he read the outer endorsements written as such endorsements always are, in almost illegible old English letters—

"Jonathan Ball, to John Ball, junior—Deed of Gift."

But, after all, there was nothing more than a coincidence in this. Of course Mr. Slow would have in his possession all the papers appertaining to the transfer of Jonathan Ball's property to the Mackenzies; or, at any rate, such as referred to Walter's share of it. Indeed, Mr. Slow, at the time of Jonathan Ball's death, acted for the two brothers, and it was probable that all the papers would be with him. John Ball had known that there had been some intention on his uncle's part, before the quarrel between his father and his uncle, to make over to him, on his coming of age, a certain property in London, and he had been told that the money which the Mackenzies had inherited had ultimately come from this very property. His uncle had been an eccentric, quarrelsome man, prone to change his mind often, and not regardful of money as far as he himself was concerned. John Ball remembered to have heard that his uncle had intended him to become possessed of certain property in his own right the day that he became of age, and that this had all been changed because of the quarrel which had taken place between his uncle and his father. His father now never spoke of this, and for many years past had seldom mentioned it. But from his mother he had often heard of the special injury which he had undergone.

"His uncle," she had said, "had given it, and had taken it back again,—had taken it back that he might waste it on those Mackenzies."

All this he had heard very often, but he had never known anything of a deed of gift. Was it not singular, he thought, that the draft of such a deed should be lying at his foot at this moment.

He showed nothing of this in his face, and still sat there with his chin resting on his umbrella. But certainly stronger ideas than usual of the great wrongs which he had suffered did come into his head as he looked upon the paper at his feet. He began to wonder whether he would be justified in taking it up and inspecting it. But as he was thinking of this the pale-faced man rose from his chair, and after moving among the papers on the ground for an instant, selected this very document, and carried it with him to his table. Mr. Ball, as his eyes followed the parchment, watched the young man dust it and open it, and then having flattened it with his hand, glance over it till he came to a certain spot. The pale-faced clerk, accustomed to such documents, glanced over the ambages, the "whereases," the "aforesaids," the rich exuberance of "admors.," "exors.," and "assigns," till he deftly came to the pith of the matter, and then he began to make extracts, a date here and a date there. John Ball watched him all the time, till the door was opened, and old Mr. Slow himself appeared in the room.

He stepped across the papers to shake hands with his client, and then shook hands also with Mr. Ball, whom he knew. His eye glanced at once down to the box, and after that over towards the pale-faced clerk. Mr. Ball perceived that the attorney had joined in his own mind the operation that was going on with these special documents, and the presence of these two special visitors; and that he, in some measure, regretted the coincidence. There was something wrong, and John Ball began to consider whether the old lawyer could be an old scoundrel. Some lawyers, he knew, were desperate scoundrels. He said nothing, however; but, obeying Mr. Slow's invitation, followed him and his cousin into the sanctum sanctorum of the chambers.

"They didn't tell me you were here at first," said the lawyer, in a tone of vexation, "or I wouldn't have had you shown in there."

John Ball thought that this was, doubtless, true, and that very probably they might not have been put in among those papers had Mr. Slow known what was being done.

"The truth is," continued the lawyer, "the Duke of F——'s man of business was with me, and they did not like to interrupt me."

Mr. Slow was a grey-haired old man, nearer eighty than seventy, who, with the exception of a fortnight's holiday every year which he always spent at Margate, had attended those same chambers in Lincoln's Inn Fields daily for the last sixty years. He was a stout, thickset man, very leisurely in all his motions, who walked slowly, talked slowly, read slowly, wrote slowly, and thought slowly; but who, nevertheless, had the reputation of doing a great deal of business, and doing it very well. He had a partner in the business, almost as old as himself, named Bideawhile; and they who knew them both used to speculate which of the two was the most leisurely. It was, however, generally felt that, though Mr. Slow was the slowest in his speech, Mr. Bideawhile was the longest in getting anything said. Mr. Slow would often beguile his time with unnecessary remarks; but Mr. Bideawhile was so constant in beguiling his time, that men wondered how, in truth, he ever did anything at all. Of both of them it may be said that no men stood higher in their profession, and that Mr. Ball's suspicions, had they been known in the neighbourhood of Lincoln's Inn, would have been scouted as utterly baseless. And, for the comfort of my readers, let me assure them that they were utterly baseless. There might, perhaps, have been a little vanity about Mr. Slow as to the names of his aristocratic clients; but he was an honest, painstaking man, who had ever done his duty well by those who had employed him.

Is it not remarkable that the common repute which we all give to attorneys in the general is exactly opposite to that which every man gives to his own attorney in particular? Whom does anybody trust so implicitly as he trusts his own attorney? And yet is it not the case that the body of attorneys is supposed to be the most roguish body in existence?

The old man seemed now to be a little fretful, and said something more about his sorrow at their having been sent into that room.

"We are so crowded," he said, "that we hardly know how to stir ourselves."

Miss Mackenzie said it did not signify in the least. Mr. Ball said nothing, but seated himself with his chin again resting on his umbrella.

"I was so sorry to see in the papers an account of your brother's death," said Mr. Slow.

"Yes, Mr. Slow; he has gone, and left a wife and very large family."

"I hope they are provided for, Miss Mackenzie."

"No, indeed; they are not provided for at all. My brother had not been fortunate in business."

"And yet he went into it with a large capital,—with a large capital in such a business as that."

John Ball, with his chin on the umbrella, said nothing. He said nothing, but he winced as he thought whence the capital had come. And he thought, too, of those much-meaning words: "Jonathan Ball to John Ball, junior—Deed of gift."

"He had been unfortunate," said Miss Mackenzie, in an apologetic tone.

"And what will you do about your loan?" said Mr. Slow, looking over to John Ball when he asked the question, as though inquiring whether all Miss Mackenzie's affairs were to be talked over openly in the presence of that gentleman.

"That was a gift," said Miss Mackenzie.

"A deed of gift," thought John Ball to himself. "A deed of gift!"

"Oh, indeed! Then there's an end of that, I suppose," said Mr. Slow.

"Exactly so. I have been explaining to my cousin all about it. I hope the firm will be able to pay my sister-in-law the interest on it, but that does not seem sure."

"I am afraid I cannot help you there, Miss Mackenzie."

"Of course not. I was not thinking of it. But what I've come about is this." Then she told Mr. Slow the whole of her project with reference to her fortune; how, on his death-bed, she had promised to give half of all that she had to her brother's wife and family, and how she had come there to him, with her cousin, in order that he might put her in the way of keeping her promise.

Mr. Slow sat in silence and patiently heard her to the end. She, finding herself thus encouraged to speak, expatiated on the solemnity of her promise, and declared that she could not be comfortable till she had done all that she had undertaken to perform. "And I shall have quite enough for myself afterwards, Mr. Slow, quite enough."

Mr. Slow did not say a word till she had done, and even then he seemed to delay his speech. John Ball never raised his face from his umbrella, but sat looking at the lawyer, whom he still suspected of roguery. And if the lawyer were a rogue, what then about his cousin? It must not be supposed that he suspected her; but what would come of her, if the fortune she held were, in truth, not her own?

"I have told my cousin all about it," continued Margaret, "and I believe that he thinks I am doing right. At any rate, I would do nothing without his knowing it."

"I think she is giving her sister-in-law too much," said John Ball.

"I am only doing what I promised," urged Margaret.

"I think that the money which she lent to the firm should, at any rate, be deducted," said John Ball, speaking this with a kind of proviso to himself, that the words so spoken were intended to be taken as having any meaning only on the presumption that that document which he had seen in the other room should turn out to be wholly inoperative and inefficient at the present moment. In answer to these side-questions or corollary points as to the deduction or non-deduction of the loan, Mr. Slow answered not a word; but when there was silence between them, he did make answer as to the original proposition.

"Miss Mackenzie," he said, "I think you had better postpone doing anything in this matter for the present."

"Why postpone it?" said she.

"Your brother's death is very recent. It happened not above a fortnight since, I think."

"And I want to have this settled at once, so that there shall be no distress. What's the good of waiting?"

"Such things want thinking of, Miss Mackenzie."

"But I have thought of it. All I want now is to have it done."

A slight smile came across the puckered grey face of the lawyer as he felt the imperative nature of the instruction given to him. The lady had come there not to be advised, but to have her work done for her out of hand. But the smile was very melancholy, and soon passed away.

"Is the widow in immediate distress?" asked Mr. Slow.

Now the fact was that Miss Mackenzie herself had been in good funds, having had ready money in her hands from the time of her brother Walter's death; and for the last year she had by no means spent her full income. She had, therefore, given her sister-in-law money, and had paid the small debts which had come in, as such small debts will come in, directly the dead man's body was under ground. Nay, some had come in and had been paid while the man was yet dying. She exclaimed, therefore, that her sister-in-law was not absolutely in immediate want.

"And does she keep the house?" asked the lawyer.

Then Miss Mackenzie explained that Mrs. Tom intended, if possible, to keep the house, and to take some lady in to lodge with her.

"Then there cannot be any immediate hurry," urged the lawyer; "and as the sum of money in question is large, I really think the matter should be considered."

But Miss Mackenzie still pressed it. She was very anxious to make him understand—and of course he did understand at once—that she had no wish to hurry him in his work. All that she required of him was an assurance that he accepted her instructions, and that the thing should be done with not more than the ordinary amount of legal delay.

"You can pay her what you like out of your own income," said the lawyer.

"But that is not what I promised," said Margaret Mackenzie.

Then there was silence among them all. Mr. Ball had said very little since he had been sitting in that room, and now it was not he who broke the silence. He was still thinking of that deed of gift, and wondering whether it had anything to do with Mr. Slow's unwillingness to undertake the commission which Margaret wished to give him. At last Mr. Slow got up from his chair, and spoke as follows:

"Mr. Ball, I hope you will excuse me; but I have a word or two to say to Miss Mackenzie, which I had rather say to her alone."

"Certainly," said Mr. Ball, rising and preparing to go.

"You will wait for me, John," said Miss Mackenzie, asking this favour of him as though she were very anxious that he should grant it.

Mr. Slow said that he might be closeted with Miss Mackenzie for some little time, perhaps for a quarter of an hour or twenty minutes. John Ball looked at his watch, and then at his cousin's face, and then promised that he would wait. Mr. Slow himself took him into the outer office, and then handed him a chair; but he observed that he was not allowed to go back into the waiting-room.

There he waited for three-quarters of an hour, constantly looking at his watch, and thinking more and more about that deed of gift. Surely it must be the case that the document which he had seen had some reference to this great delay. At last he heard a door open, and a step along a passage, and then another door was opened, and Mr. Slow reappeared with Margaret Mackenzie behind him. John Ball's eyes immediately fell on his cousin's face, and he could see that it was very pale. The lawyer's wore that smile which men put on when they wish to cover the disagreeable seriousness of the moment.

"Good morning, Miss Mackenzie," said he, pressing his client's hand.

"Good morning, sir," said she.

The lawyer and Mr. Ball then touched each other's hands, and the former followed his cousin down the steps out into the square.

Chapter XVIII

Tribulation

When they were once more out in the square, side by side, Miss Mackenzie took hold of her cousin's arm and walked on for a few steps in silence, in the direction of Great Queen Street—that is to say, away from the city, towards which she knew her cousin would go in pursuit of his own business. And indeed the hour was now close at hand in which he should be sitting as a director at the Shadrach Fire Assurance Office. If not at the Shadrach by two, or, with all possible allowance for the shortcoming of a generally punctual director, by a quarter past two, he would be too late for his guinea; and now, as he looked at his watch, it wanted only ten minutes to two. He was very particular about these guineas, and the chambers of the Shadrach were away in Old Broad Street. Nevertheless he walked on with her.

"John," she said, when they had walked half the length of that side of the square, "I have heard dreadful news."

Then that deed of gift was, after all, a fact; and Mr. Slow, instead of being a rogue, must be the honestest old lawyer in London! He must have been at work in discovering the wrong that had been done, and was now about to reveal it to the world.

Some such idea as this had glimmered across Mr. Ball's mind as he had sat in Mr. Slow's outer office, with his chin still resting on his umbrella.

But though some such idea as this did cross his mind, his thought on the instant was of his cousin.

"What dreadful news, Margaret?"

"It is about my money."

"Stop a moment, Margaret. Are you sure that you ought to tell it to me?"

"If I don't, to whom shall I tell it? And how can I bear it without telling it to some one?"

"Did Mr. Slow bid you speak of it to me?"

"No; he bade me think much of it before I did so, as you are concerned. And he said that you might perhaps be disappointed."

Then they walked on again in silence. John Ball found his position to be very difficult, and hardly knew how to speak to her, or how to carry himself. If it was to be that this money was to come back to him; if it was his now in spite of all that had come and gone; if the wrong done was to be righted, and the property wrested from him was to be restored,—restored to him who wanted it so sorely,—how could he not triumph in such an act of tardy restitution? He remembered all the particulars at this moment. Twelve thousand pounds of his uncle Jonathan's money had gone to Walter Mackenzie. The sum once intended for him had been much more than that,—more he believed than double that; but if twelve thousand pounds was now restored to him, how different would it make the whole tenor of his life; Mr. Slow said that he might be disappointed; but then Mr. Slow was not his lawyer. Did he not owe it to his family immediately to go to his own attorney? Now he thought no more of his guinea at the Shadrach, but walked on by his cousin's side with his mind intently fixed on his uncle's money. She was still leaning on his arm.

"Tell me, John, what shall I do?" said she, looking up into his face.

Would it not be better for them, better for the interests of them both, that they should be separated? Was it probable, or possible, that with interests so adverse, they should give each other good advice? Did it not behove him to explain to her that till this should be settled between them, they must necessarily regard each other as enemies? For a moment or two he wished himself away from her, and was calculating how he might escape. But then, when he looked down at her, and saw the softness of her eye, and felt the confidence implied in the weight of her hand upon his arm, his hard heart was softened, and he relented.

"It is difficult to tell you what you should do," he said. "At present nothing seems to be known. He has said nothing for certain."

"But I could understand him," she said, in reply; "I could see by his face, and I knew by the tone of his voice, that he was almost certain. I know that he is sure of it. John, I shall be a beggar, an absolute beggar! I shall have nothing; and those poor children will be beggars, and their mother. I feel as though I did not know where I am, or what I am doing."

Then an idea came into his head. If this money was not hers, it was his. If it was not his, then it was hers. Would it not be well that they should solve all the difficulty by agreeing then and there to be man and wife? It was true that since his Rachel's death he had seen no woman whom he so much coveted to have in his home as this one who now leaned on his arm. But, as he thought of it, there seemed to be a romance about such a step which would not befit him. What would his mother and father say to him if, after all his troubles, he was at last to marry a woman without a farthing? And then, too, would she consent to give up all further consideration for her brother's family? Would she agree to abandon her idea of assisting them, if ultimately it should turn out that the property was hers? No; there was certainly a looseness about such a plan which did not befit him; and, moreover, were he to attempt it, he would probably not succeed.

But something must be done, now at this moment. The guinea at the Shadrach was gone for ever, and therefore he could devote himself for the day to his cousin.

"Are you to hear again from Mr. Slow?" he said.

"I am to go to him this day week."

"And then it will be decided?"

"John, it is decided now; I am sure of it. I feel that it is all gone. A careful man like that would never have spoken as he did, unless he was sure. It will be all yours, John."

"So would have been that which your brother had," said he.

"I suppose so. It is dreadful to think of; very dreadful. I can only promise that I will spend nothing till it is decided. John, I wish you would take from me what I have, lest it should go." And she absolutely had her hand upon her purse in her pocket.

"No," said he slowly, "no; you need think of nothing of that sort."

"But what am I to do? Where am I to go while this week passes by?"

"You will stay where you are, of course."

"Oh John! if you could understand! How am I to look my aunt in the face. Don't you know that she would not wish to have me there at all if I was a poor creature without anything?" The poor creature did not know herself how terribly heavy was the accusation she was bringing against her aunt. "And what will she say when she knows that the money I have spent has never really been my own?"

Then he counselled her to say nothing about it to her aunt till after her next visit to Mr. Slow's and made her understand that he, himself, would not mention the subject at the Cedars till the week was passed. He should go, he said, to his own lawyer, and tell him the whole story as far as he knew it. It was not that he in the least doubted Mr. Slow's honesty or judgment, but it would be better that the two should act together. Then when the week was over, he and Margaret would once more go to Lincoln's Inn Fields.

"What a week I shall have!" said she.

"It will be a nervous time for us both," he answered.

"And what must I do after that?" This question she asked, not in the least as desirous of obtaining from him any assurance of assistance, but in the agony of her spirit, and in sheer dismay as to her prospects.

"We must hope for the best," he said. "God tempers the wind to the shorn lamb." He had often thought of the way in which he had been shorn, but he did not, at this moment, remember that the shearing had never been so tempered as to be acceptable to his own feelings.

"And in God only can I trust," she answered. As she said this, her mind went away to Littlebath, and the Stumfoldians, and Mr. Maguire. Was there not great mercy in the fact, that this ruin had not found her married to that unfortunate clergyman? And what would they all say at Littlebath when they heard the story? How would Mrs. Stumfold exult over the downfall of the woman who had rebelled against her! how would the nose of the coachmaker's wife rise in the air! and how would Mr. Maguire rejoice that this great calamity had not fallen upon him! Margaret Mackenzie's heart and spirit had been sullied by no mean feeling with reference to her own wealth. It had never puffed her up with exultation. But she calculated on the meanness of others, as though it was a matter of course, not, indeed, knowing that it was meanness, or blaming them in any way for that which she attributed to them. Four gentlemen had wished to marry her during the past year. It never occurred to her now, that any one of these four would on that account hold out a hand to help her. In losing her money she would have lost all that was desirable in their eyes, and this seemed to her to be natural.

They were still walking round Lincoln's Inn Fields.
"John," she exclaimed suddenly, "I must go to them in Gower
Street."

"What, now, to-day?"

"Yes, now, immediately. You need not mind me; I can
get back to Twickenham by myself. I know the trains."

"If I were you, Margaret, I would not go till all this is
decided."

"It is decided, John; I know it is. And how can I leave
them in such a condition, spending money which they will never
get? They must know it some time, and the sooner the better.
Mr. Rubb must know it too. He must understand that he is more
than ever bound to provide them with an income out of the
business."

"I would not do it to-day if I were you."

"But I must, John; this very day. If I am not home by
dinner, tell them that I had to go to Gower Street. I shall at any
rate be there in the evening. Do not you mind coming back with
me."

They were then at the gate leading into the New Square,
and she turned abruptly round, and hurried away from him up
into Holborn, passing very near to Mr. Slow's chambers. John
Ball did not attempt to follow her, but stood there awhile looking
after her. He felt, in his heart, and knew by his judgment, that
she was a good woman, true, unselfish, full of love, clever too in
her way, quick in apprehension, and endowed with an admirable
courage. He had heard her spoken of at the Cedars as a poor
creature who had money. Nay, he himself had taken a part in so
speaking of her. Now she had no money, but he knew well that
she was a creature the very reverse of poor. What should he do
for her? In what way should he himself behave towards her? In
the early days of his youth, before the cares of the world had
made him hard, he had married his Rachel without a penny, and
his father had laughed at him, and his mother had grieved over
him. Tough and hard, and careworn as he was now, defiled by

the price of stocks, and saturated with the poison of the money market, then there had been in him a touch of romance and a dash of poetry, and he had been happy with his Rachel. Should he try it again now? The woman would surely love him when she found that he came to her in her poverty as he had before come to her in her wealth. He watched her till she passed out of his sight along the wall leading to Holborn, and then he made his way to the City through Lincoln's Inn and Chancery Lane.

Margaret walked straight into Holborn, and over it towards Red Lion Square. She crossed the line of the omnibuses, feeling that now she must spend no penny which she could save. She was tired, for she had already walked much that morning, and the day was close and hot; but nevertheless she went on quickly, through Bloomsbury Square and Russell Square, to Gower Street. As she got near to the door her heart almost failed her; but she went up to it and knocked boldly. The thing should be done, let the pain of doing it be what it might.

"Laws, Miss Margaret! is that you?" said the maid. "Yes, missus is at home. She'll see you, of course, but she's hard at work on the furniture."

Then she went directly up into the drawing-room and there she found her sister-in-law, with her dress tucked up to her elbows, with a cloth in her hand, rubbing the chairs.

"What, Margaret! Whoever expected to see you? If we are to let the rooms, it's as well to have the things tidy, isn't it? Besides, a person bears it all the better when there's anything to do."

Then Mary Jane, the eldest daughter, came in from the bedroom behind the drawing-room, similarly armed for work.

Margaret sat down wearily upon the sofa, having muttered some word in answer to Mrs. Tom's apology for having been found at work so soon after her husband's death.

"Sarah," she said, "I have come to you to-day because I had something to say to you about business."

"Oh, to be sure! I never thought for a moment you had come for pleasure, or out of civility, as it might be. Of course I didn't expect that when I saw you."

"Sarah, will you come upstairs with me into your own room?"

"Upstairs, Margaret? Oh yes, if you please. We shall be down directly, my dear, and I dare say Margaret will stay to tea. We tea early, because, since you went, we have dined at one."

Then Mrs. Tom led the way up to the room in which Margaret had watched by her dying brother's bed-side.

"I'm come in here," said Mrs. Tom, again apologising, "because the children had to come out of the room behind the drawing-room. Miss Colza is staying with us, and she and Mary Jane have your room."

Margaret did not care much for all this; but the solemnity of the chamber in which, when she last saw it, her brother's body was lying, added something to her sadness at the moment.

"Sarah," she said, endeavouring to warn her sister-in-law by the tone of her voice that her news was bad news, "I have just come from Mr. Slow."

"He's the lawyer, isn't he?"

"Yes, he's the lawyer. You know what I promised my brother. I went to him to make arrangements for doing it, and when there I heard—oh, Sarah, such dreadful news!"

"He says you're not to do it, I suppose!" And in the woman's voice and eyes there were signs of anger, not against Mr. Slow alone, but also against Miss Mackenzie. "I knew how it would be. But, Margaret, Mr. Slow has got nothing to do with it. A promise is a promise; and a promise made to a dying man! Oh, Margaret!"

"If I had it to give I would give it as surely as I am standing here. When I told my brother it should be so, he believed me at once."

"Of course he believed you."

"But Sarah, they tell me now that I have nothing to give."

"Who tells you so?"

"The lawyer. I cannot explain it all to you; indeed, I do not as yet understand it myself; but I have learned this morning that the property which Walter left me was not his to leave. It had been given away before Mr. Jonathan Ball died."

"It's a lie!" said the injured woman,—the woman who was the least injured, but who, with her children, had perhaps the best excuse for being ill able to bear the injury. "It must be a lie. It's more than twenty years ago. I don't believe and won't believe that it can be so. John Ball must have something to do with this."

"The property will go to him, but he has had nothing to do with it. Mr. Slow found it out."

"It can't be so, not after twenty years. Whatever they may have done from Walter, they can't take it away from you; not if you've spirit enough to stand up for your rights. If you let them take it in that way, I can't tell you what I shall think of you."

"It is my own lawyer that says so."

"Yes, Mr. Slow; the biggest rogue of them all. I always knew that of him, always. Oh, Margaret, think of the children! What are we to do? What are we to do?" And sitting down on the bedside, she put her dirty apron up to her eyes.

"I have been thinking of them ever since I heard it," said Margaret.

"But what good will thinking do? You must do something. Oh! Margaret, after all that you said to him when he lay there dying!" and the woman, with some approach to true pathos, put her hand on the spot where her husband's head had rested. "Don't let his children come to beggary because men like that choose to rob the widow and the orphan."

"Every one has a right to what is his own," said Margaret. "Even though widows should be beggars, and orphans should want."

"That's very well of you, Margaret. It's very well for you to say that, who have friends like the Balls to stand by you. And, perhaps, if you will let him have it all without saying anything, he will stand by you firmer than ever. But who is there to stand by me and my children? It can't be that after twenty years your fortune should belong to anyone else. Why should it have gone on for more than twenty years, and nobody have found it out? I don't believe it can come so, Margaret, unless you choose to let them do it. I don't believe a word of it."

There was nothing more to be said upon that subject at present. Mrs. Tom did indeed say a great deal more about it, sometimes threatening Margaret, and sometimes imploring her; but Miss Mackenzie herself would not allow herself to speak of the thing otherwise than as an ascertained fact. Had the other woman been more reasonable or less passionate in her lamentations Miss Mackenzie might have trusted herself to tell her that there was yet a doubt. But she herself felt that the doubt was so small, and that, in Mrs. Tom's mind, it would be so magnified into nearly a certainty on the other side, that she thought it most discreet not to refer to the exact amount of information which Mr. Slow had given to her.

"It will be best for us to think, Sarah," she said, trying to turn the other's mind away from the coveted income which she would never possess—"to think what you and the children had better do."

"Oh, dear! oh, dear! oh, dear!"

"It is very bad; but there is always something to be done. We must lose no time in letting Mr. Rubb know the truth. When he hears how it is, he will understand that something must be done for you out of the firm."

"He won't do anything. He's downstairs now, flirting with that girl in the drawing-room, instead of being at his business."

"If he's downstairs, I will see him."

As Mrs. Mackenzie made no objection to this, Margaret went downstairs, and when she came near the passage at the bottom, she heard the voices of people talking merrily in the parlour. As her hand was on the lock of the door, words from Miss Colza became very audible. "Now, Mr. Rubb, be quiet." So she knocked at the door, and having been invited by Mr. Rubb to come in, she opened it.

It may be presumed that the flirting had not gone to any perilous extent, as there were three or four children present. Nevertheless Miss Colza and Mr. Rubb were somewhat disconcerted, and expressed their surprise at seeing Miss Mackenzie.

"We all thought you were staying with the baronet's lady," said Miss Colza.

Miss Mackenzie explained that she was staying at Twickenham, but that she had come up to pay a visit to her sister-in-law. "And I've a word or two I want to say to you, Mr. Rubb, if you'll allow me."

"I suppose, then, I'd better make myself scarce," said Miss Colza.

As she was not asked to stay, she did make herself scarce, taking the children with her up among the tables and chairs in the drawing-room. There she found Mary Jane, but she did not find Mrs. Mackenzie, who had thrown herself on the bed in her agony upstairs.

Then Miss Mackenzie told her wretched story to Mr. Rubb,—telling it for the third time. He was awe-struck as he listened, but did not once attempt to deny the facts, as had been done by Mrs. Mackenzie.

"And is it sure?" he asked, when her story was over.

"I don't suppose it is quite sure yet. Indeed, Mr. Slow said it was not quite sure. But I have not allowed myself to doubt it, and I do not doubt it."

"If he himself had not felt himself sure, he would not have told you."

"Just so, Mr. Rubb. That is what I think; and therefore I have given my sister-in-law no hint that there is a chance left. I think you had better not do so either."

"Perhaps not," said he. He spoke in a low voice, almost whispering, as though he were half scared by the tidings he had heard.

"It is very dreadful," she said; "very dreadful for Sarah and the children."

"And for you too, Miss Mackenzie."

"But about them, Mr. Rubb. What can you do for them out of the business?"

He looked very blank, and made no immediate answer.

"I know you will feel for their position," she said. "You do; do you not?"

"Indeed I do, Miss Mackenzie."

"And you will do what you can. You can at any rate ensure them the interest of the money—of the money you know that came from me."

Still Mr. Rubb sat in silence, and she thought that he must be stonyhearted. Surely he might undertake to do that, knowing, as he so well knew, the way in which the money had been obtained, and knowing also that he had already said that so much should be forthcoming out of the firm to make up a general income for the family of his late partner.

"Surely there will be no doubt about that, Mr. Rubb."

"The Balls will claim the debt," said he hoarsely; and then, in answer to her inquiries, he explained that the sum she had lent had not, in truth, been hers to lend. It had formed part of the money that John Ball could claim, and Mr. Slow held in his hands an acknowledgement of the debt from Rubb and Mackenzie. Of course, Mr. Ball would claim that the interest should be paid to him; and he would claim the principal too, if, on inquiry, he should find that the firm would be able to raise it. "I don't know that he wouldn't be able to come upon the firm for the money your brother put into the business," said he gloomily.

"But I don't think he'll be such a fool as that. He'd get nothing by it."

"Then may God help them!" said Miss Mackenzie.

"And what will you do?" he asked.

She shook her head, but made him no answer. As for herself she had not begun to form a plan. Her own condition did not seem to her to be nearly so dreadful as that of all these young children.

"I wish I knew how to help you," said Samuel Rubb.

"There are some positions, Mr. Rubb, in which no one but God can help one. But, perhaps—perhaps you may still do something for the children."

"I will try, Miss Mackenzie."

"Thank you, and may God bless you; and He will bless you if you try. 'Who giveth a drop of water to one of them in my name, giveth it also to me.' You will think of that, will you not?"

"I will think of you, and do the best that I can."

"I had hoped to have made them so comfortable! But God's will be done; God's will be done. I think I had better go now, Mr. Rubb. There will be no use in my going to her upstairs again. Tell her from me, with my love, that she shall hear from me when I have seen the lawyer. I will try to come to her, but perhaps I may not be able. Good-bye, Mr. Rubb."

"Good-bye, Miss Mackenzie. I hope we shall see each other sometimes."

"Perhaps so. Do what you can to support her. She will want all that her friends can do for her." So saying she went out of the room, and let herself out of the front door into the street, and began her walk back to the Waterloo Station.

She had not broken bread in her sister-in-law's house, and it was now nearly six o'clock. She had taken nothing since she had breakfasted at Twickenham, and the affairs of the day had been such as to give her but little time to think of such wants. But now as she made her weary way through the streets she became sick with hunger, and went into a baker's shop for a bun. As she ate it she felt that it was almost wrong in her to buy even that. At the present moment nothing that she possessed seemed to her to be, by right, her own. Every shilling in her purse was the property of John Ball, if Mr. Slow's statement were true. Then, when the bun was finished, as she went down by Bloomsbury church and the region of St Giles's back to the Strand, she did begin to think of her own position. What should she do, and how should she commence to do it? She had declared to herself but lately that the work for which she was fittest was that of nursing the sick. Was it not possible that she might earn her bread in this way? Could she not find such employment in some quarter where her labour would be worth the food she must eat and the raiment she would require? There was a hospital somewhere in London with which she thought she had heard that John Ball was connected. Might not he obtain for her a situation such as that?

It was past eight when she reached the Cedars, and then she was very tired,—very tired and nearly sick also with want. She went first of all up to her room, and then crept down into the drawing-room, knowing that she should find them at tea. When she entered there was a large party round the table, consisting of the girls and children and Lady Ball. John Ball, who never took tea, was sitting in his accustomed place near the lamp, and the old baronet was half asleep in his arm-chair.

"If you were going to dine in Gower Street, Margaret, why didn't you say so?" said Lady Ball.

In answer to this, Margaret burst out into tears. It was not the unkindness of her aunt's voice that upset her so much as her own weakness, and the terrible struggle of the long day.

"What on earth is the matter?" said Sir John.

One of the girls brought her a cup of tea, but she felt herself to be too weak to take it in her hand, and made a sign that it should be put on the table. She was not aware that she had ever fainted, but a fear came upon her that she might do so now. She rallied herself and struggled, striving to collect her strength.

"Do you know what is the matter with her, John?" said Lady Ball.

Then John Ball asked her if she had had dinner, and when she did not answer him he saw how it was.

"Mother," he said, "she has had no food all day; I will get it for her."

"If she wants anything, the servants can bring it to her, John," said the mother.

But he would not trust the servants in this matter, but went out himself and fetched her meat and wine, and pressed her to take it, and sat himself beside her, and spoke kind words into her ear, and at last, in some sort, she was comforted.

Chapter XIX

Showing How Two of Miss Mackenzie's Lovers Behaved

Mr. Ball, on his return home to the Cedars, had given no definite answer to his mother's inquiries as to the day's work in London, and had found it difficult to make any reply to her that would for the moment suffice. She was not a woman easily satisfied with evasive answers; but, nevertheless, he told her nothing of what had occurred, and left her simply in a bad humour. This conversation had taken place before dinner, but after dinner she asked him another question.

"John, you might as well tell me this; are you engaged to Margaret Mackenzie?"

"No, I am not," said her son, angrily.

After that his mother's humour had become worse than before, and in that state her niece had found her when she returned home in the evening, and had suffered in consequence.

On the next morning Miss Mackenzie sent down word to say she was not well, and would not come down to breakfast. It so happened that John Ball was going into town on this day also, the Abednego Life Office holding its board day immediately after that of the Shadrach Fire Office, and therefore he was not able to see her before she encountered his mother. Lady Ball went up to her in her bedroom immediately after breakfast, and there remained with her for some time. Her aunt at first was tender with her, giving her tea and only asking her gentle little questions at intervals; but as the old lady became impatient at learning nothing, she began a system of cross-questions, and at last grew to be angry and disagreeable. Her son had distinctly told her that he was not engaged to his cousin, and had in fact told her nothing else distinctly; but she, when she had seen how careful he had been in supplying Margaret's wants himself, with what anxious solicitude he had pressed wine on her; how he had sat by her saying soft words to her—Lady Ball, when she remembered this, could not but think that her son had deceived her. And if so, why had he wished to deceive her? Could it be that he had allowed her to give away half her money, and had promised to marry her with the other half? There were moments in which her dear son John could be very foolish, in spite of that life-long devotion to the price of stocks, for which he was conspicuous. She still remembered, as though it were but the other day, how he had persisted in marrying Rachel, though Rachel brought nothing with her but a sweet face, a light figure, a happy temper, and the clothes on her back. To all mothers their sons are ever young, and to old Lady Ball John Ball was still young, and still, possibly, capable of some such folly as that of which she was thinking. If it were not so, if there were not something of that kind in the wind why should he—why should she—be so hard and uncommunicative in all their answers? There lay her niece, however, sick with the headache, and therefore weak, and very much in Lady Ball's power. The evil to be done was great, and the necessity for preventing it might be immediate. And Lady Ball was a lady who did not like to be kept in the dark in reference to anything concerning her family. Having gone downstairs, therefore, for an hour or so to look after her servants, or, as she had said, to allow Margaret to have a little sleep, she returned again to the charge, and sitting close to Margaret's pillow, did her best to find out the truth.

If she could only have known the whole truth; how her son's thoughts were running throughout the day, even as he sat at the Abednego board, not on Margaret with half her fortune, but on Margaret with none! how he was recalling the sweetness of her face as she looked up to him in the square, and took him by his coat, and her tears as she spoke of the orphan children, and the grace of her figure as she had walked away from him, and the persistency of her courage in doing what she thought to be right! how he was struggling within himself with an endeavour, a vain endeavour, at a resolution that such a marriage as that must be out of the question! Had Lady Ball known all that, I think she would have flown to the offices of the Abednego after her son, and never have left him till she had conquered his heart and trampled his folly under her feet.

But she did not conquer Margaret Mackenzie. The poor creature lying there, racked, in truth, with pain and sorrow, altogether incapable of any escape from her aunt's gripe, would not say a word that might tend to ease Lady Ball's mind. If she had told all that she knew, all that she surmised, how would her aunt have rejoiced? That the money should come without the wife would indeed have been a triumph! And Margaret in telling all would have had nothing to tell of those terribly foolish thoughts which were then at work in the City. To her such a state of things as that which I have hinted would have seemed quite as improbable, quite as unaccountable, as it would have done to her aunt. But she did not tell all, nor in truth did she tell anything.

"And John was with you at the lawyer's," said Lady Ball, attempting her cross-examination for the third time. "Yes; he was with me there."

"And what did he say when you asked Mr. Slow to make such a settlement as that?"

"He didn't say anything, aunt. The whole thing was put off."

"I know it was put off; of course it was put off. I didn't suppose any respectable lawyer in London would have dreamed of doing such a thing. But what I want to know is, how it was put off. What did Mr. Slow say?"

"I am to see him again next week."

"But not to get him to do anything of that kind?"

"I can't tell, aunt, what he is to do then."

"But what did he say when you made such a proposition as that? Did he not tell you that it was quite out of the question?"

"I don't think he said that, aunt."

"Then what did he say? Margaret, I never saw such a person as you are. Why should you be so mysterious? There can't be anything you don't want me to know, seeing how very much I am concerned; and I do think you ought to tell me all that occurred, knowing, as you do, that I have done my very best to be kind to you."

"Indeed there isn't anything I can tell—not yet."

Then Lady Ball remained silent at the bed-head for the space, perhaps, of ten minutes, meditating over it all. If her son was, in truth, engaged to this woman, at any rate she would find that out. If she asked a point-blank question on that subject, Margaret would not be able to leave it unanswered, and would hardly be able to give a directly false answer.

"My dear," she said, "I think you will not refuse to tell me plainly whether there is anything between you and John. As his mother, I have a right to know?"

"How anything between us?" said Margaret, raising herself on her elbow.

"Are you engaged to marry him?"

"Oh, dear! no."

"And there is nothing of that sort going on?"

"Nothing at all."

"You are determined still to refuse him?"

"It is quite out of the question, aunt. He does not wish it at all. You may be sure that he has quite changed his mind about it."

"But he won't have changed his mind if you have given up your plan about your sister-in-law."

"He has changed it altogether, aunt. You needn't think anything more about that. He thinks no more about it."

Nevertheless he was thinking about it this very moment, as he voted for accepting a doubtful life at the Abednego, which was urged on the board by a director, who, I hope, had no intimate personal relations with the owner of the doubtful life in question.

Lady Ball did not know what to make of it. For many years past she had not seen her son carry himself so much like a lover as he had done when he sat himself beside his cousin pressing her to drink her glass of sherry. Why was he so anxious for her comfort? And why, before that, had he been so studiously reticent as to her affairs?

"I can't make anything out of you," said Lady Ball, getting up from her chair with angry alacrity; "and I must say that I think it very ungrateful of you, seeing all that I have done for you."

So saying, she left the room.

What, oh, what would she think when she should come to know the truth? Margaret told herself as she lay there, holding her head between her hands, that she was even now occupying that room and enjoying the questionable comfort of that bed under false pretences. When it was known that she was absolutely a pauper, would she then be made welcome to her uncle's house? She was now remaining there without divulging her circumstances, under the advice and by the authority of her cousin; and she had resolved to be guided by him in all things as long as he would be at the trouble to guide her. On whom else could she depend? But, nevertheless, her position was very grievous to her, and the more so now that her aunt had twitted her with ingratitude. When the servant came to her, she felt that she had no right to the girl's services; and when a message was brought to her from Lady Ball, asking whether she would be taken out in the carriage, she acknowledged to herself that such courtesy to her was altogether out of place.

On that evening her cousin said nothing to her, and on the next day he went again up to town.

"What, four days running, John!" said Lady Ball, at breakfast.

"I have particular business to-day, mother," said he.

On that evening, when he came back, he found a moment to take Margaret by the hand and tell her that his own lawyer also was to meet them at Mr. Slow's chambers on the day named. He took her thus, and held her hand closely in his while he was speaking, but he said nothing to her more tender than the nature of such a communication required.

"You and John are terribly mysterious," said Lady Ball to her, a minute or two afterwards. "If there is anything I do hate it's mystery in families. We never had any with us till you came."

On the next day a letter reached her which had been redirected from Gower Street. It was from Mr. Maguire; and she took it up into her own room to read it and answer it. The letter and reply were as follows:

Littlebath, Oct., 186—.

DEAREST MARGARET,

I hope the circumstances of the case will, in your opinion, justify me in writing to you again, though I am sorry to intrude upon you at a time when your heart must yet be sore with grief for the loss of your lamented brother. Were we now all in all to each other, as I hope we may still be before long, it would be my sweet privilege to wipe your eyes, and comfort you in your sorrow, and bid you remember that it is the Lord who giveth and the Lord who taketh away. Blessed be the name of the Lord. I do not doubt that you have spoken to yourself daily in those words, nay, almost hourly, since your brother was taken from you. I had not the privilege of knowing him, but if he was in any way like his sister, he would have been a friend whom I should have delighted to press to my breast and carry in my heart of hearts.

But now, dearest Margaret, will you allow me to intrude upon you with another theme? Of course you well know the subject upon which, at present, I am thinking more than on any other. May I be permitted to hope that that subject sometimes presents itself to you in a light that is not altogether disagreeable. When you left Littlebath so suddenly, carried away on a mission of love and kindness, you left me, as you will doubtlessly remember, in a state of some suspense. You had kindly consented to acknowledge that I was not altogether indifferent to you.

"That's not true," said Margaret to herself, almost out loud; "I never told him anything of the kind."

And it was arranged that on that very day we were to have had a meeting, to which—shall I confess it?—I looked forward as the happiest moment of my life. I can hardly tell you what my feelings were when I found that you were going, and that I could only just say to you, farewell. If I could only have been with you when that letter came I think I could have softened your sorrow, and perhaps then, in your gentleness, you might have said a word which would have left me nothing to wish for in this world. But it has been otherwise ordered, and, Margaret, I do not complain.

But what makes me write now is the great necessity that I should know exactly how I stand. You said something in your last dear letter which gave me to understand that you wished to do something for your brother's family. Promises made by the bed-sides of the dying are always dangerous, and in the cases of Roman Catholics have been found to be replete with ruin.

Mr. Maguire, no doubt, forgot that in such cases the promises are made by, and not to, the dying person.

Nevertheless, I am far from saying that they should not be kept in a modified form, and you need not for a moment think that I, if I may be allowed to have an interest in the matter, would wish to hinder you from doing whatever may be becoming. I think I may promise you that you will find no mercenary spirit in me, although, of course, I am bound, looking forward to the tender tie which will, I hope, connect us, to regard your interests above all other worldly affairs. If I may then say a word of advice, it is to recommend that nothing permanent be done till we can act together in this matter. Do not, however, suppose that anything you can do or have done, can alter the nature of my regard.

But now, dearest Margaret, will you not allow me to press for an immediate answer to my appeal? I will tell you exactly how I am circumstanced, and then you will see how strong is my reason that there should be no delay. Very many people here, I may say all the elite of the evangelical circles, including Mrs. Perch—[Mrs. Perch was the coachmaker's wife, who had always been so true to Mrs. Stumfold]—desired that I should establish a church here, on my own bottom, quite independent of Mr. Stumfold. The Stumfolds would then soon have to leave Littlebath, there is no doubt of that, and she has already made herself so unendurable, and her father and she together are so distressing, that the best of their society has fallen away from them. Her treatment to you was such that I could never endure her afterwards. Now the opening for a clergyman with pure Gospel doctrines would be the best thing that has turned up for a long time. The church would be worth over six hundred a year, besides the interest of the money which would have to be laid out. I could have all this commenced at once, and secure the incumbency, if I could myself head the subscription list with two thousand pounds. It should not be less than that. You will understand that the money would not be given, though, no doubt, a great many persons would, in this way, be induced to give theirs. But the pew rents would go in the first instance to provide interest for the money not given, but lent; as would of course be the case with your money, if you would advance it.

I should not think of such a plan as this if I did not feel that it was the best thing for your interests; that is, if, as I fondly hope, I am ever to call you mine. Of course, in that case, it is only common prudence on my part to do all I can to insure for myself such a professional income, for your sake. For, dearest Margaret, my brightest earthly hope is to see you with everything comfortable around you. If that

could be arranged, it would be quite within our means to
keep some sort of carriage.

Here would be a fine opportunity for rivalling Mrs. Stumfold!
That was the temptation with which he hoped to allure her.

> But the thing must be done quite immediately; therefore let
> me pray you not to postpone my hopes with unnecessary
> delay. I know it seems unromantic to urge a lady with any
> pecuniary considerations, but I think that under the
> circumstances, as I have explained them, you will forgive
> me.
>
> Believe me to be, dearest Margaret,
>
> Yours, with truest,
>
> Most devoted affection,
>
> JEREH. MAGUIRE.

One man had wanted her money to buy a house on a mortgage,
and another now asked for it to build a church, giving her, or
promising to give her, the security of the pew rents. Which of
the two was the worst? They were both her lovers, and she
thought that he was the worst who first made his love and then
tried to get her money. These were the ideas which at once
occurred to her upon her reading Mr. Maguire's letter. She had
quite wit enough to see through the whole project; how outsiders
were to be induced to give their money, thinking that all was to
be given; whereas those inside the temple,—those who knew all
about it,—were simply to make for themselves a good
speculation. Her cousin John's constant solicitude for money
was bad; but, after all, it was not so bad as this. She told herself
at once that the letter was one which would of itself have ended
everything between her and Mr. Maguire, even had nothing
occurred to put an absolute and imperative stop to the affair. Mr.
Maguire pressed for an early answer, and before she left the
room she sat down and wrote it.

The Cedars, Twickenham, October, 186—.

DEAR SIR

Before she wrote the words, "Dear Sir," she had to think much of them, not having had as yet much experience in writing letters to gentlemen; but she concluded at last that if she simply wrote "Sir," he would take it as an insult, and that if she wrote "My dear Mr. Maguire," it would, under the circumstances, be too affectionate.

> DEAR SIR
>
> I have got your letter to-day, and I hasten to answer it at once. All that to which you allude between us must be considered as being altogether over, and I am very sorry that you should have had so much trouble. My circumstances are altogether changed. I cannot explain how, as it would make my letter very long; but you may be assured that such is the case, and to so great an extent that the engagement you speak of would not at all suit you at present. Pray take this as being quite true, and believe me to be
>
> Your very humble servant,
>
> MARGARET MACKENZIE.

I feel that the letter was somewhat curt and dry as an answer to an effusion so full of affection as that which the gentleman had written; and the fair reader, when she remembers that Miss Mackenzie had given the gentleman considerable encouragement, will probably think that she should have expressed something like regret at so sudden a termination to so tender a friendship. But she, in truth, regarded the offer as having been made to her money solely, and as in fact no longer existing as an offer, now that her money itself was no longer in existence. She was angry with Mr. Maguire for the words he had written about her brother's affairs; for his wish to limit her kindness to her nephews and nieces, and also for his greediness in being desirous of getting her money at once; but as to the main question, she thought herself bound to answer him plainly, as she would have answered a man who came to buy from her a house, which house was no longer in her possession.

Mr. Maguire when he received her letter, did not believe a word of it. He did not in the least believe that she had actually lost everything that had once belonged to her, or that he, if he married her now, would obtain less than he would have done had he married her before her brother's death. But he thought that her brother's family and friends had got hold of her in London; that Mr. Rubb might very probably have done it; and that they were striving to obtain command of her money, and were influencing her to desert him. He thinking so, and being a man of good courage, took a resolution to follow his game, and to see whether even yet he might not obtain the good things which had made his eyes glisten and his mouth water. He knew that there was very much against him in the race that he was desirous of running, and that an heiress with—he did not know how much a year, but it had been rumoured among the Stumfoldians that it was over a thousand—might not again fall in his way. There were very many things against him, of which he was quite conscious. He had not a shilling of his own, and was in receipt of no professional income. He was not altogether a young man. There was in his personal appearance a defect which many ladies might find it difficult to overcome; and then that little story about his debts, which Miss Todd had picked up, was not only true, but was some degrees under the truth. No doubt, he had a great wish that his wife should be comfortable; but he also, for himself, had long been pining after those eligible comforts, which when they appertain to clergymen, the world, with so much malice, persists in calling the flesh-pots of Egypt. Thinking of all this, of the position he had already gained in spite of his personal disadvantages, and of the great chance there was that his Margaret might yet be rescued from the Philistines, he resolved upon a journey to London.

In the meantime Miss Mackenzie's other lover had not been idle, and he also was resolved by no means to give up the battle.

It cannot be said that Mr. Rubb was not mercenary in his views, but with his desire for the lady's money was mingled much that was courageous, and something also that was generous. The whole truth had been told to him as plainly as it had been told to Mr. Ball, and nevertheless he determined to persevere. He went to work diligently on that very afternoon, deserting the smiles of Miss Colza, and made such inquiries into the law of the matter as were possible to him; and they resulted, as far as Miss Mackenzie was concerned, in his appearing late one afternoon at the front door of Sir John Ball's house. On the day following this Miss Mackenzie was to keep her appointment with Mr. Slow, and her cousin was now up in London among the lawyers.

Miss Mackenzie was sitting with her aunt when Mr. Rubb called. They were both in the drawing-room; and Lady Ball, who had as yet succeeded in learning nothing, and who was more than ever convinced that there was much to learn, was not making herself pleasant to her companion. Throughout the whole week she had been very unpleasant. She did not quite understand why Margaret's sojourn at the Cedars had been and was to be so much prolonged. Margaret, feeling herself compelled to say something on the subject, had with some hesitation told her aunt that she was staying till she had seen her lawyer again, because her cousin wished her to stay.

In answer to this, Lady Ball had of course told her that she was welcome. Her ladyship had then cross-questioned her son on that subject also, but he had simply said that as there was law business to be done, Margaret might as well stay at Twickenham till it was completed.

"But, my dear," Lady Ball had said, "her law business might go on for ever, for what you know."

"Mother," said the son, sternly, "I wish her to stay here at present, and I suppose you will not refuse to permit her to do so."

After this, Lady Ball could go no further.

On the day on which Mr. Rubb was announced in the drawing-room, the aunt and niece were sitting together. "Mr. Rubb—to see Miss Mackenzie," said the old servant, as he opened the door.

Miss Mackenzie got up, blushing to her forehead, and Lady Ball rose from her chair with an angry look, as though asking the oilcloth manufacturer how he dared to make his way in there. The name of the Rubbs had been specially odious to all the family at the Cedars since Tom Mackenzie had carried his share of Jonathan Ball's money into the firm in the New Road. And Mr. Rubb's appearance was not calculated to mitigate this anger. Again he had got on those horrid yellow gloves, and again had dressed himself up to his idea of the garb of a man of fashion. To Margaret's eyes, in the midst of her own misfortunes, he was a thing horrible to behold, as he came into that drawing-room. When she had seen him in his natural condition, at her brother's house, he had been at any rate unobjectionable to her; and when, on various occasions, he had talked to her about his own business, pleading his own cause and excusing his own fault, she had really liked him. There had been a moment or two, the moments of his bitterest confessions, in which she had in truth liked him much. But now! What would she not have given that the old servant should have taken upon himself to declare that she was not at home.

But there he was in her aunt's drawing-room, and she had nothing to do but to ask him to sit down.

"This is my aunt, Lady Ball," said Margaret.

"I hope I have the honour of seeing her ladyship quite well," said Mr. Rubb, bowing low before he ventured to seat himself.

Lady Ball would not condescend to say a word, but stared at him in a manner that would have driven him out of the room had he understood the nature of such looks on ladies' faces.

"I hope my sister-in-law and the children are well," said Margaret, with a violent attempt to make conversation.

"Pretty much as you left them, Miss Mackenzie; she takes on a good deal; but that's only human nature; eh, my lady?"

But her ladyship still would not condescend to speak a word.

Margaret did not know what further to say. All subjects on which it might have been possible for her to speak to Mr. Rubb were stopped from her in the presence of her aunt. Mr. Rubb knew of that great calamity of which, as yet, Lady Ball knew nothing,—of that great calamity to the niece, but great blessing, as it would be thought by the aunt. And she was in much fear lest Mr. Rubb should say something which might tend to divulge the secret.

"Did you come by the train?" she said, at last, reduced in her agony to utter the first unmeaning question of which she could think.

"Yes, Miss Mackenzie, I came by the train, and I am going back by the 5.45, if I can just be allowed to say a few words to you first."

"Does the gentleman mean in private?" asked Lady Ball.

"If you please, my lady," said Mr. Rubb, who was beginning to think that he did not like Lady Ball.

"If Miss Mackenzie wishes it, of course she can do so."

"It may be about my brother's affairs," said Margaret, getting up.

"It is nothing to me, my dear, whether they are your brother's or your own," said Lady Ball; "you had better not interrupt your uncle in the study; but I daresay you'll find the dining-room disengaged."

So Miss Mackenzie led the way into the dining-room, and Mr. Rubb followed. There they found some of the girls, who stared very hard at Mr. Rubb, as they left the room at their cousin's request. As soon as they were left alone Mr. Rubb began his work manfully.

"Margaret," said he, "I hope you will let me call you so now that you are in trouble?"

To this she made no answer.

"But perhaps your trouble is over? Perhaps you have found out that it isn't as you told us the other day?"

"No, Mr. Rubb; I have found nothing of that kind; I believe it is as I told you."

"Then I'll tell you what I propose. You haven't given up the fight, have you? You have not done anything?"

"I have done nothing as yet."

"Then I'll tell you my plan. Fight it out."

"I do not want to fight for anything that is not my own."

"But it is your own. It is your own of rights, even though it should not be so by some quibble of the lawyers. I don't believe twelve Englishmen would be found in London to give it to anybody else; I don't indeed."

"But my own lawyer tells me it isn't mine, Mr. Rubb."

"Never mind him; don't you give up anything. Don't you let them make you soft. When it comes to money nobody should give up anything. Now I'll tell you what I propose."

She now sat down and listened to him, while he stood over her. It was manifest that he was very eager, and in his eagerness he became loud, so that she feared his words might be heard out of the room.

"You know what my sentiments are," he said. At that moment she did not remember what his sentiments were, nor did she know what he meant. "They're the same now as ever. Whether you have got your fortune, or whether you've got nothing, they're the same. I've seen you tried alongside of your brother, when he was a-dying, and, Margaret, I like you now better than ever I did."

"Mr. Rubb, at present, all that cannot mean anything."

"But doesn't it mean anything? By Jove! it does though. It means just this, that I'll make you Mrs. Rubb to-morrow, or as soon as Doctors' Commons, and all that, will let us do it; and I'll chance the money afterwards. Do you let it just go easy, and say nothing, and I'll fight them. If the worst comes to the worst, they'll be willing enough to cry halves with us. But, Margaret, if the worst does come to be worse than that you won't find me hard to you on that account. I shall always remember who helped me when I wanted help."

"I am sure, Mr. Rubb, I am much obliged to you."

"Don't talk about being obliged, but get up and give me your hand, and say it shall be a bargain." Then he tried to take her by the hand and raise her from the chair up towards him.

"No, no, no!" said she.

"But I say yes. Why should it be no? If there never should come a penny out of this property I will put a roof over your head, and will find you victuals and clothes respectably. Who will do better for you than that? And as for the fight, by Jove! I shall like it. You'll find they'll get nothing out of my hands till they have torn away my nails."

Here was a new phase in her life. Here was a man willing to marry her even though she had no assured fortune.

"Margaret," said he, pleading his cause again, "I have that love for you that I would take you though it was all gone, to the last farthing."

"It is all gone."

"Let that be as it may, we'll try it. But though it should be all gone, every shilling of it, still, will you be my wife?"

It was altogether a new phase, and one that was inexplicable to her. And this came from a man to whom she had once thought that she might bring herself to give her hand and her heart, and her money also. She did not doubt that if she took

ANTHONY TROLLOPE

him at his word he would be good to her, and provide her with shelter, and food and raiment, as he had promised her. Her heart was softened towards him, and she forgot his gloves and his shining boots. But she could not bring herself to say that she would love him, and be his wife. It seemed to her now that she was under the guidance of her cousin, and that she was pledged to do nothing of which he would disapprove. He would not approve of her accepting the hand of a man who would be resolved to litigate this matter with him.

"It cannot be," she said. "I feel how generous you are, but it cannot be."

"And why shouldn't it be?"

"Oh, Mr. Rubb, there are things one cannot explain."

"Margaret, think of it. How are you to do better?"

"Perhaps not; probably not. In many ways I am sure I could not do better. But it cannot be."

Not then, nor for the next twenty minutes, but at last he took his answer and went. He did this when he found that he had no more minutes to spare if he intended to return by the 5.45 train. Then, with an angry gesture of his head, he left her, and hurried across to the front door. Then, as he went out, Mr. John Ball came in.

"Good evening, sir," said Mr. Rubb. "I am Mr. Samuel Rubb. I have just been seeing Miss Mackenzie, on business. Good evening, sir."

John Ball said never a word, and Samuel Rubb hurried across the grounds to the railway station.

Chapter XX

Showing How the Third Lover Behaved

"What has that man been here for?" Those were the first words which Mr. Ball spoke to his cousin after shutting the hall-door behind Mr. Rubb's back. When the door was closed he turned round and saw Margaret as she was coming out of the dining-room, and in a voice that sounded to her as though he were angry, asked her the above question.

"He came to see me, John," said Miss Mackenzie, going back into the dining-room. "He was my brother's partner."

"He said he came upon business; what business could he have?"

It was not very easy for her to tell him what had been Mr. Rubb's business. She had no wish to keep anything secret from her cousin, but she did not know how to describe the scene which had just taken place, or how to acknowledge that the man had come there to ask her to marry him.

"Does he know anything of this matter of your money?" continued Mr. Ball.

"Oh yes; he knows it all. He was in Gower Street when I told my sister-in-law."

"And he came to advise you about it?"

"Yes; he did advise me about it. But his advice I shall not take."

"And what did he advise?"

Then Margaret told him that Mr. Rubb had counselled her to fight it out to the last, in order that a compromise might at any rate be obtained.

"If it has no selfish object in view I am far from saying that he is wrong," said John Ball. "It is what I should advise a friend to do under similar circumstances."

"It is not what I shall do, John."

"No; you are like a lamb that gives itself up to the slaughterer. I have been with one lawyer or the other all day, and the end of it is that there is no use on earth in your going to London to-morrow, nor, as far as I can see, for another week to come. The two lawyers together have referred the case to counsel for opinion,—for an amicable opinion as they call it. From what they all say, Margaret, it seems to me clear that the matter will go against you."

"I have expected nothing else since Mr. Slow spoke to me."

"But no doubt you can make a fight, as your friend says."

"I don't want to fight, John; you know that."

"Mr. Slow won't let you give it up without a contest. He suggested a compromise,—that you and I should divide it. But I hate compromises." She looked up into his face but said nothing. "The truth is, I have been so wronged in the matter, the whole thing has been so cruel, it has, all of it together, so completely ruined me and my prospects in life, that were it any one but you, I would sooner have a lawsuit than give up one penny of what is left." Again she looked at him, but he went on speaking of it without observing her. "Think what it has been, Margaret! The whole of this property was once mine! Not the half of it only that has been called yours, but the whole of it! The income was actually paid for one half-year to a separate banking account on my behalf, before I was of age. Yes, paid to me, and I had it! My uncle Jonathan had no more legal right to take it away from me than you have to take the coat off my back. Think of that, and of what four-and-twenty thousand pounds would have done for me and my family from that time to this. There have been nearly thirty years of this robbery!"

"It was not my fault, John."

"No; it was not your fault. But if your brothers could pay me back all that they really owe me, all that the money would now be worth, it would come to nearly a hundred thousand pounds. After that, what is a man to say when he is asked to compromise? As far as I can see, there is not a shadow of doubt about it. Mr. Slow does not pretend that there is a doubt. How they can fail to see the justice of it is what passes my understanding!"

"Mr. Slow will give up at once, I suppose, if I ask him?"

"I don't want you to ask him. I would rather that you didn't say a word to him about it. There is a debt too from that man Rubb which they advise me to abandon."

In answer to this, Margaret could say nothing, for she knew well that her trust in the interest of that money was the only hope she had of any maintenance for her sister-in-law.

After a few minutes' silence he again spoke to her. "He desires to know whether you want money for immediate use."

"Who wants to know?"

"Mr. Slow."

"Oh no, John. I have money at the bankers', but I will not touch it."

"How much is there at the bankers?"

"There is more than three hundred pounds; but very little more; perhaps three hundred and ten."

"You may have that."

"John, I don't want anything that is not my own; not though I had to walk out to earn my bread in the streets to-morrow."

"That is your own, I tell you. The tenants have been ordered not to pay any further rents, till they receive notice. You can make them pay, nevertheless, if you wish it; at least, you might do so, till some legal steps were taken."

"Of course, I shall do nothing of the kind. It was Mr. Slow's people who used to get the money. And am I not to go up to London to-morrow?"

"You can go if you choose, but you will learn nothing. I told Mr. Slow that I would bid you wait till I heard from him again. It is time now for us to get ready for dinner."

Then, as he was going to leave the room, she took him by the coat and held him again,—held him as fast as she had done on the pavement in Lincoln's Inn Fields. There was a soft, womanly, trusting weakness in the manner of her motion as she did this, which touched him now as it had touched him then.

"John," she said, "if there is to be so much delay, I must not stay here."

"Why not, Margaret?"

"My aunt does not like my staying; I can see that; and I don't think it is fair to do so while she does not know all about it. It is something like cheating her out of the use of the house."

"Then I will tell her."

"What, all? Had I not better go first?"

"No; you cannot go. Where are you to go to? I will tell her everything to-night. I had almost made up my mind to do so already. It will be better that they should both know it,—my father and my mother. My father probably will be required to say all that he knows about the matter."

"I shall be ready to go at once if she wishes it," said Margaret.

To this he made no answer, but went upstairs to his bedroom, and there, as he dressed, thought again, and again, and again of his cousin Margaret. What should he do for her, and in what way should he treat her? The very name of the Mackenzies he had hated of old, and their names were now more hateful to him than ever. He had correctly described his own feelings towards them when he said, either truly or untruly, that they had deprived him of that which would have made his whole life prosperous instead of the reverse. And it seemed as though he had really thought that they had been in fault in this,—that they had defrauded him. It did not, apparently, occur to him that the only persons he could blame were his uncle Jonathan and his own lawyers, who, at his uncle's death, had failed to discover on his behalf what really were his rights. Walter Mackenzie had been a poor creature who could do nothing. Tom Mackenzie had been a mean creature who had allowed himself to be cozened in a petty trade out of the money which he had wrongfully acquired. They were odious to him, and he hated their memories. He would fain have hated all that belonged to them, had he been able. But he was not able to hate this woman who clung to him, and trusted him, and felt no harsh feelings towards him, though he was going to take from her everything that had been hers. She trusted him for advice even though he was her adversary! Would he have trusted her or any other human being under such circumstances? No, by heavens! But not the less on that account did he acknowledge to himself that this confidence in her was very gracious.

That evening passed by very quietly as far as Miss Mackenzie was concerned. She had some time since, immediately on her last arrival at the Cedars, offered to relieve her aunt from the trouble of making tea, and the duty had then been given up to her. But since Lady Ball's affair in obtaining possession of her niece's secret, the post of honour had been taken away.

"You don't make it as your uncle likes it," Lady Ball had said.

She made her little offer again on this evening, but it was rejected.

"Thank you, no; I believe I had better do it myself," had been the answer.

"Why can't you let Margaret make tea? I'm sure she does it very well," said John.

"I don't see that you can be a judge, seeing that you take none," his mother replied; "and if you please, I'd rather make the tea in my own house as long as I can."

This little allusion to her own house was, no doubt, a blow at her son, to punish him in that he had dictated to her in that matter of the continued entertainment of her guest; but Margaret also felt it to be a blow at her, and resolved that she would escape from the house with as little further delay as might be possible. Beyond this, the evening was very quiet, till Margaret, a little after tea, took her candle and went off wearily to her room.

But then the business of the day as regarded the Cedars began; for John Ball, before he went to bed, told both his father and his mother the whole story,—the story, that is, as far as the money was concerned, and also as far as Margaret's conduct to him was concerned; but of his own feelings towards her he said nothing.

"She has behaved admirably, mother," he said; "you must acknowledge that, and I think that she is entitled to all the kindness we can show her."

"I have been kind to her," Lady Ball answered.

This had taken place in Lady Ball's own room, after they had left Sir John. The tidings had taken the old man so much by surprise, that he had said little or nothing. Even his caustic ill-nature had deserted him, except on one occasion, when he remarked that it was like his brother Jonathan to do as much harm with his money as was within his reach.

"My memory in such a matter is worth nothing,— absolutely nothing," the old man had said. "I always supposed something was wrong. I remember that. But I left it all to the lawyers."

In Lady Ball's room the conversation was prolonged to a late hour of the night, and took various twists and turns, as such conversations will do.

"What are we to do about the young woman?" That was Lady Ball's main question, arising, no doubt, from the reflection that the world would lean very heavily on them if they absolutely turned her out to starve in the streets.

John Ball made no proposition in answer to this, having not as yet made up his mind as to what his own wishes were with reference to the young woman. Then his mother made her proposition.

"Of course that money due by the Rubbs must be paid. Let her take that." But her son made no reply to this other than that he feared the Rubbs were not in a condition to pay the money.

"They would pay her the interest at any rate," said Lady Ball, "till she had got into some other way of life. She would do admirably for a companion to an old lady, because her manners are good, and she does not want much waiting upon herself."

On the next morning Miss Mackenzie trembled in her shoes as she came down to breakfast. Her uncle, whom she feared the most, would not be there; but the meeting with her aunt, when her aunt would know that she was a pauper and that she had for the last week been an impostor, was terrible to her by anticipation. But she had not calculated that her aunt's triumph in this newly-acquired wealth for the Ball family would, for the present, cover any other feeling that might exist. Her aunt met her with a gracious smile, was very urbane in selecting a chair for her at prayers close to her own, and pressed upon her a piece of buttered toast out of a little dish that was always prepared for her ladyship's own consumption. After breakfast John Ball again went to town. He went daily to town during the present crisis; and, on this occasion, his mother made no remark as to the urgency of his business. When he was gone Lady Ball began to potter about the house, after her daily custom, and was longer in her pottering than was usual with her. Miss Mackenzie helped the younger children in their lessons, as she often did; and when time for luncheon came, she had almost begun to think that she was to be allowed to escape any conversation with her aunt touching the great money question. But it was not so. At one she was told that luncheon and the children's dinner was postponed till two, and she was asked by the servant to go up to Lady Ball in her own room.

"Come and sit down, my dear," said Lady Ball, in her sweetest voice. "It has got to be very cold, and you had better come near the fire." Margaret did as she was bidden, and sat herself down in the chair immediately opposite to her aunt.

"This is a wonderful story that John has told me," continued her aunt—"very wonderful."

"It is sad enough for me," said Margaret, who did not feel inclined to be so self-forgetful in talking to her aunt as she had been with her cousin.

"It is sad for you, Margaret, no doubt. But I am sure you have within you that conscientious rectitude of purpose that you would not wish to keep anything for yourself that in truth belongs to another."

To this Margaret answered nothing, and her aunt went on.

"It is a great change to you, no doubt; and, of course, that is the point on which I wish to speak to you most especially. I have told John that something must be done for you."

This jarred terribly on poor Margaret's feelings. Her cousin had said nothing, not a word as to doing anything for her. The man who had told her of his love, and asked her to be his wife, not twelve months since,—who had pressed her to be of all women the dearest to him and the nearest,—had talked to her of her ruin without offering her aid, although this ruin to her would enrich him very greatly. She had expected nothing from him, had wanted nothing from him; but by degrees, when absent from him, the feeling had grown upon her that he had been hard to her in abstaining from expressions of commiseration. She had yielded to him in the whole affair, assuring him that nothing should be done by her to cause him trouble; and she would have been grateful to him if in return he had said something to her of her future mode of life. She had intended to speak to him about the hospital; but she had thought that she might abstain from doing so till he himself should ask some question as to her plans. He had asked no such question, and she was now almost determined to go away without troubling him on the subject. But if he, who had once professed to love her, would make no suggestion as to her future life, she could ill bear that any offer of the kind should come from her aunt, who, as she knew, had only regarded her for her money.

"I would rather," she replied, "that nothing should be said to him on the subject."

"And why not, Margaret?"

"I desire that I may be no burden to him or anybody. I will go away and earn my bread; and even if I cannot do that, my relations shall not be troubled by hearing from me."

She said this without sobbing, but not without that almost hysterical emotion which indicates that tears are being suppressed with pain.

"That is false pride, my dear."

"Very well, aunt. I daresay it is false; but it is my pride. I may be allowed to keep my pride, though I can keep nothing else."

"What you say about earning your bread is very proper; and I and John and your uncle also have been thinking of that. But I should be glad if some additional assistance should be provided for you, in the event of old age, you know, or illness. Now, as to earning your bread, I remarked to John that you were peculiarly qualified for being a lady's companion."

"For being what, aunt?"

"For being companion to some lady in the decline of life, who would want to have some nice mannered person always with her. You have the advantage of being ladylike and gentle, and I think that you are patient by disposition."

"Aunt," said Miss Mackenzie, and her voice as she spoke was hardly gentle, nor was it indicative of much patience. Her hysterics also seemed for the time to have given way to her strong passionate feeling. "Aunt," she said, "I would sooner take a broom in my hand, and sweep a crossing in London, than lead such a life as that. What! make myself the slave of some old woman, who would think that she had bought the power of tyrannising over me by allowing me to sit in the same room with her? No, indeed! It may very likely be the case that I may have to serve such a one in the kitchen, but it shall be in the kitchen, and not in the drawing-room. I have not had much experience in life, but I have had enough to learn that lesson!"

Lady Ball, who during the first part of the conversation had been unrolling and winding a great ball of worsted, now sat perfectly still, holding the ball in her lap, and staring at her niece. She was a quick-witted woman, and it no doubt occurred to her that the great objection to living with an old lady, which her niece had expressed so passionately, must have come from the trial of that sort of life which she had had at the Cedars. And there was enough in Miss Mackenzie's manner to justify Lady Ball in thinking that some such expression of feeling as this had been intended by her. She had never before heard Margaret speak out so freely, even in the days of her undoubted heiress-ship; and now, though she greatly disliked her niece, she could not avoid mingling something of respect and something almost amounting to fear with her dislike. She did not dare to go on unwinding her worsted, and giving the advantage of her condescension to a young woman who spoke out at her in that way.

"I thought I was advising you for the best," she said, "and I hoped that you would have been thankful."

"I don't know what may be for the best," said Margaret, again bordering upon the hysterical in the tremulousness of her voice, "but that I'm sure would be for the worst. However, I've made up my mind to nothing as yet."

"No, my dear; of course not; but we all must think of it, you know."

Her cousin John had not thought of it, and she did not want any one else to do so. She especially did not want her aunt to think of it. But it was no doubt necessary that her aunt should consider how long she would be required to provide a home for her impoverished niece, and Margaret's mind at once applied itself to that view of the subject. "I have made up my mind that I will go to London next week, and then I must settle upon something."

"You mean when you go to Mr. Slow's?"

"I mean that I shall go for good. I have a little money by me, which John says I may use, and I shall take a lodging till—till—till—" Then she could not go on any further.

"You can stay here, Margaret, if you please;—that is till something more is settled about all this affair."

"I will go on Monday, aunt. I have made up my mind to that." It was now Saturday. "I will go on Monday. It will be better for all parties that I should be away." Then she got up, and waiting no further speech from her aunt, took herself off to her own room.

She did not see her aunt again till dinner-time, and then neither of them spoke to each other. Lady Ball thought that she had reason to be offended, and Margaret would not be the first to speak. In the evening, before the whole family, she told her cousin that she had made up her mind to go up to London on Monday. He begged her to reconsider her resolution, but when she persisted that she would do so, he did not then argue the question any further. But on the Sunday he implored her not to go as yet, and did obtain her consent to postpone her departure till Tuesday. He wished, he said, to be at any rate one day more

in London before she went. On the Sunday she was closeted
with her uncle who also sent for her, and to him she suggested
her plan of becoming nurse at a hospital. He remarked that he
hoped that would not be necessary.

"Something will be necessary," she said, "as I don't
mean to eat anybody's bread but my own."

In answer to this he said that he would speak to John, and
then that interview was over. On the Monday morning John Ball
said something respecting Margaret to his mother which
acerbated that lady more than ever against her niece. He had not
proposed that anything special should be done; but he had
hinted, when his mother complained of Margaret, that
Margaret's conduct was everything that it ought to be.

"I believe you would take anybody's part against me,"
Lady Ball had said, and then as a matter of course she had been
very cross. The whole of that day was terrible to Miss
Mackenzie, and she resolved that nothing said by her cousin
should induce her to postpone her departure for another day.

In order to insure this by a few minutes' private
conversation with him, and also with the view of escaping for
some short time from the house, she walked down to the station
in the evening to meet her cousin. The train by which he arrived
reached Twickenham at five o'clock, and the walk occupied
about twenty minutes. She met him just as he was coming out of
the station gate, and at once told him that she had come there for
the sake of walking back with him and talking to him. He
thanked her, and said that he was very glad to meet her. He also
wanted to speak to her very particularly. Would she take his
arm?

She took his arm, and then began with a quick tremulous
voice to tell him of her sufferings at the house. She threw no
blame on her aunt that she could avoid, but declared it to be
natural that under such circumstances as those now existing her
prolonged sojourn at her aunt's house should be unpleasant to
both of them. In answer to all this, John Ball said nothing, but

once or twice lifted up his left hand so as to establish Margaret's arm more firmly on his own. She hardly noticed the motion, but yet she was aware that it was intended for kindness, and then she broke forth with a rapid voice as to her plan about the hospital. "I think we can manage better than that, at any rate," said he, stopping her in the path when this proposal met his ear. But she went on to declare that she would like it, that she was strong and qualified for such work, that it would satisfy her aspirations, and be fit for her. And then, after that, she declared that nothing should induce her to undertake the kind of life that had been suggested by her aunt. "I quite agree with you there," said he; "quite. I hate tabbies as much as you do."

They had now come to a little gate, of which John Ball kept a key, and which led into the grounds belonging to the Cedars. The grounds were rather large, and the path through them extended for half a mile, but the land was let off to a grazier. When inside the wall, however, they were private; and Mr. Ball, as soon as he had locked the gate behind him, stopped her in the dark path, and took both her hands in his. The gloom of the evening had now come round them, and the thick trees which formed the belt of the place, joined to the high wall, excluded from them nearly all what light remained.

"And now," said he, "I will tell you my plan."

"What plan?" said she; but her voice was very low.

"I proposed it once before, but you would not have it then."

When she heard this, she at once drew both her hands from him, and stood before him in an agony of doubt. Even in the gloom, the trees were going round her, and everything, even her thoughts, were obscure and misty.

"Margaret," said he, "you shall be my wife, and the mother of my children, and I will love you as I loved Rachel before. I loved you when I asked you at Christmas, but I did not love you then as I love you now."

She still stood before him, but answered him not a word. How often since the tidings of her loss had reached her had the idea of such a meeting as this come before her! how often had she seemed to listen to such words as those he now spoke to her! Not that she had expected it, or hoped for it, or even thought of it as being in truth possible; but her imagination had been at work, during the long hours of the night, and the romance of the thing had filled her mind, and the poetry of it had been beautiful to her. She had known—she had told herself that she knew—that no man would so sacrifice himself; certainly no such man as John Ball, with all his children and his weary love of money! But now the poetry had come to be fact, and the romance had turned itself into reality, and the picture formed by her imagination had become a living truth. The very words of which she had dreamed had been spoken to her.

"Shall it be so, my dear?" he said, again taking one of her hands. "You want to be a nurse; will you be my nurse? Nay; I will not ask, but it shall be so. They say that the lovers who demand are ever the most successful. I make my demand. Tell me, Margaret, will you obey me?"

He had walked on now, but in order that his time might be sufficient, he led her away from the house. She was following him, hardly knowing whither she was going.

"Susanna," said he, "shall come and live with the others; one more will make no difference."

"And my aunt?" said Margaret.

It was the first word she had spoken since the gate had been locked behind her, and this word was spoken in a whisper.

"I hope my mother may feel that such a marriage will best conduce to my happiness; but, Margaret, nothing that my mother can say will change me. You and I have known something of each other now. Of you, from the way in which things have gone, I have learned much. Few men, I take it, see so much of their future wives as I have seen of you. If you can love me as your husband, say so at once honestly, and then leave the rest to me."

"I will," she said, again whispering; and then she clung to his hand, and for a minute or two he had his arm round her waist. Then he took her, and kissed her lips, and told her that he would take care of her, and watch for her, and keep her, if possible, from trouble.

Ah, me, how many years had rolled by since last she had been kissed in that way! Once, and once only, had Harry Handcock so far presumed, and so far succeeded. And now, after a dozen years or more, that game had begun again with her! She had boxed Harry Handcock's ears when he had kissed her; but now, from her lover of to-day, she submitted to the ceremony very tamely.

"Oh, John," she said, "how am I to thank you?" But the thanks were tendered for the promise of his care, and not for the kiss.

I think there was but little more said between them before they reached the door-step. When there, Mr. Ball, speaking already with something of marital authority, gave her his instructions.

"I shall tell my mother this evening," he said, "as I hate mysteries; and I shall tell my father also. Of course there may be something disagreeable said before we all shake down happily in our places, but I shall look to you, Margaret, to be firm."

"I shall be firm," she said, "if you are."

"I shall be firm," was the reply; and then they went into the house.

Chapter XXI

Mr. Maguire Goes to London on Business

Mr. Maguire made up his mind to go to London, to look after his lady-love, but when he found himself there he did not quite know what to do. It is often the case with us that we make up our minds for great action,—that in some special crisis of our lives we resolve that something must be done, and that we make an energetic start; but we find very soon that we do not know how to go on doing anything. It was so with Mr. Maguire. When he had secured a bed at a small public house near the Great Western railway station,—thinking, no doubt that he would go to the great hotel on his next coming to town, should he then have obtained the lady's fortune,—he scarcely knew what step he would next take. Margaret's last letter had been written to him from the Cedars, but he thought it probable that she might only have gone there for a day or two. He knew the address of the house in Gower Street, and at last resolved that he would go boldly in among the enemy there; for he was assured that the family of the lady's late brother were his special enemies in this case. It was considerably past noon when he reached London, and it was about three when, with a hesitating hand, but a loud knock, he presented himself at Mrs. Mackenzie's door.

He first asked for Miss Mackenzie, and was told that she was not staying there. Was he thereupon to leave his card and go away? He had told himself that in this pursuit of the heiress he would probably be called upon to dare much, and if he did not begin to show some daring at once, how could he respect himself, or trust to himself for future daring? So he boldly asked for Mrs. Mackenzie, and was at once shown into the parlour. There sat the widow, in her full lugubrious weeds, there sat Miss Colza, and there sat Mary Jane, and they were all busy hemming, darning, and clipping; turning old sheets into new ones; for now it was more than ever necessary that Mrs. Mackenzie should make money at once by taking in lodgers. When Mr. Maguire was shown into the room each lady rose from her chair, with her sheet in her hands and in her lap, and then, as he stood before them, at the other side of the table, each lady again sat down.

"A gentleman as is asking for Miss Margaret," the servant had said; that same cook to whom Mr. Grandairs had been so severe on the occasion of Mrs. Mackenzie's dinner party. The other girl had been unnecessary to them in their poverty, and had left them.

"My name is Maguire, the Rev. Mr. Maguire, from Littlebath, where I had the pleasure of knowing Miss Mackenzie."

Then the widow asked him to take a chair, and he took a chair.

"My sister-in-law is not with us at present," said Mrs. Mackenzie.

"She is staying for a visit with her aunt, Lady Ball, at the Cedars, Twickenham," said Mary Jane, who had contrived to drop her sheet, and hustle it under the table with her feet, as soon as she learned that the visitor was a clergyman.

"Lady Ball is the lady of Sir John Ball, Baronet," said Miss Colza, whose good nature made her desirous of standing up for the honour of the family with which she was, for the time, domesticated.

"I knew she had been at Lady Ball's," said the clergyman, "as I heard from her from thence; but I thought she had probably returned."

"Oh dear, no," said the widow, "she ain't returned here, nor don't mean. We haven't the room for her, and that's the truth. Have we, Mary Jane?"

"That we have not, mamma; and I don't think aunt Margaret would think of such a thing."

Then, thought Mr. Maguire, the Balls must have got hold of the heiress, and not the Mackenzies, and my battle must be fought at the Cedars, and not here. Still, as he was there, he thought possibly he might obtain some further information; and this would be the easier, if, as appeared to be the case, there was enmity between the Gower Street family and their relative.

"Has Miss Mackenzie gone to live permanently at the Cedars?" he asked.

"Not that I know of," said the widow.

"It isn't at all unlikely, mamma, that it may be so, when you consider everything. It's just the sort of way in which they'll most likely get over her."

"Mary Jane, hold your tongue," said her mother; "you shouldn't say things of that sort before strangers."

"Though I may not have the pleasure of knowing you and your amiable family," said Mr. Maguire, smiling his sweetest, "I am by no means a stranger to Miss Mackenzie."

Then the ladies all looked at him, and thought they had never seen anything so terrible as that squint.

"Miss Mackenzie is making a long visit at the Cedars," said Miss Colza, "that is all we know at present. I am told the Balls are very nice people, but perhaps a little worldly-minded; that's to be expected, however, from people who live out of the west-end from London. I live in Finsbury Square, or at least, I did before I came here, and I ain't a bit ashamed to own it. But of course the west-end is the nicest."

Then Mr. Maguire got up, saying that he should probably do himself the pleasure of calling on Miss Mackenzie at the Cedars, and went his way.

"I wonder what he's after," said Mrs. Mackenzie, as soon as the door was shut.

"Perhaps he came to tell her to bear it all with Christian resignation," said Miss Colza; "they always do come when anything's in the wind like that; they like to know everything before anybody else."

"It's my belief he's after her money," said Mrs. Mackenzie.

"With such a squint as that!" said Mary Jane; "I wouldn't have him though he was made of money, and I hadn't a farthing."

"Beauty is but skin deep," said Miss Colza.

"And it's manners to wait till you are asked," said Mrs. Mackenzie.

Mary Jane chucked up her head with disdain, thereby indicating that though she had not been asked, and though beauty is but skin deep, still she held the same opinion.

Mr. Maguire, as he went away to a clerical advertising office in the neighbourhood of Exeter Hall, thought over the matter profoundly. It was clear enough to him that the Mackenzies of Gower Street were not interfering with him; very probably they might have hoped and attempted to keep the heiress among them; that assertion that there was no room for her in the house—as though they were and ever had been averse to having her with them—seemed to imply that such was the case. It was the natural language of a disappointed woman. But if so, that hope was now over with them. And then the young lady had plainly exposed the suspicions which they all entertained as to the Balls. These grand people at the Cedars, this baronet's family at Twickenham, must have got her to come among them with the intention of keeping her there. It did not occur to him that the baronet or the baronet's son would actually want Miss Mackenzie's money. He presumed baronets to be rich people; but still they might very probably be as dogs in the manger, and desirous of preventing their relative from doing with her money that active service to humanity in general which would be done were she to marry a deserving clergyman who had nothing of his own.

He made his visit to the advertising office, and learned that clergymen without cures were at present drugs in the market. He couldn't understand how this should be the case, seeing that the newspapers were constantly declaring that the supply of university clergymen were becoming less and less every day. He had come from Trinity, Dublin and after the success of his career at Littlebath, was astonished that he should not be snapped at by the retailers of curacies.

On the next day he visited Twickenham. Now, on the morning of that very day Margaret Mackenzie first woke to the consciousness that she was the promised wife of her cousin John Ball. There was great comfort in the thought.

It was not only, nor even chiefly, that she who, on the preceding morning, had awakened to the remembrance of her utter destitution, now felt that all those terrible troubles were over. It was not simply that her great care had been vanquished for her. It was this, that the man who had a second time come to her asking for her love, had now given her all-sufficient evidence that he did so for the sake of her love. He, who was so anxious for money, had shown her that he could care for her more even than he cared for gold. As she thought of this, and made herself happy in the thought, she would not rise at once from her bed, but curled herself in the clothes and hugged herself in her joy.

"I should have taken him before, at once, instantly, if I could have thought that it was so," she said to herself; "but this is a thousand times better."

Then she found that the pillow beneath her cheek was wet with her tears.

On the preceding evening she had been very silent and demure, and her betrothed had also been silent. There had been no words about the tea-making, and Lady Ball had been silent also. As far as she knew, Margaret was to go on the following day, but she would say nothing on the subject. Margaret, indeed, had commenced her packing, and did not know when she went to bed whether she was to go or not. She rather hoped that she might be allowed to go, as her aunt would doubtless be disagreeable; but in that, and in all matters now, she would of course be guided implicitly by Mr. Ball. He had told her to be firm, and of her own firmness she had no doubt whatever. Lady Ball, with all her anger, or with all her eloquence, should not talk her out of her husband. She could be firm, and she had no doubt that John Ball could be firm also.

Nevertheless, when she was dressing, she did not fail to tell herself that she might have a bad time of it that morning,— and a bad time of it for some days to come, if it was John's intention that she should remain at the Cedars. She was convinced that Lady Ball would not welcome her as a daughter-in-law now as she would have done when the property was thought to belong to her. What right had she to expect such welcome? No doubt some hard things would be said to her; but she knew her own courage, and was sure that she could bear any hard things with such a hope within her breast as that which she now possessed. She left her room a little earlier than usual, thinking that she might thus meet her cousin and receive his orders. And in this she was not disappointed; he was in the hall as she came down, and she was able to smile on him, and press his hand, and make her morning greetings to him with some tenderness in her voice. He looked heavy about the face, and almost more careworn than usual, but he took her hand and led her into the breakfast-room.

"Did you tell your mother, John?" she said, standing very close to him, almost leaning upon his shoulder.

He, however, did not probably want such signs of love as this, and moved a step away from her.

"Yes," said he, "I told both my father and my mother. What she says to you, you must hear, and bear it quietly for my sake."

"I will," said Margaret.

"I think that she is unreasonable, but still she is my mother."

"I shall always remember that, John."

"And she is old, and things have not always gone well with her. She says, too, that you have been impertinent to her."

Margaret's face became very red at this charge, but she made no immediate reply.

"I don't think you could mean to be impertinent."

"Certainly not, John; but, of course, I shall feel myself much more bound to her now than I was before."

"Yes, of course; but I wish that nothing had occurred to make her so angry with you."

"I don't think that I was impertinent, John, though perhaps it might seem so. When she was talking about my being a companion to a lady, I perhaps answered her sharply. I was so determined that I wouldn't lead that sort of life, that, perhaps I said more than I should have done. You know, John, that it hasn't been quite pleasant between us for the last few days."

John did know this, and he knew also that there was not much probability of pleasantness for some days to come. His mother's last words to him on the preceding evening, as he was leaving her after having told his story, did not give much promise of pleasantness for Margaret. "John," she had said, "nothing on earth shall induce me to live in the same house with Margaret Mackenzie as your wife. If you choose to break up everything for her sake, you can do it. I cannot control you. But remember, it will be your doing."

Margaret then asked him what she was to do, and where she was to live. She would fain have asked him when they were to be married, but she did not dare to make inquiry on that point. He told her that, for the present, she must remain at the Cedars. If she went away it would be regarded as an open quarrel, and moreover, he did not wish that she should live by herself in London lodgings. "We shall be able to see how things go for a day or two," he said. To this she submitted without a murmur, and then Lady Ball came into the room.

They were both very nervous in watching her first behaviour, but were not at all prepared for the line of conduct which she adopted. John Ball and Margaret had separated when they heard the rustle of her dress. He had made a step towards the window, and she had retreated to the other side of the fire-place. Lady Ball, on entering the room, had been nearest to Margaret, but she walked round the table away from her usual place for prayers, and accosted her son.

"Good-morning, John," she said, giving him her hand.

Margaret waited a second or two, and then addressed her aunt.

"Good-morning, aunt," she said, stepping half across the rug.

But her aunt, turning her back to her, moved into the embrasure of the window. It had been decided that there was to be an absolute cut between them! As long as she remained in that house Lady Ball would not speak to her. John said nothing, but a black frown came upon his brow. Poor Margaret retired, rebuked, to her corner by the chimney. Just at that moment the girls and children rushed in from the study, with the daily governess who came every morning, and Sir John rang for the servants to come to prayers.

I wonder whether that old lady's heart was at all softened as she prayed? whether it ever occurred to her to think that there was any meaning in that form of words she used, when she asked her God to forgive her as she might forgive others? Not that Margaret had in truth trespassed against her at all; but, doubtless, she regarded her niece as a black trespasser, and as being quite qualified for forgiveness, could she have brought herself to forgive. But I fear that the form of words on that occasion meant nothing, and that she had been delivered from no evil during those moments she had been on her knees. Margaret sat down in her accustomed place, but no notice was taken of her by her aunt. When the tea had been poured out, John got up from his seat and asked his mother which was Margaret's cup.

"My dear," said she, "if you will sit down, Miss Mackenzie shall have her tea."

"I will take it to her," said he.

"John," said his mother, drawing her chair somewhat away from the table, "if you flurry me in this way, you will drive me out of the room."

Then he had sat down, and Margaret received her cup in the usual way. The girls and children stared at each other, and the governess, who always breakfasted at the house, did not dare to lift her eyes from off her plate.

Margaret longed for an opportunity of starting with John Ball, and walking with him to the station, but no such opportunity came in her way. It was his custom always to go up to his father before he left home, and on this occasion Margaret did not see him after he quitted the breakfast table. When the clatter of the knives and cups was over, and the eating and drinking was at an end, Lady Ball left the room and Margaret began to think what she would do. She could not remain about the house in her aunt's way, without being spoken to, or speaking. So she went to her room, resolving that she would not leave it till the carriage had taken off Sir John and her aunt. Then she would go out for a walk, and would again meet her cousin at the station.

From her bedroom window she could see the sweep before the front of the house, and at two o'clock she saw and heard the lumbering of the carriage as it came to the door, and then she put on her hat to be ready for her walk; but her uncle and aunt did not, as it seemed, come out, and the carriage remained there as a fixture. This had been the case for some twenty minutes, when there came a knock at her own door, and the maid-servant told her that her aunt wished to see her in the drawing-room.

"To see me?" said Margaret, thoroughly surprised, and not a little dismayed.

"Yes, Miss; and there's a gentleman there who asked for you when he first come."

Now, indeed, she was dismayed. Who could be the gentleman? Was it Mr. Slow, or a myrmidon from Mr. Slow's legal abode? Or was it Mr. Rubb with his yellow gloves again? Whoever it was there must be something very special in his mission, as her aunt had, in consequence, deferred her drive, and was also apparently about to drop her purpose of cutting her niece's acquaintance in her own house.

But we will go back to Mr. Maguire. He had passed the evening and the morning in thinking over the method of his attack, and had at last resolved that he would be very bold. He would go down to the Cedars, and claim Margaret as his affianced bride. He went, therefore, down to the Cedars, and in accordance with his plan as arranged, he gave his card to the servant, and asked if he could see Sir John Ball alone. Now, Sir John Ball never saw any one on business, or, indeed, not on business; and, after a while, word was brought out to Mr. Maguire that he could see Lady Ball, but that Sir John was not well enough to receive any visitors. Lady Ball, Mr. Maguire thought, would suit him better than Sir John. He signified his will accordingly, and on being shown into the drawing-room, found her ladyship there alone.

It must be acknowledged that he was a brave man, and that he was doing a bold thing. He knew that he should find himself among enemies, and that his claim would be ignored and ridiculed by the persons whom he was about to attack; he knew that everybody, on first seeing him, was affrighted and somewhat horrified; he knew too,—at least, we must presume that he knew,—that the lady herself had given him no promise. But he thought it possible, nay, almost probable, that she would turn to him if she saw him again; that she might own him as her own; that her feelings might be strong enough in his favour to induce her to throw off the thraldom of her relatives, and that he might make good his ground in her breast, even if he could not bear her away in triumph out of the hands of his enemies.

When he entered the room Lady Ball looked at him and shuddered. People always did shudder when they saw him for the first time.

"Lady Ball," said he, "I am the Rev. Mr. Maguire, of Littlebath."

She was holding his card in her hand, and having notified to him that she was aware of the fact he had mentioned, asked him to sit down.

"I have called," said he, taking his seat, "hoping to be allowed to speak to you on a subject of extreme delicacy."

"Indeed," said Lady Ball, thinking to catch his eye, and failing in the effort.

"I may say of very extreme delicacy. I believe your niece, Miss Margaret Mackenzie, is staying here?" In answer to this, Lady Ball acknowledged that Miss Mackenzie was now at the Cedars.

"Have you any objection, Lady Ball, to allowing me to see her in your presence?"

Lady Ball was a quick-thinking, intelligent, and, at the same time, prudent old lady, and she gave no answer to this before she had considered the import of the question. Why should this clergyman want to see Margaret? And would his seeing her conduce most to her own success, or to Margaret's? Then there was the fact that Margaret was of an age which entitled her to the right of seeing any visitor who might call on her. Thinking over all this as best she could in the few moments at her command, and thinking also of this clergyman's stipulation that she was to be present at the interview, she said that she had no objection whatever. She would send for Miss Mackenzie.

She rose to ring the bell, but Mr. Maguire, also rising from his chair, stopped her hand.

"Pardon me for a moment," said he. "Before you call Margaret to come down I would wish to explain to you for what purpose I have come here."

Lady Ball, when she heard the man call her niece by her Christian name, listened with all her ears. Under no circumstances but one could such a man call such a woman by her Christian name in such company.

"Lady Ball," he said, "I do not know whether you may be aware of it or no, but I am engaged to marry your niece."

Lady Ball, who had not yet resumed her seat, now did so.

"I had not heard of it," she said.

"It may be so," said Mr. Maguire.

"It is so," said Lady Ball.

"Very probably. There are many reasons which operate upon young ladies in such a condition to keep their secret even from their nearest relatives. For myself, being a clergyman of the Church of England, professing evangelical doctrines, and therefore, as I had need not say, averse to everything that may have about it even a seeming of impropriety, I think it best to declare the fact to you, even though in doing so I may perhaps give some offence to dear Margaret."

It must, I think, be acknowledged that Mr. Maguire was true to himself, and that he was conducting his case at any rate with courage.

Lady Ball was doubtful what she would do. It was on her tongue to tell the man that her niece's fortune was gone. But she remembered that she might probably advance her own interests by securing an interview between the two lovers of Littlebath in her own presence. She never for a moment doubted that Mr. Maguire's statement was true. It never occurred to her that there had been no such engagement. She felt confident from the moment in which Mr. Maguire's important tidings had reached her ears that she had now in her hands the means of rescuing her son. That Mr. Maguire would cease to make his demand for his bride when he should hear the truth, was of course to be expected; but her son would not be such an idiot, such a soft fool, as to go on with his purpose when he should learn that such a secret as this had been kept back from him. She had refused him, and taken up with this horrid, greasy, evil-eyed parson when she was rich; and then, when she was poor,—even before she had got rid of her other engagement, she had come back upon him, and, playing upon his pity, had secured him in her toils. Lady Ball felt well inclined to thank the clergyman for coming to her relief at such a moment.

"It will be best that I should ask my niece to come down to you," said she, getting up and walking out of the room.

But she did not go up to her niece. She first went to Sir John and quieted his impatience with reference to the driving, and then, after a few minutes' further delay for consideration, she sent the servant up to her niece. Having done this she returned to the drawing-room, and found Mr. Maguire looking at the photographs on the table.

"It is very like dear Margaret, very like her, indeed," said he, looking at one of Miss Mackenzie. "The sweetest face that ever my eyes rested on! May I ask you if you have just seen your niece, Lady Ball?"

"No, sir, I have not seen her; but I have sent for her."

There was still some little delay before Margaret came down. She was much fluttered, and wanted time to think, if only time could be allowed to her. Perhaps there had come a man to say that her money was not gone. If so, with what delight would she give it all to her cousin John! That was her first thought. But if so, how then about the promise made to her dying brother? She almost wished that the money might not be hers. Looking to herself only, and to her own happiness, it would certainly be better for her that it should not be hers. And if it should be Mr. Rubb with the yellow gloves! But before she could consider that alternative she had opened the door, and there was Mr. Maguire standing ready to receive her.

"Dearest Margaret!" he exclaimed. "My own love!" And there he stood, with his arms open, as though he expected Miss Mackenzie to rush into them. He was certainly a man of very great courage.

"Mr. Maguire!" said she, and she stood still near the door. Then she looked at her aunt, and saw that Lady Ball's eyes were keenly fixed upon her. Something like the truth, some approximation to the facts as they were, flashed upon her in a moment, and she knew that she had to bear herself in this difficulty with all her discretion and all her fortitude.

"Margaret," exclaimed Mr. Maguire, "will you not come to me?"

"What do you mean, Mr. Maguire?" said she, still standing aloof from him, and retreating somewhat nearer to the door.

"The gentleman says that you are engaged to marry him," said Lady Ball.

Margaret, looking again into her aunt's face, saw the smile of triumph that sat there, and resolved at once to make good her ground.

"If he has said that, he has told an untruth,—an untruth both unmanly and unmannerly. You hear, sir, what Lady Ball has stated. Is it true that you have made such an assertion?"

"And will you contradict it, Margaret? Oh, Margaret! Margaret! you cannot contradict it."

The reader must remember that this clergyman no doubt thought and felt that he had a good deal of truth on his side. Gentlemen when they make offers to ladies, and are told by ladies that they may come again, and that time is required for consideration, are always disposed to think that the difficulties of the siege are over. And in nine cases out of ten it is so. Mr. Maguire, no doubt, since the interview in question, had received letters from the lady which should at any rate have prevented him from uttering any such assertion as that which he had now made; but he looked upon those letters as the work of the enemy, and chose to go back for his authority to the last words which Margaret had spoken to him. He knew that he was playing an intricate game,—that all was not quite on the square; but he thought that the enemy was playing him false, and that falsehood in return was therefore fair. This that was going on was a robbery of the Church, a spoiling of Israel, a touching with profane hands of things that had already been made sacred.

"But I do contradict it," said Margaret, stepping forward into the room, and almost exciting admiration in Lady Ball's breast by her demeanour. "Aunt," said she, "as this gentleman has chosen to come here with such a story as this, I must tell you all the facts."

"Has he ever been engaged to you?" asked Lady Ball.

"Never."

"Oh, Margaret!" again exclaimed Mr. Maguire.

"Sir, I will ask you to let me tell my aunt the truth. When I was at Littlebath, before I knew that my fortune was not my own,"—as she said this she looked hard into Mr. Maguire's face—"before I had become penniless, as I am now,"—then she paused again, and still looking at him, saw with inward pleasure the elongation of her suitor's face, "this gentleman asked me to marry him."

"He did ask you?" said Lady Ball.

"Of course I asked her," urged Mr. Maguire. "There can be no denying that on either side."

He did not now quite know what to do. He certainly did not wish to impoverish the Church by marrying Miss Mackenzie without any fortune. But might it not all be a trick? That she had been rich he knew, and how could she have become poor so quickly?

"He did ask me, and I told him that I must take a fortnight to consider of it."

"You did not refuse him, then?" said Lady Ball.

"Not then, but I have done so since by letter. Twice I have written to him, telling him that I had nothing of my own, and that there could be nothing between us."

"I got her letters," said Mr. Maguire, turning round to Lady Ball. "I certainly got her letters. But such letters as those, if they are written under dictation—"

He was rather anxious that Lady Bell should quarrel with him. In the programme which he had made for himself when he came to the house, a quarrel to the knife with the Ball family was a part of his tactics. His programme, no doubt, was disturbed by the course which events had taken, but still a quarrel with Lady Ball might be the best for him. If she were to quarrel with him, it would give him some evidence that this story about the loss of the money was untrue. But Lady Ball would not quarrel with him. She sat still and said nothing. "Nobody dictated them," said Margaret. "But now you are here, I will tell you the facts. The money which I thought was mine, in truth belongs to my cousin, Mr. John Ball, and I—"

So far she spoke loudly, With her face raised, and her eyes fixed upon him. Then as she concluded, she dropped her voice and eyes together. "And I am now engaged to him as his wife."

"Oh, indeed!" said Mr. Maguire.

"That statement must be taken for what it is worth," said Lady Ball, rising from her seat. "Of what Miss Mackenzie says now, I know nothing. I sincerely hope that she may find that she is mistaken."

"And now, Margaret," said Mr. Maguire, "may I ask to see you for one minute alone?"

"Certainly not," said she. "If you have anything more to say I will hear it in my aunt's presence." She waited a few moments, but as he did not speak, she took herself back to the door and made her escape to her own room.

How Mr. Maguire took himself out of the house we need not stop to inquire. There must, I should think, have been some difficulty in the manoeuvre. It was considerably past three when Sir John was taken out for his drive, and while he was in the carriage his wife told him what had occurred.

Chapter XXII

Still at the Cedars

Margaret, when she had reached her own room, and seated herself so that she could consider all that had occurred in quietness, immediately knew her own difficulty. Of course Lady Ball would give her account of what had occurred to her son, and of course John would be angry when he learned that there had been any purpose of marriage between her and Mr. Maguire. She herself took a different view of the matter now than that which had hitherto presented itself. She had not thought much of Mr. Maguire or his proposal. It had been made under a state of things differing much from that now existing, and the change that had come upon her affairs had seemed to her to annul the offer. She had learned to regard it almost as though it had never been. There had been no engagement; there had hardly been a purpose in her own mind; and the moment had never come in which she could have spoken of it to her cousin with propriety.

That last, in truth, was her valid excuse for not having told him the whole story. She had hardly been with him long enough to do more than accept the offer he had himself made. Of course she would have told him of Mr. Maguire,—of Mr. Maguire and of Mr. Rubb also, when first an opportunity might come for her to do so. She had no desire to keep from his knowledge any tittle of what had occurred. There had been nothing of which she was ashamed. But not the less did she feel that it would have been well for her that she should have told her own story before that horrid man had come to the Cedars. The story would now first be told to him by her aunt, and she knew well the tone in which it would be told.

It occurred to her that she might even yet go and meet him at the station. But if so, she must tell him at once, and he would know that she had done so because she was afraid of her aunt, and she disliked the idea of excusing herself before she was accused. If he really loved her, he would listen to her, and believe her. If he did not—why then let Lady Ball have her own way. She had promised to be firm, and she would keep her promise; but she would not intrigue with the hope of making him firm. If he was infirm of purpose, let him go. So she sat in her room, even when she heard the door close after his entrance, and did not go down till it was time for her to show herself in the drawing-room before dinner. When she entered the room was full. He nodded at her with a pleasant smile, and she made up her mind that he had heard nothing as yet. Her uncle had excused himself from coming to table, and her aunt and John were talking together in apparent eagerness about him. For one moment her cousin spoke to her before dinner.

"I am afraid," he said, "that my father is sinking fast."

Then she felt quite sure that he had as yet heard nothing about Mr. Maguire.

But it was late in the evening, when other people had gone to bed, that Lady Ball was in the habit of discussing family affairs with her son, and doubtless she would do so to-night. Margaret, before she went up to her room, strove hard to get from him a few words of kindness, but it seemed as though he was not thinking of her.

"He is full of his father," she said to herself.

When her bed-candle was in her hand she did make an opportunity to speak to him.

"Has Mr. Slow settled anything more as yet?" she asked.

"Well, yes. Not that he has settled anything, but he has made a proposition to which I am willing to agree. I don't go up to town to-morrow, and we will talk it over. If you will agree to it, all the money difficulties will be settled."

"I will agree to anything that you tell me is right."

"I will explain it all to you to-morrow; and, Margaret, I have told Mr. Slow what are my intentions,—our intentions, I ought to say." She smiled at him with that sweet smile of hers, as though she thanked him for speaking of himself and her together, and then she took herself away. Surely, after speaking to her in that way, he would not allow any words from his mother to dissuade him from his purpose?

She could not go to bed. She knew that her fate was being discussed, and she knew that her aunt at that very time was using every argument in her power to ruin her. She felt, moreover, that the story might be told in such a way as to be terribly prejudicial to her. And now, when his father was so ill, might it not be very natural that he should do almost anything to lessen his mother's troubles? But to her it would be absolute ruin; such ruin that nothing which she had yet endured would be in any way like it. The story of the loss of her money had stunned her, but it had not broken her spirit. Her misery from that had arisen chiefly from the wants of her brother's family. But if he were now to tell her that all must be over between them, her very heart would be broken.

She could not go to bed while this was going on, so she sat listening, till she should hear the noise of feet about the house. Silently she loosened the lock of her own door, so that the sound might more certainly come to her, and she sat thinking what she might best do. It had not been quite eleven when she came upstairs, and at twelve she did not hear anything. And yet she was almost sure that they must be still together in that small room downstairs, talking of her and of her conduct. It was past one before she heard the door of the room open. She heard it so plainly, that she wondered at herself for having supposed for a moment that they could have gone without her noticing them. Then she heard her cousin's heavy step coming upstairs. In passing to his room he would not go actually by her door, but would be very near it. She looked through the chink, having carefully put away her own candle, and could see his face as he came upon the top stair. It wore a look of trouble and of pain, but not, as she thought, of anger. Her aunt, she knew, would go to her room by the back stairs, and would go through the kitchen and over the whole of the lower house, before she would come out on the landing to which Margaret's room opened. Then, seeing her cousin, the idea occurred to her that she would have it all over on that very night. If he had heard that which changed his purpose, why should she be left in suspense? He should tell her at once, and at once she would prepare herself for her future life.

So she opened the door a little way, and called to him.

"John," she said, "is that you?"

She spoke almost in a whisper, but, nevertheless, he heard her very clearly, and at once turned towards her room.

"Come in, John," she said, opening the door wider. "I wish to speak to you. I have been waiting till you should come up."

She had taken off her dress, and had put on in place of it a white dressing-gown; but of this she had not thought till he was already within the room. "I hope you won't mind finding me like this, but I did so want to speak to you to-night."

He, as he looked at her, felt that he had no objection to make to her appearance. If that had been his only trouble concerning her he would have been well satisfied. When he was within the room, she closed the lock of the door very softly, and then began to question him.

"Tell me," she said, "what my aunt has been saying to you about that man that came here to-day."

He did not answer her at once, but stood leaning against the bed.

"I know she has been telling you," continued Margaret. "I know she would not let you go to bed without accusing me. Tell me, John, what she has told you."

He was very slow to speak. As he had sat listening to his mother's energetic accusation against the woman he had promised to marry, hearing her bring up argument after argument to prove that Margaret had, in fact, been engaged to that clergyman,—that she had intended to marry that man while she had money, and had not, up to that day, made him fully understand that she would not do so,—he had himself said little or nothing, claiming to himself the use of that night for consideration. The circumstances against Margaret he owned to be very strong. He felt angry with her for having had any lover at Littlebath. It was but the other day, during her winter visit to the Cedars, that he had himself proposed to her, and that she had rejected him. He had now renewed his proposal, and he did not like to think that there had been any one else between his overtures. And he could not deny the strength of his mother's argument when she averred that Mr. Maguire would not have come down there unless he had had, as she said, every encouragement. Indeed, throughout the whole affair, Lady Ball believed Mr. Maguire, and disbelieved her niece; and something of her belief, and something also of her disbelief, communicated itself to her son. But, still, he reserved to himself the right of postponing his own opinion till the morrow; and as he was coming upstairs, when Margaret saw him through the chink of the door, he was thinking of her smiles, of her graciousness, and her goodness. He was remembering the touch of her hand when they were together in the square, and the feminine sweetness with which she had yielded to him every point regarding her fortune. When he did not speak to her at once, she questioned him again.

"I know she has told you that Mr. Maguire has been here, and that she has accused me of deceiving you."

"Yes, Margaret, she has."

"And what have you said in return; or rather, what have you thought?"

He had been leaning, or half sitting, on the bed, and she had placed herself beside him. How was it that she had again taken him by the coat, and again looked up into his face with those soft, trusting eyes? Was it a trick with her? Had she ever taken that other man by the coat in the same way, and smitten him also with the battery of her eyes? The loose sleeve of her dressing-gown had fallen back, and he could see that her arm was round and white, and very fair. Was she conversant with such tricks as these? His mother had called her clever and cunning as a serpent. Was it so? Had his mother seen with eyes clearer than his own, and was he now being surrounded by the meshes of a false woman's web? He moved away from her quickly, and stood upon the hearth-rug with his back to the empty fire grate.

Then she stood up also.

"John," she said, "if you have condemned me, say so. I shall defend myself for the sake of my character, but I shall not ask you to come back to me."

But he had not condemned her. He had not condemned her altogether, neither had he acquitted her. He was willing enough to hear her defence, as he had heard his mother's accusation; but he was desirous of hearing it without committing himself to any opinion.

"I have been much surprised," he said, "by what my mother has now told me,—very much surprised indeed. If Mr. Maguire had any claim upon your hand, should you not have told me?"

"He had no claim; but no doubt it was right that I should tell you. I was bound by my duty to tell you everything that had occurred."

"Of course you were—and yet you did not do it."

"But I was not so bound before what you said to me in the shrubbery last night? Remember, John, it was but last night. Have I had a moment to speak to you?"

"If there was any question of engagement between you and him, you should have told it me then, on the instant."

"But there was no question. He came to me one day and made me an offer. I will tell you everything, and I think you will believe me. I found him holding a position of respect, at Littlebath, and I was all alone in the world. Why should I not listen to him? I gave him no answer, but told him to speak to me again after a while. Then came my poor brother's illness and death; and after that came, as you know, the loss of all my money. In the meantime Mr. Maguire had written, but as I knew that my brother's family must trust to me for their support—that, at least, John was my hope then—I answered him that my means were not the same as before, and that everything must be over. Then he wrote to me again after I had lost my money, and once I answered him. I wrote to him so that he should know that nothing could come of it. Here are all his letters, and I have a copy of the last I wrote to him." So saying, she pulled the papers out of her desk,—the desk in which still lay the torn shreds of her poetry,—and handed them to him. "After that, what right had he to come here and make such a statement as he did to my aunt? How can he be a gentleman, and say what was so false?"

"No one says that he is a gentleman," replied John Ball, as he took the proffered papers.

"I have told you all now," said she; and as she spoke, a gleam of anger flashed from her eyes, for she was not in all respects a Griselda such as she of old. "I have told you all now, and if further excuse be wanting, I have none further to make."

Slowly he read the letters, still standing up on the hearth-rug, and then he folded them again into their shapes, and slowly gave them back to her.

"There is no doubt," said he, "as to his being a blackguard. He was hunting for your money, and now that he knows you have got none, he will trouble you no further." Then he made a move from the place on which he stood, as if he were going.

"And is that to be all, John?" she said.

"I shall see you to-morrow," he replied. "I am not going to town."

"But is that to be all to-night?"

"It is very late," and he looked at his watch. "I do not see that any good can come of talking more about it now. Good-night to you."

"Good-night," she said. Then she waited till the door was closed, and when he was gone she threw herself upon the bed. Alas! alas! Now once more was she ruined, and her present ruin was ruin indeed.

She threw herself on the bed, and sobbed as though she would have broken her heart in the bitterness of her spirit. She had told him the plainest, simplest truest story, and he had received it without one word of comment in her favour,—without one sign to show that her truthfulness had been acknowledged by him! He had told her that this man, who had done her so great an injury, was a blackguard; but of her own conduct he had not allowed himself to speak. She knew that his judgment had gone against her, and though she felt it to be hard,—very hard,—she resolved that she would make no protest against it. Of course she would leave the Cedars. Only a few hours since she had assured herself that it was her duty henceforward to obey him in everything. But that was now all changed. Whatever he might say to the contrary, she would go. If he chose to follow her whither she went, and again ask her to be his wife she would receive him with open arms. Oh, yes; let him only once again own that she was worthy of him, and then she would sit at his feet and confess her folly, and ask his pardon a thousand times for the trouble she had given him. But unless he were to do this she would never again beg for favour. She had made her defence, and had, as she felt, made it in vain. She would not condescend to say one other word in excuse of her conduct.

As for her aunt, all terms between Lady Ball and herself must be at an end. Lady Ball had passed a day with her in the house without speaking to her, except when that man had come, and then she had taken part with him! Her aunt, she thought, had been untrue to hospitality in not defending the guest within her own walls; she had been untrue to her own blood, in not defending her husband's niece; but, worse than all that, ten times worse, she had been untrue as from one woman to another! Margaret, as she thought of this, rose from the bed and walked wildly through the room unlike any Griselda. No; she would have no terms with Lady Ball. Lady Ball had understood it all, though John had not done so! She had known how it all was, and had pretended not to know. Because she had an object of her own to gain, she had allowed these calumnies to be believed! Let come what might, they should all know that Margaret Mackenzie, poor, wretched, destitute as she was, had still spirit enough to resent such injuries as these.

In the morning she sent down word by one of her young cousins that she would not come to breakfast, and she asked that some tea might be sent up to her.

"Is she in bed, my dear?" asked Lady Ball.

"No, she is not in bed," said Jane Ball. "She is sitting up, and has got all her things about the room as though she were packing."

"What nonsense!" said Lady Ball; "why does she not come down?"

Then Isabella, the eldest girl, was sent up to her, but Margaret refused to show herself.

"She says she would rather not; but she wants to know if papa will walk out with her at ten."

Lady Ball again said that this was nonsense, but tea and toast were at last supplied to her, and her cousin promised to be ready at the hour named. Exactly at ten o'clock, Margaret opened the schoolroom door, and asked one of the girls to tell her father that she would be found on the walk leading to the long shrubbery.

There on the walk she remained, walking slowly backwards and forwards over a space of twenty yards, till he joined her. She gave him her hand, and then turned towards the long shrubbery, and he, following her direction, walked at her side.

"John," she said, "you will not be surprised at my telling you that, after what has occurred, I shall leave this place to-day."

"You must not do that," he said.

"Ah, but I must do it. There are some things John, which no woman should bear or need bear. After what has occurred it is not right that I should incur your mother's displeasure any longer. All my things are ready. I want you to have them taken down to the one o'clock train."

"No, Margaret; I will not consent to that."

"But, John, I cannot consent to anything else. Yesterday was a terrible day for me. I don't think you can know how terrible. What I endured then no one has a right to expect that I should endure any longer. It was necessary that I should say something to you of what had occurred, and that I said last night. I have no further call to remain here, and, most positively, I shall go to-day."

He looked into her face and saw that she was resolved, but yet he was not minded to give way. He did not like to think that all authority over her was passing out of his hands. During the night he had not made up his mind to pardon her at once. Nay, he had not yet told himself that he would pardon her at all. But he was prepared to receive her tears and excuses, and we may say that, in all probability, he would have pardoned her had she wept before him and excused herself. But though she could shed tears on this matter,—though, doubtless, there were many tears to be shed by her,—she would shed no more before him in token of submission. If he would first submit, then, indeed, she might weep on his shoulder or laugh on his breast, as his mood might dictate.

"Margaret," he said, "we have very much to talk over before you can go."

"There will be time for that between this and one. Look here, John; I have made up my mind to go. After what took place yesterday, it will be better for us all that we should be apart."

"I don't see that, unless, indeed, you are determined to quarrel with us altogether. I suppose my wishes in the matter will count for something."

"Yesterday morning they would have counted for everything; but not this morning."

"And why not, Margaret?"

This was a question to which it was so difficult to find a reply, that she left it unanswered. They both walked on in silence for some paces, and then she spoke again.

"You said yesterday that you had been with Mr. Slow, and that you had something to tell me. If you still wish to tell me anything, perhaps you can do so now."

"Everything seems to be so much changed," said he, speaking very gloomily.

"Yes," said she; "things are changed. But my confidence in Mr. Slow, and in you, is not altered. If you like it, you can settle everything about the money without consulting me. I shall agree to anything about that."

"I was going to propose that your brother's family should have the debt due by the Rubbs. Mr. Slow thinks he might so manage as to secure the payment of the interest."

"Very well; I shall be delighted that it should be so. I had hoped that they would have had more, but that of course is all over. I cannot give them what is not mine."

But this arrangement, which would have been pleasant enough before,—which seemed to be very pleasant when John Ball was last in Mr. Slow's chambers, telling that gentleman that he was going to make everything smooth by marrying his cousin,—was not by any means so pleasant now. He had felt, when he was mentioning the proposed arrangement to Margaret, that the very naming of it seemed to imply that Mr. Maguire and his visit were to go for nothing. If Mr. Maguire and his visit were to go for much—to go for all that which Lady Ball wished to make of them—then, in such a case as that, the friendly arrangement in question would not hold water. If that were to be so, they must all go to work again, and Mr. Slow must be told to do the best in his power for his own client. John Ball was by no means resolved to obey his mother implicitly and make so much of Mr. Maguire and his visit as all this; but how could he help doing so if Margaret would go away? He could not as yet bring himself to tell her that Mr. Maguire and the visit should go altogether for nothing. He shook his head in his trouble, and pished and pshawed.

"The truth is, Margaret, you can't go to-day."

"Indeed I shall, John," said she, smiling. "You would hardly wish to keep me a prisoner, and the worst you could do would be to keep my luggage from me."

"Then I must say that you are very obstinate."

"It is not very often that I resolve to have my own way; but I have resolved now, and you should not try to balk me."

They had now come round nearly to the house, and she showed, by the direction that she took, that she was going in.

"You will go?" said he.

"Yes," said she; "I will go. My address will be at the old house in Arundel Street. Shall I see you again before I go?" she asked him, when she stood on the doorstep. "Perhaps you will be busy, and I had better say goodbye."

"Good-bye," said he, very gloomily; but he took her hand.

"I suppose I had better not disturb my uncle. You will give him my love. And, John, you will tell some one about my luggage; will you not?"

He muttered some affirmative, and then went round from the front of the house, while she entered the hall.

It was now half-past eleven, and she intended to start at half-past twelve. She went into the drawing-room and not finding her aunt, rang the bell. Lady Ball was with Sir John, she was told. She then wrote a note on a scrap of paper, and sent it in:

DEAR AUNT,

    I leave here at half-past twelve. Perhaps you would like to see me before I go.

                           M. M.

Then, while she was waiting for an answer, she went into the school room, and said good-bye to all the children.

"But you are coming back, aunt Meg," said the youngest girl.

Margaret stooped down to kiss her, and, when the child saw and felt the tears, she asked no further questions.

"Lady Ball is in the drawing-room, Miss," a servant said at that moment, and there she went to fight her last battle!

"What's the meaning of this, Margaret?" said her aunt.

"Simply that I am going. I was to have gone on Monday, as you will remember."

"But it was understood that you were to stop."

For a moment or two Margaret said nothing.

"I hate these sudden changes," said Lady Ball; "they are hardly respectable. I don't think you should leave the house in this way, without having given notice to any one. What will the servants think of it?"

"They will probably think the truth, aunt. They probably thought that, when they saw that you did not speak to me yesterday morning. You can hardly imagine that I should stay in the house under such circumstances as that."

"You must do as you like, of course."

"In this instance I must, aunt. I suppose I cannot see my uncle?"

"It is quite out of the question."

"Then I will say good-bye to you. I have said good-bye to John. Good-bye, aunt," and Margaret put out her hand.

But Lady Ball did not put out hers.

"Good-bye, Margaret," she said. "There are circumstances under which it is impossible for a person to make any expression of feeling that may be taken for approbation. I hope a time may come when these things shall have passed away, and that I may be able to see you again." Margaret's eyes, as she made her way out of the room were full of tears, and when she found herself outside the hall door, and at the bottom of the steps, she was obliged to put her handkerchief up to them. Before her on the road was a boy with a donkey cart and her luggage. She looked round furtively, half-fearing, half hoping—hardly expecting, but yet thinking, that she might again see her cousin. But he did not show himself to her as she walked down to the railway station by herself. As she went she told herself that she was right; she applauded her own courage, but what, oh! what was she to do? Everything now was over for her. Her fortune was gone. The man whom she had learned to love had left her. There was no place in the world on which her feet might rest till she had made one for herself by the work of her hands. And as for friends—was there a single being in the world whom she could now call her friend?

Chapter XXIII

The Lodgings of Mrs. Buggins, Née Protheroe

It was nearly the end of October when Miss Mackenzie left the Cedars and at that time of the year there is not much difficulty in getting lodgings in London. The house which her brother Walter occupied in Arundel Street had, at his death, remained in the hands of an old servant of his, who had bought her late master's furniture with her savings, and had continued to live there, letting out the house in lodgings. Her former mistress had gone to see her once or twice during the past year, and it had been understood between them, that if Miss Mackenzie ever wanted a room for a night or two in London, she could be accommodated at the old house. She would have preferred to write to Hannah Protheroe,—or Mrs. Protheroe, as she was now called by brevet rank since she had held a house of her own,—had time permitted her to do so. But time and the circumstances did not permit this, and therefore she had herself driven to Arundel Street without any notice.

Mrs. Protheroe received her with open arms, and with many promises of comfort and attendance,—as was to be expected, seeing that Mrs. Protheroe was, as she thought, receiving into her house the rich heiress. She proffered at once the use of her drawing-room and of the best bedroom, and declared that as the house was now empty, with the exception of one young gentleman from Somerset House upstairs, she would be able to devote herself almost exclusively to Miss Mackenzie. Things were much changed from those former days in which Hannah Protheroe used frequently to snub Margaret Mackenzie, being almost of equal standing in the house with her young mistress. And now Margaret was called upon to explain, that low as her standing might have been then, at this present moment it was even lower. She had indeed the means of paying for her lodgings, but these she was called upon to husband with the minutest economy. The task of telling all this was difficult. She began it by declining the drawing-room, and by saying that a bedroom upstairs would suffice for her.

"You haven't heard, Hannah, what has happened to me," she said, when Mrs. Protheroe expressed her surprise at this decision. "My brother's will was no will at all. I do not get any of his property. It all goes under some other will to my cousin, Mr. John Ball."

By these tidings Hannah was of course prostrated, and driven into a state of excitement that was not without its pleasantness as far as she was concerned. Of course she objected that the last will must be the real will, and in this way the matter came to full discussion between them.

"And, after all, that John Ball is to have everything!" said Mrs. Protheroe, holding up both her hands. By this time Hannah Protheroe had got herself comfortably into a chair, and no doubt her personal pleasure in the evening's occupation was considerably enhanced by the unconscious feeling that she was the richer woman of the two. But she behaved very well, and I am inclined to think, in preparing buttered muffins for her guest, she was more particular in the toasting, and more generous with the butter, than she would have been had she been preparing the dainty for drawing-room use. And when she learned that Margaret had eaten nothing since breakfast, she herself went out and brought in a sweetbread with her own hand, though she kept a servant whom she might have sent to the shop. And, for the honour of lodging-house keepers, I protest that that sweetbread never made its appearance in any bill.

"You will be more comfortable down here with me, won't you, my dear, than up there, with not a creature to speak to?"

In this way Mrs. Protheroe made her apology for giving Miss Mackenzie her tea downstairs, in a little back parlour behind the kitchen. It was a tidy room, with two wooden armchairs, and a bit of carpet over the flags in the centre, and a rug before the fire. Margaret did not inquire why it smelt of tobacco, nor did Mrs. Protheroe think it necessary to give any explanation why she went up herself at half-past seven to answer the bell at the area; nor did she say anything then of the office messenger from Somerset House, who often found this little room convenient for his evening pipe. So was passed the first evening after our Griselda had left the Cedars.

The next day she sat at home doing nothing,—still talking to Hannah Protheroe, and thinking that perhaps John Ball might come. But he did not come. She dined downstairs, at one o'clock, in the same room behind the kitchen, and then she had tea at six. But as Hannah intimated that perhaps a gentleman friend would look in during the evening, she was obliged to betake herself, after tea, to the solitude of her own room. As Hannah was between fifty and sixty, and nearer the latter age than the former, there could be no objection to her receiving what visitors she pleased. The third day passed with Miss Mackenzie the same as the second, and still no cousin came to see her. The next day, being Sunday, she diversified by going to church three times; but on the Sunday she was forced to dine alone, as the gentleman friend usually came in on that day to eat his bit of mutton with his friend, Mrs. Protheroe.

"A most respectable man, in the Admiralty branch, Miss Margaret, and will have a pension of twenty-seven shillings and sixpence a week in a year or two. And it is so lonely by oneself, you know."

Then Miss Mackenzie knew that Hannah Protheroe intended to become Hannah Buggins, and she understood the whole mystery of the tobacco smoke.

On the Monday she went to the house in Gower Street, and communicated to them the fact that she had left the Cedars. Miss Colza was in the room with her sister-in-law and nieces, and as it was soon evident that Miss Colza knew the whole history of her misfortune with reference to the property, she talked about her affairs before Miss Colza as though that young lady had been one of her late brother's family. But yet she felt that she did not like Miss Colza, and once or twice felt almost inclined to resent certain pushing questions which Miss Colza addressed to her.

"And have you quarrelled with all the Ball family?" the young lady asked, putting great emphasis on the word all.

"I did not say that I had quarrelled with any of them," said Miss Mackenzie.

"Oh! I beg pardon. I thought as you came away so sudden like, and as you didn't see any of them since, you know—"

"It is a matter of no importance whatever," said Miss Mackenzie.

"No: none in the least," said Miss Colza. And in this way they made up their minds to hate each other.

But what did the woman mean by talking in this way of all the Balls, as though a quarrel with one of the family was a thing of more importance than a quarrel with any of the others? Could she know, or could she even guess, anything of John Ball and of the offer he had made? But this mystery was soon cleared up in Margaret's mind, when, at Mrs. Mackenzie's request, they two went upstairs into that lady's bedroom for a little private conversation.

The conversation was desired for purposes appertaining solely to the convenience of the widow. She wanted some money, and then, with tears in her eyes, she demanded to know what was to be done. Miss Colza paid her eighteen shillings a week for board and lodging, and that was now two weeks in arrear; and one bedroom was let to a young man employed in the oilcloth factory, at seven shillings a week.

"And the rent is ninety pounds, and the taxes twenty-two," said Mrs. Mackenzie, with her handkerchief up to her eyes; "and there's the taxman come now for seven pound ten, and where I'm to get it, unless I coined my blood, I don't know."

Margaret gave her two sovereigns which she had in her purse, and promised to send her a cheque for the amount of the taxes due. Then she told as much as she could tell of that proposal as to the interest of the money due from the firm in the New Road.

"If it could only be made certain," said the widow, who had fallen much from her high ideas since Margaret had last seen her. Things were greatly changed in that house since the day on which the dinner, à la Russe, had been given under the auspices of Mr. Grandairs. "If it can only be made certain. They still keep his name up in the firm. There it is as plain as life over the place of business"—she would not even yet call it a shop—"Rubb and Mackenzie; and yet they won't let me know anything as to how matters are going on. I went there the other day, and they would tell me nothing. And as for Samuel Rubb, he hasn't been here this last fortnight, and I've got no one to see me righted. If you were to ask Mr. Slow, wouldn't he be able to see me righted?"

Margaret declared that she hardly knew whether that would come within Mr. Slow's line of business, and that she did not feel herself competent to give advice on such a point as that. She then explained, as best she could, that her own affairs were not as yet settled, but that she was led to hope, from what had been said to her, that the interest due by the firm on the money borrowed might become a fixed annual income for Mrs. Mackenzie's benefit.

After that it came out that Mr. Maguire had again been in Gower Street.

"And he was alone, for the best part of half an hour, with that young woman downstairs," said Mrs. Mackenzie.

"And you saw him?" Margaret asked.

"Oh, yes; I saw him afterwards."

"And what did he say?"

"He didn't say much to me. Only he gave me to understand—at least, that is what I suppose he meant—that you and he—He meant to say, that you and he had been courting, I suppose."

Then Margaret understood why Miss Colza had desired to know whether she had quarrelled with all the Balls. In her open and somewhat indignant speech in the drawing-room at the Cedars, she had declared before Mr. Maguire, in her aunt's presence, that she was engaged to marry her cousin, John Ball. Mr. Maguire had now enlisted Miss Colza in his service, and had told Miss Colza what had occurred. But still Miss Mackenzie did not thoroughly understand the matter. Why, she asked herself, should Mr. Maguire trouble himself further, now that he knew that she had no fortune? But, in truth, it was not so easy to satisfy Mr. Maguire on that point, as it was to satisfy Miss Mackenzie herself. He believed that the relatives of his lady-love were robbing her, or that they were, at any rate, taking advantage of her weakness. If it might be given to him to rescue her and her fortune from them, then, in such case as that, surely he would get his reward. The reader will therefore understand why Miss Colza was anxious to know whether Miss Mackenzie had quarrelled with all the Balls.

Margaret's face became unusually black when she was told that she and Mr. Maguire had been courting, but she did not contradict the assertion. She did, however, express her opinion of that gentleman.

"He is a mean, false, greedy man," she said, and then paused a moment; "and he has been the cause of my ruin." She would not, however, explain what she meant by this, and left the house, without going back to the room in which Miss Colza was sitting.

About a week afterwards she got a letter from Mr. Slow, in which that gentleman,—or rather the firm, for the letter was signed Slow and Bideawhile,—asked her whether she was in want of immediate funds. The affair between her and her cousin was not yet, they said, in a state for final settlement, but they would be justified in supplying her own immediate wants out of the estate. To this she sent a reply, saying that she had money for her immediate wants, but that she would feel very grateful if anything could be done for Mrs. Mackenzie and her family. Then she got a further letter, very short, saying that a half-year's interest on the loan had, by Mr. Ball's consent, been paid to Mrs. Mackenzie by Rubb and Mackenzie.

On the day following this, when she was sitting up in her bedroom, Mrs. Protheroe came to her, dressed in wonderful habiliments. She wore a dark-blue bonnet, filled all round with yellow flowers, and a spotted silk dress, of which the prevailing colour was scarlet. She was going, she said, to St Mary-le-Strand, "to be made Mrs. Buggins of." She tried to carry it off with bravado when she entered the room, but she left it with a tear in her eye, and a whimper in her throat. "To be sure, I'm an old woman," she said before she went. "Who has said that I ain't? Not I; nor yet Buggins. We is both of us old. But I don't know why we is to be desolate and lonely all our days, because we ain't young. It seems to me that the young folks is to have it all to themselves, and I'm sure I don't know why." Then she went, clearly resolved, that as far as she was concerned, the young people shouldn't have it all to themselves; and as Buggins was of the same way of thinking, they were married at St Mary-le-Strand that very morning.

And this marriage would have been of no moment to us or to our little history, had not Mr. Maguire chosen that morning, of all mornings in the year, to call on Miss Mackenzie in Arundel Street. He had obtained her address—of course, from Miss Colza; and, not having been idle the while in pushing his inquiries respecting Miss Mackenzie's affairs, had now come to Arundel Street to carry on the battle as best he might. Margaret was still in her room as he came, and as the girl could not show the gentleman up there, she took him into an empty parlour, and brought the tidings up to the lodger. Mr. Maguire had not sent up his name; but a personal description by the girl at once made Margaret know who was there.

"I won't see him," said she, with heightened colour, grieving greatly that the strong-minded Hannah Protheroe,—or Buggins, as it might probably be by that time,—was not at home. "Martha, don't let him come up. Tell him to go away at once."

After some persuasion, the girl went down with the message, which she softened to suit her own idea of propriety. But she returned, saying that the gentleman was very urgent. He insisted that he must see Miss Mackenzie, if only for an instant, before he left the house.

"Tell him," said Margaret, "that nothing shall induce me to see him. I'll send for a policeman. If he won't go when he's told, Martha, you must go for a policeman."

Martha, when she heard that, became frightened about the spoons and coats, and ran down again in a hurry. Then she came up again with a scrap of paper, on which a few words had been written with a pencil. This was passed through a very narrow opening in the door, as Margaret stood with it guarded, fearing lest the enemy might carry the point by an assault.

"You are being robbed," said the note, "you are, indeed,—and my only wish is to protect you."

"Tell him that there is no answer, and that I will receive no more notes from him," said Margaret. Then, at last, when he received that message, Mr. Maguire went away.

About a week after that, another visitor came to Miss Mackenzie, and him she received. But he was not the man for whose coming she in truth longed. It was Mr. Samuel Rubb who now called, and when Mrs. Buggins told her lodger that he was in the parlour, she went down to see him willingly. Her life was now more desolate than it had been before the occurrence of that ceremony in the church of St Mary-le-Strand; for, though she had much respect for Mr. Buggins, of whose character she had heard nothing that was not good, and though she had given her consent as to the expediency of the Buggins' alliance, she did not find herself qualified to associate with Mr. Buggins.

"He won't say a word, Miss," Hannah had pleaded, "and he'll run and fetch for you like a dog."

But even when recommended so highly for his social qualities, Buggins, she felt, would be antipathetic to her; and, with many false assurances that she did not think it right to interrupt a newly-married couple, she confined herself on those days to her own room.

But when Mr. Rubb came, she went down to see him. How much Mr. Rubb knew of her affairs,—how far he might be in Miss Colza's confidence,—she did not know; but his conduct to her had not been offensive, and she had been pleased when she learned that the first half year's interest had been paid to her sister-in-law.

"I'm sorry to hear of all this, Miss Mackenzie," said he, when he came forward to greet her. He had not thought it necessary, on this occasion, to put on his yellow gloves or his shiny boots, and she liked him the better on that account.

"Of all what, Mr. Rubb?" said she.

"Why, about you and the family at the Cedars. If what I hear is true, they've just got you to give up everything, and then dropped you."

"I left Sir John Ball's house on my own account, Mr. Rubb; I was not turned out."

"I don't suppose they'd do that. They wouldn't dare to do that; not so soon after getting hold of your money. Miss Mackenzie, I hope I shall not anger you; but it seems to me to be the most horridly wicked piece of business I ever heard of."

"You are mistaken, Mr. Rubb. You forget that the thing was first found out by my own lawyer."

"I don't know how that may be, but I can't bring myself to believe that it all is as they say it is; I can't, indeed."

She merely smiled, and shook her head. Then he went on speaking.

"I hope I'm not giving offence. It's not what I mean, if I am."

"You are not giving any offence, Mr. Rubb; only I think you are mistaken about my relatives at Twickenham."

"Of course, I may be; there's no doubt of that. I may be mistaken, like another. But, Miss Mackenzie, by heavens, I can't bring myself to think it." As he spoke in this energetic way, he rose from his chair, and stood opposite to her. "I cannot bring myself to think that the fight should be given up."

"But there has been no fight."

"There ought to be a fight, Miss Mackenzie; I know that there ought. I believe I'm right in supposing, if all this is allowed to go by the board as it is going, that you won't have, so to say, anything of your own."

"I shall have to earn my bread like other people; and, indeed, I am endeavouring now to put myself in the way of doing so."

"I'll tell you how you shall earn it. Come and be my wife. I think we've got a turn for good up at the business. Come and be my wife. That's honest, any way."

"You are honest," said she, with a tear in her eye.

"I am honest now," said he, "though I was not honest to you once;" and I think there was a tear in his eye also.

"If you mean about that money that you have borrowed, I am very glad of it—very glad of it. It will be something for them in Gower Street."

"Miss Mackenzie, as long as I have a hand to help myself with, they shall have that at least. But now, about this other thing. Whether there's nothing to come or anything, I'll be true to my offer. I'll fight for it, if there's to be a fight, and I'll let it go if there's to be no fight. But whether one way or whether the other, there shall be a home for you when you say the word. Say it now. Will you be my wife?"

"I cannot say that word, Mr. Rubb."

"And why not?"

"I cannot say it; indeed, I cannot."

"Is it Mr. Ball that prevents you?"

"Do not ask me questions like that. Indeed, indeed, indeed, I cannot do as you ask me."

"You despise me, like enough, because I am only a tradesman?"

"What am I myself, that I should despise any man? No, Mr. Rubb, I am thankful and grateful to you; but it cannot be."

Then he took up his hat, and, turning away from her without any word of adieu, made his way out of the house.

"He really do seem a nice man, Miss," said Mrs. Buggins. "I wonder you wouldn't have him liefer than go into one of them hospitals."

Whether Miss Mackenzie had any remnant left of another hope, or whether all such hope had gone, we need not perhaps inquire accurately. Whatever might be the state of her mind on that score, she was doing her best to carry out her purpose with reference to the plan of nursing; and as she could not now apply to her cousin, she had written to Mr. Slow upon the subject.

Late in November yet another gentleman came to see her, but when he came she was unfortunately out. She had gone up to the house in Gower Street, and had there been so cross-questioned by the indefatigable Miss Colza that she had felt herself compelled to tell her sister-in-law that she could not again come there as long as Miss Colza was one of the family. It was manifest to her that these questions had been put on behalf of Mr. Maguire, and she had therefore felt more indignant than she would have been had they originated in the impertinent curiosity of the woman herself. She also informed Mrs. Mackenzie that, in obedience to instructions from Mr. Slow, she intended to postpone her purpose with reference to the hospital till some time early in the next year. Mr. Slow had sent a clerk to her to explain that till that time such amicable arrangement as that to which he looked forward to make could not be completed. On her return from this visit to Gower Street she found the card,—simply the card,—of her cousin, John Ball.

Why had she gone out? Why had she not remained a fixture in the house, seeing that it had always been possible that he should come? But why! oh, why! had he treated her in this way, leaving his card at her home, as though that would comfort her in her grievous desolation? It would have been far better that he should have left there no intimation of his coming. She took the card, and in her anger threw it from her into the fire.

But yet she waited for him to come again. Not once during the next ten days, excepting on the Sunday, did she go out of the house during the hours that her cousin would be in London. Very sad and monotonous was her life, passed alone in her own bedroom. And it was the more sad, because Mrs. Buggins somewhat resented the manner in which her husband was treated. Mrs. Buggins was still attentive, but she made little speeches about Buggins' respectability, and Margaret felt that her presence in the house was an annoyance.

At last, at the end of the ten days, John Ball came again, and Margaret, with a fluttering heart, descended to meet him in the empty parlour.

She was the first to speak. As she had come downstairs, she had made up her mind to tell him openly what were her thoughts.

"I had hoped to have seen you before this, John," she said, as she gave him her hand.

"I did call before. Did you not get my card?"

"Oh, yes; I got your card. But I had expected to see you before that. The kind of life that I am leading here is very sad, and cannot be long continued."

"I would have had you remain at the Cedars, Margaret; but you would not be counselled by me."

"No; not in that, John."

"I only mention it now to excuse myself. But you are not to suppose that I am not anxious about you, because I have not seen you. I have been with Mr. Slow constantly. These law questions are always very tedious in being settled."

"But I want nothing for myself."

"It behoves Mr. Slow, for that very reason, to be the more anxious on your behalf; and, if you will believe me, Margaret, I am quite as anxious as he is. If you had remained with us, I could have discussed the matter with you from day to day; but, of course, I cannot do so while you are here."

As he was talking in this way, everything with reference to their past intercourse came across her mind. She could not tell him that she had been anxious to see him, not with reference to the money, but that he might tell her that he did not find her guilty on that charge which her aunt had brought against her concerning Mr. Maguire. She did not want assurances of solicitude as to her future means of maintenance. She cared little or nothing about her future maintenance, if she could not get from him one kind word with reference to the past. But he went on talking to her about Mr. Slow, and the interest, and the property, and the law, till, at last, in her anger, she told him that she did not care to hear further about it, till she should be told at last what she was to do.

"As I have got nothing of my own," she said, "I want to be earning my bread, and I think that the delay is cruel."

"And do you think," said he, "that the delay is not cruel to me also?"

She thought that he alluded to the fact that he could not yet obtain possession of the income for his own purposes.

"You may have it all at once, for me," she said.

"Have all what?" he replied. "Margaret, I think you fail to see the difficulties of my position. In the first place, my father is on his deathbed!"

"Oh, John, I am sorry for that."

"And, then, my mother is very bitter about all this. And how can I, at such a time, tell her that her opinion is to go for nothing? I am bound to think of my own children, and cannot abandon my claim to the property."

"No one wants you to abandon it. At least, I do not."

"What am I to do, then? This Mr. Maguire is making charges against me."

"Oh, John!"

"He is saying that I am robbing you, and trying to cover the robbery by marrying you. Both my own lawyer, and Mr. Slow, have told me that a plain statement of the whole case must be prepared, so that any one who cares to inquire may learn the whole truth, before I can venture to do anything which might otherwise compromise my character. You do not think of all this, Margaret, when you are angry with me." Margaret, hanging down her head, confessed that she had not thought of it.

"The difficulty would have been less, had you remained at the Cedars."

Then she again lifted her head, and told him that that would have been impossible. Let things go as they might, she knew that she had been right in leaving her aunt's house.

There was not much more said between them, nor did he give her any definite promise as to when he would see her again. He told her that she might draw on Mr. Slow for money if she wanted it, but that she again declined. And he told her also not to withdraw Susanna Mackenzie from her school at Littlebath—at any rate, not for the present; and intimated also that Mr. Slow would pay the schoolmistress's bill. Then he took his leave of her. He had spoken no word of love to her; but yet she felt, when he was gone, that her case was not as hopeless now as it had seemed to be that morning.

Chapter XXIV

The Little Story of the Lion and the Lamb

During those three months of October, November, and December, Mr. Maguire was certainly not idle. He had, by means of pertinacious inquiry, learned a good deal about Miss Mackenzie; indeed, he had learned most of the facts which the reader knows, though not quite all of them. He had seen Jonathan Ball's will, and he had seen Walter Mackenzie's will. He had ascertained, through Miss Colza, that John Ball now claimed the property by some deed said to have been executed by Jonathan Ball previous to the execution of his will; and he had also learned, from Miss Mackenzie's own lips, in Lady Ball's presence, that she had engaged herself to marry the man who was thus claiming her property. Why should Mr. Ball want to marry her,—who would in such a case be penniless,—but that he felt himself compelled in that way to quell all further inquiry into the thing that he was doing? And why should she desire to marry him, but that in this way she might, as it were, go with her own property, and not lose the value of it herself when compelled to surrender it to her cousin? That she would have given herself, with all her property, to him,—Maguire,—a few months ago, Mr. Maguire felt fully convinced, and, as I have said before, had some ground for such conviction. He had learned also from Miss Colza, that Miss Mackenzie had certainly quarrelled with Lady Ball, and that she had, so Miss Colza believed, been turned out of the house at the Cedars. Whether Mr. Ball had or had not abandoned his matrimonial prospects, Miss Colza could not quite determine. Having made up her mind to hate Miss Mackenzie, and therefore, as was natural, thinking that no gentleman could really like such "a poor dowdy creature," she rather thought that he had abandoned his matrimonial prospects. Mr. Maguire had thus learned much on the subject; but he had not learned this:—that John Ball was honest throughout in the matter, and that the lawyers employed in it were honest also.

And now, having got together all this information, and he himself being in a somewhat precarious condition as to his own affairs, Mr. Maguire resolved upon using his information boldly. He had a not incorrect idea of the fitness of things, and did not fail to tell himself that were he at that moment in possession of those clerical advantages which his labours in the vineyard should have earned for him, he would not have run the risk which he must undoubtedly incur by engaging himself in this matter. Had he a full church at Littlebath depending on him, had Mr. Stumfold's chance and Mr. Stumfold's success been his, had he still even been an adherent of the Stumfoldian fold, he would have paused before he rushed to the public with an account of Miss Mackenzie's grievance. But as matters stood with him, looking round upon his own horizon, he did not see that he had any course before him more likely to lead to good pecuniary results, than this.

The reader has been told how Mr. Maguire went to Arundel Street, and how he was there received. But that reception did not at all daunt his courage. It showed him that the lady was still under the Ball influence, and that his ally, Miss

Colza, was probably wrong in supposing that the Ball marriage was altogether off. But this only made him the more determined to undermine that influence, and to prevent that marriage. If he could once succeed in convincing the lady that her best chance of regaining her fortune lay in his assistance, or if he could even convince her that his interference must result, either with or without her good wishes, in dividing her altogether from the Ball alliance, then she would be almost compelled to throw herself into his arms. That she was violently in love with him he did not suppose, nor did he think it at all more probable that she should be violently in love with her cousin. He put her down in his own mind as one of those weak, good women, who can bring themselves easily to love any man, and who are sure to make useful wives, because they understand so thoroughly the nature of obedience. If he could secure for her her fortune, and could divide her from John Ball, he had but little doubt that she would come to him, in spite of the manner in which she had refused to receive him in Arundel Street. Having considered all this, after the mode of thinking which I have attempted to describe, he went to work with such weapons as were readiest to his hands.

As a first step, he wrote boldly to John Ball. In this letter he reasserted the statement he had made to Lady Ball as to Miss Mackenzie's engagement to himself, and added some circumstances which he had not mentioned to Lady Ball. He said, that having become engaged to that lady, he had, in consequence, given up his curacy at Littlebath, and otherwise so disarranged his circumstances, as to make it imperative upon him to take the steps which he was now taking. He had come up to London, expecting to find her anxious to receive him in Gower Street, and had then discovered that she had been taken away to the Cedars. He could not, he said, give any adequate description of his surprise, when, on arriving there, he heard from the mouth of his own Margaret that she was now engaged to her cousin. But if his surprise then had been great and terrible, how much greater and more terrible must it have been when, step by step, the story of that claim upon her fortune revealed itself to him! He pledged himself, in his letter, as a gentleman and as a Christian minister, to see the matter out. He would not allow Miss Mackenzie to be despoiled of her fortune and her hand,—both of which he had a right to regard as his own,— without making known to the public a transaction which he regarded as nefarious. Then there was a good deal of eloquent indignation the nature and purport of which the reader will probably understand.

Mr. Ball did not at all like this letter. He had that strong feeling of disinclination to be brought before the public with reference to his private affairs, which is common to all Englishmen; and he specially had a dislike to this, seeing that there would be a question not only as to money, but also as to love. A gentleman does not like to be accused of a dishonest attempt to possess himself of a lady's property; but, at the age of fifty, even that is almost better than one which charges him with such attempt against a lady's heart. He knew that he was not dishonest, and therefore could endure the first. He was not quite sure that he was not, or might not become, ridiculous, and therefore feared the latter very greatly. He could not ignore the letter, and there was nothing for it but to show it to his lawyer. Unfortunately, he had told this lawyer, on the very day of Mr. Maguire's visit to the Cedars, that all was to be made smooth by his marriage with Miss Mackenzie; and now, with much misery and many inward groanings, he had to explain all this story of Mr. Maguire. It was the more painful in that he had to admit that an offer had been made to the lady by the clergyman, and had not been rejected.

"You don't think there was more than that?" asked the lawyer, having paved the way for his question with sundry apologetic flourishes.

"I am sure there was not," said John Ball. "She is as true as the Gospel, and he is as false as the devil."

"Oh, yes," said the lawyer; "there's no doubt about his falsehood. He's one of those fellows for whom nothing is too dirty. Clergymen are like women. As long as they're pure, they're a long sight purer than other men; but when they fall, they sink deeper."

"You needn't be afraid of taking her word," said John Ball. "If all women were as pure as she is, there wouldn't be much amiss with them." His eyes glittered as he spoke of her, and it was a pity that Margaret could not have heard him then, and seen him there.

"You don't think she has been—just a little foolish, you know?"

"I think she was very foolish in not bidding such a man to go about his business, at once. But she has not been more so than what she owns. She is as brave as she is good, and I don't think she would keep anything back."

The result was that a letter was written by the lawyer to Mr. Maguire, telling Mr. Maguire that any further communication should be made to him; and also making a slight suggestion as to the pains and penalties which are incurred in the matter of a libel. Mr. Maguire had dated his letter from Littlebath, and there the answer reached him. He had returned thither, having found that he could take no further immediate steps towards furthering his cause in London.

And now, what steps should he take next? More than once he thought of putting his own case into the hands of a lawyer; but what was a lawyer to do for him? An action for breach of promise was open to him, but he had wit enough to feel that there was very little chance of success for him in that line. He might instruct a lawyer to look into Miss Mackenzie's affairs, and he thought it probable that he might find a lawyer to take such instructions. But there would be much expense in this, and, probably, no result. Advancing logically from one conclusion to another, he at last resolved that he must rush boldly into print, and lay the whole iniquity of the transaction open to the public.

He believed—I think he did believe—that the woman was being wronged. Some particle of such belief he had, and fostering himself with this, he sat himself down, and wrote a leading article.

Now there existed in Littlebath at this time a weekly periodical called the *Christian Examiner*, with which Mr. Maguire had for some time had dealings. He had written for the paper, taking an earnest part in local religious subjects; and the paper, in return, had very frequently spoken highly of Mr. Maguire's eloquence, and of Mr. Maguire's energy. There had been a give and take in this, which all people understand who are conversant with the provincial, or perhaps I might add, with the metropolitan press of the country. The paper in question was not a wicked paper, nor were the gentlemen concerned in its publication intentionally scurrilous or malignant; but it was subject to those great temptations which beset all class newspapers of the kind, and to avoid which seems to be almost more difficult, in handling religious subjects, than in handling any other. The editor of a *Christian Examiner*, if, as is probable, he have, of his own, very strong and one-sided religious convictions, will think that those who differ from him are in a perilous way, and so thinking, will feel himself bound to tell them so. The man who advocates one line of railway instead of another, or one prime minister as being superior to all others, does not regard his opponents as being fatally wrong,—wrong for this world and for the next,—and he can restrain himself. But how is a newspaper writer to restrain himself when his opponent is incurring everlasting punishment, or, worse still, carrying away others to a similar doom, in that they read, and perhaps even purchase, that which the lost one has written? In this way the contents of religious newspapers are apt to be personal; and heavy, biting, scorching attacks, become the natural vehicle of *Christian Examiners*.

Mr. Maguire sat down and wrote his leading article, which on the following Saturday appeared in all the glory of large type. The article shall not be repeated here at length, because it contained sundry quotations from Holy Writ which may as well be omitted, but the purport of it shall be explained. It commenced with a dissertation against an undue love of wealth,—the *auri sacra fames*, as the writer called it; and described with powerful unction the terrible straits into which, when indulged, it led the vile, wicked, ugly, hideous, loathsome, devilish human heart. Then there was an eloquent passage referring to worms and dust and grass, and a quotation respecting treasures both corruptible and incorruptible. Not at once, but with crafty gradations, the author sloped away to the point of his subject. How fearful was it to watch the way in which the strong, wicked ones,—the roaring lions of the earth, beguiled the ignorance of the innocent, and led lonely lambs into their slaughter-houses. All this, much amplified, made up half the article; and then, after the manner of a pleasant relater of anecdotes, the clerical story-teller began his little tale. When, however, he came to the absolute writing of the tale, he found it to be prudent for the present to omit the names of his hero and heroine—to omit, indeed, the names of all the persons concerned. He had first intended boldly to dare it all, and perhaps would yet have done so had he been quite sure of his editor. But his editor he found might object to these direct personalities at the first sound of the trumpet, unless the communication were made in the guise of a letter, with Mr. Maguire's name at the end of it. After a while the editor might become hot in the fight himself, and then the names could be blazoned forth. And there existed some chance,—some small chance,—that the robber-lion, John Ball, might be induced to drop his lamb from his mouth when he heard this premonitory blast, and then the lion's prey might be picked up by—"the bold hunter," Mr. Maguire would probably have said, had he been called upon to finish the sentence himself; anyone else might, perhaps, say, by the jackal. The little story was told, therefore, without the mention of any names. Mr. Maguire had read other little stories told in another way in other newspapers, of greater weight, no doubt, than the Littlebath *Christian Examiner*, and had thought that he could wield a thunderbolt as well as any other Jupiter; but in wielding thunderbolts, as in all other operations of skill, a man must first try his 'prentice hand with some reticence; and thus he reconciled himself to prudence, not without some pangs of conscience which accused him inwardly of cowardice.

"Not long ago there was a lady in this town, loved and respected by all who knew her." Thus he began, and then gave a not altogether inaccurate statement of the whole affair, dropping, of course, his own share in the concern, and accusing the vile, wicked, hideous, loathsome human heart of the devouring lion, who lived some miles to the west end of London, of a brutal desire and a hellish scheme to swallow up the inheritance of the innocent, loved, and respected lamb, in spite of the closest ties of consanguinity between them. And then he went on to tell how, with a base desire of covering up from the eyes of an indignant public his bestial greediness in having made this dishonest meal, the lion had proposed to himself the plan of marrying the lamb! It was a pity that Maguire had not learned—that Miss Colza had not been able to tell him—that the lion had once before expressed his wish to take the lamb for his wife. Had he known that, what a picture he would have drawn of the disappointed vindictive king of the forest, as lying in his lair at Twickenham he meditated his foul revenge! This unfortunately was unknown to Mr. Maguire and unsuspected by him.

But the article did not end here. The indignant writer of it went on to say that he had buckled on his armour in support of the lamb, and that he was ready to meet the lion either in the forest or in any social circle; either in the courts of law or before any Christian arbitrator. With loud trumpetings, he summoned the lion to appear and plead guilty, or to stand forward, if he dared, and declare himself innocent with his hand on his heart. If the lion could prove himself to be innocent the writer of that article offered him the right hand of fellowship, an offer which the lion would not, perhaps, regard as any strong inducement; but if the lion were not innocent—if, as the writer of that article was well aware was the case, the lion was basely, greedily, bestially guilty, then the writer of that article pledged himself to give the lion no peace till he had disgorged his prey, and till the lamb was free to come back, with all her property, to that Christian circle in Littlebath which had loved her so warmly and respected her so thoroughly.

Such was the nature of the article, and the editor put it in. After all, what, in such matters, is an editor to do? Is it not his business to sell his paper? And if the editor of a *Christian Examiner* cannot trust the clergyman he has sat under, whom can he trust? Some risk an editor is obliged to run, or he will never sell his paper. There could be little doubt that such an article as this would be popular among the religious world of Littlebath, and that it would create a demand. He had his misgivings—had that poor editor. He did not feel quite sure of his lion and his lamb. He talked the matter over vehemently with Mr. Maguire in the little room in which he occupied himself with his scissors and his paste; but ultimately the article was inserted. Who does not know that interval of triumph which warms a man's heart when he has delivered his blow, and the return blow has not been yet received? The blow has been so well struck that it must be successful, nay, may probably be death-dealing. So felt Mr. Maguire when two dozen copies of the *Christian Examiner* were delivered at his lodgings on the Saturday morning. The article, though printed as a leading article, had been headed as a little story,—"The Lion and the Lamb,"—so that it might more readily attract attention. It read very nicely in print. It had all that religious unction which is so necessary for *Christian Examiners*, and with it that spice of devilry, so delicious to humanity that without it even *Christian Examiners* cannot be made to sell themselves. He was very busy with his two dozen damp copies before him,—two dozen which had been sent to him, by agreement, as the price of his workmanship. He made them up and directed them with his own hand. To the lion and the lamb he sent two copies, two to each. To Mr. Slow he sent a copy, and another to Messrs Slow and Bideawhile, and a third to the other lawyer. He sent a copy to Lady Ball and one to Sir John. Another he sent to the old Mackenzie, baronet at Incharrow, and two more to the baronet's eldest son, and the baronet's eldest son's wife. A copy he sent to Mrs. Tom Mackenzie, and a copy to Miss Colza; and a copy also he sent to Mrs. Buggins. And he sent a copy to the Chairman of the Board at the Shadrach Fire Office, and another to the Chairman at the Abednego Life Office. A copy he sent to Mr. Samuel Rubb, junior, and a copy to Messrs Rubb and Mackenzie. Out of his own pocket he supplied the postage stamps, and with his own hand he dropped the papers into the Littlebath post-office.

Poor Miss Mackenzie, when she read the article, was stricken almost to the ground. How she did hate the man whose handwriting on the address she recognised at once! What should she do? In her agony she almost resolved that she would start at once for the Cedars and profess her willingness to go before all the magistrates in London and Littlebath, and swear that her cousin was no lion and that she was no lamb. At that moment her feelings towards the Christians and *Christian Examiners* of Littlebath were not the feelings of a Griselda. I think she could have spoken her mind freely had Mr. Maguire come in her way. Then, when she saw Mrs. Buggins's copy, her anger blazed up afresh, and her agony became more intense. The horrid man must have sent copies all over the world, or he would never have thought of sending a copy to Mrs. Buggins!

But she did not go to the Cedars. She reflected that when there she might probably find her cousin absent, and in such case she would hardly know how to address herself to her aunt. Mr. Ball, too, might perhaps come to her, and for three days she patiently awaited his coming. On the evening of the third day there came to her, not Mr. Ball, but a clerk from Mr. Slow, the same clerk who had been with her before, and he made an appointment with her at Mr. Slow's office on the following morning. She was to meet Mr. Ball there, and also to meet Mr. Ball's lawyer. Of course she consented to go, and of course she was on Mr. Slow's staircase exactly at the time appointed. Of what she was thinking as she walked round Lincoln's Inn Fields to kill a quarter of an hour which she found herself to have on hand, we will not now inquire.

She was shown at once into Mr. Slow's room, and the first thing that met her eyes was a copy of that horrible *Christian Examiner*, lying on the table before him. She knew it instantly, and would have known it had she simply seen a corner of the printing. To her eyes and to her mind, no other printed paper had ever been so ugly and so vicious. But she saw that there was also another newspaper under the *Christian Examiner*. Mr. Slow brought her to the fire, and gave her a chair, and was very courteous. In a few moments came the other lawyer, and with him came John Ball.

Mr. Slow opened the conference, all the details of which need not be given here. He first asked Miss Mackenzie whether she had seen that wicked libel. She, with much energy and, I may almost say, with virulence, declared that the horrid paper had been sent to her. She hoped that nobody suspected that she had known anything about it. In answer to this, they all assured her that she need not trouble herself on that head. Mr. Slow then told her that a London paper had copied the whole story of the "Lion and the Lamb," expressing a hope that the lion would be exposed if there was any truth in it, and the writer would be exposed if there was none.

"The writer was Mr. Maguire, a clergyman," said Miss Mackenzie, with indignation.

"We all know that," said Mr. Slow, with a slight smile on his face. Then he went on reading the remarks of the London paper, which declared that the Littlebath *Christian Examiner*, having gone so far, must, of necessity, go further. The article was calculated to give the greatest pain to, no doubt, many persons; and the innocence or guilt of "the Lion," as poor John Ball was called, must be made manifest to the public.

"And now, my dear Miss Mackenzie, I will tell you what we propose to do," said Mr. Slow. He then explained that it was absolutely necessary that a question of law should be tried and settled in a court of law, between her and her cousin. When she protested against this, he endeavoured to explain to her that the cause would be an amicable cause, a simple reference, in short, to a legal tribunal. Of course, she did not understand this, and, of course, she still protested; but after a while, when she began to perceive that her protest was of no avail, she let that matter drop. The cause should be brought on as soon as possible, but could not be decided till late in the spring. She was told that she had better make no great change in her own manner of life till that time, and was again informed that she could have what money she wanted for her own maintenance. She refused to take any money: but when the reference was made to some proposed change in her life, she looked wistfully into her cousin's face. He, however, had nothing to say then, and kept his eyes intently fixed upon the carpet.

Mr. Slow then took up the *Christian Examiner*, and declared to her what was their intention with reference to that. A letter should be written from his house to the editor of the London newspaper, giving a plain statement of the case, with all the names, explaining that all the parties were acting in perfect concert, and that the matter was to be decided in the only way which could be regarded as satisfactory. In answer to this, Miss Mackenzie, almost in tears, pointed out how distressing would be the publicity thus given to her name "particularly"—she said, "particularly—" But she could not go on with the expression of her thoughts, or explain that so public a reference to a proposal of marriage from her cousin must be doubly painful to her, seeing that the idea of such a marriage had been abandoned. But Mr. Slow understood all this, and, coming over to her, took her gently by the hand.

"My dear," he said, "you may trust me in this as though I were your father. I know that such publicity is painful; but, believe me, it is the best that we can do."

Of course she had no alternative but to yield.

When the interview was over, her cousin walked home with her to Arundel Street, and said much to her as to the necessity for this trial. He said so much, that she, at last, dimly understood that the matter could not be set at rest by her simple renouncing of the property. Her own lawyer could not allow her to do so; nor could he, John Ball, consent to receive the property in such a manner. "You see, by that newspaper, what people would say of me."

But had he not the power of making everything easy by doing that which he himself had before proposed to do? Why did he not again say, "Margaret, come and be my wife?" She acknowledged to herself that he had a right to act as though he had never said those words,—that the facts elicited by Mr. Maguire's visit to the Cedars were sufficient to absolve him from his offer. But yet she thought that they should have been sufficient also to induce him to renew it.

On that occasion, when he left her at the door in Arundel Street, he had not renewed his offer.

Chapter XXV

Lady Ball in Arundel Street

On Christmas Day Miss Mackenzie was pressed very hard to eat her Christmas dinner with Mr. and Mrs. Buggins, and she almost gave way. She had some half-formed idea in her head that should she once sit down to table with Buggins, she would have given up the fight altogether. She had no objection to Buggins, and had, indeed, no strong objection to put herself on a par with Buggins; but she felt that she could not be on a par with Buggins and with John Ball at the same time. Why it should be that in associating with the man she would take a step downwards, and might yet associate with the man's wife without taking any step downwards, she did not attempt to explain to herself. But I think that she could have explained it had she put herself to the task of analysing the question, and that she felt exactly the result of such analysis without making it. At any rate, she refused the invitation persistently, and ate her wretched dinner alone in her bedroom.

She had often told herself, in those days of her philosophy at Littlebath, that she did not care to be a lady; and she told herself now the same thing very often when she was thinking of the hospital. She cosseted herself with no false ideas as to the nature of the work which she proposed to undertake. She knew very well that she might have to keep rougher company than that of Buggins if she put her shoulder to that wheel. She was willing enough to do this, and had been willing to encounter such company ever since she left the Cedars. She was prepared for the roughness. But she would not put herself beyond the pale, as it were, of her cousin's hearth, moved simply by a temptation to relieve the monotony of her life. When the work came within her reach she would go to it, but till then she would bear the wretchedness of her dull room upstairs. She wondered whether he ever thought how wretched she must be in her solitude.

On New Year's Day she heard that her uncle was dead. She was already in mourning for her brother, and was therefore called upon to make no change in that respect. She wrote a note of condolence to her aunt, in which she strove much, and vainly, to be cautious and sympathetic at the same time, and in return received a note, in which Lady Ball declared her purpose of coming to Arundel Street to see her niece as soon as she found herself able to leave the house. She would, she said, give Margaret warning the day beforehand, as it would be very sad if she had her journey all for nothing.

Her aunt, Lady Ball, was coming to see her in Arundel Street! What could be the purpose of such a visit after all that had passed between them? And why should her aunt trouble herself to make it at a period of such great distress? Lady Ball must have some very important plan to propose, and poor Margaret's heart was in a flutter. It was ten days after this before the second promised note arrived, and then Margaret was asked to say whether she would be at home and able to receive her aunt's visit at ten minutes past two on the day but one following. Margaret wrote back to say that she would be at home at ten minutes past two on the day named.

Her aunt was old, and she again borrowed the parlour, though she was not now well inclined to ask favours from Mrs.

Buggins. Mrs. Buggins had taken to heart the slight put upon her husband, and sometimes made nasty little speeches.

"Oh dear, yes, in course, Miss Margaret; not that I ever did think much of them Ballses, and less than ever now, since the gentleman was kind enough to send me the newspaper. But she's welcome to the room, seeing as how Mr. Tiddy will be in the City, of course; and you're welcome to it, too, though you do keep yourself so close to yourself, which won't ever bring you round to have your money again; that it won't."

Lady Ball came and was shown into the parlour, and her niece went down to receive her.

"I would have been here before you came, aunt, only the room is not mine."

In answer to this, Lady Ball said that it did very well. Any room would answer the present purpose. Then she sat down on the sofa from which she had risen. She was dressed, of course, in the full weeds of her widowhood, and the wide extent of her black crape was almost awful in Margaret's eyes. She did not look to be so savage as her niece had sometimes seen her, but there was about her a ponderous accumulation of crape, which made her even more formidable than she used to be. It would be almost impossible to refuse anything to a person so black, so grave, so heavy, and so big.

"I have come to you, my dear," she said, "as soon as I possibly could after the sad event which we have had at home."

In answer to this, Margaret said that she was much obliged, but she hoped that her aunt had put herself to no trouble. Then she said a word or two about her uncle,—a word or two that was very difficult, as of course it could mean nothing.

"Yes," said the widow, "he has been taken from us after a long and useful life. I hope his son will always show himself to be worthy of such a father."

After that there was silence in the room for a minute or two, during which Margaret waited for her aunt to begin; but

Lady Ball sat there solid, grave, and black, as though she thought that her very presence, without any words, might be effective upon Margaret as a preliminary mode of attack. Margaret herself could find nothing to say to her aunt, and she, therefore, also remained silent. Lady Ball was so far successful in this, that when three minutes were over her niece had certainly been weakened by the oppressive nature of the meeting. She had about her less of vivacity, and perhaps also less of vitality, than when she first entered the room.

"Well, my dear," said her aunt at last, "there are things, you know, which must be talked about, though they are ever so disagreeable;" and then she pulled out of her pocket that abominable number of the Littlebath *Christian Examiner*.

"Oh, aunt, I hope you are not going to talk about that."

"My dear, that is cowardly; it is, indeed. How am I to help talking about it? I have come here, from Twickenham, on purpose to talk about it."

"Then, aunt, I must decline; I must, indeed."

"My dear!"

"I must, indeed, aunt."

Let a man or a woman's vitality be ever so thoroughly crushed and quenched by fatigue or oppression—or even by black crape—there will always be some mode of galvanising which will restore it for a time, some specific either of joy or torture which will produce a return of temporary energy. This Littlebath newspaper was a battery of sufficient power to put Margaret on her legs again, though she perhaps might not be long able to keep them.

"It is a vile, lying paper, and it was written by a vile, lying man, and I hope you will put it up and say nothing about it."

"It is a vile, lying paper, Margaret; but the lies are against my son, and not against you."

"He is a man, and knows what he is about, and it does not signify to him. But, aunt, I won't talk about it, and there's an end of it."

"I hope he does know what he is about," said Lady Ball. "I hope he does. But you, as you say, are a woman, and therefore it specially behoves you to know what you are about."

"I am not doing anything to anybody," said Margaret.

Lady Ball had now refolded the offensive newspaper, and restored it to her pocket. Perhaps she had done as much with it as she had from the first intended. At any rate, she brought it forth no more, and made no further intentionally direct allusion to it. "I don't suppose you really wish to do any injury to anybody," she said.

"Does anybody accuse me of doing them an injury?" Margaret asked.

"Well, my dear, if I were to say that I accused you, perhaps you would misunderstand me. I hope—I thoroughly expect, that before I leave you, I may be able to say that I do not accuse you. If you will only listen to me patiently for a few minutes, Margaret—which I couldn't get you to do, you know, before you went away from the Cedars in that very extraordinary manner—I think I can explain to you something which—" Here Lady Ball became embarrassed, and paused; but Margaret gave her no assistance, and therefore she began a new sentence. "In point of fact, I want you to listen to what I say, and then, I think—I do think—you will do as we would have you."

Whom did she include in that word "we"? Margaret had still sufficient vitality not to let the word pass by unquestioned. "You mean yourself and John?" said she.

"I mean the family," said Lady Ball rather sharply. "I mean the whole family, including those dear girls to whom I have been in the position of a mother since my son's wife died. It is in the name of the Ball family that I now speak, and surely I have a right."

Margaret thought that Lady Ball had no such right, but she would not say so at that moment.

"Well, Margaret, to come to the point at once, the fact is this. You must renounce any idea that you may still have of becoming my son's wife." Then she paused.

"Has John sent you here to say this?" demanded Margaret.

"I don't wish you to ask any such question as that. If you had any real regard for him I don't think you would ask it. Consider his difficulties, and consider the position of those poor children! If he were your brother, would you advise him, at his age, to marry a woman without a farthing, and also to incur the certain disgrace which would attach to his name after—after all that has been said about it in this newspaper?"—then, Lady Ball put her hand upon her pocket—"in this newspaper, and in others?"

This was more than Margaret could bear. "There would be no disgrace," said she, jumping to her feet.

"Margaret, if you put yourself into a passion, how can you understand reason? You ought to know, yourself, by the very fact of your being in a passion, that you are wrong. Would there be no disgrace, after all that has come out about Mr. Maguire?"

"No, none—none!" almost shouted this modern Griselda. "There could be no disgrace. I won't admit it. As for his marrying me, I don't expect it. There is nothing to bind him to me. If he doesn't come to me I certainly shall not go to him. I have looked upon it as all over between him and me; and as I have not troubled him with any importunities, nor yet you, it is cruel in you to come to me in this way. He is free to do what he likes—why don't you go to him? But there would be no disgrace."

"Of course he is free. Of course such a marriage never can take place now. It is quite out of the question. You say that it is all over, and you are quite right. Why not let this be settled in a friendly way between you and me, so that we might be friends again? I should be so glad to help you in your difficulties if you would agree with me about this."

"I want no help."

"Margaret, that is nonsense. In your position you are very wrong to set your natural friends at defiance. If you will only authorise me to say that you renounce this marriage—"

"I will not renounce it," said Margaret, who was still standing up. "I will not renounce it. I would sooner lose my tongue than let it say such a word. You may tell him, if you choose to tell him anything, that I demand nothing from him; nothing. All that I once thought mine is now his, and I demand nothing from him. But when he asked me to be his wife he told me to be firm, and in that I will obey him. He may renounce me, and I shall have nothing with which to reproach him; but I will never renounce him—never." And then the modern Griselda, who had been thus galvanised into vitality, stood over her aunt in a mood that was almost triumphant.

"Margaret, I am astonished at you," said Lady Ball, when she had recovered herself.

"I can't help that, aunt."

"And now let me tell you this. My son is, of course, old enough to do as he pleases. If he chooses to ruin himself and his children by marrying, anybody—even if it were out of the streets—I can't help it. Stop a moment and hear me to the end." This she said, as her niece had made a movement as though towards the door. "I say, even if it were out of the streets, I couldn't help it. But nothing shall induce me to live in the same house with him if he marries you. It will be on your conscience for ever that you have brought ruin on the whole family, and that will be your punishment. As for me, I shall take myself off to some solitude, and—there—I—shall—die." Then Lady Ball put her handkerchief up to her face and wept copiously.

Margaret stood still, leaning upon the table, but she spoke no word, either in answer to the threat or to the tears. Her immediate object was to take herself out of the room, but this she did not know how to achieve. At last her aunt spoke again: "If you please, I will get you to ask your landlady to send for a cab." Then the cab was procured, and Buggins, who had come home for his dinner, handed her ladyship in. Not a word had been spoken during the time that the cab was being fetched, and when Lady Ball went down the passage, she merely said, "I wish you good-bye, Margaret."

"Good-bye," said Margaret, and then she escaped to her own bedroom.

Lady Ball had not done her work well. It was not within her power to induce Margaret to renounce her engagement, and had she known her niece better, I do not think that she would have made the attempt. She did succeed in learning that Margaret had received no renewal of an offer from her son,—that there was, in fact, no positive engagement now existing between them; and with this, I think, she should have been satisfied. Margaret had declared that she demanded nothing from her cousin, and with this assurance Lady Ball should have been contented. But she had thought to carry her point, to obtain the full swing of her will, by means of a threat, and had forgotten that in the very words of her own menace she conveyed to Margaret some intimation that her son was still desirous of doing that very thing which she was so anxious to prevent. There was no chance that her threat should have any effect on Margaret. She ought to have known that the tone of the woman's mind was much too firm for that. Margaret knew—was as sure of it as any woman could be sure—that her cousin was bound to her by all ties of honour. She believed, too, that he was bound to her by love, and that if he should finally desert it, he would be moved to do so by mean motives. It was no anger on the score of Mr. Maguire that would bring him to such a course, no suspicion that she was personally unworthy of being his wife. Our Griselda, with all her power of suffering and willingness to suffer, understood all that, and was by no means disposed to give way to any threat from Lady Ball.

When she was upstairs, and once more in solitude, she disgraced herself again by crying. She could be strong enough when attacked by others, but could not be strong when alone. She cried and sobbed upon her bed, and then, rising, looked at herself in the glass, and told herself that she was old and ugly, and fitted only for that hospital nursing of which she had been thinking. But still there was something about her heart that bore her up. Lady Ball would not have come to her, would not have exercised her eloquence upon her, would not have called upon her to renounce this engagement, had she not found all similar attempts upon her own son to be ineffectual. Could it then be so, that, after all, her cousin would be true to her? If it were so, if it could be so, what would she not do for him and for his children? If it were so, how blessed would have been all these troubles that had brought her to such a haven at last! Then she tried to reconcile his coldness to her with that which she so longed to believe might be the fact. She was not to expect him to be a lover such as are young men. Was she young herself, or would she like him better if he were to assume anything of youth in his manners? She understood that life with him was a serious thing, and that it was his duty to be serious and grave in what he did. It might be that it was essential to his character, after all that had passed, that the question of the property should be settled finally, before he could come to her, and declare his wishes. Thus flattering herself, she put away from her her tears, and dressed herself, smoothing her hair, and washing away the traces of her weeping; and then again she looked at herself in the glass to see if it were possible that she might be comely in his eyes.

The months of January and February slowly wore themselves away, and during the whole of that time Margaret saw her cousin but once, and then she met him at Mr. Slow's chambers. She had gone there to sign some document, and there she had found him. She had then been told that she would certainly lose her cause. No one who had looked into the matter had any doubt of that. It certainly was the case that Jonathan Ball had bequeathed property which was not his at the time he made the will, but which at the time of his death, in fact, absolutely belonged to his nephew, John Ball. Old Mr. Slow, as he explained this now for the seventh or eighth time, did it without a tone of regret in his voice, or a sign of sorrow in his eye. Margaret had become so used to the story now, that it excited no strong feelings within her. Her wish, she said, was, that the matter should be settled. The lawyer, with almost a smile on his face, but still shaking his head, said that he feared it could not be settled before the end of April. John Ball sat by, leaning his face, as usual, upon his umbrella, and saying nothing. It did, for a moment, strike Miss Mackenzie as singular, that she should be reduced from affluence to absolute nothingness in the way of property, in so very placid a manner. Mr. Slow seemed to be thinking that he was, upon the whole, doing rather well for his client.

"Of course you understand, Miss Mackenzie, that you can have any money you require for your present personal wants."

This had been said to her so often, that she took it as one of Mr. Slow's legal formulas, which meant nothing to the laity.

On that occasion also Mr. Ball walked home with her, and was very eloquent about the law's delays. He also seemed to speak as though there was nothing to be regretted by anybody, except the fact that he could not get possession of the property as quick as he wished. He said not a word of anything else, and Margaret, of course, submitted to be talked to by him rather than to talk herself. Of Lady Ball's visit he said not a word, nor did she. She asked after the children, and especially after Jack. One word she did say:

"I had hoped Jack would have come to see me at my lodgings."

"Perhaps he had better not," said Jack's father, "till all is settled. We have had much to trouble us at home since my father's death."

Then of course she dropped that subject. She had been greatly startled on that day on hearing her cousin called Sir John by Mr. Slow. Up to that moment it had never occurred to her that the man of whom she was so constantly thinking as her possible husband was a baronet. To have been Mrs. Ball seemed to her to have been possible; but that she should become Lady Ball was hardly possible. She wished that he had not been called Sir John. It seemed to her to be almost natural that people should be convinced of the impropriety of such a one as her becoming the wife of a baronet.

During this period she saw her sister-in-law once or twice, who on those occasions came down to Arundel Street. She herself would not go to Gower Street, because of the presence of Miss Colza. Miss Colza still continued to live there, and still continued very much in arrear in her contributions to the household fund. Mrs. Mackenzie did not turn her out, because she would,—so she said,—in such case get nothing. Mrs. Tom was by this time quite convinced that the property would, either justly or unjustly, go into the hands of John Ball, and she was therefore less anxious to make any sacrifice to please her sister-in-law.

"I'm sure I don't see why you should be so bitter against her," said Mrs. Tom. "I don't suppose she told the clergyman a word that wasn't true."

Miss Mackenzie declined to discuss the subject, and assured Mrs. Tom that she only recommended the banishment of Miss Colza because of her apparent unwillingness to pay.

"As for the money," said Mrs. Tom, "I expect Mr. Rubb to see to that. I suppose he intends to make her Mrs. Rubb sooner or later."

Miss Mackenzie, having some kindly feeling towards Mr. Rubb, would have preferred to hear that Miss Colza was likely to become Mrs. Maguire. During these visits, Mrs. Tom got more than one five-pound note from her sister-in-law, pleading the difficulty she had in procuring breakfast for lodgers without any money for the baker. Margaret protested against these encroachments, but, still, the money would be forthcoming.

Once, towards the end of February, Mrs. Buggins seduced her lodger down into her parlour in the area, and Miss Mackenzie thought she perceived that something of the old servant's manners had returned to her. She was more respectful than she had been of late, and made no attempts at smart, ill-natured speeches.

"It's a weary life, Miss, this you're living here, isn't it?" said she.

Margaret said that it was weary, but that there could be no change till the lawsuit should be settled. It would be settled, she hoped, in April.

"Bother it for a lawsuit," said Mrs. Buggins. "They all tells me that it ain't any lawsuit at all, really."

"It's an amicable lawsuit," said Miss Mackenzie.

"I never see such amicableness! 'Tis a wonder to hear, Miss, how everybody is talking about it everywheres. Where we was last night—that is, Buggins and I—most respectable people in the copying line—it isn't only he as does the copying, but she too; nurses the baby, and minds the kitchen fire, and goes on, sheet after sheet, all at the same time; and a very tidy thing they make of it, only they do straggle their words so;—well, they were saying as it's one of the most remarkablest cases as ever was know'd."

"I don't see that I shall be any the better because it's talked about."

"Well, Miss Margaret, I'm not so sure of that. It's my belief that if one only gets talked about enough, one may have a'most anything one chooses to ask for."

"But I don't want to ask for anything."

"But if what we heard last night is all true, there's somebody else that does want to ask for something, or, as has asked, as folks say."

Margaret blushed up to the eyes, and then protested that she did not know what Mrs. Buggins meant.

"I never dreamed of it, my dear; indeed, I didn't, when the old lady come here with her tantrums; but now, it's as plain as a pikestaff. If I'd a' known anything about that, my dear, I shouldn't have made so free about Buggins; indeed, I shouldn't."

"You're talking nonsense, Mrs. Buggins; indeed, you are."

"They have the whole story all over the town at any rate, and in the lane, and all about the courts; and they declare it don't matter a toss of a halfpenny which way the matter goes, as you're to become Lady Ball the very moment the case is settled."

Miss Mackenzie protested that Mrs. Buggins was a stupid woman,—the stupidest woman she had ever heard or seen; and then hurried up into her own room to hug herself in her joy, and teach herself to believe that what so many people said must at last come true.

Three days after this, a very fine, private carriage, with two servants on a hammer cloth, drove up to the door in Arundel Street, and the maid-servant, hurrying upstairs, told Miss Mackenzie that a beautifully-dressed lady downstairs was desirous of seeing her immediately.

Chapter XXVI

Mrs. Mackenzie of Cavendish Square

"My dear," said the beautifully-dressed lady, "you don't know me, I think;" and the beautifully-dressed lady came up to Miss Mackenzie very cordially, took her by the hand, smiled upon her, and seemed to be a very good-natured person indeed. Margaret told the lady that she did not know her, and at that moment was altogether at a loss to guess who the lady might be. The lady might be forty years of age, but was still handsome, and carried with her that easy, self-assured, well balanced manner, which, if it be not overdone, goes so far to make up for beauty, if beauty itself be wanting.

"I am your cousin, Mrs. Mackenzie,—Clara Mackenzie. My husband is Walter Mackenzie, and his father is Sir Walter Mackenzie, of Incharrow. Now you will know all about me."

"Oh, yes, I know you," said Margaret.

"I ought, I suppose, to make ever so many apologies for not coming to you before; but I did call upon you, ever so long ago; I forget when, and after that you went to live at Littlebath. And then we heard of you as being with Lady Ball, and for some reason, which I don't quite understand, it has always been supposed that Lady Ball and I were not to know each other. And now I have heard this wonderful story about your fortune, and about everything else, too, my dear; and it seems all very beautiful, and very romantic; and everybody says that you have behaved so well; and so, to make a long story short, I have come to find you out in your hermitage, and to claim cousinship, and all that sort of thing."

"I'm sure I'm very much obliged to you, Mrs. Mackenzie—"

"Don't say it in that way, my dear, or else you'll make me think you mean to turn a cold shoulder on me for not coming to you before."

"Oh, no."

"But we've only just come to town; and though of course I heard the story down in Scotland—"

"Did you?"

"Did I? Why, everybody is talking about it, and the newspapers have been full of it."

"Oh, Mrs. Mackenzie, that is so terrible."

"But nobody has said a word against you. Even that stupid clergyman, who calls you the lamb, has not pretended to say that you were his lamb. We had the whole story of the Lion and the Lamb in the *Inverary Interpreter*, but I had no idea that it was you, then. But the long and the short of it is, that my husband says he must know his cousin; and to tell the truth, it was he that sent me; and we want you to come and stay with us in Cavendish Square till the lawsuit is over, and everything is settled."

Margaret was so startled by the proposition, that she did not know how to answer it. Of course she was at first impressed with a strong idea of the impossibility of her complying with such a request, and was simply anxious to find some proper way of refusing it. The Incharrow Mackenzies were great people who saw much company, and it was, she thought, quite out of the

question that she should go to their house. At no time of her
career would she have been, as she conceived, fit to live with
such grand persons; but at the present moment, when she
grudged herself even a new pair of gloves out of the money
remaining to her, while she was still looking forward to a future
life passed as a nurse in a hospital, she felt that there would be
an absolute unfitness in such a visit.

"You are very kind," she said at last with faltering voice,
as she meditated in what words she might best convey her
refusal.

"No, I'm not a bit kind; and I know from the tone of your
voice that you are meditating a refusal. But I don't mean to
accept it. It is much better that you should be with us while all
this is going on, than that you should be living here alone. And
there is no one with whom you could live during this time so
properly, as with those who are your nearest relatives."

"But, Mrs. Mackenzie—"

"I suppose you are thinking now of another cousin, but
it's not at all proper that you should go to his house;—not as yet,
you know. And you need not suppose that he'll object because
of what I said about Lady Ball and myself. The Capulets and the
Montagues don't intend to keep it up for ever; and, though we
have never visited Lady Ball, my husband and the present Sir
John know each other very well."

Mrs. Mackenzie was not on that occasion able to
persuade Margaret to come at once to Cavendish Square, and
neither was Margaret able to give a final refusal. She did not
intend to go, but she could not bring herself to speak a positive
answer in such a way as to have much weight with Mrs.
Mackenzie. That lady left her at last, saying that she would send
her husband, and promising Margaret that she would herself
come in ten days to fetch her.

"Oh no," said Margaret; "it will be very good-natured of
you to come, but not for that."

"But I shall come, and shall come for that," said Mrs. Mackenzie; and at the end of the ten days she did come, and she did carry her husband's cousin back with her to Cavendish Square.

In the meantime Walter Mackenzie had called in Arundel Street, and had seen Margaret. But there had been given to her advice by a counsellor whom she was more inclined to obey than any of the Mackenzies. John Ball had written to her, saying that he had heard of the proposition, and recommending her to accept the invitation given to her.

"Till all this trouble about the property is settled," said he, "it will be much better that you should be with your cousins than living alone in Mrs. Buggins' lodgings."

After receiving this Margaret held out no longer but was carried off by the handsome lady in the grand carriage, very much to the delight of Mrs. Buggins.

Mrs. Buggins' respect for Miss Mackenzie had returned altogether since she had heard of the invitation to Cavendish Square, and she apologised, almost without ceasing, for the liberty she had taken in suggesting that Margaret should drink tea with her husband.

"And indeed, Miss, I shouldn't have proposed such a thing, were it ever so, if I had suspected for a hinstant how things were a going to be. For Buggins is a man as knows his place, and never puts himself beyond it! But you was that close, Miss—"

In answer to this Margaret would say that it didn't signify, and that it wasn't on that account; and I have no doubt but that the two women thoroughly understood each other.

There was a subject on which, in spite of all her respect, Mrs. Buggins ventured to give Miss Mackenzie much advice, and to insist on that advice strongly. Mrs. Buggins was very anxious that the future "baronet's lady" should go out upon her grand visit with a proper assortment of clothing. That argument of the baronet's lady was the climax of Mrs. Buggins' eloquence: "You, my dear, as is going to be one baronet's lady is going to a lady who is going to be another baronet's lady, and it's only becoming you should go as is becoming."

Margaret declared that she was not going to be anybody's lady, but Mrs. Buggins altogether pooh-poohed this assertion.

"That, Miss, is your predestation," said Mrs. Buggins, "and well you'll become it. And as for money, doesn't that old party who found it all out say reg'lar once a month that there's whatever you want to take for your own necessaries? and you that haven't had a shilling from him yet! If it was me, I'd send him in such a bill for necessaries as 'ud open that old party's eyes a bit, and hurry him up with his lawsuits."

The matter was at last compromised between her and Margaret, and a very moderate expenditure for smarter clothing was incurred.

On the day appointed Mrs. Mackenzie again came, and Margaret was carried off to Cavendish Square. Here she found herself suddenly brought into a mode of life altogether different from anything she had as yet experienced. The Mackenzies were people who went much into society, and received company frequently at their own house. The first of these evils for a time Margaret succeeded in escaping, but from the latter she had no means of withdrawing herself. There was very much to astonish her at this period of her life, but that which astonished her perhaps more than anything else was her own celebrity. Everybody had heard of the Lion and the Lamb, and everybody was aware that she was supposed to represent the milder of those two favourite animals. Everybody knew the story of her property, or rather of the property which had never in truth been hers, and which was now being made to pass out of her hands by means of a lawsuit, of which everybody spoke as though it were the best thing in the world for all the parties concerned. People, when they mentioned Sir John Ball to her—and he was often so mentioned—never spoke of him in harsh terms, as though he were her enemy. She observed that he was always named before her in that euphuistic language which we naturally use when we speak to persons of those who are nearest to them and dearest to them. The romance of the thing, and not the pity of it, was the general subject of discourse, so that she could not fail to perceive that she was generally regarded as the future wife of Sir John Ball.

It was the sudden way in which all this had come upon her that affected her so greatly. While staying in Arundel Street she had been altogether ignorant that the story of the Lion and the Lamb had become public, or that her name had been frequent in men's mouths. When Mrs. Buggins had once told her that she was thus becoming famous, she had ridiculed Mrs. Buggins' statement. Mrs. Buggins had brought home word from some tea-party that the story had been discussed among her own friends; but Miss Mackenzie had regarded that as an accident. A lawyer's clerk or two about Chancery Lane or Carey Street might by chance hear of the matter in the course of their daily work;—that it should be so, and that such people talked of her affairs distressed her; but that had, she was sure, been all. Now, however, in her new home she had learned that Mr. Maguire's efforts had become notorious, and that she and her history were public property. When all this first became plain to her, it overwhelmed her so greatly that she was afraid to show her face; but this feeling gradually wore itself away, and she found herself able to look around upon the world again, and ask herself new questions of the future, as she had done when she had first found herself to be the possessor of her fortune.

When she had been about three weeks with the Mackenzies, Sir John Ball came to see her. He had written to her once before that, but his letter had referred simply to some matter of business. When he was shown into the drawing-room in Cavendish Square, Mrs. Mackenzie and Margaret were both there, but the former in a few minutes got up and left the room. Margaret had wished with all her heart that her hostess would remain with them. She was sure that Sir John Ball had nothing to say that she would care to hear, and his saying nothing would seem to be of no special moment while three persons were in the room. But his saying nothing when special opportunity for speaking had been given to him would be of moment to her. Her destiny was in his hands to such a degree that she felt his power over her to amount almost to a cruelty. She longed to ask him what her fate was to be, but it was a question that she could not put to him. She knew that he would not tell her now; and she knew also that the very fact of his not telling her would inflict upon her a new misery, and deprive her of the comfort which she was beginning to enjoy. If he could not tell her at once how all this was to be ended, it would be infinitely better for her that he should remain away from her altogether.

As soon as Mrs. Mackenzie had left the room he began to describe to her his last interview with the lawyers. She listened to him, and pretended to interest herself, but she did not care two straws about the lawyers. Point after point he explained to her, showing the unfortunate ingenuity with which his uncle Jonathan had contrived to confuse his affairs, and Margaret attempted to appear concerned. But her mind had now for some months past refused to exert itself with reference to the mode in which Mr. Jonathan Ball had disposed of his money. Two years ago she had been told that it was hers; since that, she had been told that it was not hers. She had felt the hardship of this at first; but now that feeling was over with her, and she did not care to hear more about it. But she did care very much to know what was to be her future fate.

"And when will be the end of it, John?" she asked him.

"Ha! that seems so hard to say. They did name the first of April, but it won't be so soon as that. Mr. Slow said to-day about the end of April, but his clerk seems to think it will be the middle of May."

"It is very provoking," said Margaret.

"Yes, it is," said John Ball, "very provoking; I feel it so. It worries me so terribly that I have no comfort in life. But I suppose you find everything very nice here."

"They are very kind to me."

"Very kind, indeed. It was quite the proper thing for them to do; and when I heard that Mrs. Mackenzie had been to you in Arundel Street, I was delighted."

Margaret did not dare to tell him that she would have preferred to have been left in Arundel Street; but that, at the moment, was her feeling. If, when all this was over, she would still have to earn her bread, it would have been much better for her not to have come among her rich relations. What good would it then do her to have lived two or three months in Cavendish Square?

"I wish it were all settled, John," she said; and as she spoke there was a tear standing in the corner of each eye.

"I wish it were, indeed," said John Ball; but I think that he did not see the tears.

It was on her tongue to speak some word about the hospital; but she felt that if she did so now, it would be tantamount to asking him that question which it did not become her to ask; so she repressed the word, and sat in silence.

"When the day is positively fixed for the hearing," said he, "I will be sure to let you know."

"I wish you would let me know nothing further about it, John, till it is all settled."

"I sometimes almost fancy that I wish the same thing," said he, with a faint attempt at a smile; and after that he got up and went his way.

This was not to be endured. Margaret declared to herself that she could not live and bear it. Let the people around her say what they would, it could not be that he would treat her in this way if he intended to make her his wife. It would be better for her to make up her mind that it was not to be so, and to insist on leaving the Mackenzies' house. She would go, not again to

Arundel Street, but to some lodging further away, in some furthest recess of London, where no one would come to her and flurry her with false hopes, and there remain till she might be allowed to earn her bread. That was the mood in which Mrs. Mackenzie found her late in the afternoon on the day of Sir John Ball's visit. There was to be a dinner party in the house that evening, and Margaret began by asking leave to absent herself.

"Nonsense, Margaret," said Mrs. Mackenzie; "I won't have anything of the kind."

"I cannot come down, Mrs. Mackenzie; I cannot, indeed."

"That is absolute nonsense. That man has been saying something unkind to you. Why do you mind what he says?"

"He has not said anything unkind; he has not said anything at all."

"Oh, that's the grief, is it?"

"I don't know what you mean by grief; but if you were situated as I am you would perceive that you were in a false position."

"I am sure he has been saying something unkind to you."

Margaret hardly knew how to tell her thoughts and feelings, and yet she wished to tell them. She had resolved that she would tell the whole to Mrs. Mackenzie, having convinced herself that she could not carry out her plan of leaving Cavendish Square without some explanation of the kind. She did not know how to make her speech with propriety, so she jumped at the difficulty boldly. "The truth is, Mrs. Mackenzie, that he has no more idea of marrying me than he has of marrying you."

"Margaret, how can you talk such nonsense?"

"It is not nonsense; it is true; and it will be much better that it should all be understood at once. I have nothing to blame him for, nothing; and I don't blame him; but I cannot bear this kind of life any longer. It is killing me. What business have I to be living here in this way, when I have got nothing of my own, and have no one to depend on but myself?"

"Then he must have said something to you; but, whatever it was, you cannot but have misunderstood him."

"No; he has said nothing, and I have not misunderstood him." Then there was a pause. "He has said nothing to me, and I am bound to understand what that means."

"Margaret, I want to put one question to you," said Mrs. Mackenzie, speaking with a serious air that was very unusual with her,—"and you will understand, dear, that I only do so because of what you are saying now."

"You may put any question you please to me," said Margaret.

"Has your cousin ever asked you to be his wife, or has he not?"

"Yes, he has. He has asked me twice."

"And what answer did you make him?"

"When I thought all the property was mine, I refused him. Then, when the property became his, he asked me again, and I accepted him. Sometimes, when I think of that, I feel so ashamed of myself, that I hardly dare to hold up my head."

"But you did not accept him simply because you had lost your money."

"No; but it looks so like it; does it not? And of course he must think that I did so."

"I am quite sure he thinks nothing of the kind. But he did ask you, and you did accept him?"

"Oh, yes."

"And since that, has he ever said anything to you to signify that the match should be broken off?"

"The very day after he had asked me, Mr. Maguire came to the Cedars and saw me, and Lady Ball was there too. And he was very false, and told my aunt things that were altogether untrue. He said that—that I had promised to marry him, and Lady Ball believed him."

"But did Mr. Ball believe him?"

"My aunt said all that she could against me, and when John spoke to me the next day, it was clear that he was very angry with me."

"But did he believe you or Mr. Maguire when you told him that Mr. Maguire's story was a falsehood from beginning to end?"

"But it was not a falsehood from beginning to end. That's where I have been so very, very unfortunate; and perhaps I ought to say, as I don't want to hide anything from you, so very, very wrong. The man did ask me to marry him, and I had given him no answer."

"Had you thought of accepting him?"

"I had not thought about that at all, when he came to me. So I told him that I would consider it all, and that he must come again."

"And he came again."

"Then my brother's illness occurred, and I went to London. After that Mr. Maguire wrote to me two or three times, and I refused him in the plainest language that I could use. I told him that I had lost all my fortune, and then I was sure that there would be an end of any trouble from him; but he came to the Cedars on purpose to do me all this injury; and now he has put all these stories about me into the newspapers, how can I think that any man would like to make me his wife? I have no right to be surprised that Lady Ball should be so eager against it."

"But did Mr. Ball believe you when you told him the story?"

"I think he did believe me."

"And what did he say?"

Margaret did not answer at once, but sat with her fingers up among her hair upon her brow:

"I am trying to think what were his words," she said, "but I cannot remember. I spoke more than he did. He said that I should have told him about Mr. Maguire, and I tried to explain to him that there had been no time to do so. Then I said that he could leave me if he liked."

"And what did he answer?"

"If I remember rightly, he made no answer. He left me saying that he would see me again the next day. But the next day I went away. I would not remain in the house with Lady Ball after what she had believed about me. She took that other man's part against me, and therefore I went away."

"Did he say anything as to your going?"

"He begged me to stay, but I would not stay. I thought it was all over then. I regarded him as being quite free from any engagement, and myself as being free from any necessity of obeying him. And it was all over. I had no right to think anything else."

"And what came next?"

"Nothing. Nothing else has happened, except that Lady Ball came to me in Arundel Street, asking me to renounce him."

"And you refused?"

"Yes; I would do nothing at her bidding. Why should I? She had been my enemy throughout, since she found that the money belonged to her son and not to me."

"And all this time you have seen him frequently?"

"I have seen him sometimes about the business."

"And he has never said a word to you about your engagement to him?"

"Never a word."

"Nor you to him?"

"Oh, no! how could I speak to him about it?"

"I would have done so. I would not have had my heart crushed within me. But perhaps you were right. Perhaps it was best to be patient."

"I know that I have been wrong to expect anything or to hope for anything," said Margaret. "What right have I to hope for anything when I refused him while I was rich?"

"That has nothing to do with it."

"When he asked me again, he only did it because he pitied me. I don't want to be any man's wife because he pities me."

"But you accepted him."

"Yes; because I loved him."

"And now?" Again Miss Mackenzie sat silent, still moving her fingers among the locks upon her brow. "And now, Margaret?" repeated Mrs. Mackenzie.

"What's the use of it now?"

"But you do love him?"

"Of course I love him. How shall it be otherwise? What has he done to change my love? His feelings have changed, and I have no right to blame him. He has changed; and I hate myself, because I feel that in coming here I have, as it were, run after him. I should have put myself in some place where no thought of marrying him should ever have come again to me."

"Margaret, you are wrong throughout."

"Am I? Everybody always says that I am always wrong."

"If I can understand anything of the matter, Sir John Ball has not changed."

"Then, why—why—why?"

"Ah, yes, exactly; why? Why is it that men and women cannot always understand each other; that they will remain for hours in each other's presence without the power of expressing, by a single word, the thoughts that are busy within them? Who can say why it is so? Can you get up and make a clean breast of it all to him?"

"But I am a woman, and am very poor."

"Yes, and he is a man, and, like most men, very dumb when they have anything at heart which requires care in the speaking. He knows no better than to let things be as they are; to leave the words all unspoken till he can say to you, 'Now is the time for us to go and get ourselves married;' just as he might tell you that now was the time to go and dine."

"But will he ever say that?"

"Of course he will. If he does not say so when all this business is off his mind, when Mr. Maguire and his charges are put at rest, when the lawyers have finished their work, then come to me and tell me that I have deceived you. Say to me then, 'Clara Mackenzie, you have put me wrong, and I look to you to put me right.' You will find I will put you right."

In answer to this, Margaret was able to say nothing further. She sat for a while with her face buried in her hands thinking of it all, asking herself whether she might dare to believe it all. At last, however, she went up to dress for dinner; and when she came down to the drawing-room there was a smile upon her face.

After that a month or six weeks passed in Cavendish Square, and there was, during all that time, no further special reference to Sir John Ball or his affairs. Twice he was asked to dine with the Mackenzies, and on both occasions he did so. On neither of those evenings did he say very much to Margaret; but, on both of them he said some few words, and it was manifestly his desire that they should be regarded as friends.

And as the spring came on, Margaret's patience returned to her, and her spirits were higher than they had been at any time since she first discovered that success among the Stumfoldians at Littlebath did not make her happy.

Chapter XXVII

The Negro Soldiers' Orphan Bazaar

In the spring days of the early May there came up in London
that year a great bazaar,—a great charity bazaar on behalf of
the orphan children of negro soldiers who had fallen in the
American war. Tidings had come to this country that all slaves
taken in the revolted States had been made free by the Northern
invaders, and that these free men had been called upon to show
their immediate gratitude by becoming soldiers in the Northern
ranks. As soldiers they were killed in battle, or died, and as dead
men they left orphans behind them. Information had come that
many of these orphans were starving, and hence had arisen the
cause for the Negro Soldiers' Orphan Bazaar. There was still in
existence at that time, down at South Kensington, some
remaining court or outstanding building which had belonged to
the Great International Exhibition, and here the bazaar was to be
held. I do not know that I can trace the way in which the idea
grew and became great, or that anyone at the time was able to
attribute the honour to the proper founder. Some gave it all to the
Prince of Wales, declaring that his royal highness had done it out
of his own head; and others were sure that the whole business
had originated with a certain philanthropical Mr. Manfred Smith

who had lately come up in the world, and was supposed to have
a great deal to do with most things. Be that as it may, this thing
did grow and become great, and there was a list of lady
patronesses which included some duchesses, one marchioness,
and half the countesses in London. It was soon manifest to the
eyes of those who understood such things, that the Negro
Soldiers' Orphan Bazaar was to be a success, and therefore there
was no difficulty whatsoever in putting the custody of the stalls
into the hands of proper persons. The difficulty consisted in
rejecting offers from persons who undoubtedly were quite
proper for such an occasion. There came to be interest made for
permission to serve, and boastings were heard of unparalleled
success in the bazaar line. The Duchess of St Bungay had a
happy bevy of young ladies who were to act as counter
attendants under her grace; and who so happy as any young lady
who could get herself put upon the duchess's staff? It was even
rumoured that a certain very distinguished person would have
shown herself behind a stall, had not a certain other more
distinguished person expressed an objection; and while the
rumour was afloat as to the junior of those two distinguished
persons, the young-ladydom of London was frantic in its
eagerness to officiate. Now at that time there had become
attached to the name of our poor Griselda a romance with which
the west-end of London had become wonderfully well
acquainted. The story of the Lion and the Lamb was very
popular. Mr. Maguire may be said to have made himself odious
to the fashionable world at large, and the fate of poor Margaret
Mackenzie with her lost fortune, and the additional misfortune
of her clerical pledged protector, had recommended itself as
being truly interesting to all the feeling hearts of the season.
Before May was over, gentlemen were enticed to dinner parties
by being told—and untruly told—that the Lamb had been
"secured;" as on the previous year they had been enticed by a
singular assurance as to Bishop Colenso; and when Margaret on
one occasion allowed herself to be taken to Covent Garden

Theatre, every face from the stalls was turned towards her between the acts.

Who then was more fit to take a stall, or part of a stall at the Negro Soldiers' Orphan Bazaar, than our Griselda? When the thing loomed so large, lady patronesses began to be aware that mere nobodies would hardly be fit for the work. There would have been little or no difficulty in carrying out a law that nobody should take a part in the business who had not some handle to her name, but it was felt that such an arrangement as that might lead to failure rather than glory. The commoner world must be represented but it should be represented only by ladies who had made great names for themselves. Mrs. Conway Sparkes, the spiteful poetess, though she was old and ugly as well as spiteful, was to have a stall and a bevy, because there was thought to be no doubt about her poetry. Mrs. Chaucer Munro had a stall and a bevy; but I cannot clearly tell her claim to distinction, unless it was that she had all but lost her character four times, but had so saved it on each of those occasions that she was just not put into the Index Expurgatorius of fashionable society in London. It was generally said by those young men who discussed the subject, that among Mrs. Chaucer Munro's bevy would be found the most lucrative fascination of the day. And then Mrs. Mackenzie was asked to take a stall, or part of a stall, and to bring Griselda with her as her assistant. By this time the Lamb was most generally known as "Griselda" among fashionable people.

Now Mrs. Mackenzie was herself a woman of fashion, and quite open to the distinction of having a part assigned to her at the great bazaar of the season. She did not at all object to a booth on the left hand of the Duchess of St Bungay, although it was just opposite to Mrs. Chaucer Munro. She assented at once.

"But you must positively bring Griselda," said Lady Glencora Palliser, by whom the business of this mission was conducted.

"Of course, I understand that," said Mrs. Mackenzie. "But what if she won't come?"

"Griseldas are made to do anything," said Lady Glencora, "and of course she must come."

Having settled the difficulty in this way, Lady Glencora went her way, and Mrs. Mackenzie did not allow Griselda to go to her rest that night till she had extracted from her a promise of acquiescence, which, I think, never would have been given had Miss Mackenzie understood anything of the circumstances under which her presence was desired.

But the promise was given, and Margaret knew little or nothing of what was expected from her till there came up, about a fortnight before the day of the bazaar, the great question of her dress for the occasion. Previous to that she would fain have been energetic in collecting and making things for sale at her stall, for she really taught herself to be anxious that the negro soldiers' orphans should have provision made for them; but, alas! her energy was all repressed, and she found that she was not to be allowed to do anything in that direction.

"Things of that sort would not go down at all now-a-days, Margaret," said Mrs. Mackenzie. "Nobody would trouble themselves to carry them away. There are tradesmen who furnish the stalls, and mark their own prices, and take back what is not sold. You charge double the tradesman's price, that's all."

Margaret, when her eyes were thus opened, of course ceased to make little pincushions, but she felt that her interest in the thing was very much lowered. But a word must be said as to that question of the dress. Miss Mackenzie, when she was first interrogated as to her intentions, declared her purpose of wearing a certain black silk dress which had seen every party at Mrs. Stumfold's during Margaret's Littlebath season. To this her cousin demurred, and from demurring proceeded to the enunciation of a positive order. The black silk dress in question should not be worn. Now Miss Mackenzie chose to be still in mourning on the second of June, the day of the bazaar, her brother having died in September, and had no fitting garment, so she said, other than the black silk in question. Whereupon Mrs. Mackenzie, without further speech to her cousin on the subject, went out and purchased a muslin covered all over with the prettiest little frecks of black, and sent a milliner to Margaret, and provided a bonnet of much the same pattern, the gayest, lightest, jauntiest, falsest, most make-belief-mourning bonnet that ever sprang from the art of a designer in bonnets—and thus nearly broke poor Margaret's heart.

"People should never have things given them, who can't buy for themselves," she said, with tears in her eyes, "because of course they know what it means."

"But, my dearest," said Mrs. Mackenzie, "young ladies who never have any money of their own at all always accept presents from all their relations. It is their special privilege."

"Oh, yes, young ladies; but not women like me who are waiting to find out whether they are ruined or not."

The difficulty, however, was at last overcome, and Margaret, with many inward upbraidings of her conscience, consented to wear the black-freckled dress.

"I never saw anybody look so altered in my life," said Mrs. Mackenzie, when Margaret, apparelled, appeared in the Cavendish Square drawing-room on the morning in question. "Oh, dear, I hope Sir John Ball will come to look at you."

"Nonsense! he won't be such a fool as to do anything of the kind."

"I took care to let him know that you would be there;" said Mrs. Mackenzie.

"You didn't?"

"But I did, my dear."

"Oh, dear, what will he think of me?" ejaculated Margaret; but nevertheless I fancy that there must have been some elation in her bosom when she regarded herself and the freckled muslin in the glass.

Both Mrs. Mackenzie and Miss Mackenzie had more than once gone down to the place to inspect the ground and make themselves familiar with the position they were to take. There were great stalls and little stalls, which came alternately; and the Mackenzie stall stood next to a huge centre booth at which the duchess was to preside. On their other hand was the stall of old Lady Ware, and opposite to them, as has been before said, the doubtful Mrs. Chaucer Munro was to hold difficult sway over her bevy of loud nymphs. Together with Mrs. Mackenzie were two other Miss Mackenzies, sisters of her husband, handsome, middle-aged women, with high cheek-bones and fine brave-looking eyes. All the Mackenzies, except our Griselda, were dressed in the tartan of their clan; and over the stall there was some motto in Gaelic, *"Dhu dhaith donald dhuth,"* which nobody could understand, but which was not the less expressive. Indeed, the Mackenzie stall was got up very well; but then was it not known and understood that Mrs. Mackenzie did get up things very well? It was acknowledged on all sides that the Lamb, Griselda, was uncommonly well got up on this occasion.

It was understood that the ladies were to be assembled in the bazaar at half-past two, and that the doors were to be thrown open to the public at three o'clock. Soon after half-past two Mrs. Mackenzie's carriage was at the door, and the other Mackenzies having come up at the same time, the Mackenzie phalanx entered the building together. There were many others with them, but as they walked up they found the Countess of Ware standing alone in the centre of the building, with her four daughters behind her. She had on her head a wonderful tiara, which gave to her appearance a ferocity almost greater than was natural to her. She was a woman with square jaws, and a big face, and stout shoulders: but she was not, of her own unassisted height, very tall. But of that tiara and its altitude she was proud, and as she stood in the midst of the stalls, brandishing her umbrella-sized parasol in her anger, the ladies, as they entered, might well be cowed by her presence.

"When ladies say half-past two," said she, "they ought to come at half-past two. Where is the Duchess of St Bungay? I shall not wait for her."

But there was a lady there who had come in behind the Mackenzies, whom nothing ever cowed. This was the Lady Glencora Palliser, the great heiress who had married the heir of a great duke, pretty, saucy, and occasionally intemperate, in whose eyes Lady Ware with her ferocious tiara was simply an old woman in a ridiculous head-gear. The countess had apparently addressed herself to Mrs. Mackenzie, who had been the foremost to enter the building, and our Margaret had already begun to tremble. But Lady Glencora stepped forward, and took the brunt of the battle upon herself.

"Nobody ever yet was so punctual as my Lady Ware," said Lady Glencora.

"It is very annoying to be kept waiting on such occasions," said the countess.

"But my dear Lady Ware, who keeps you waiting? There is your stall, and why on earth should you stand here and call us all over as we come in, like naughty schoolboys?"

"The duchess said expressly that she would be here at half-past two."

"Who ever expects the dear duchess to keep her word?" said Lady Glencora.

"Or whoever cared whether she does or does not?" said Mrs. Chaucer Munro, who, with her peculiar bevy, had now made her way up among the front rank.

Then to have seen the tiara of Lady Ware, as it wagged and nodded while she looked at Mrs. Munro, and to have witnessed the high moral tone of the ferocity with which she stalked away to her own stall with her daughters behind her,—a tragi-comedy which it was given to no male eyes to behold,— would have been worth the whole after-performance of the bazaar. No male eyes beheld that scene, as Mr. Manfred Smith, the manager, had gone out to look for his duchess, and missing her carriage in the crowd, did not return till the bazaar had been opened. That Mrs. Chaucer Munro did not sink, collapsed, among her bevy, must have been owing altogether to that callousness which a long habit of endurance produces. Probably she did feel something as at the moment there came no titter from any other bevy corresponding to the titter which was raised by her own. She and her bevy retired to their allotted place, conscious that their time for glory could not come till the male world should appear upon the scene. But Lady Ware's tiara still wagged and nodded behind her counter, and Margaret, looking at her, thought that she must have come there as the grand duenna of the occasion.

Just at three o'clock the poor duchess hurried into the building in a terrible flurry, and went hither and thither among the stalls, not knowing at first where was her throne. Unkind chance threw her at first almost into the booth of Mrs. Conway Sparkes, the woman whom of all women she hated the most; and from thence she recoiled into the arms of Lady Hartletop who was sitting serene, placid, and contented in her appointed place.

"Opposite, I think, duchess," Mrs. Conway Sparkes had said. "We are only the small fry here."

"Oh, ah; I beg pardon. They told me the middle, to the left."

"And this is the middle to the right," said Mrs. Conway Sparkes. But the duchess had turned round since she came in, and could not at all understand where she was.

"Under the canopy, duchess," just whispered Lady Hartletop. Lady Hartletop was a young woman who knew her right hand from her left under all circumstances of life, and who never made any mistakes. The duchess looked up in her confusion to the centre of the ceiling, but could see no canopy. Lady Hartletop had done all that could be required of her, and if the duchess were to die amidst her difficulties it would not be her fault. Then came forth the Lady Glencora, and with true charity conducted the lady-president to her chair, just in time to avoid the crush, which ensued upon the opening of the doors.

The doors were opened, and very speedily the space of the bazaar between the stalls became too crowded to have admitted the safe passage of such a woman as the Duchess of St Bungay; but Lady Glencora, who was less majestic in her size and gait, did not find herself embarrassed. And now there arose, before the general work of fleecing the wether lambs had well commenced, a terrible discord, as of a brass band with broken bassoons, and trumpets all out of order, from the further end of the building,—a terrible noise of most unmusical music, such as Bartholomew Fair in its loudest days could hardly have known. At such a diapason one would have thought that the tender ears of May Fair and Belgravia would have been crushed and cracked and riven asunder; that female voices would have shrieked, and the intensity of fashionable female agony would have displayed itself in all its best recognised forms. But the crash of brass was borne by them as though they had been rough schoolboys delighting in a din. The duchess gave one jump, and then remained quiet and undismayed. If Lady Hartletop heard it, she did not betray the hearing. Lady Glencora for a moment put her hands to her ears as she laughed, but she did it as though the prettiness of the motion were its only one cause. The fine nerves of Mrs. Conway Sparkes, the poetess, bore it all without flinching; and Mrs. Chaucer Munro with her bevy rushed forward so that they might lose nothing of what was coming.

"What are they going to do?" said Margaret to her cousin, in alarm.

"It's the play part of the thing. Have you not seen the bills?" Then Margaret looked at a great placard which was exhibited near to her, which, though by no means intelligible to her, gave her to understand that there was a show in progress. The wit of the thing seemed to consist chiefly in the wonderful names chosen. The King of the Cannibal Islands was to appear on a white charger. King Chrononhotonthologos was to be led in chains by Tom Thumb. Achilles would drag Hector thrice round the walls of Troy; and Queen Godiva would ride through Coventry, accompanied by Lord Burghley and the ambassador from Japan. It was also signified that in some back part of the premises a theatrical entertainment would be carried on throughout the afternoon, the King of the Cannibal Islands, with his royal brother and sister Chrononhotonthologos and Godiva, taking principal parts; but as nobody seemed to go to the theatre the performers spent their time chiefly in making processions through and amidst the stalls, when, as the day waxed hot, and the work became heavy, they seemed to be taken much in dudgeon by the various bevies with whose business they interfered materially.

On this, their opening march, they rushed into the bazaar with great energy, and though they bore no resemblance to the characters named in the playbill, and though there was among them neither a Godiva, a Hector, a Tom Thumb, or a Japanese, nevertheless, as they were dressed in paint and armour after the manner of the late Mr. Richardson's heroes, and as most of the ladies had probably been without previous opportunity of seeing such delights, they had their effect. When they had made their twenty-first procession the thing certainly grew stale, and as they brought with them an infinity of dirt, they were no doubt a nuisance. But no one would have been inclined to judge these amateur actors with harshness who knew how much they themselves were called on to endure, who could appreciate the disgusting misery of a hot summer afternoon spent beneath dust and paint and tin-plate armour, and who would remember that the performers received payment neither in *éclat* nor in thanks, nor even in the smiles of beauty.

"Can't somebody tell them not to come any more?" said the duchess, almost crying with vexation towards the end of the afternoon.

Then Mr. Manfred Smith, who managed everything, went to the rear, and the king and warriors were sent away to get beer or cooling drinks at their respective clubs.

Poor Mr. Manfred Smith! He had not been present at the moment in which he was wanted to lead the duchess to her stall, and the duchess never forgave him. Instead of calling him by his name from time to time, and enabling him to shine in public as he deserved to shine,—for he had worked at the bazaar for the last six weeks as no professional man ever worked at his profession,—the duchess always asked for "somebody" when she wanted Mr. Smith, and treated him when he came as though he had been a servant hired for the occasion. One very difficult job of work was given to him before the day was done; "I wish you'd go over to those young women," said the duchess, "and say that if they make so much noise, I must go away."

The young women in question were Mrs. Chaucer Munro and her bevy, and the commission was one which poor Manfred Smith found it difficult to execute.

"Mrs. Munro," said he, "you'll be sorry to hear—that the duchess—has got—a headache, and she thinks we all might be a little quieter."

The shouts of the loud nymphs were by this time high. "Pooh!" said one of them. "Headache indeed!" said another. "Bother her head!" said a third. "If the duchess is ill, perhaps she had better retire," said Mrs. Chaucer Munro. Then Mr. Manfred Smith walked off sorrowfully towards the door, and seating himself on the stool of the money-taker by the entrance, wiped off the perspiration from his brow. He had already put on his third pair of yellow kid gloves for the occasion, and they were soiled and torn and disreputable; his polished boots were brown with dust; the magenta ribbon round his neck had become a moist rope; his hat had been thrown down and rumpled; a drop of oil had made a spot upon his trousers; his whiskers were draggled and out of order, and his mouth was full of dirt. I doubt if Mr. Manfred Smith will ever undertake to manage another bazaar.

The duchess I think was right in her endeavour to mitigate the riot among Mrs. Munro's nymphs. Indeed there was rioting among other nymphs than hers, though her noise and their noise was the loudest; and it was difficult to say how there should not be riot, seeing what was to be the recognised manner of transacting business. At first there was something of prettiness in the rioting. The girls, who went about among the crowd, begging men to put their hands into lucky bags, trading in rose-buds, and asking for half-crowns for cigar lighters, were fresh in their muslins, pretty with their braided locks, and perhaps not impudently over-pressing in their solicitations to male strangers. While they were not as yet either aweary or habituated to the necessity of importunity, they remembered their girlhood and their ladyhood, their youth and their modesty, and still carried with them something of the bashfulness of maidenhood; and the young men, the wether lambs, were as yet flush with their half-crowns, and the elder sheep had not quite dispensed the last of their sovereigns or buttoned up their trousers pockets. But as the work went on, and the dust arose, and the prettinesses were destroyed, and money became scarce, and weariness was felt, and the heat showed itself, and the muslins sank into limpness, and the ribbons lost their freshness, and braids of hair grew rough and loose, and sidelocks displaced themselves—as girls became used to soliciting and forgetful of their usual reticences in their anxiety for money, the charm of the thing went, and all was ugliness and rapacity. Young ladies no longer moved about, doing works of charity; but harpies and unclean birds were greedy in quest of their prey.

"Put a letter in my post-office," said one of Mrs. Munro's bevy, who officiated in a postal capacity behind a little square hole, to a young man on whom she pounced out and had caught him and brought up, almost with violence.

The young man tendered some scrap of paper and a sixpence.

"Only sixpence!" said the girl.

A cabman could not have made the complaint with a more finished accent of rapacious disgust.

"Never mind," said the girl, "I'll give you an answer."

Then, with inky fingers and dirty hands, she tendered him some scrawl, and demanded five shillings postage. "Five shillings!" said the young man. "Oh, I'm d——"

Then he gave her a shilling and walked away. She ventured to give one little halloa after him, but she caught the duchess's eye looking at her, and was quiet.

I don't think there was much real flirting done. Men won't flirt with draggled girls, smirched with dust, weary with work, and soiled with heat; and especially they will not do so at the rate of a shilling a word. When the whole thing was over, Mrs. Chaucer Munro's bevy, lying about on the benches in fatigue before they went away, declared that, as far as they were concerned, the thing was a mistake. The expenditure in gloves and muslin had been considerable, and the returns to them had been very small. It is not only that men will not flirt with draggled girls, but they will carry away with them unfortunate remembrances of what they have seen and heard. Upon the whole it may be doubted whether any of the bevies were altogether contented with the operations on the occasion of the Negro Soldiers' Orphan Bazaar.

Miss Mackenzie had been, perhaps, more fortunate than some of the others. It must, however, be remembered that there are two modes of conducting business at these bazaars. There is the travelling merchant, who roams about, and there is the stationary merchant, who remains always behind her counter. It is not to be supposed that the Duchess of St Bungay spent the afternoon rushing about with a lucky bag. The duchess was a stationary trader, and so were all the ladies who belonged to the Mackenzie booth. Miss Mackenzie, the lamb, had been much regarded, and consequently the things at her disposal had been quickly sold. It had all seemed to her to be very wonderful, and as the fun grew fast and furious, as the young girls became eager in their attacks, she made up her mind that she would never occupy another stall at a bazaar. One incident, and but one, occurred to her during the day; and one person came to her that she knew, and but one. It was nearly six, and she was beginning to think that the weary work must soon be over, when, on a sudden, she found Sir John Ball standing beside her.

"Oh, John!" she said, startled by his presence, "who would have thought of seeing you here?"

"And why not me as well as any other fool of my age?"

"Because you think it is foolish," she answered, "and I suppose the others don't."

"Why should you say that I think it foolish? At any rate, I'm glad to see you looking so nice and happy."

"I don't know about being happy," said Margaret,—"or nice either for the matter of that."

But there was a smile on her face as she spoke, and Sir John smiled also when he saw it.

"Doesn't she look well in that bonnet?" said Mrs. Mackenzie, turning round to the side of the counter at which he was standing. "It was my choice, and I absolutely made her wear it. If you knew the trouble I had!"

"It is very pretty," said Sir John.

"Is it not? And are you not very much obliged to me? I'm sure you ought to be, for nobody before has ever taken the trouble of finding out what becomes her most. As for herself, she's much too well-behaved a young woman to think of such vanities."

"Not at present, certainly," said Margaret.

"And why not at present? She looks on those lawyers and their work as though there was something funereal about them. You ought to teach her better, Sir John."

"All that will be over in a day or two now," said he.

"And then she will shake off her dowdiness and her gloom together," said Mrs. Mackenzie. "Do you know I fancy she has a liking for pretty things at heart as well as another woman."

"I hope she has," said he.

"Of course you do. What is a woman worth without it? Don't be angry, Margaret, but I say a woman is worth nothing without it, and Sir John will agree with me if he knows anything about the matter. But, Margaret, why don't you make him buy something? He can't refuse you if you ask him."

If Miss Mackenzie could thereby have provided for all the negro soldiers' orphans in existence, I do not think that she could at that moment have solicited him to make a purchase.

"Come, Sir John," continued Mrs. Mackenzie, "you must buy something of her. What do you say to this paper-knife?"

"How much does the paper-knife cost?" said he, still smiling. It was a large, elaborate, and perhaps, I may say, unwieldy affair, with a great elephant at the end of it.

"Oh! that is terribly dear," said Margaret, "it costs two pounds ten."

Thereupon he put his hand into his pocket, and taking out his purse, gave her a five-pound note.

"We never give change," said Mrs. Mackenzie: "do we, Margaret?"

"I'll give him change," said Margaret.

"I'll be extravagant for once," said Sir John, "and let you keep the whole."

"Oh, John!" said Margaret.

"You have no right to scold him yet," said Mrs. Mackenzie.

Margaret, when she heard this, blushed up to her forehead, and in her confusion forgot all about the paper-knife and the money. Sir John, I fancy, was almost as much confused himself, and was quite unable to make any fitting reply. But, just at that moment, there came across two harpies from the realms of Mrs. Chaucer Munro, eagerly intent upon their prey.

"Here are the lion and the lamb together," said one harpy. "The lion must buy a rose to give to the lamb. Sir Lion, the rose is but a poor half-crown." And she tendered him a battered flower, leering at him from beneath her draggled, dusty bonnet as she put forth her untempting hand for the money.

"Sir Lion, Sir Lion," said the other harpy, "I want your name for a raffle."

But the lion was off, having pushed the first harpy aside somewhat rudely. That tale of the Lion and the Lamb had been very terrible to him; but never till this occasion had any one dared to speak of it directly to his face. But what will not a harpy do who has become wild and dirty and disgusting in the pursuit of half-crowns?

"Now he is angry," said Margaret. "Oh, Mrs. Mackenzie, why did you say that?"

"Yes; he is angry," said Mrs. Mackenzie, "but not with you or me. Upon my word, I thought he would have pushed that girl over; and if he had, he would only have served her right."

"But why did you say that? You shouldn't have said it."

"About your not scolding him yet? I said it, my dear, because I wanted to make myself certain. I was almost certain before, but now I am quite certain."

"Certain of what, Mrs. Mackenzie?"

"That you'll be a baronet's wife before me, and entitled to be taken out of a room first as long as dear old Sir Walter is alive."

Soon after that the bazaar was brought to an end, and it was supposed to have been the most successful thing of the kind ever done in London. Loud boasts were made that more than eight hundred pounds had been cleared; but whether any orphans of any negro soldiers were ever the better for the money I am not able to say.

Chapter XXVIII

Showing How the Lion Was Stung by the Wasp

It may be remembered that Mr. Maguire, when he first made public that pretty story of the Lion and the Lamb, declared that he would give the lion no peace till that beast had disgorged his prey, and that he had pledged himself to continue the fight till he should have succeeded in bringing the lamb back to the pleasant pastures of Littlebath. But Mr. Maguire found some difficulty in carrying out his pledge. He was willing enough to fight, but the weapons with which to do battle were wanting to him. The *Christian Examiner*, having got so far into the mess, and finding that a ready sale did in truth result from any special article as to the lion and the lamb, was indeed ready to go on with the libel. The *Christian Examiner* probably had not much to lose. But there arose a question whether fighting simply through the columns of the *Christian Examiner* was not almost tantamount to no fight at all. He wanted to bring an action against Sir John Ball, to have Sir John Ball summoned into court and examined about the money, to hear some truculent barrister tell Sir John Ball that he could not conceal himself from the scorn of an indignant public behind the spangles of his parvenu baronetcy. He had a feeling that the lion would be torn to pieces, if only a properly truculent barrister could be got to fix his claws into him. But, unfortunately, no lawyer,—not even Solomon Walker, the Low Church attorney at Littlebath,—would advise him that he had any ground for an action. If indeed he chose to proceed against the lady for a breach of promise of marriage, then the result would depend on the evidence. In such case as that the Low Church attorney at Littlebath was willing to take the matter up. "But Mr. Maguire was, of course, aware," said Solomon Walker, "that there was a prejudice in the public mind against gentlemen appearing as parties to such suits." Mr. Maguire was also aware that he could adduce no evidence of the fact beyond his own unsupported, and, in such case, untrue word, and declared therefore to the attorney, in a very high tone indeed, that on no account would he take any step to harass the lady. It was simply against Sir John Ball that he wished to proceed. "Things would come out in that trial, Mr. Walker," he said, "which would astonish you and all the legal world. A rapacious scheme of villainy has been conceived and brought to bear, through the stupidity of some people and the iniquity of others, which would unroll itself fold by fold as certainly as I stand here, if it were properly handled by a competent barrister in one of our courts of law." And I think that Mr. Maguire believed what he was saying, and that he believed, moreover, that he was speaking the truth when he told Mr. Walker that the lady had promised to marry him. Men who can succeed in deceiving no one else will succeed at last in deceiving themselves. But the lawyer told him, repeating the fact over and over again, that the thing was impracticable; that there was no means of carrying the matter so far that Sir John Ball should be made to appear in a witness box. Everything that Sir John had done he had done legally; and even at that moment of the discussion between Mr. Walker and Mr. Maguire, the question of the ownership of the property was being tried before a proper tribunal in London. Mr. Maguire still thought Mr. Walker to be wrong,—thought that his attorney was a weak and ignorant man; but he acknowledged to himself the fact that he in his unhappy position was unable to get any more cunning attorney to take the matter in hand.

But the *Christian Examiner* still remained to him, and that he used with diligence. From week to week there appeared in it articles attacking the lion, stating that the lion was still being watched, that his prey would be snatched from him at last, that the lamb should even yet have her rights, and the like. And as the thing went on, the periodical itself and the writer of the article became courageous by habit, till things were printed which Sir John Ball found it almost impossible to bear. It was declared that he was going to desert the lamb, now that he had taken all the lamb's property; and that the lamb, shorn of all her fleece, was to be condemned to earn her bread as a common nurse in the wards of a common hospital,—all which information came readily enough to Mr. Maguire by the hands of Miss Colza. The papers containing these articles were always sent to Sir John Ball and to Miss Mackenzie, and the articles were always headed, "The Lion and the Lamb." Miss Mackenzie, in accordance with an arrangement made to that purpose, sent the papers as soon as they came to Mr. Slow, but Sir John Ball had no such ready way of freeing himself from their burden. He groaned and toiled under them, going to his lawyer with them, and imploring permission to bring an action for libel against Mr. Maguire. The venom of the unclean animal's sting had gone so deep into him, that, fond as he was of money, he had told his lawyer that he would not begrudge the expense if he could only punish the man who was hurting him. But the attorney, who understood something of feeling as well as something of money, begged him to be quiet at any rate till the fate of the property should be settled. "And if you'll take my advice, Sir John, you will not notice him at all. You may be sure that he has not a shilling in the world, and that he wants you to prosecute him. When you have got damages against him, he will be off out of the country."

"But I shall have stopped his impudent ribaldry," said Sir John Ball. Then the lawyer tried to explain to him that no one read the ribaldry. It was of no use. Sir John read it himself, and that was enough to make him wretched.

The little fable which made Sir John so unhappy had not, for some months past, appeared in any of the metropolitan newspapers; but when the legal inquiry into the proper disposition of Mr. Jonathan Ball's property was over, and when it was known that, as the result of that inquiry, the will in favour of the Mackenzies was to be set aside and the remains of the property handed over to Sir John, then that very influential newspaper, which in the early days of the question had told the story of the Lion and the Lamb, told it all again, tearing, indeed, the Littlebath *Christian Examiner* into shreds for its iniquity, but speaking of the romantic misfortune of the lamb in terms which made Sir John Ball very unhappy. The fame which accrued to him from being so publicly pointed out as a lion, was not fame of which he was proud. And when the writer in this very influential newspaper went on to say that the world was now looking for a termination of this wonderful story, which would make it pleasant to all parties, he was nearly beside himself in his misery. He, a man of fifty, of slow habits, with none of the buoyancy of youth left in him, apt to regard himself as older than his age, who had lived with his father and mother almost on an equality in regard to habits of life, the father of a large family, of which the eldest was now himself a man! Could it be endured that such a one as he should enter upon matrimony amidst the din of public trumpets and under a halo of romance? The idea of it was frightful to him. On the very day on which the result of the legal investigation was officially communicated to him, he sat in the old study at the Cedars with two newspapers before him. In one of these there was a description of his love, which he knew was intended as furtive ridicule, and an assurance to the public that the lamb's misfortunes would all be remedied by the sweet music of the marriage bell. What right had any one to assert publicly that he intended to marry any one? In his wretchedness and anger he would have indicted this newspaper also for a libel, had not his lawyer assured him that, according to law, there was no libel in stating that a man was going to be married. The other paper accused him of rapacity and dishonesty in that he would not marry the lamb, now that he had secured the lamb's fleece; so that, in truth, he had no escape on either side; for Mr. Maguire, having at last ascertained that the lamb had, in very truth, lost all her fleece, was no longer desirous of any personal connection, and felt that he could best carry out his pledge by attacking the possessor of the fleece on that side. Under such circumstances, what was such a man as Sir John Ball to do? Could he marry his cousin amidst the trumpets, and the halo, and the doggrel poetry which would abound? Was it right that he should be made a mark for the finger of scorn? Had he done anything to deserve this punishment?

And it must be remembered that from day to day his own mother, who lived with him, who sat with him late every night talking on this one subject, was always instigating him to abandon his cousin. It had been admitted between them that he was no longer bound by his offer. Margaret herself had admitted it,—"does not attempt to deny it," as Lady Ball repeated over and over again. When he had made his offer he had known nothing of Mr. Maguire's offer, nor had Margaret then told him of it. Such reticence on her part of course released him from his bond. So Lady Ball argued, and against this argument her son made no demur. Indeed it was hardly possible that he should comprehend exactly what had taken place between his cousin and Mr. Maguire. His mother did not scruple to assure him that she must undoubtedly at one time have accepted the man's proposal. In answer to this John Ball would always assert his entire reliance on his cousin's word.

"She did it without knowing that she did so," Lady Ball would answer; "but in some language she must have assented."

But the mother was never able to extract from the son any intimation of his intention to give up the marriage, though she used threats and tears, ridicule and argument,—appeals to his pride and appeals to his pocket. He never said that he certainly would marry her; he never said so at least after that night on which Margaret in her bedroom had told him her story with reference to Mr. Maguire; but neither did he ever say that he certainly would not marry her. Lady Ball gathered from all his words a conviction that he would be glad to be released, if he could be released by any act on Margaret's behalf, and therefore she had made her attempt on Margaret. With what success the reader will, I hope, remember. Margaret, when she accepted her cousin's offer, had been specially bidden by him to be firm. This bidding she obeyed, and on that side there was no hope at all for Lady Ball.

I fear there was much of cowardice on Sir John's part. He had, in truth, forgiven Margaret any offence that she had committed in reference to Mr. Maguire. She had accepted his offer while another offer was still dragging on an existence after a sort, and she had not herself been the first to tell him of these circumstances. There had been offence to him in this, but that offence he had, in truth, forgiven. Had there been no Littlebath *Christian Examiner*, no tale of the Lion and the Lamb, no publicity and no ridicule, he would quietly have walked off with his cousin to some church, having gone through all preliminary ceremonies in the most silent manner possible for them, and would have quietly got himself married and have carried Margaret home with him. Now that his father was dead and that his uncle Jonathan's money had come to him, his pecuniary cares were comparatively light, and he believed that he could be very happy with Margaret and his children. But then to be pointed at daily as a lion, and to be asked by all his acquaintances after the lamb! It must be owned that he was a coward; but are not most men cowards in such matters as that?

But now the trial was over, the money was his own, Margaret was left without a shilling in the world, and it was quite necessary that he should make up his mind. He had once told his lawyer, in his premature joy, on that very day on which Mr. Maguire had come to the Cedars, that everything was to be made smooth by a marriage between himself and the disinherited heiress. He had since told the lawyer that something had occurred which might, perhaps, alter this arrangement. After that the lawyer had asked no question about the marriage; but when he communicated to his client the final intelligence that Jonathan Ball's money was at his client's disposal, he said that it would be well to arrange what should be done on Miss Mackenzie's behalf. Sir John Ball had assumed very plainly a look of vexation when the question was put to him.

"I promised Mr. Slow that I would ask you," said the lawyer. "Mr. Slow is of course anxious for his client."

"It is my business and not Mr. Slow's," said Sir John Ball, "and you may tell him that I say so."

Then there had been a moment's silence, and Sir John had felt himself to be wrong.

"Pray tell him also," said Sir John, "that I am very grateful to him for his solicitude about my cousin, and that I fully appreciate his admirable conduct both to her and me throughout all this affair. When I have made up my mind what shall be done, I will let him know at once."

As he walked down from his lawyer's chambers in Bedford Row to the railway station he thought of all this, and thought also of those words which Mrs. Mackenzie had spoken to him in the bazaar. "You have no right to scold him yet," she had said to Margaret. Of course he had understood what they meant, and of course Margaret had understood them also. And he had not been at all angry when they were spoken. Margaret had been so prettily dressed, and had looked so fresh and nice, that at that moment he had forgotten all his annoyances in his admiration, and had listened to Mrs. Mackenzie's cunning speech, not without confusion, but without any immediate desire to contradict its necessary inference. A moment or two afterwards the harpies had been upon him, and then he had gone off in his anger. Poor Margaret had been unable to distinguish between the effects produced by the speech and by the harpies; but Mrs. Mackenzie had been more clever, and had consequently predicted her cousin's speedy promotion in the world's rank.

Sir John, as he went home, made up his mind to one of two alternatives. He would either marry his cousin or halve Jonathan Ball's money with her. He wanted to marry her, and he wanted to keep the money. He wanted to marry her especially since he had seen how nice she looked in black-freckled muslin; but he wanted to marry her in silence, without any clash of absurd trumpets, without ridicule-moving leading articles, and fingers pointed at the triumphant lion. He made up his mind to one of those alternatives, and resolved that he would settle which on that very night. His mind should be made up and told to his mother before he went to bed. Nevertheless, when the girls and Jack were gone, and he was left alone with Lady Ball, his mind had as yet been made up to nothing!

His mother gave him no peace on this subject. It was she who began the conversation on this occasion.

"John," she said, "the time has come for me to settle the question of my residence."

Now the house at Twickenham was the property of the present baronet, but Lady Ball had a jointure of five hundred a year out of her late husband's estate. It had always been intended that the mother should continue to live with her son and grandchildren in the very probable event of her being left a widow; and it was felt by them all that their means were not large enough to permit, with discretion, separate households; but Lady Ball had declared more than once with extreme vehemence that nothing should induce her to live at the Cedars if Margaret Mackenzie should be made mistress of the house.

"Has the time come especially to-day?" he asked in reply.

"I think we may say it has come especially to-day. We know now that you have got this increase to your income, and nothing is any longer in doubt that we cannot ourselves settle. I need not say that my dearest wish is to remain here, but you know my mind upon that subject."

"I cannot see any possible reason for your going."

"Nor can I—except the one. I suppose you know yourself what you mean to do about your cousin. Everybody knows what you ought to do after the disgraceful things that have been put into all the newspapers."

"That has not been Margaret's fault."

"I am by no means so sure of that. Indeed, I think it has been her fault; and now she has made herself notorious by being at this bazaar, and by having herself called a ridiculous name by everybody. Nothing will make me believe but what she likes it."

"You are ready to believe any evil of her, mother; and yet it is not two years since you yourself wished me to marry her."

"Things are very different since that; very different indeed. And I did not know her then as I do now, or I should never have thought of such a thing, let her have had all the money in the world. She had not misbehaved herself then with that horrible curate."

"She has not misbehaved herself now," said the son, in an angry voice.

"Yes, she has, John," said the mother, in a voice still more angry.

"That's a matter for me to judge. She has not misbehaved herself in my eyes. It is a great misfortune,—a great misfortune for us both,—the conduct of this man; but I won't allow it to be said that it was her fault."

"Very well. Then I suppose I may arrange to go. I did not think, John, that I should be turned out of your father's house so soon after your father's death. I did not indeed."

Thereupon Lady Ball got out her handkerchief, and her son perceived that real tears were running down her face.

"Nobody has ever spoken of your going except yourself, mother."

"I won't live in the house with her."

"And what would you have me do? Would you wish me to let her go her way and starve by herself?"

"No, John; certainly not. I think you should see that she wants for nothing. She could live with her sister-in-law, and have the interest of the money that the Rubbs took from her. It was your money."

"I have explained to you over and over again, mother, that that has already been made over to Mrs. Tom Mackenzie; and that would not have been at all sufficient. Indeed, I have altogether made up my mind upon that. When the lawyers and all the expenses are paid, there will still be about eight hundred a year. I shall share it with her."

"John!"

"That is my intention; and therefore if I were to marry her I should get an additional income of four hundred a year for myself and my children."

"You don't mean it, John?"

"Indeed I do, mother. I'm sure the world would expect me to do as much as that."

"The world expect you! And are you to rob your children, John, because the world expects it? I never heard of such a thing. Give away four hundred a year merely because you are afraid of those wretched newspapers! I did expect you would have more courage."

"If I do not do one, mother, I shall do the other certainly."

"Then I must beg you to tell me which you mean to do. If you gave her half of all that is coming to you, of course I must remain here because you could not live here without me. Your income would be quite insufficient. But you do owe it to me to tell me at once what I am to do."

To this her son made no immediate answer, but sat with his elbow on the table, and his head upon his hand looking moodily at the fire-place. He did not wish to commit himself if he could possibly avoid it.

"John, I must insist upon an answer," said his mother. "I have a right to expect an answer."

"You must do what you like, mother, independently of me. If you think you can live here on your income, I will go away, and you shall have the place."

"That's nonsense, John. Of course you want a large house for the children, and I, if I must be alone, shall only want one room for myself. What should I do with the house?" Then there was silence again for a while.

"I will give you a final answer on Saturday," he said at last. "I shall see Margaret before Saturday."

After that he took his candle and went to bed. It was then Tuesday, and Lady Ball was obliged to be contented with the promise thus made to her.

On Wednesday he did nothing. On the Thursday morning he received a letter which nearly drove him mad. It was addressed to him at the office of the Shadrach Fire Insurance Company, and it reached him there. It was as follows—

Littlebath, — June, 186—.

SIR,

You are no doubt fully aware of all the efforts which I have made during the last six months to secure from your grasp the fortune which did belong to my dear— my dearest friend, Margaret Mackenzie. For as my dearest friend I shall ever regard her, though she and I have been separated by machinations of the nature of which she, as I am fully sure, has never been aware. I now ascertain that some of the inferior law courts have, under what pressure I know not, set aside the will which was made twenty years ago in favour of the Mackenzie family, and given to you the property which did belong to them. That a superior court would reverse the judgment, I believe there is little doubt; but whether or no the means exist for me to bring the matter before the higher tribunals of the country I am not yet aware. Very probably I may have no such power, and in such case, Margaret Mackenzie is, to-day, through your means, a beggar.

Since this matter has been before the public you have ingeniously contrived to mitigate the wrath of public opinion by letting it be supposed that you purposed to marry the lady whose wealth you were seeking to obtain by legal quibbles. You have made your generous intentions very public, and have created a romance that has been, I must say, but little becoming to your age. If all be true that I heard when I last saw Miss Mackenzie at Twickenham, you have gone through some ceremony of proposing to her. But, as I understand, that joke is now thought to have been carried far enough; and as the money is your own, you intend to enjoy yourself as a lion, leaving the lamb to perish in the wilderness.

Now I call upon you to assert, under your own name and with your own signature, what are your intentions with reference to Margaret Mackenzie. Her property, at any rate for the present, is yours. Do you intend to make her your wife, or do you not? And if such be your intention, when do you purpose that the marriage shall take place, and where?

I reserve to myself the right to publish this letter and your answer to it; and of course shall publish the fact if your cowardice prevents you from answering it. Indeed nothing shall induce me to rest in this matter till I know that I have been the means of restoring to Margaret Mackenzie the means of decent livelihood.

I have the honour to be, Sir,

Your very humble servant,

JEREMIAH MAGUIRE.

Sir John Ball, Bart., &c., &c, Shadrach Fire Office.

Sir John, when he had read this, was almost wild with agony and anger. He threw up his hands with dismay as he walked along the passages of the Shadrach Office, and fulminated mental curses against the wasp that was able to sting him so deeply. What should he do to the man? As for answering the letter, that was of course out of the question; but the reptile would carry out his threat of publishing the letter, and then the whole question of his marriage would be discussed in the public prints. An idea came across him that a free press was bad and rotten from the beginning to the end. This creature was doing him a terrible injury, was goading him almost to death, and yet he could not punish him. He was a clergyman, and could not be beaten and kicked, or even fired at with a pistol. As for prosecuting the miscreant, had not his own lawyer told him over and over again that such a prosecution was the very thing which the miscreant desired. And then the additional publicity of such a prosecution, and the twang of false romance which would follow and the horrid alliteration of the story of the two beasts, and all the ridicule of the incidents, crowded upon his mind, and he walked forth from the Shadrach office among the throngs of the city a wretched and almost despairing man.

Chapter XXIX

A Friend in Need Is a Friend Indeed

When the work of the bazaar was finished all the four Mackenzie ladies went home to Mrs. Mackenzie's house in Cavendish Square, very tired, eager for tea, and resolved that nothing more should be done that evening. There should be no dressing for dinner, no going out, nothing but idleness, tea, lamb chops, and gossip about the day's work. Mr. Mackenzie was down at the House, and there was no occasion for any domestic energy. And thus the evening was passed. How Mrs. Chaucer Munro and the loud bevy fared among them, or how old Lady Ware and her daughters, or the poor, dear, bothered duchess or Mr. Manfred Smith, or the kings and heroes who had appeared in paint and armour, cannot be told. I fear that the Mackenzie verdict about the bazaar in general was not favourable and that they agreed among themselves to abstain from such enterprises of charity in future. It concerns us now chiefly to know that our Griselda held up her head well throughout that evening, and made herself comfortable and at her ease among her cousins, although it was already known to her that the legal decision had gone against her in the great case of Ball *v.* Mackenzie. But had that decision been altogether in her favour the result would not have been so favourable to her spirits, as had been that little speech made by Mrs. Mackenzie as to her having no right as yet to scold Sir John for his extravagance,—that little speech made in good humour, and apparently accepted in good humour even by him. But on that evening Mrs. Mackenzie was not able to speak to Margaret about her prospects, or to lecture her on the expediency of regarding the nicenesses of her dress in Sir John's presence, because of the two other cousins. The two other cousins, no doubt, knew all the story of the Lion and the Lamb, and talked to their sister-in-law, Clara, of their other cousin, Griselda, behind Griselda's back; and were no doubt very anxious that Griselda should become a baronet's wife; but among so large a party there was no opportunity for confidential advice.

On the next morning Mrs. Mackenzie and Margaret were together, and then Mrs. Mackenzie began:

"Margaret, my dear," said she, "that bonnet I gave you has been worth its weight in gold."

"It cost nearly as much," said Margaret, "for it was very expensive and very light."

"Or in bank-notes either, because it has shown him and me and everybody else that you needn't be a dowdy unless you please. No man wishes to marry a dowdy, you know."

"I suppose I was a dowdy when he asked me."

"I wasn't there, and didn't know you then, and can't say. But I do know that he liked the way you looked yesterday. Now, of course, he'll be coming here before long."

"I dare say he won't come here again the whole summer."

"If he did not, I should send for him."

"Oh, Mrs. Mackenzie!"

"And oh, Griselda! Why should I not send for him? You don't suppose I'm going to let this kind of thing go on from month to month, till that old woman at the Cedars has contrived to carry her point. Certainly not."

"Now that the matter is settled, of course, I shall not go on staying here."

"Not after you're married, my dear. We couldn't well take in Sir John and all the children. Besides, we shall be going down to Scotland for the grouse. But I mean you shall be married out of this house. Don't look so astonished. Why not? There's plenty of time before the end of July."

"I don't think he means anything of the kind; I don't indeed."

"Then he must be the queerest man that ever I met; and I should say about the falsest and most heartless also. But whether he means to do that or does not, he must mean to do something. You don't suppose he'll take all your fortune away from you, and then leave you without coming to say a word to you about it? If you had disputed the matter, and put him to all manner of expense; if, in short, you had been enemies through it all, that might have been possible. But you have been such a veritable lamb, giving your fleece to the shearer so meekly,—such a true Griselda, that if he were to leave you in that way, no one would ever speak to him again."

"But you forget Lady Ball."

"No, I don't. He'll have a disagreeable scene with his mother, and I don't pretend to guess what will be the end of that; but when he has done with his mother, he'll come here. He must do it. He has no alternative. And when he does come, I want you to look your best. Believe me, my dear, there would be no muslins in the world and no starch, if it was not intended that people should make themselves look as nice as possible."

"Young people," suggested Margaret.

"Young people, as you call them, can look well without muslin and without starch. Such things were intended for just such persons as you and me; and as for me, I make it a rule to take the goods the gods provide me."

Mrs. Mackenzie's philosophy was not without its result, and her prophecy certainly came true. A few days passed by and no lover came, but early on the Friday morning after the bazaar, Margaret, who at the moment was in her own room, was told that Sir John was below in the drawing-room with Mrs. Mackenzie. He had already been there some little time, the servant said, and Mrs. Mackenzie had sent up with her love to know if Miss Mackenzie would come down. Would she go down? Of course she would go to her cousin. She was no coward. Indeed, a true Griselda can hardly be a coward. So she made up her mind to go to her cousin and hear her fate.

The last four-and-twenty hours had been very bitter with Sir John Ball. What was he to do, walking about with that man's letter in his pocket—with that reptile's venom still curdling through his veins? On that Thursday morning, as he went towards his office, he had made up his mind, as he thought, to go to Margaret and bid her choose her own destiny. She should become his wife, or have half of Jonathan Ball's remaining fortune, as she might herself elect. "She refused me," he said to himself, "when the money was all hers. Why should she wish to come to such a house as mine, to marry a dull husband and undertake the charge of a lot of children? She shall choose herself." And then he thought of her as he had seen her at the bazaar, and began to flatter himself that, in spite of his dullness and his children, she would choose to become his wife. He was making some scheme as to his mother's life, proposing that two of his girls should live with her, and that she should be near to him, when the letter from Mr. Maguire was put into his hands.

How was he to marry his cousin after that? If he were to do so, would not that wretch at Littlebath declare, through all the provincial and metropolitan newspapers, that he had compelled the marriage? That letter would be published in the very column that told of the wedding. But yet he must decide. He must do something. They who read this will probably declare that he was a weak fool to regard anything that such a one as Mr. Maguire could say of him. He was not a fool, but he was so far weak and foolish; and in such matters such men are weak and foolish, and often cowardly.

It was, however, absolutely necessary that he should do something. He was as well aware as was Mrs. Mackenzie that it was essentially his duty to see his cousin, now that the question of law between them had been settled. Even if he had no thought of again asking her to be his wife, he could not confide to any one else the task of telling her what was to be her fate. Her conduct to him in the matter of the property had been exemplary, and it was incumbent on him to thank her for her generous forbearance. He had pledged himself also to give his mother a final answer on Saturday.

On the Friday morning, therefore, he knocked at the Mackenzies' house door in Cavendish Square, and soon found himself alone with Mrs. Mackenzie. I do not know that even then he had come to any fixed purpose. What he would himself have preferred would have been permission to postpone any action as regards his cousin for another six months, and to have been empowered to use that time in crushing Mr. Maguire out of existence. But this might not be so, and therefore he went to Cavendish Square that he might there decide his fate.

"You want to see Margaret, no doubt," said Mrs. Mackenzie, "that you may tell her that her ruin is finally completed;" and as she thus spoke of her cousin's ruin, she smiled her sweetest smile and put on her pleasantest look.

"Yes, I do want to see her presently," he said.

Mrs. Mackenzie had stood up as though she were about to go in quest of her cousin, but had sat down again when the word presently was spoken. She was by no means averse to having a few words of conversation about Margaret, if Sir John should wish it. Sir John, I fear, had merely used the word through some instinctive idea that he might thereby stave off the difficulty for a while.

"Don't you think she looked very well at the Bazaar?" said Mrs. Mackenzie.

"Very well, indeed," he answered; "very well. I can't say I liked the place."

"Nor any of us, I can assure you. Only one must do that sort of thing sometimes, you know. Margaret was very much admired there. So much has been said of this singular story about her fortune, that people have, of course, talked more of her than they would otherwise have done."

"That has been a great misfortune," said Sir John, frowning.

"It has been a misfortune, but it has been one of those things that can't be helped. I don't think you have any cause to complain, for Margaret has behaved as no other woman ever did behave, I think. Her conduct has been perfect."

"I don't complain of her."

"As for the rest, you must settle that with the world yourself. I don't care for any one beyond her. But, for my part, I think it is the best to let those things die away of themselves. After all, what does it matter as long as one does nothing to be ashamed of oneself? People can't break any bones by their talking."

"Wouldn't you think it very unpleasant, Mrs. Mackenzie, to have your name brought up in the newspapers?"

"Upon my word I don't think I should care about it as long as my husband stood by me. What is it after all? People say that you and Margaret are the Lion and the Lamb. What's the harm of being called a lamb or a lion either? As long as people are not made to believe that you have behaved badly, that you have been false or cruel, I can't see that it comes to much. One does not, of course, wish to have newspaper articles written about one."

"No, indeed."

"But they can't break your bones, nor can they make the world think you dishonest, as long as you take care that you are honest. Now, in this matter, I take it for granted that you and Margaret are going to make a match of it—"

"Has she told you so?"

Mrs. Mackenzie paused a moment to collect her thoughts before she answered; but it was only for a moment, and Sir John Ball hardly perceived that she had ceased to speak.

"No," she said; "she has not told me so. But I have told her that it must be so."

"And she does not wish it?"

"Do you want me to tell a lady's secret? But in such a case as this the truth is always the best. She does wish it, with all her heart,—as much as any woman ever wished for anything. You need have no doubt about her loving you."

"Of course, Mrs. Mackenzie, I should take care in any case that she were provided for amply. If a single life will suit her best, she shall have half of all that she ever thought to be her own."

"And do you wish it to be so?"

"I have not said that, Mrs. Mackenzie. But it may be that I should wish her to have the choice fairly in her own power."

"Then I can tell you at once which she would choose. Your offer is very generous. It is more than generous. But, Sir John, a single life will not suit her; and my belief is, that were you to offer her the money without your hand, she would not take a farthing of it."

"She must have some provision."

"She will take none from you but the one, and you need be under no doubt whatsoever that she will take that without a moment's doubt as to her own future happiness. And, Sir John, I think you would have the best wife that I know anywhere among my acquaintance." Then she stopped, and he sat silent, making no reply. "Shall I send to her now?" said Mrs. Mackenzie.

"I suppose you might as well," said Sir John.

Then Mrs. Mackenzie got up and left the room, but she did not herself go up to her cousin. She felt that she could not see Margaret without saying something of what had passed between herself and Sir John, and that it would be better that nothing should be said. So she went away to her own room, and dispatched her maid to send the lamb to the lion. Nevertheless, it was not without compunction, some twang of feminine conscience, that Mrs. Mackenzie gave up this opportunity of saying some last important word, and perhaps doing some last important little act with regard to those nicenesses of which she thought perhaps too much. Mrs. Mackenzie's philosophy was not without its truth; but a man of fifty should not be made to marry a woman by muslin and starch, if he be not prepared to marry her on other considerations.

When the message came, Margaret thought nothing of the muslin and starch. The bonnet that had been worth its weight in gold, and the black-freckled dress, were all forgotten. But she thought of the words which her cousin John had spoken to her as soon as they had got through the little gate into the grounds of the Cedars when they had walked back together from the railway station at Twickenham; and she remembered that she had then pledged herself to be firm. If he alluded to the offer he had then made, and repeated it, she would throw herself into his arms at once, and tell him that she would serve him with all her heart and all her strength as long as God might leave them together. But she was quite as strongly determined to accept from him for herself no other kind of provision. That money which for a short while had been hers was now his; and she could have no claim upon him unless he gave her the claim of a wife. After what had passed between them she would not be the recipient of his charity. Certain words had been written and spoken from which she had gathered the existence, in Mr. Slow's mind, of some such plan as this. His client should lose her cause meekly and graciously, and should then have a claim for alms. That had been the idea on which Mr. Slow had worked. She had long made up her mind that Mr. Slow should be taught to know her better, if the day for such offering of alms should ever come. Perhaps it had come now. She took up a little scarf that she wore ordinarily and folded it tight across her shoulders, quite forgetful of muslin and starch, as she descended to the drawing-room in order that this question might be solved for her.

Sir John met her almost at the door as she entered.

"I'm afraid you've been expecting me to come sooner," he said.

"No, indeed; I was not quite sure that you would come at all."

"Oh, yes; I was certain to come. You have hardly received as yet any official notification that your cause has been lost."

"It was not my cause, John," she said, smiling, "and I received no other notification than what I got through Mrs. Mackenzie. Indeed, as you know, I have regarded this law business as nonsense all through. Since what you and Mr. Slow told me, I have known that the property was yours."

"But it was quite necessary to have a judgment."

"I suppose so, and there's an end of it. I, for one, am not in the least disappointed,—if it will give you any comfort to know that."

"I don't believe that any other woman in England would have lost her fortune with the equanimity that you have shown."

She could not explain to him that, in the first days of dismay caused by that misfortune, he had given her such consolation as to make her forget her loss, and that her subsequent misery had been caused by the withdrawal of that consolation. She could not tell him that the very memory of her money had been, as it were, drowned by other hopes in life,—by other hopes and by other despair. But when he praised her for her equanimity, she thought of this. She still smiled as she heard his praise.

"I suppose I ought to return the compliment," she said, "and declare that no cousin who had been kept so long out of his own money ever behaved so well as you have done. I can assure you that I have thought of it very often,—of the injustice that has been involuntarily done to you."

"It has been unjust, has it not?" said he, piteously, thinking of his injuries. "So much of it has gone in that oilcloth business, and all for nothing!"

"I'm glad at any rate that Walter's share did not go."

He knew that this was not the kind of conversation which he had desired to commence, and that it must be changed before anything could be settled. So he shook himself and began again.

"And now, Margaret, as the lawyers have finished their part of the business, ours must begin."

She had been standing hitherto and had felt herself to be strong enough to stand, but at the sound of these words her knees had become weak under her, and she found a retreat upon the sofa. Of course she said nothing as he came and stood over her.

"I hope you have understood," he continued, "that while all this was going on I could propose no arrangement of any kind."

"I know you have been very much troubled."

"Indeed I have. It seems that any blackguard has a right to publish any lies that he likes about any one in any of the newspapers, and that nobody can do anything to protect himself! Sometimes I have thought that it would drive me mad!"

But he again perceived that he was getting out of the right course in thus dwelling upon his own injuries. He had come there to alleviate her misfortunes, not to talk about his own.

"It is no good, however, talking about all that; is it, Margaret?"

"It will cease now, will it not?"

"I cannot say. I fear not. Whichever way I turn, they abuse me for what I do. What business is it of theirs?"

"You mean their absurd story—calling you a lion."

"Don't talk of it, Margaret."

Then Margaret was again silent. She by no means wished to talk of the story, if he would only leave it alone.

"And now about you."

Then he came and sat beside her, and she put her hand back behind the cushion on the sofa so as to save herself from trembling in his presence. She need not have cared much, for, let her tremble ever so much, he had then no capacity for perceiving it.

"Come, Margaret; I want to do what is best for us both. How shall it be?"

"John, you have children, and you should do what is best for them."

Then there was a pause again, and when he spoke after a while, he was looking down at the floor and poking among the pattern on the carpet with his stick.

"Margaret, when I first asked you to marry me, you refused me."

"I did," said she; "and then all the property was mine."

"But afterwards you said you would have me."

"Yes; and when you asked me the second time I had nothing. I know all that."

"I thought nothing about the money then. I mean that I never thought you refused me because you were rich and took me because you were poor. I was not at all unhappy about that when we were walking round the shrubbery. But when I thought you had cared for that man—"

"I had never cared for him," said Margaret, withdrawing her hand from behind the pillow in her energy, and fearing no longer that she might tremble. "I had never cared for him. He is a false man, and told untruths to my aunt."

"Yes, he is, a liar,—a damnable liar. That is true at any rate."

"He is beneath your notice, John, and beneath mine. I will not speak of him."

Sir John, however, had an idea that when he felt the wasp's venom through all his blood, the wasp could not be altogether beneath his notice.

"The question is," said he, speaking between his teeth, and hardly pronouncing his words, "the question is whether you care for me."

"I do," said she turning round upon him; and as she did so our Griselda took both his hands in hers. "I do, John. I do care for you. I love you better than all the world besides. Whom else have I to love at all? If you choose to think it mean of me, now that I am so poor, I cannot help it. But who was it told me to be firm? Who was it told me? Who was it told me?"

Lady Ball had lost her game, and Mrs. Mackenzie had been a true prophet. Mrs. Mackenzie had been one of those prophets who knew how to assist the accomplishment of their own prophecies, and Lady Ball had played her game with very indifferent skill. Sir John endeavoured to say a word as to that other alternative that he had to offer, but the lamb was not lamb-like enough to listen to it. I doubt even whether Margaret knew, when at night she thought over the affairs of the day, that any such offer had been made to her. During the rest of the interview she was by far the greatest talker, and she would not rest till she had made him swear that he believed her when she said, that both in rejecting him and accepting him, she had been guided simply by her affection. "You know, John," she said, "a woman can't love a man all at once."

They had been together for the best part of two hours, when Mrs. Mackenzie knocked at the door. "May I come in?"

"Oh, yes," said Margaret.

"And may I ask a question?" She knew by the tone of her cousin's voice that no question could come amiss.

"You must ask him," said Margaret, coming to her and kissing her.

"But, first of all," said Mrs. Mackenzie, shutting the door and assuming a very serious countenance, "I have news of my own to tell. There is a gentleman downstairs in the dining-room who has sent up word that he wants to see me. He says he is a clergyman."

Then Sir John Ball ceased to smile, and look foolish, but doubled his fist, and went towards the door.

"Who is it?" said Margaret, whispering.

"I have not heard his name, but from the servant's account of him I have not much doubt myself; I suppose he comes from Littlebath. You can go down to him, if you like, Sir John; but I would not advise it."

"No," said Margaret, clinging to his arm, "you shall not go down. What good can you do? He is beneath you. If you beat him he will have the law of you—and he is a clergyman. If you do not, he will only revile you, and make you wretched." Thus between the two ladies the baronet was restrained.

It was Mr. Maguire. Having learned from his ally, Miss Colza, that Margaret was staying with her cousins in Cavendish Square, he had resolved upon calling on Mrs. Mackenzie, and forcing his way, if possible, into Margaret's presence. Things were not going well with him at Littlebath, and in his despair he had thought that the best chance to him of carrying on the fight lay in this direction. Then there was a course of embassies between the dining-room and drawing-room in the Mackenzie mansion. The servant was sent to ask the gentleman his name, and the gentleman sent up to say that he was a clergyman,—that his name was not known to Mrs. Mackenzie, but that he wanted to see her most particularly for a few minutes on very special business. Then the servant was despatched to ask him whether or no he was the Rev. Jeremiah Maguire, of Littlebath, and under this compulsion he sent back word that such was his designation. He was then told to go. Upon that he wrote a note to Mrs. Mackenzie, setting forth that he had a private communication to make, much to the advantage of her cousin, Miss Margaret Mackenzie. He was again told to go; and then told again, that if he did not leave the house at once, the assistance of the police would be obtained. Then he went. "And it was frightful to behold him," said the servant, coming up for the tenth time. But the servant no doubt enjoyed the play, and on one occasion presumed to remark that he did not think any reference to the police was necessary. "Such a game as we've had up!" he said to the coachman that afternoon in the kitchen.

And the game that they had in the drawing-room was not a bad game either. When Mr. Maguire would not go, the two women joined in laughing, till at last the tears ran down Mrs. Mackenzie's face.

"Only think of our being kept prisoners here by a one-eyed clergyman."

"He has got two eyes," said Margaret. "If he had ten he shan't see us."

And at last Sir John laughed; and as he laughed he came and stood near Margaret; and once he got his arm round her waist, and Griselda was very happy. At the present moment she was quite indifferent to Mr. Maguire and any mode of fighting that he might adopt.

Chapter XXX

Conclusion

Things had not been going well with Mr. Maguire when, as a last chance, he attempted to force an entrance into Mrs. Mackenzie's drawing-room. Things, indeed, had been going very badly with him. Mr. Stumfold at Littlebath had had an interview with the editor of the *Christian Examiner*, and had made that provincial Jupiter understand that he must drop the story of the Lion and the Lamb. There had been more than enough of it, Mr. Stumfold thought; and if it were continued, Mr. Stumfold would—would make Littlebath too hot to hold the *Christian Examiner*. That was the full meaning of Mr. Stumfold's threat; and, as the editor knew Mr. Stumfold's power, the editor wisely turned a cold shoulder upon Mr. Maguire. When Mr. Maguire came to the editor with his letter for publication, the editor declared that he should be happy to insert it—as an advertisement. Then there had been a little scene between Mr. Maguire and the editor, and Mr. Maguire had left the editorial office shaking the dust from off his feet. But he was a persistent man, and, having ascertained that Miss Colza was possessed of some small share in her brother's business in the city, he thought it expedient to betake himself again to London.

He did so, as we have seen; and with some very faint hope of obtaining collateral advantage for himself, and some stronger hope that he might still be able to do an injury to Sir John Ball, he went to the Mackenzies' house in Cavendish Square. There his success was not great; and from that time forward the wasp had no further power of inflicting stings upon the lion whom he had persecuted.

But some further annoyance he did give to Griselda. He managed to induce Mrs. Tom Mackenzie to take him in as a lodger in Gower Street, and Margaret very nearly ran into his way in her anxiety to befriend her sister-in-law. Luckily she heard from Mr. Rubb that he was there on the very day on which she had intended to visit Gower Street. Poor Mrs. Mackenzie got the worst of it; for of course Mr. Maguire did not pay for his lodgings. But he did marry Miss Colza, and in some way got himself instituted to a chapel at Islington. There we will leave him, not trusting much in his connubial bliss, but faintly hoping that his teaching may be favourable to the faith and morals of his new flock.

Of Mr. Samuel Rubb, junior, we must say a few words. His first acquaintance with our heroine was not made under circumstances favourable to him. In that matter of the loan, he departed very widely from the precept which teaches us that honesty is the best policy. And when I feel that our Margaret was at one time really in danger of becoming Mrs. Rubb,—that in her ignorance of the world, in the dark gropings of her social philosophy, amidst the difficulties of her solitude, she had not known whether she could do better with herself and her future years, than give herself, and them, and her money to Mr. Samuel Rubb, I tremble as I look back upon her danger. It has been said of women that they have an insane desire for matrimony. I believe that the desire, even if it be as general as is here described, is no insanity. But when I see such a woman as Margaret Mackenzie in danger from such a man as Samuel Rubb, junior, I am driven to fear that there may sometimes be a maniacal tendency. But Samuel Rubb was by no means a bad man. He first hankered after the woman's money, but afterwards he had loved the woman; and my female reader, if she agrees with me, will feel that that virtue covers a multitude of sins.

And he was true to the promise that he made about the loan. He did pay the interest of the money regularly to Mrs. Mackenzie in Gower Street, and after a while was known in that house as the recognised lover of Mary Jane, the eldest daughter. It this way it came to pass that he occasionally saw the lady to whose hand he had aspired; for Margaret, when she was assured that Mr. Maguire and his bride were never likely to be seen in that locality, did not desert her nephews and nieces in Gower Street.

But we must go back to Sir John Ball. As soon as the coast was clear in Cavendish Square, he took his leave of Margaret. Mrs. Mackenzie had left the room, desiring to speak a word to him alone as he came down.

"I shall tell my mother to-night," he said to Margaret. "You know that all this is not exactly as she wishes it."

"John," she said, "if it is as you wish it, I have no right to think of anything beyond that."

"It is as I wish it," said he.

"Then tell my aunt, with my love, that I shall hope that she will receive me as her daughter."

Then they parted, and Margaret was left alone to congratulate herself over her success.

"Sir John," said Mrs. Mackenzie, calling him into the drawing-room; "you must hear my congratulations; you must, indeed."

"Thank you," said he, looking foolish; "you are very good."

"And so is she. She is what you may really call good. She is as good as gold. I know a woman when I see her; and I know that for one like her there are fifty not fit to hold a candle to her. She has nothing mean or little about her—nothing. They may call her a lamb, but she can be a lioness too when there is an occasion."

"I know that she is steadfast," said he.

"That she is, and honest, and warm hearted; and—and Oh! Sir John, I am so happy that it is all to be made right, and nice, and comfortable. It would have been very sad if she hadn't gone with the money; would it not?"

"I should not have taken the money—not all of it."

"And she would not have taken any. She would not have taken a penny of it, though we need not mind that now; need we? But there is one thing I want to say; you must not think I am interfering."

"I shan't think that after all that you have done."

"I want her to be married from here. It would be quite proper; wouldn't it? Mr. Mackenzie is a little particular about the grouse, because there is to be a large party at Incharrow; but up to the 10th of August you and she should fix any day you like."

Sir John showed by his countenance that he was somewhat taken aback. The 10th of August, and here they were far advanced into June! When he had left home this morning he had not fully made up his mind whether he meant to marry his cousin or not; and now, within a few hours, he was being confined to weeks and days! Mrs. Mackenzie saw what was passing in his mind; but she was not a woman to be driven easily from her purpose.

"You see," she said, "there is so much to think of. What is Margaret to do, if we leave her in London when we go down? And it would really be better for her to be married from her cousin's house; it would, indeed. Lady Ball would like it better—I'm sure she would—than if she were to be living alone in the town in lodgings. There is always a way of doing things; isn't there? And Walter's sisters, her own cousins, could be her bridesmaids, you know."

Sir John said that he would think about it.

"I haven't spoken to her, of course," said Mrs. Mackenzie; "but I shall now."

Sir John, as he went eastwards into the city, did think about it; and before he had reached his own house that evening, he had brought himself to regard Mrs. Mackenzie's scheme in a favourable light. He was not blind to the advantage of taking his wife from a house in Cavendish Square, instead of from lodgings in Arundel Street; and he was aware that his mother would not be blind to that advantage either. He did not hope to be able to reconcile her to his marriage at once; and perhaps he entertained some faint idea that for the first six months of his new married life the Cedars would be quite as pleasant without his mother as with her; but a final reconciliation would be more easy if he and his wife had the Mackenzies of Incharrow to back them, than it could be without such influence. And as for the London gossip of the thing, the finale to the romance of the Lion and the Lamb, it would be sure to come sooner or later. Let them have their odious joke and have done with it!

"Mother," he said, as soon as he could find himself alone with Lady Ball that day, not waiting for the midnight conference; "mother, I may as well tell you at once. I have proposed to Margaret Mackenzie again to-day."

"Oh! very well."

"And she has accepted me."

"Accepted you! of course she has; jumped at the chance, no doubt. What else should a pauper do?"

"Mother, that is ungenerous."

"She did not accept you when she had got anything."

"If I can reconcile myself to that, surely you can do so. The matter is settled now, and I think I have done the best in my power for myself and my children."

"And as for your mother, she may go and die anywhere."

"Mother, that is unfair. As long as I have a house over my head, you shall share it, if you please to do so. If it suits you to go elsewhere, I will be with you as often as may be possible. I hope, however, you will not leave us."

"That I shall certainly do."

"Then I hope you will not go far from me."

"And when is it to be?" said his mother, after a pause.

"I cannot name any day; but some time before the 10th of August."

"Before the 10th of August! Why, that is at once. Oh! John; and your father not dead a year!"

"Margaret has a home now with her cousins in Cavendish Square; but she cannot stay there after they go to Scotland. It will be for her welfare that she should be married from their house. And as for my father's death, I know that you do not suspect me of disrespect to his memory."

And in this way it was settled at the Cedars; and his mother's question about the time drove him to the resolution which he himself had not reached. When next he was in Cavendish Square he asked Margaret whether she could be ready so soon, and she replied that she would be ready on any day that he told her to be ready.

Thus it was settled, and with a moderate amount of nuptial festivity the marriage feast was prepared in Mrs. Mackenzie's house. Margaret was surprised to find how many dear friends she had who were interested in her welfare. Miss Baker wrote to her most affectionately; and Miss Todd was warm in her congratulations. But the attention which perhaps surprised her most was a warm letter of sisterly affection from Mrs. Stumfold, in which that lady rejoiced with an exceeding joy in that the machinations of a certain wolf in sheep's clothing had been unsuccessful. "My anxiety that you should not be sacrificed I once before evinced to you," said Mrs. Stumfold; "and within the last two months Mr. Stumfold has been at work to put an end to the scurrilous writings which that wolf in sheep's clothing has been putting into the newspapers." Then Mrs. Stumfold very particularly desired to be remembered to Sir John Ball, and expressed a hope that, at some future time, she might have the honour of being made acquainted with "the worthy baronet."

They were married in the first week in August, and our modern Griselda went through the ceremony with much grace. That there was much grace about Sir John Ball, I cannot say; but gentlemen, when they get married at fifty, are not expected to be graceful.

"There, my Lady Ball," said Mrs. Mackenzie, whispering into her cousin's ear before they left the church; "now my prophecy has come true; and when we meet in London next spring, you will reward me for all I have done for you by walking out of a room before me."

But all these honours, and, what was better, all the happiness that came in her way, Lady Ball accepted thankfully, quietly, and with an enduring satisfaction, as it became such a woman to do.

THE END

CPSIA information can be obtained
at www.ICGtesting.com
Printed in the USA
BVOW08s1957020417

480064BV00001B/80/P